Tanners' Close

Also by Inga Dunbar

THE CHEQUERBOARD
CANDLEMAKER ROW

TANNERS' CLOSE

Inga Dunbar

SIMON & SCHUSTER

LONDON·SYDNEY·NEW YORK·TOKYO·SINGAPORE·TORONTO

F

493331

First published in Great Britain by
Simon & Schuster Ltd in 1993
A Paramount Communications Company

Simon & Schuster Ltd
West Garden Place
Kendal Street
London W2 2AQ

Simon & Schuster of Australia Pty Ltd
Sydney

A CIP catalogue record for this book is
available from the British Library
ISBN 0-671-71788-X

Typeset in Sabon 11/13 by
Hewer Text Composition Services, Edinburgh
Printed and bound in Great Britain by
Butler & Tanner Ltd, Frome

In memory of my uncle
William Cameron Mitchell (Mitch), O.B.E. (Burma), M.B., CH.B.
who told me many a tale.

This book has been written for his son,
my cousin Ian Mitchell, and his wife Diana.

'Up the close and down the stair,
But and ben wi' Burke and Hare,
Burke's the butcher, Hare's the thief,
Knox the boy that buys the beef.'

Scottish Children's Song, Anon

'Though the mills of God grind slowly,
Yet they grind exceeding small.'

Retribution, Longfellow

1

BILLY WAS ELEVEN years old when the Burkes' fifteenth child was born.

'Run and fetch Father Ryan, Billy,' said the midwife. 'Tell him there's another Catholic soul come into the world, if he's after wanting to give her a blessing. And then fetch your father.'

Glad to get out of it, Billy set off for the Spread Eagle, the logical place to go since it was the only tavern for miles around, and inside its smoky interior he spied Patsy Burke in his usual seat in the corner. 'Come quick, Da,' he said. 'It's another girl.'

'A girl, is it? Begod and bedammed' – his father peered first at him and then at the other men through a drunken haze before he moaned and slumped forward on his stool – 'another bloody useless mouth to feed, then!'

His cronies rallied round to help him up and out, and Billy ran on to the priest's along the wet dark road. It wasn't a road, really, he was thinking to himself. It was just a muddy path getting muddier all the time in the pouring rain, and as it got muddier he got angrier. A flame of red-hot rebellion shot through him suddenly. He was sick of it, sick of the miserable cabin that was his home, sick of never having enough to eat, sick of rags for clothes, sick of the never-ending babies. If only he could run away! *Well, why didn't he run away, then?* Now, tonight?

He ran straight past the priest's house. If he called in there, Father Ryan would drag him back to the cabin with him. Instead he slushed past as quietly as he could, and when he thought he was safely out of earshot he took to his heels. The thought occurred to him that he had nowhere to go, but, as sure as God, nowhere must be better than where he'd come from, and he had no sooner agreed with himself on that score than he heard the sound of a horse and wheels behind him. Filthy and soaking wet already, he leaped into the ditch at the side of the road.

'Whoa! Haud still, beastie!' said a voice that sounded Scottish. Who could it be, and he a Scotsman begod, as far west in Ireland as this? Then there was the sound of someone splashing down into the mud. 'Who's there? You, laddie, get oot o' that ditch! Come on, noo. Up ye come!'

A strong arm hauled Billy up, and he saw that the man was tall with a face of whiskers – and, if that wasn't frightening enough, underneath his beard a white dog-collar gleamed in the murky light. God be present! Not another priest?

'I'm Reverend Horace Watt,' he said. 'And who might you be?'

'Billy Burke, begging your pardon, your Reverence.'

'I'll have none o' that Popish talk around me, laddie. Plain sir or Mr Watt is how to address me.'

Ah, so he wasn't a priest! He must be a minister, which was just as bad, but the face under the whiskers was kind enough.

'Yes, sir.'

'So where were ye running to when ye jumped into that ditch?'

'Nowhere, sir,' Billy said truthfully.

'The first thing to learn is not to tell me lies.'

'It's the truth, sir.' Billy was nearly in tears. 'I was running away from home.'

'And what'll yer poor mother say to that, Billy Burke?'

'Not much. She's just had her fifteenth.'

'I see. Where is yer home?'

'One of the cabins, sir, on the hillside.'

'Seventeen o' ye, then, in one room?'

Billy shook his head, sobbing in earnest now, in case Mr Watt forced him back home. 'Sixteen. My brother Con ran away last year, when the last bairn was born.'

'Then ye'd better come wi' me. There's a few boys just like yersel' back at the manse.' Mr Watt hauled him up into the gig beside him, took up the ribbons and drove Billy away out of Orrey in County Tyrone, over the border to Donegal and into a new life.

Four years later Billy looked much the same, only bigger. His nose was still short and snub in his round face, but his chin seemed stronger and his jaw firmer. At first he had been afraid that Mr Watt was one of those 'queer fellows' that his older brother Constantine used to warn him about before he had run away from home.

'What does that mean, Con?'

'They like boys better than girls.'

'What do you mean – to . . . do it with?' Billy was shocked. 'But how?'

He was even more shocked when Con told him in graphic detail. Now he was only thankful that Mr Watt did not turn out to be a 'queer fellow' after all, and quite the reverse. The four other homeless boys in his charge loved him like a father, and with Mistress Clara Watt's help he fed them and clothed them, taught them to read and write and gave them a grounding in a few trades before he sent them out one by one into the world.

In the meantime he made it clear that their payment for this was to attend his kirk, and Billy went to Mr Watt's services in the Presbyterian church with perfect equanimity. He missed the rituals, the incense and the saints of his own religion. In this church there seemed to be an awful lot of droning psalms, but he put up with it all because some of the music for the hymns was quite lively, and music was the breath of life to Billy.

From the day he left home he never gave another thought to the Burke family he had left behind. He was perfectly happy. He thrived and grew, and alongside his dedication to music grew his interest in the opposite sex, often to bursting point in his sleep.

'Ay, Billy,' Mr Watt said, 'it's wet dreams ye're having. It happens to a boy when he changes into a man. It's nothing to be ashamed of. Let's see – ye're fifteen now, and it's time to be deciding yer future. Ha'e ye any ideas o' yer ain?'

'No, sir,' Billy admitted in his soft Irish. 'But I like singing in the choir.'

Mr Watt sighed and patted his shoulder. 'We'll just wait and see,' he said, but later that night he talked anxiously to his wife. 'What we're going to do with him I don't know, Clara. All the other boys have shown a bent of some sort by the time they were fifteen. This one is different.'

'Yes, he's different, Horace. He was born without feelings, for one thing.'

'What does that mean?'

'When Ruff was so ill six months ago he simply was not interested in whether the poor dog lived or died. He never sat with him like the other boys did. In fact he even asked me if there wasn't some way to make him die quicker, and when at last he did die he didn't shed a tear. He's heartless, that's what he is.'

'Na, na, Clara. He's probably just one of those people who don't care for animals.'

'He doesn't care for anything or anyone, believe me.'

'But I thought ye liked Billy.'

'So I do. He has nice manners now, and a nice smile. He's just different, that's all.'

Mrs Watt had an uncanny way of seeing through people. Her husband stared at her with a worried expression on his face. 'I wonder what we're going to do with him, then?'

'Just come through from the study for yer soup a bit earlier tomorrow,' she said with a smile. 'He's been doing something lately that might give ye an idea.'

The following day was a Wednesday, a rainy grey Wednesday, when the boys at the manse crawled back into themselves, depressed and silent as they sat round the large dining-table waiting for Mrs Watt to fetch in the tattie soup.

Billy broke out of the cloud. That was the way it always seemed to happen. He just lost patience and burst out, and it happened again when he seized two spoons lying on the table, laid them on his knee and started to play them together in a rapid and insistent staccato.

The other boys shook their heads and smiled. Mrs Watt screeched and spilled a little out of the first two bowls in her hands on to the already stained tablecloth. 'Och, ye gave me a right fright, Billy! Horace, are ye there? Horace!'

Billy carried on, in a world of his own by this time, and Mr Watt stood in the doorway and listened. 'It's the rhythm in yer soul, Billy,' he pronounced at last. 'Ye can hear music when none o' the rest o' us can. Ye're a musician, that's what ye are, and it's given me an idea. Just leave it wi' me, laddie.'

In a few weeks, just as Billy was approaching his sixteenth birthday, Mr Watt sent for him to come to the study. It must be serious. Billy could see that it was, because standing there too was a soldier with gold braid decorating his dark green uniform, in flashes down the front of his coat and on the epaulettes.

Mr Watt did not introduce the man to him at first. He just handed him a drum and two sticks. 'See what ye can do wi' these, laddie.'

The pleasure it gave Billy just to grasp those two drumsticks he could never have described. He felt the blood flooding into his heart as he beat out his first roll. The two men listened to him for a while, but he had forgotten their presence until the soldier stopped him. 'Here,' he said. 'Try the fife.'

Billy laid down the sticks reluctantly and blew into the pipes. It was a sheer experiment, but to his intense interest and surprise he soon went up and down the scales and then broke into a tune.

'He's a natural,' his quick ears heard the soldier say to Mr Watt in the background. 'We can sign him up.'

'Billy, this is Drum Major Harrington,' the minister held up his hand to stop him playing, 'and he's short o' drummers. It's a wonderful opportunity for ye, to be taken into the Donegal Militia as a musician. How would ye like that?'

How would he like that? He was speechless with delight. For the first time in five years Mr Watt actually saw tears in Billy's eyes. 'When can I go?' he managed at last. 'Now?'

So for the second time in his life Billy Burke left home

5

without a backward glance or another thought, and not long afterwards he was measured for his nankeens and his boots, fitted for his dark green tight-fitting coat with the yellow flashes and epaulettes and issued with his flat round hat with the red and white plume and the strap under his chin. When he donned his uniform and pulled on his short white gloves he was every inch a drummer boy in the Donegals.

Left, right! Left, right! All along the stone-flagged passage the small detail of musicians was marching, their footsteps falling as one. Billy's fingers itched for his drumsticks. He longed to beat out the rhythm for the Drum Major leading the way, the two big bruisy boys behind him, and himself the youngest bringing up the rear on this bright, crisp September morning of 1809.

He was in his eighteenth year now and the blood was singing through his veins. He felt on top of the world. 'It's the music I'm after having in my soul,' he told himself. 'That, and the rhythm of life, to be sure.'

The Drum Major brought them to a stamping, almost dancing, halt outside the cell. 'Out ye come, Mickey O'Rourke! Let's be having ye!' he commanded as the guard unlocked the door. 'Drunk and disorderly, were ye? Bloody idiot!'

His two husky soldiers grasped Mickey O'Rourke's arms, marched him the rest of the way to the Punishment Room and manacled his wrists to the chains hanging from the roof.

Stupid bugger, Billy thought, glancing at the dangling Mickey. Pissing in the street was neither here nor there. They all did it, as far out of sight as possible, of course, when they were caught short. Waggling his bare arse at the officers who came upon him in such a drunken state was another matter – just plain asking for trouble – for in Billy's book there was no harm in doing anything you felt like doing, so long as you never got caught. That was Rule Number One.

So would you be looking at Mickey O'Rourke now, come to this! And still drunk, by the look of him! When he was sober he was as straight as the rest of them. It was only when the drink was in that his right leg seemed to give way and bend in towards his left one, as it was doing right now. Billy shook

6

his head and sighed; then, in case his sigh was mistaken for an admission of weakness, he came to attention with a clatter, snapping his eyes dead ahead in his round young face, which he'd learned to keep more expressionless than ever after a year in the Donegal Militia.

The large clock on the wall said it was almost half past six as they all waited for the doctor to arrive. In the silence Billy reflected that Reverend Horace Watt had never warned him what, exactly, enlisting in the Donegals as a drummer would mean. He should have explained a musician's two other duties to him at the time: to be a hospital orderly, and to administer the punishments as he was about to do this morning for the first time. Well, the lashing wouldn't worry him, if he even got a turn to do it after these two big boys obviously chosen for the job had finished. He could rise above it all because of the music in his soul and the rhythm of life.

Yes, the rhythm of life was what mattered most to Billy, and especially the rhythm of life with women. There he was, a raw recruit walking down the main street of Ballina one sunny afternoon, and there *she* was, this lady at least ten years older, descending from a carriage and straight into a shop with MICHAEL COLEMAN above the door. In just one glance he knew she burned for him, and in that same glance she lit a little fire in him.

Whether it was just by pure chance or whether she manoeuvred it he didn't know, but only a few days later he met her again in the street and without a word she dragged him up a long narrow alleyway, round a dark corner into a small dark slit of a place and lifted up her skirts.

It was an invitation that Billy couldn't resist, and it was only the first of many. Not that he particularly liked Margaret Coleman upon further acquaintance. Her invitations began to sound more and more like orders, and he didn't like taking orders from a woman, even if she *was* rich, as she constantly told him she was.

Before long she had his feet under the Colemans' table and he soon found out that the women in that family wore the breeches.

Margaret's mother said that if her daughter had to get married it should not be to a mere drummer in the Donegal Militia, but all the same she lost no time in arranging a shotgun wedding.

It was conducted in the Colemans' parlour by a Protestant minister. Billy didn't mind whether he was a minister or a priest, so long as they got it over and done with and they could get out of this ugly, freezing room and upstairs to bed as fast as possible. But Mrs Coleman had other, very strong ideas. 'Margaret will sleep in a bed in our room while she is pregnant. We want this baby to arrive safely,' she said sourly. She was a sour old bitch, right enough.

For a while he got Margaret to meet him outside in the evenings, until the weather became too cold, and their meetings too difficult to arrange. 'Why can we not sleep together like any other married couple?' he demanded on the last of these occasions.

'She thinks you'll demand your rights and crush the child inside me. God knows, that's what you may have done already, Billy Burke.' Margaret shivered. 'You'd better stay in the barracks until after the birth. You can come home at the weekends if you like.'

'What for?' he asked bitterly. 'It was all a trick to make you look respectable.'

Margaret smiled quietly in the darkness. 'Oh, it was more than that,' she said mysteriously.

'My coat, Burke,' said a voice in his ear, scattering these dark thoughts.

'Yes, sir. Certainly, sir.' Billy took the coat and hung it up on the same peg from which he took down a large stained apron. He held it up for Dr Corcoran to put on. 'Your apron, sir, and the top o' the morning to ye.'

The doctor ignored him and looked at the Drum Major enquiringly.

'Six hundred lashes, sir. In turns, a hundred each. I'll take the first turn,' said the Major.

Six hundred! Jesus and Mary! With an effort Billy managed

to disguise his shock. He kept his face very plain because och
– they'd only be wee lashes at that rate.

Dr Corcoran took his watch out of his pocket and held it
to his ear. 'You understand that I must take his pulse at the
end of every fifty?'

'Yes, sir,' said the Drum Major.

'Get on with it, then,' he snapped.

It was plain to them all that the doctor was nervous at the
prospect of the next few hours. After all, he wouldn't treat his
horse in such a way. But the Major began with a practised hand,
one, pause, two, pause, three, pause, four, pause, and made it
look very easy, though Billy suspected it wasn't. He could tell
the Major was restraining himself, landing the whip as lightly
as it would allow on Mickey's back. At the end of fifty lashes
Dr Corcoran took Mickey's pulse, nodded, and so it went on
until the count stood at one hundred.

Next it was the turn of the first big soldier, Callum Carruthers.
He stepped forward and grasped the whip with a nasty smile on
his bullying face. He never should have been allowed to do the
job, in Billy's opinion, but it was none of his business and he
kept his eyes straight ahead until Carruthers was ten strokes
into it, the count was only a hundred and ten, and Mickey
began to moan.

Billy stole a glance. Carruthers' method was not so gentle as
the Drum Major's. He lashed first one way so that angry weals
appeared, going from left to right. Then he lashed the other
way so that the weals became criss-crossed and very red. At a
hundred and fifty the doctor took the pulse again, clucked his
tongue, but allowed the flogging to continue. Mickey's moans
became groans and sobs as the weals became purple mounds
of flesh with opening slits of blood.

Surely the doctor would stop it at two hundred! Mickey was
by now a poor wretch, a very different sight from the rollicking
drinker of the night before. But Dr Corcoran only pursed his lips
and nodded, and the whip was handed over to Tim Donelly.

It was then that the real torture began. Donelly had got the
wielding of a whip down to a fine art. He took a step back,
raised the whip above and behind his head with a snap, there

9

was an instant's terrible pause, and then it landed, whining, not only across Mickey's back but curling cruelly round his chest as well. The slits of blood became streams. Mickey screamed and the streams became rivers, as his once healthy torso turned into a hideous pulp of raw flesh. Even Carruthers, bad as he was, turned pale.

Tim Donelly was allowed to carry on to three hundred, the halfway mark of the punishment, and still the doctor only shook his head. Why didn't he stop it? Doctors must know some quick way to put men out of their agony for ever. That's what Billy would have done, but he had no more time to speculate about it. The whip was thrust into his hand next by a Tim Donelly who was beginning to look pale himself.

Before he had even laid on, Billy heard the soft sigh as Mickey O'Rourke's soul left his body. He always knew when people died. There was that sound of breath expiring, and then a loud silence. It came of long experience in the filthy, overcrowded and miserable cabins where he'd been brought up and thankfully escaped. He laid down the whip and looked enquiringly at the doctor, who pretended not to see anything amiss and merely gestured to him to carry on.

For the first time in his life Billy could find no rhythm. A few half-hearted strokes later Dr Corcoran stopped him, took Mickey's pulse again and then looked up into Billy's face. 'No use flogging a dead horse, Burke,' he said dispassionately. 'Wait behind. You are probably aware that, should death occur during punishment, the last man with the whip in his hand is held responsible for dealing with the remains.'

Billy looked at him, his pleasant face as impassive as ever, and the Drum Major withdrew with the two hard men. *Responsible!* Who the hell was responsible if not this doctor? Hadn't he been the one taking the pulse all the way through? He had simply allowed Mickey O'Rourke to die. Why? Billy was not only burning with indignation at having to take the blame for it – he was becoming very curious by now. 'Yes, sir,' he said smoothly. 'Would I be after bagging him, then?'

'No,' Dr Corcoran said. 'Help me to carry him to the mortuary. You take the head and shoulders. I'll take the feet.'

Poor Mickey's remains were bundled almost secretly out of sight back along the stone corridor. 'Now,' the doctor panted, 'lay him up here on the slab. We'll undress him and give him time to cool down. He should be ready for me tomorrow night. I have always been curious why that right leg seemed to atrophy in drink. There has to be a reason.' The fanatical brilliance in his eyes dulled momentarily under Billy's hard grey stare. 'Just report back here at six o'clock tomorrow night, Burke. You shall be my assistant when I conduct the investigation.'

'Six o'clock tomorrow night, sir?'

'Six o'clock, man, dammit!' The doctor did not look up. Daniel Corcoran had been studying Billy Burke for a long time, and found him strangely unemotional. That was why he had asked for him to be included in the punishment detail, to see if he would remain so hard in the presence of death. Burke hadn't even batted an eyelid.

'Very good, sir.'

Billy saluted and retired, absolutely seething, to his billet to change his clothes. There were better things to be doing at six o'clock at night than watching a doctor fiddle about with a dead body, so there was. He was still angry when he reported for band practice, but as soon as the band struck up the old familiar tunes and he grasped his drumsticks to beat out the tattoo he was on familiar ground again. He felt a bit better.

Still, there it was, niggling away in the back of his mind all the time. Everyone knew that Mickey had been all alone in the world except for the regiment. That bastard doctor had let him die quite deliberately just so that he could cut him up afterwards. There would be no relatives to ask for his body to bury decently. They were a queer bloody lot, these doctors. They would do anything under Heaven to get a corpse. No wonder there were grave-robbers.

It was the first lesson in the real education of William Burke.

2

EVERY SATURDAY AFTERNOON the band went marching through the streets, to the quivering excitement of all the girls in Ballina. Two of them grasped each other by the hand and raced, giggling, across the cobbles to the place where they knew by experience they could get the best view.

Every soldier there recognised pretty Bridie Sullivan for one of them, with that cloud of fair curls that frothed halfway down her back. It was just that none of them ever went with her, to be accused of taking advantage. 'Oh, God, would you be looking at that, Helen?' she moaned, feasting her eyes on Billy, who had laid down his sticks in the drum slots, taken up his fife and as usual kept his eyes dead ahead. 'When did you ever see such a pretty man? What's his name, I wonder?'

'I see him. John MacDougal told me his name when he joined up, not very long ago. It's Billy Burke. He's married, ye ken. He had to marry Margaret Coleman.'

'*Her?* Why her? Why didn't he come to me? Sure and I wouldn't have made him get married. He could have had it for nothing.'

Helen laughed. 'We all know that, Bridie. It was Margaret's mother made them get married, although they say he's not been going back to the house lately.'

'Ah.' Bridie smiled, and in no time at all she was waylaying

13

him in the street or waiting for him at the gates of the barracks.

'She's here again,' one of the sentries muttered as Billy was going off duty one summer evening. 'For God's sake tell her to hide around the corner, at least. She's an embarrassment.'

'What's the matter? Jealous?' Billy laughed, but he took Bridie's arm and quickly led her away out of sight down to the riverside.

To look at her nobody would have guessed that she was a wee shilling short of the guinea, he thought, although he had sensed it in the first five minutes of their acquaintance. Well, he was not the sort to let the green grass of Ireland grow under his feet. He was a man of action, and all he hoped was that the Colemans never got to hear about it, or else all hell would be let loose.

He thought it had a few months later, when he was summoned back to their house. 'Margaret's had a miscarriage,' Mistress Coleman told him instead, with a sniff, 'and she's told me why she thinks it happened. It's all your fault. God knows why, but she wants you to go upstairs and see her.'

'Oh, Billy,' Margaret sobbed, 'I've lost the baby.'

'So I hear,' he said grimly. 'I've also heard why, from that old bitch down the stairs. What have you two been saying about me?'

'None of it was my idea, Billy. She doesn't approve of sex.'

'How did you get here on the face of this earth, then?'

'As far as I can make out, it was just that one time, and then I was on the way.'

Billy thought of Michael Coleman's sour face. 'I can well believe it,' he said.

'But, Billy, I still love you, and I still want your baby.'

'And how are you going to manage that, as things are?'

'Come back home. Give me a month to get over this, and then come back home.'

He knew he should, and he probably would, but to tell the truth he liked Bridie better now, even if she was still only ten years old in her head. Quite clearly, he was a man very much in demand by the ladies, so the thing to do was to make the

14

most of his freedom for the next four weeks. But at the present moment it was six o'clock in the evening, the appointed hour for Dr Corcoran to examine Mickey O'Rourke's remains, when Billy reported to the mortuary.

The doctor was already there, wearing his waterproof apron. In fact, he had already begun, making a flowing incision from the chest down to the pubic bone before he started to cut down through the fat and the cartilages with his long sharp knife.

'The heart,' he announced, lifting it out. 'And the lungs,' a minute later.

Billy looked round the chilly little room and wondered what cutting out Mickey's organs had to do with the weakness in his leg, sincerely hoping that the doctor did not intend to cut up the entire body. Bridie would be at the gates at seven o'clock. She would wait faithfully for an hour before she went home, but at this rate he would be lucky if they were finished by midnight.

The doctor looked up for an instant at him, remembering that he had chosen Burke after studying his pitiless eyes, his inscrutable expression and apparent insensibility, and now he could detect no flinching or pallor on his assistant's face. He was simply a cold fish, with no qualms whatsoever about the dissection of the human body. That was good. That was part of his plan, but he was offended, all the same, when Billy showed little or no interest in his lively running commentary.

Instead, Billy was examining the mortuary. It was a room that had never seen the sunshine, nor ever would, and he realised the reason for that was to keep its inhabitants nice and cold. Furthermore, it was built at the north-west corner of the hospital, in the path of the prevailing wind from the sea – perhaps so the smells would be blown away – and appeared to be carved out of the rocks. The walls were of stone, as was the floor, which was tilted and furrowed to drain into a large channel at the far end.

He discovered why at about half past ten when, at the doctor's orders, and not faltering in spite of the terrible smell, he had to sluice away the bits and pieces of Mickey that had escaped on to the floor.

'Yes, I thought you would be satisfactory,' Dr Daniel

15

Corcoran said, 'so you may be my assistant again, the next time I am so lucky.'

'Thank you, sir,' Billy said as they were parting company, 'but was there not an easier way out for Mickey O'Rourke?'

'Of course there was.' The doctor smiled. 'I could have put my hand over his mouth and his nose so that he couldn't breathe. It would have taken only a few minutes. But a soldier has to die in the hospital or on the battlefield before I can legally appropriate his body, and only then if there is nobody to claim it.'

'Yes, sir. I see,' Billy said thoughtfully.

The following afternoon he managed to get away. Bridie had remembered what he told her. If ever one evening he was delayed, he would get time off the following afternoon to make up for it, with any luck. He hardly expected to see her down by the river in the pouring rain, but Bridie was there waiting patiently. He helped her into their favourite place on a patch of soft grass under a densely overhanging bush, and immediately she began to take off her dress.

'Come on, Billy,' she said, smiling eagerly. 'The rain can't get in here, so it can't.'

'No,' he teased her, and lay still.

Idly he watched her undress, admiring the fine body on her and comparing it with Margaret's thin one. God, her breasts were fuller than ever, and her stomach was plump and round. *Too plump and round!* He sat up suddenly in alarm. 'Bridie!'

'What is it, then?'

'You're expecting, begod!'

'So, what of it, Billy darlin'? Wait and see. It'll be a wee boy just like his daddy, with golden hair. Just like you, Billy-boy.'

'How far gone are you?'

'Nearly five months!' Bridie giggled. 'But don't worry. Ma'll take care of it.'

'Oh, Bridie, and it's me here to tell you today that I won't be seeing you for a while. I've got to go on a special duty.'

'I can wait.' She smiled. 'Love me now, anyway.'

After that, Billy stayed in the barracks until the month's separation from his wife was up, and he was accepted back into the Coleman family, but only with a grudge. It was not a happy life. Four months later, one cold snowy night when he was helping Dr Corcoran again, a sentry came knocking on the hospital door in great agitation.

'What is it, Thomson?' the doctor answered him shortly. 'Can't you see we're busy in here?'

'Begging your pardon, sir, but there's a young woman at the gates lying down in the snow. She's screaming something wicked. We think she's giving birth!'

'Good God! Did you hear that, Burke? Get a stretcher and go and fetch her. We can't have a woman in that state at the very gates of the barracks!'

Billy gave no indication that he knew Bridie, and Bridie was too far gone in pain to see who was putting her on to her back in a narrow iron bed and tying her legs up on a contraption like ram's horns.

'There's not much call for this in a military hospital,' said the doctor, laughing at his own joke, 'but there's nothing like being prepared.' Then he seated himself comfortably at the lower end of the bed, with Billy behind him, and began to encourage Bridie over the mountain of her swollen belly. 'Push, mother!' he shouted.

Bridie groaned and screamed until it became obvious that something was happening. Billy had never seen a birth from this angle before, nor indeed from any angle, having run as far away as possible from his mother at her birthings. It wasn't long before he vowed to himself he would never witness another, either.

'Push, mother, push!' Dr Corcoran was on his feet when Bridie's screams took on a different pitch. He guided the baby out with his left hand while he protected the bottom of its spine with his right. Then there was one last terrible scream.

'It's here, mother! Grand! It's a girl. Burke, the twine.' The doctor laid down the baby on a sheet, took the twine and tied two knots round the cord. Then, after cutting in between them to separate mother and child, he lifted the infant by her feet and smacked her back until there was a little wail. 'Show the woman her child,' he said impatiently, handing her over to Billy, who scarcely glanced at the baby. He was more concerned to wink at Bridie when he showed her their daughter. She entered into the spirit of the game at once, and merely smiled as she took the baby into her arms.

'Now, Burke, watch this,' Corcoran muttered, and approached Bridie with a smile. She was so relaxed now as to be almost sleeping, and still on her back. 'You're fine now, my dear,' he said gently, rolling back the sheet that was covering her and pressing down on her pelvis. 'You see that I am pulling on the cord, Burke? It's to bring away the afterbirth. It is dangerous to leave it in there,' he added, as a lump like a red umbrella with trailing bloody ribbons fell on to the floor.

It was the most shattering experience of Billy's life so far, from every point of view. How he had managed not only secretly to father the child but also to be so unlucky as to be present at her birth, he did not know. But at least nobody else knew, either. As for his daughter, he simply wasn't interested. He took one corner of the stretcher and, along with three other soldiers, carried Bridie home with her baby. That, so far as he was concerned, was the end of it.

It was not the end of it in the Sullivans' cottage.

'Thanks be to Mary and Jesus your father's gone to his last rest long ago,' said Bryde Sullivan, crossing herself devoutly, 'or else he would have battered the life out of you for sure, Bridie Sullivan.'

'Ach, Ma, no he would not! He would be proud of his little granddaughter.'

'Proud, did you say?'

Bridie opened her wide blue eyes even further and tossed back her dishevelled mass of yellow curls. 'Sure he would! And her born in a proper hospital with a proper doctor and even with her own dada watching her come into the world!'

'Oh,' Bryde said patiently. 'So the dada was there, was he? So he's a soldier, is he? What's his name?'

'Billy Burke. He's a drummer. The musicians are nearly doctors themselves, you know. Sure, and he's a bonny, bonny man.'

'Oh, yes, he's a bonny one all right, Bridie.' Bryde looked at her sadly. 'He'll be going to marry you, is he?'

'No, Ma. He has to go away on another duty.'

Why did her beautiful daughter have to be born so simple? Bryde Sullivan asked God yet again. She kept having to remind herself that Bridie was not like everyone else. She mustn't be hard on her. She just couldn't help herself, poor girl. 'Well,' she asked more gently, 'what are you going to call the little one?'

'Oh, Ma, she's a gift from Heaven, straight from the Blessed Lady herself, so she is! It'll have to be Mary.'

'Ay,' Bryde sighed, taking the infant in her arms and looking down into her face. 'She's just the very picture of you yourself when you were born, alanna. A gift from Our Lady right enough – and not forgetting Billy Burke.'

A day or two later Bryde went to the priest and asked him to write a letter for her.

'It's to my sister Madge in Edinburgh, Father. It was one of the soldiers fathered Bridie's child. Before you know it, there'll be another soldier and another and another. It's too much temptation for my poor Bridie, living right next to a barracks, so it is.'

'Ah, yes – Madge! Of course I hadn't forgotten Madge. And how is she getting on in Edinburgh?'

'Not too well in her health, the last I heard of her, Father. I was thinking of offering her Bridie's services.'

'Uh huh. Of course, we won't mention the baby?'

'No, although I don't think she would object. She always loved children. But her prayers for a husband were never answered, as you know.'

'God works in mysterious ways, Bryde.'

Two months later, on a Saturday afternoon, Bridie caught sight of Billy again, marching with the band, and held up baby Mary to let him see how big the fruit of his passion was growing. 'It's wonderful, so it is, that Billy's back!' she said excitedly to Helen standing beside her.

Billy didn't want to see her, or the baby, and his eyes slid away and came to rest on Helen's face instead, a pale fragile face with high blue eyes under dark hair. God, why had he never looked properly at Bridie's friend before? He glanced back for an instant and straight into those blue eyes, and for some odd reason felt tears at the back of his own.

Christ Jesus and Mary His Mother!

Billy called down the name of every saint he could remember. He was already married to Margaret Coleman, and a savage lady she was turning out to be, the same as her mother. Bridie was his mistress any time he liked. But now had come the love of his life. He knew it without fail in just one meeting of their eyes. What was her name again? Bridie used to speak about her. He would have to ask her, and that meant he would have to see her again – and he knew what *that* would lead to.

He took to walking down by the river, and sure enough one afternoon Bridie turned up with little Mary. They crept into their usual hiding-place. 'Ach, Billy, I know you wanted a boy,' she hung her head, 'but can you not see how pretty your little girl is?'

'Not so loud, Bridie, for God's sake!' he hissed. 'Anyone might be passing by this bush. Yes, she's pretty. Of course she is. She's like her mother.'

'You do like her, then?'

'And you, Bridie Sullivan.' Billy was very excited now. Her breasts were larger than ever, swollen with milk.

'Then give me a wee boy this time, Billy darlin'.' She set Mary down on the grass and flung her arms round him. 'You're still my sweetheart, aren't you, Billy? Tell me you are.'

'You know I am,' he panted. 'Oh, God, yes, yes, yes!' They lay still in their embrace for a while afterwards before he asked her what he wanted to know. 'That girl you go with, what's her name again?'

'You mean Helen?' No matter how simple, Bridie was very much a woman. 'Now, it's funny you asking about Helen today of all days.' She smiled with a flash of malice.

'Why's that?'

'She's just got married this very afternoon, to John MacDougal. He's taking her to Scotland tomorrow.'

'Where in Scotland? Edinburgh?'

'I can't remember. Why?' Bridie was beginning to look a little tearful. 'Oh, Billy, what does it matter. You don't like her better than me, do you? She's not even Irish! She's Scottish! She only came over here when her mother and father died, to be with her grandma.'

'Helen? Don't be silly,' he lied. God, he would have to shake Bridie off somehow. 'It's just that the regiment has to do a tour in Edinburgh shortly, that's all.'

'You could take me with you. Lots of women follow the army.'

'But not you, Bridie, with our sweet little daughter. You're not going to be a camp-follower. No. You just stay at home with your ma.'

Bridie went home with Mary and a smile on her face. Billy was such a dear sweet man, and she had forgotten already that he might be going away. She found her mother packing a fardel. 'What are you doing, Ma?' she asked, putting the baby down in the cradle.

'Sit down, Bridie. I've got something to tell you.' Bryde produced a letter out of her pocket. 'This is from your Auntie Madge.'

'Auntie Madge?' Bridie wrinkled her brow and tried to go over all her mother's and father's sisters in her mind. It was too big a task.

'Yes: Madge, my sister. The one who went to Edinburgh.'

That was the second time within an hour that Edinburgh had been mentioned, and it jogged Bridie's memory. 'Edinburgh?'

'She hasn't been keeping too well, Bridie, and she's no one there belonging to her. She was asking if you would go and help her.'

'Go to Edinburgh?' The sun shone out of Bridie's face again. She would be in Edinburgh before Billy after all. She would be there waiting for him. 'When?'

'With the wagon very early tomorrow morning. You can get on the boat by nightfall and sleep on it until it sails. For a mercy to God, John MacDougal and Helen are going on the boat too. They'll look after you all the way.'

'I'll have to take Mary, Ma.'

21

Bryde picked the baby up again and cuddled her. 'I suppose you will,' she said, sighing. 'Well, I'll look after her just now. Get to your bed early tonight, though. I'll wake you in the morning.'

Bridie's eyes were shining when she climbed up on the wagon beside Helen and John MacDougal the following morning. She looked much happier than the bride.

'Going to help your Auntie Madge, are you?' Helen asked, a little sourly.

'I am.' Bridie smiled, and for once kept her secret to herself. 'Me and Mary, we're going to Edinburgh!'

3

MADGE CONNELLY HUNCHED over the dying embers of her fire, doing her best to extract the last remnants of heat from it before she must crawl into the damp iciness of the bed in the corner. She wasn't well.

Forty-nine years of age she was, and she knew she was dying. Hadn't she got the letterwriter to answer her sister in Ballina and tell her she was dying? No good had come of that, of course. Bryde Connelly, or Sullivan, or whatever she called herself nowadays, would pay no attention to *that*, even if the message ever got to her.

Bryde with her frizzy fair curls and her slack mouth, not to mention that Sammy Sullivan she lived with – well, until he died – and their parcel of brats would pay no attention at all. Bridie, she'd called the last one. The girl must be fifteen or sixteen by now.

Yes, Madge could bet that as long as Sammy had lived Bryde was always kept warm – and, in her opinion now, any way of keeping warm must be heaven. Her thoughts went back to thirty years ago. They always went back to thirty years ago, with bitter regret. What a fool she had been!

Thirty years ago Madge had experienced the hottest contact of her life, with Bernard Hanley. It was up a close in the town, with his huge bulk blotting out the one dim lamp, and his tremendous heat searching out the way into her, bringing her out in beads of sweat and almost giving him entry, until at the last minute she had somehow pulled away from him, twisted off and had run for home, fanning her heated cheeks as she went.

Every five minutes after that she had crossed herself and asked the Blessed Lady's forgiveness for being such a bad girl. Thirty years on, she was still bitterly regretting she hadn't been a very, very bad girl instead. Bernard Hanley would have turned out – he *did* turn out – to be a drunken, ugly, wife-beating lump of a man, but he would have been warm at least, and here she was dying of the cold tonight as sure as God.

Dying of the cold she was, without even a drop o' the cratur to give her some inner heat, she grumbled away to herself as at last she lay down in her bed, fully clothed. Madge hadn't taken her clothes off since the month of July and now it was March and long into the new year. As the weather got colder she just kept adding another layer on top of what she was wearing already.

A knock sounded at the door. But that was impossible. No one ever knocked on her door, except Mabel Milligan, but never at this time of night. There it was again! It wasn't fair, with the life oozing out of her, to have to get up and answer it. 'Who is it?' she shouted crossly. 'Go away, whoever ye are!'

'Ach, Auntie Madge,' said a young laughing voice outside, 'sure and it's Bridie, come all the way from Ireland to see you. Open the door!'

'*Bridie!* Oh, my God, is it really you?' Madge cried when she saw her. 'Ye're the very picture o' yer ma! The same hair! And the same bonny skin, but then our Bryde was aye bonny. I see ye've got two bundles wi' ye.'

'This one's Mary.' Bridie uncovered her sleeping child.

'Holy Mary!' Madge crossed herself. 'Are ye married?'

'No, not yet. I'm too young.'

'Then ye've sinned.' Madge's voice took on a hard note.

'Ach, she's only a wee sin. Look at her! And let me show you what I've got in my fardel for you.' Birdie untied the bundle under her other arm and took out a bottle. 'A man on the boat gave me it. He wanted to come with me to see you, but John MacDougal wouldn't let him.'

'God bless ye, Bridie Sullivan!' Madge almost wept. 'It's poteen.'

'What's happened to your fire, Auntie Madge?' Bridie asked a few drinks later.

'Don't call me Auntie. It makes me feel too old, as if I was going to die. Just Madge. I've no coal, and no money to pay for any, or for a carrier to drag it up these stairs.'

'Is that all? Have another dram and hold Mary. I'll get coal, don't you be worrying.'

Half an hour later Madge heard Bridie giggling outside. When she opened the door her neighbour Mabel Milligan had opened hers too, to see the girl looking flushed, dishevelled and smudged with black. Madge didn't know whether to be more annoyed with Mabel Milligan's long nose or the cheek of the man carrying the bag of coal. He was more than willing to follow Bridie in, but Madge slammed the door in his face. 'How much did ye pay him?' she asked.

'Never you mind. I got another bottle as well, Madge. It's Scotch whisky this time. Between the fire and the booze we'll soon be warm.'

'I'm right glad ye've come, Bridie,' Madge said a few hours later when they went to bed. 'It's fine and warm in here now.' She peered drunkenly at her niece's hair in the firelight when she joined her. 'Tell me, why is yer hair brown all over and shining yellow at the bottom o' yer curls?'

'The yellow bits are what the plaid didn't cover and the rain must have washed.'

'Never mind, ye're a grand lassie, whether yer hair's dirty or no'.'

'Now that I think about it, my hair hasn't been washed for a long time, not since Mary was born and long before that.'

'Well, I've no soap.'

'I'll get soap, the same way as I got coal,' Bridie slurred as she fell into bed beside her aunt.

'God, I feel I might live up again, after all. I might start another life.'

'Christ, Madge, that's the booze talking.' Bridie laughed as

25

she snuggled down. 'But I'll wash your hair as well, if you like. You never can tell.'

Next morning they woke up and thank God there was still a dram left for each of them in the bottom of the bottle.

'What about something to eat?' Bridie asked.

Madge lifted the lid off a big black pot on the hearth and then slammed it down again. 'There's enough soup for one,' she said sullenly. 'I canna afford to pay a water-carrier to bring water up here, and I've no' been able to get to the market stalls to try and swipe a few cabbage leaves.'

'Just get the fire going again,' Bridie told her, flinging on her plaid as she went out, 'and look after Mary.'

She wasn't surprised when Madge didn't wash out the soup pot later that morning, after the water-carrier had been. In their family soup pots just kept going and going. You poured in more water and flung in what you had – an onion, a carrot and some praties if you were very lucky, and today they were luckier than ever.

'Oh – where did ye get this knuckle-bone?' Madge asked disbelievingly.

'Count on me,' Bridie laughed, 'but maybe it could do with a wee wash before we put it in the pot. I found it rumbling about on the ground under one of the stalls.'

'And what's this? Soap? So ye got some after all! But soap was never rumbling aboot on the ground, Bridie Sullivan! It costs too much. Ye havena been stealing, have ye?'

'It's got a fine, sweet smell, hasn't it, Madge?' Bridie smiled innocently. 'No, it was on a stall, right on the edge of it. It just slipped into my pocket, that's all. It was easy in such a crowd.'

'Wheesht! There's someone outside the door! Oh ay, it's you, is it, Mabel Milligan?'

'Wouldn't ye be after asking me in, then?' A tall, very thin woman with a long nose and small deep-set eyes, aged perhaps thirty, took a step inside. 'I've come with some bread rolls. My, that's an awful fine smell, Madge! What is it? Pratie soup?'

'It is, thanks to my niece here, lately come over from Ireland. It was Bridie got the stuff to go in it.' Madge was unable to keep the pride out of her voice as she sat her neighbour down with a bowl and a spoon.

'A right bonnie girl she is, too,' Mabel Milligan said between spoonfuls. Her lips framed the words with a smile, but her hard jealous eyes said something else. 'And her wi' a wee bairn, as well.'

'Mary.' Bridie nodded. 'That's her name, so it is. She's four months old.'

'So where's her father? Is he here, too?'

'He's coming, with the Donegals.'

'The Donegals?' Mabel Milligan sneered. 'The Donegals never come to Edinburgh. Someone's been telling ye lies.'

Bridie received this like a slap on the face. She turned to her aunt, her face crumpling and tears welling into her eyes.

'Now then, Bridie, dinna cry.' Madge put her arms around her. 'If he said he was coming, he'll be coming. If ye're finished wi' that soup, Mabel Milligan, Bridie's going to get her hair washed. Ye might as well go home."

Thus dismissed, Mabel Milligan walked out. She wasn't sorry to go, for the girl Bridie sent shivers up and down her spine just to look at her, and the shivers didn't stop until she got inside the door of her own land, as the flats were called in the tall tenements crowding the Royal Mile of Edinburgh.

Her land consisted of a single room, the same as Madge Connelly's next door. In fact Madge had come over from Ireland along with the Milligans and their young daughter Mabel fifteen years ago. That tenement in World's End Close was ramshackle then, and now that it had become a stepping-off place for many Irish immigrants it was in a worse state than ever.

But Mabel, like Madge, had never dreamed of leaving it, not even when her parents died. It was her home, and in it she was determined to stay until one day, when she had enough money, she would go back to Ireland and buy a farm of her own. Just a wee one. Then, with money *and* a farm, some Irishman would want to marry her and her dream would come true.

For now, at thirty, she could see that she would never get a man, at least not here in Edinburgh where there were plenty of pretty women. Everywhere she looked there were pretty women, and she hated them every one, so she did. The last straw was this Bridie come to live right next door to her, for she must be the prettiest one ever. The world was ill-parted, Mabel decided when she looked in her own bit of looking-glass. Shaking her head, she put her hand up the chimney and brought down a tin box.

What was inside made up for her own deficiencies and the deficiencies of all the rest of her life. She counted her money over and over again, putting it in this pile and that and adding it all up once more, and very soon she began to feel better. Better, but hungry, as usual. Mabel was always hungry. She went into her cupboard, took out another bread roll, crumbled it up in a drop of milk, sprinkled it with sugar and raisins and heated it up in her pan.

That was how she had managed to save nearly all her wages from the bake-shop where she had worked for fifteen years. Second-day bread was sold at half-price. Third-day bread, if any, she was allowed to take home, and that was her diet, along with a blood pudding – a gift now and then from the kindly butcher next door to the bake-shop who worried about her scrawny frame.

Mabel Milligan ate her bread pudding thoughtfully before she went to bed that night. What she really needed was a stroke of luck in what had been so far a luckless life. She thought about that every night before she went to sleep, waiting patiently for her stroke of luck to come. Tonight, somehow and in some way she thought it had, and it was all through that girl Bridie.

'She eats end on, that one,' Madge flung after Mabel Milligan's departing figure, 'and yet she's as thin as a rake, so she is. Of course, she must have a worm.'

'A worm?' Bridie asked uncomprehendingly.

'Yes. A worm. A tapeworm.'

'What's that?'

'A great big worm living inside ye that eats yer food so that ye get none. Believe me, that's why she's so thin.'

Until that black day Bridie's short life had been sunny and

untroubled. Her mother and everyone who knew her had seen to that. Now nasty things were coming at her thick and fast. She gazed at her aunt in horror and promptly fainted on the floor.

Madge was sorry. The poor child had no idea of the afflictions of this world, she thought, sprinkling her with water to bring her round.

'What happened?' Bridie asked, white-faced. 'My stomach turned, all of a sudden.'

'It was nothing,' Madge assured her. 'There's water heating. Ye were going to wash yer hair.'

Instantly diverted, Bridie sat up and smiled. The colour came back to her cheeks. 'Oh yes, Madge, now I remember.' She got to her feet. 'Where did we put the soap?'

'It won't be so easy for the stuff to fall off the stalls and into yer pocket now, my lassie,' Madge said, once Bridie had washed her hair and stuck her head out of the window to let the rain wash all the soap away. 'Ye'll stand out in the crowd wi' that mass o' yellow ringlets.'

'I was after thinking that meself.' Bridie looked at her strangely. 'It's money we need next, to keep us going.'

'A bar o' soap's one thing, Bridie,' Madge resumed her lecture. 'Stealing money is another. If ye're caught ye'll land up in the Tolbooth – that's the prison, sticking oot in the Lawnmarket, beside the Luckenbooths and the stalls. Ye shouldna ha'e gone and washed yer hair.' Madge paused for breath, gazing almost in fear at Bridie's glorious blonde mane. 'Ye'll be too easy seen now.'

'That's what I mean. I want to be easy seen, Madge. I've got to earn some money, not steal it.'

'Oh, yes? How?'

'Am I really pretty, Madge?'

Madge caught her breath at the childish words. 'Very pretty, dearie,' she said, smoothing down the soft blonde curls.

'And you're sure the Donegals are never coming here?' Bridie asked, her blue eyes bleak.

'Never.'

'Then it doesn't matter any more. It was all lies that Billy told me. I'm not very bright, Madge.'

'Och, ye're all right,' her aunt comforted her.

'Well, then, I might make a few coppers in amongst the drinking men, in the taverns of the town. I'll start tonight.'

'And why would they give ye a few coppers, Bridie Sullivan? Ye dinna mean . . . ye'd sell yersel'?'

'If I have to – and maybe take home a bottle or two, besides. You'd like that, wouldn't you?'

'Och, Bridie!' Madge Connelly sighed, but her eyes brightened. The pain she sometimes had in her stomach only went away nowadays when she had a good drink in.

It was in the month of July that Bridie was positioned between Madge and the window, stirring the latest pot of soup on the fire. This time it was as they liked it, the old Irish way, thick with praties and onions.

'By God, ye're pregnant!' Madge said.

'I am, a bit,' Bridie acknowledged. 'Five months.'

'But that means it happened before ye ever came to Edinburgh.'

'It did, and it was the same man that fathered Mary, that lying, deceiving Billy Burke! But I've got over him now.' Bridie tossed her head. 'I've got a new man now, Madge.'

'Who? Where did ye meet him?'

'In the White Hart, along the Grassmarket a bit. His name's John Smith. He's a traveller. He sells things.'

'What things?'

'I don't know. What does it matter? He's going to marry me, Madge, as sure as God.'

'Oh, Bridie . . .'

'Yes, he is, the next time he's here. November nineteenth, that's the date.'

'And when's the baby due?'

'November eleventh, maybe,' Bridie hazarded a guess, for counting was not one of her accomplishments.

'By Christ, ye're cutting it fine.'

'I know, but I've been along to Rhymer's and got this.' Bridie showed her a thin tattered cloak.

'To cover yer shame?' Madge sighed, and clutched her stomach. Heat and good soup and many a bottle brought by Bridie could not stop the agonising pains now.

'Yes.' Bridie took no offence, but looked across at her aunt's pale mauve face with concern. 'I hope it'll be another beautiful little girl, just like Mary. Will you help me, Madge, when that time comes?'

'If I'm still living,' Madge Connelly gasped.

'You'll still be living. I told John I knew someone with bad pains in her stomach and he gave me this.' Bridie held out a bottle, and then snatched it back. 'No, you're not to touch it! I'll give you your doses. It's called laudanum, and too much could kill you, he said.'

The laudanum dulled Madge's pains, right up to November the tenth, when Bridie went into labour. Madge had never seen a baby born before. She had only the sketchiest idea of what should be done, and no idea at all what could go wrong, but her niece guided her through it until the cord was cut. It was another little girl, just like Mary. Without Bridie to supervise her, Madge took the rest of the laudanum, washed down with half a pint of neat whisky after such an ordeal, and fell down on the floor.

In the morning Bridie woke up to hear two howling infants, and to find her aunt stark dead in the same position as she had fallen the night before. Somehow she crawled to Mabel Milligan's door and asked for help.

'My God,' Mabel Milligan said, for in spite of all her bitterness she was shocked at the sight of Bridie's ashen face, 'are ye all right?'

'No,' Bridie sobbed, 'and I don't know what to do.'

'Leave it to me,' Mabel Milligan said immediately. There was money to be made out of this situation. 'I ken a man who'll see to Madge. Ye'd better go back to bed. Are ye bleeding?'

'No, but I should be. There's something wrong.'

Mabel Milligan shrugged her bony shoulders and waited until nightfall before she went, well wrapped up in her dark cloak, to find the man – and a nasty furtive-looking man he was, stuffing

31

poor Madge into a sack and putting it over his shoulder. Then Mabel Milligan said something queer.

'I know where ye live,' she said, glaring at him. 'So ye'd better come back with my share, or I'll get a few Irishmen to come after ye.'

Bridie didn't know what she was talking about. It was not the way they did it in Ireland, that's all she knew. At home you were put into a proper coffin and they had a wake for you. The Irish showed some respect. But she couldn't be worrying any more about that. She had enough to worry about, wondering what she was going to do next, with two baby girls with only a year between them, and John Smith going to marry her in less than a week.

He didn't know about Mary, let alone this second child she'd managed to disguise from him. It came to her suddenly that John Smith wouldn't want either of the little ones, and if she was ever to live a proper life with a man to look after her she would have to get rid of them both. Bridie shed bitter tears, said her prayers over and over again and then cried some more. She loved her babies with all her heart. No matter what happened to her – in York, as John had promised – no harm must ever come to them.

4

AFTER A WEEK Bridie still hadn't bounced back to health the way she had after having Mary, but her mind was made up to go and meet John Smith in Gilmerton, no matter how ill she was feeling, and before she did there were two heart-breaking tasks she had to face.

'Holy Mother of God, preserve us,' she moaned five minutes after she took her babies and left Madge Connelly's house for the last time. Nobody looked at her. Nobody was paying any attention to her shadowy figure lingering in a doorway of Candlemaker Row, or so she thought. Another ferocious gust of wind tore at her bedraggled cloak, but how could she put out her hands to clutch it back round her? The burdens she carried inside it were becoming heavier by the minute, and she must keep them hidden. Turning slightly, she allowed the wind to blow the cloak back into place, shuddering violently all the while in the pitiless cold, and Mabel Milligan, following her, darted into the next doorway.

Motionless, Bridie began to watch. From where she stood she had a good view of everything, the White Hart inn with all its comings and goings, the towering grandeur of Edinburgh Castle up behind like the backcloth on a stage, and straight ahead the whole length and breadth of the Grassmarket.

By three o'clock on that merciless afternoon of Wednesday,

nineteenth November, still nobody had spared her a glance, and still Mabel Milligan waited close by, silent and hidden.

Bit by bit, and despite her desperation, Bridie began to feel slightly encouraged. The few people who were out hurried by, their heads bent low before the brutal wind, scurrying for shelter, for warmth, for any kind of refuge. She could tell which of them had money; they were the ones who headed for the White Hart. She continued to watch it all, and waited for her opportunity.

The wind whipped a storm of leaves into a swirling dance of death, leaves that must have been blown down from Greyfriars' churchyard. Some of them stuck to the mud filming the cobbles. By dawn their brave scarlets and yellows would be grimed and blackened like everything else down here in the Grassmarket.

But not all the leaves had stuck. A sudden flurry hurtled towards her, slapping her face and blinding her before they rustled to rest in the far corner of the doorway. Afterwards, blinking, she saw that the moment had come at last when the whole street was deserted, a moment she knew would not last long. Even now there was a cackling and a squawking as first a few geese and then more and more straggled down from the West Port. Soon the man who was driving them would be in sight.

'Mother of God, forgive me . . .'

She bent down and laid the smaller bundle of the two on the heap of dry leaves behind her. A moment later the doorway yawned dark and empty. Bridie was gone.

Mabel Milligan never saw her going, for all her long vigil. The next thing she knew was that she was in danger of being attacked by a large grey squawking shape in the darkening doorway. She flapped her cloak at it in terror and pressed herself against the door at the far end until the gooseman came running and poked the goose out with his long stick.

It had been a frightening experience in the gathering darkness, and she longed for Bridie to make a move one way or another, so that she could get back home herself. But she was determined to wait and see, no matter what happened, for she just knew in her bones that somehow Bridie was in some strange way her stroke of luck or would lead her to it.

It was a long way to walk to Gilmerton, and battling against the wind and the bitter cold the six miles seemed like sixty, as sure as God. Bridie didn't understand how the Blessed Virgin had ever allowed her to be in these straits, even yet, and she began to cry – for hadn't she always been a good Catholic girl?

John Smith was her one and only consolation now, and she forced herself to forget the cold and the sin of what she'd done, and think of him instead. She'd met him over a glass of gin in the White Hart. Ever so nice, he was, dressed posh, a travelling man, and like herself only out for a laugh. They were laughing when he said her loved her, but the funniest thing of all was that she believed him.

She told him bits of her story, but not the bits that mattered, and he never suspected a thing. He said to meet him at nine o'clock on the night of the 19th of November at Gilmerton – which was where he would have some business the next time he came this way – and then they would take the coach to York and a fine new life together.

Dry-eyed now, Bridie peered through the darkness at the cottage nearest to the crossroads of Gilmerton. It was low and mean, but it was lamplit and there was smoke coming out of the chimney. Mercifully the wind suffocated suddenly, but it was in the grip of a deadly frost, and the moon shone hard and fierce.

It lit up a tumbledown cottage indeed, although the lamp behind the rough orange curtain gave a glow of homeliness. A dog barked and rattled on its chain, and she fled behind a bush. A minute later the door opened and a man came out and went across to the dog's shed. In a few minutes the dog's barks eased, and a woman stood framed in the doorway, tall and plump. 'What is it?' she called to her husband.

'There's nobody here. It's only Bess a wee bit restless with her so near her time.'

'Och, you and yer dogs, Joe Paterson! Come awa' in. Bess'll look after hersel'.'

35

It seemed a long time after that, while Bridie said one Hail Mary after another right through to the end, before she stole like a shadow up to the cottage door, terrified that every stealthy footfall would alert the dog again.

The child she had left in Candlemaker Row had been her newborn baby. She didn't expect her to survive. But this one ... She opened the newspaper wrapper a bit further, and then the thin shawl, and gazed in the orange glow at the tiny flower face of her Mary. Mary would be a beauty. She crossed herself and laid the child on the doorstep and crept back behind the bush.

She felt dreadfully unwell. For hours on end she had been exposed to the cold and she was not properly recovered from the birthing. She swayed and shuddered, and tried to summon up strength from somewhere.

What time was it? Steadying herself, she examined the sky. Ach, it was never nine o'clock yet! She would wait a wee while longer to see what happened now that Mary had begun to cry. Maybe her opening the shawl had disturbed her. Maybe she was hungry. The dog started to bark again, and the door opened.

'It was no cat, Molly,' the man called Joe Paterson said as he bent down to pick up the bundle. 'Come and see.'

'The bonny wee bairn! And hardly a year old yet, by the look o' it!' exclaimed Molly Paterson as she opened up the newspaper and then the shawl. 'Now, who would leave a baby on a doorstep on a night like this? Och, it's a wee lass, too! And me wi' four boys! Nothing but boys! Ay, the world's ill-pairted, right enough.'

'Well, ye've got yer wish now,' Joe said grimly. 'The mother will be miles away by this time. So what is it to be, Molly?'

'Another mouth to feed, Joe?'

'We've aye managed, lass.'

'Sent from Heaven, she is! We'll call her Mary – what else? Mary Paterson.'

'Well, get her in to the warmth, woman!'

The door slammed shut, and Bridie turned on her heel and ran without a backward glance at the scarlet drops that stained the sparkling frost where she had been standing.

The coach hesitated briefly at the Gilmerton crossroads at nine o'clock. Bridie was so stiff with cold by then that John Smith had to lift her up into it. When he slammed the door behind him the driver whipped up the horses, and they found themselves the only two passengers speeding through the dark countryside. John Smith turned up the inside lamp a little and looked at her.

'What's happened to you?' he asked. 'My God, you look terrible!'

'I'm cold,' Bridie told him through chattering teeth.

'Lie down, then, and I'll soon heat you up!' Laughing, he stretched his whole length on top of her on the seat of the coach.

'Oh – oh, *God!*' Bridie screamed, as a terrible pain seared through her, and she felt something sliding down her legs to land wetly on the floor, the blood pouring out of it, and out of her, in rivers.

'What is it? For God's sake, what is it?' John Smith jumped up and stood pressed to the furthest corner of the coach.

But Bridie didn't answer. Her head lolled over to the side and her face was snow-white. He wasted no time in trying to find out whether she was alive or dead, but stood her upright while he tore off her cloak, then opened the door and pushed her out.

After that he wiped all the blood off the seat and off the floor with the old tattered cloak, and threw it out behind her.

At four o'clock in the afternoon of that same terrible Wednesday, 19th November, it was that last half-hour of daylight merging into dusk when the elegant coach with its gilded crests began its cautious descent of the steep zigzag of Candlemaker Row. The horses were reined in and the brake half on as it groaned down the almost perpendicular road to the Cowgate. Only when it turned into the broad flatness of the Grassmarket did its occupants breathe sighs of relief, and the coach gathered a little speed.

'Is it not too late in the day, my lady? For this place, I mean?'

Lady Alison Hamilton stared bleakly around the inside of the coach. Perhaps she had made a mistake in choosing lime-green for the upholstery. Owing to this slight worry and the stiffness of the seats, she was not enjoying her first trip out since her illness.

She had stayed too late at the Tea Afternoon. It was so very difficult to get away from Effie Henderson, but at least she had been spared the effort of talking. For a whole hour Effie's voice, recounting every item of the formidable list of gossip she had gathered together over the past month with which to entertain her guests, had washed relentlessly over her head. It was only when she stood up to go that Effie turned her attention to her.

'You are quite well again, Alison? Just one of your usual chills, I suppose? Well, if you *must* go, dear . . .'

And so Effie Henderson never found out that Alison's illness had been her second miscarriage, or that the flyleaf of the large family Bible remained obstinately blank below the record of their marriage:

Mr Eden Hamilton and Lady Alison Kyle
married this day, June 3rd, 1805,
in the church of St Giles, Edinburgh.

'That'll be the finish, noo, Alison.' Dr Chisholm's words still rang in her ears. 'Ye canna ha'e another bairn. Eden never wanted ye to try for this one.'

'He has been in a dreadful state,' she had agreed, with a smile that was almost bitter on so gentle a face. 'Trying for another baby so soon was all my idea. And once again, it all went wrong.'

'Ye canna blame yersel', my dear. It's just that ye ha'e sic a delicate constitution.'

'I do blame myself, for being nearly forty before I found the perfect husband.'

'Nor for that, either. But there are plenty of perfect babies — too many — thrown to the wall, abandoned in this toon. Would ye no' consider adopting one o' them?'

'Adopting?'

Alison had gazed at her old doctor blankly. Such a thing had never occurred to her. She wanted her own child, hers and Eden's, and the ache and the longing for it in her arms refused to go away. It made her feel so tired, every day. Painfully she dragged herself from her recent unhappiness back into the present, into the Grassmarket, which did nothing to uplift her. It was so dirty and so very depressing.

'Of course it is too late to be in the Grassmarket, Liza,' she agreed with her maid, 'but mercifully it is almost deserted on such a day. We should not be here at all if anyone else in Edinburgh could boil a ham like David Rhymer. Ugh! The nearer we get to the West Port, the worse it becomes, with that terrible wind blowing the smells all this way.'

She pressed her lace-bordered handkerchief to her nose, glad of its whiff of lavender, and turned her attention to her maid's three-year-old daughter whom Liza was trying in vain to subdue.

'Please excuse her, my lady! I said we should never have taken her.'

'Oh, don't hold her little hands so, Liza! She is still only a baby and she has so much energy! She has been trying to sit still for far too long. Kathy, dear, you may come out with us when we stop at Mr Rhymer's, if you are a good girl.'

'I'm sure no other lady but you would have been so kind as to take on a widow wi' a bairn! Well, just so long as she doesn't run off. It's her latest mischief. She's started to run away at every opportunity.'

'That's what three-year-olds do, Liza. They have arrived at the stage where they want to discover the rest of the world, especially the other children and animals in it, and they are too innocent to know any fear. We'll just have to watch her, that's all.'

The coach bowled up smartly and stopped with a flourish outside Rhymer's shop. It gave the impression to anyone who happened to be looking that of course it did not belong here in the bowels of the Old Town. It belonged to Edinburgh's grand and elegant New Town, where the houses were built of honey-coloured sandstone and never more than three storeys high, to the most splendid street of all, in fact, Charlotte Square. It gleamed richly green, spotless in the dying light, except for the sparks of mud splashed up on it from the Grassmarket.

From her doorway Mabel Milligan watched it sourly, by this time almost frozen as stiff as a statue, but still determined. Her nerves had relaxed slightly, now that the noise of the cackling geese had faded away, and she could understand how impatient Bridie must be feeling with this latest invasion of the Grassmarket, if waiting for it to be empty was the reason for this great long wait.

'You will wait here, Fergus,' Lady Alison instructed her driver, who was handing her out. He, too, was resplendent in dark-green livery. 'We shall not be more than ten minutes.'

'It will give me time to light the lamps then, my lady. In ten minutes it will be dark.'

Lady Alison proceeded into Mr Rhymer's establishment followed by Liza and little Kathy, and they crossed the threshold of an Aladdin's cave brightly lit with oil lamps and crammed with goods from the roof to the sawdust on the floor. A disembodied face appeared in a small space between the boxes piled on the counter.

'It's yersel', my lady,' David Rhymer said. 'Welcome back.'

'How do you manage it?' Lady Alison asked. 'You have packed in more than ever!'

'Ay. "Everything and anything", that's my motto. It has to be. I've got competition now, you see. There's a Jew opened up along a bit, selling second-hand clothes, next.'

'Well, I am relieved to see that your hams are wrapped and hooked up in a different corner from your old clothes, Mr Rhymer.'

From somewhere on the other side of the counter a ladder seemed to be moving along of its own volition before it was propped up and David Rhymer came into view grinning, his red hair on end. He wore a white apron and his hands were quite clean, his customers noted thankfully. 'It'll be the smoked ham as usual, my lady?' he asked, lifting one off its hook. He climbed down again and cleared some of the boxes away to lay the ham down on the counter. Under its paper skirt it was speckled yellow with breadcrumbs and wrapped in fine muslin.

'We will have that skirt off, and the ham wrapped in clean white paper, Mr Rhymer, if you please. There is nobody else in Edinburgh who can produce it like you.'

'Ay, it's the best, right enough, my lady. That's because it's from Irish pigs, born and bred, as ye might say.'

'Surely not!' Lady Alison said. 'This has not come all the way from Ireland?'

'It was bred from pigs brought over by the Irish contingent, who have settled at the West Port. There's quite a few of them now in Tanner's Close, and they all have pigs.'

Lady Alison shuddered delicately. She could well believe it. Mr Rhymer handed the parcel to Liza and Lady Alison looked round for Kathy. The little girl was nowhere to be seen. 'Where is she, Liza?' They looked at each other with the same dread in their eyes before they rushed out to the coach. 'Did you see her, Fergus?'

'See who, my lady?'

'Kathy. Did you see her running off this way?'

'My bairn! Oh, my bairn!' Liza wailed.

'No, I did not, and that'll be enough o' that, Liza Fraser,' Fergus said firmly. 'Ye're upsetting her ladyship. No, my lady, she didn't run this way, or I would have seen her. She must be back the way we came. We'll find her, Liza, don't worry.'

All the time he was speaking he was settling them back into the coach, which had been turned round and lit and made ready. Now Fergus drove it slowly back along the Grassmarket.

Listening intently, Mabel Milligan was astonished to hear the pattering of tiny feet, and more astonished still to see a tiny child out alone at that time of night in the winter darkness, running as hard as her little legs could carry her.

Where was she going? The child ran past the doorway where she was hiding, and after a pause dodged straight into the next one, where Bridie, Mabel Milligan thought, stood with her two bundles. But there wasn't a word from Bridie, only a rustling and a mewing, the mewing of a cat.

Fergus put the horses to the steep incline of Candlemaker

Row and the coach began its slow grinding ascent. Not far up, Liza's anxious eyes noticed a movement in one of the doorways.

'Stop, Fergus!' Lady Alison commanded, and before he could dismount they were out and into the dark entrance. 'Liza, have you found her?'

'Yes, thanks be to God. She's got something wi' her – a bundle of some sort.'

'Take her out into the light, then. What is it?'

'It's a cat,' Kathy said, blinking in the coach lights. 'It was crying. Listen, Mam, it's crying again!'

Lady Alison's shocked eyes met those of her maid, and for a moment neither of them could speak. Then Liza pulled Kathy's head into the shelter of her skirts, and Lady Alison came to herself suddenly and took charge, trembling.

'That's no cat, my lady,' Liza whispered.

No, it certainly wasn't a cat. Mabel Milligan was trembling herself, for she, too, had seen that it was a human child inside that bundle. It was Bridie's newborn daughter, still living.

'We shall just go home as fast as we can. Mr Eden will know what to do,' Lady Alison said shakily, tucking the bundle inside her fur-lined cloak. Then, with a warning glance at Liza, 'We will say nothing about this, not to anyone.'

'No, my lady,' Liza promised, lifting her dazed half-sleeping child into the coach behind her mistress. No, it certainly didn't belong to a cat, that little blue foot they had seen dangling from a corner of the bundle.

As soon as the coach was out of sight Mabel Milligan left her hiding-place, and clasping her bony arms around her body, stiff with the cold, she gloated all the way home. Her long, freezing watch had borne fruit, after all. But where was Bridie? She must have slipped away when she hadn't been looking.

Which way had she gone? It didn't matter. In the whole of Edinburgh only she, Mabel Milligan, knew the secret of a poor little orphan girl gone now to some prosperous home, no doubt in the rich, posh part of the town called the New Town, and all she had to do, if it took her ten years to do it, was to track her down. Then she could milk the rich so-called parents dry of money to keep her mouth shut.

At last she gained the shelter of her room, where she stirred up the dying embers of her fire and stoked it with a few well-chosen lumps of coal. When they took up she made another bread pudding, because by now she was positively ravenous.

In a small but significant celebration, for raisins cost money, she flung in every last raisin she possessed. Now she knew for certain she would get her farm in Ireland. She *would*. She would. Her dreams would come true in the end. And then, after she had eaten, the warmth of the room overtook her, and she slept, a happy woman, the sleep of the dead.

Twenty minutes later, with Liza dismissed to put Kathy to bed, Eden Hamilton joined his wife in front of their parlour fire.

'Don't stop me!' Her eyes met his in a blaze he recognised at once as mother-love, extinguished for the past few very sad months. 'Oh, don't stare at me so, Eden! It's a long story, but we found this little child abandoned in a doorway, and she's still living, by the Grace of God. *Please* let me keep her! Say I can!'

There was a long silence while he considered it. He and his wife could never have a child of their own now, and he could see how desperate she was in every tender loving movement of her hands, the way she fondled the child, fed her with drops of milk and rubbed her tiny limbs back into life.

The father might have been some passing stranger in the night, the mother no better, to have left the baby on a doorstep to live or to die, but the important thing was there would be no record whatsoever.

'Only Liza knows?' he asked.

'Only Liza. Kathy will have forgotten it already. She's only three. And Fergus saw none of it.'

'Dr Chisholm will have to know, of course.'

'That makes it the four of us, then. You; me; Liza, who will never breathe a word; and the doctor, who dare not betray the confidence.'

'She's a beautiful little thing.' Eden stared down at the naked child lying on a shawl in his wife's lap and now turning almost pink.

'And she's ours,' Alison insisted. 'What shall we call her? I always thought I would have a son, and I would call him Eden after the best husband in the world.'

'She was found on the streets of Edinburgh, wasn't she?' Eden Hamilton bent and kissed his wife. 'And Edina is the old name for Edinburgh. Also, you did say by the Grace of God, Alison. So we'll call our little girl Edina Grace Hamilton, a good Scottish name.'

B ILLY BURKE SKULKED in the barracks for the best part of the
month's separation from his wife, spending most of his
spare time brooding about Helen MacDougal. Why, oh why,
had she gone and married a brute like John MacDougal, great
fat slob that he was? Drunk half the time, and, he could bet,
violent with it. What could a delicate creature like Helen see
in the likes of him?

For days on end he visualised her narrow pale face, those
strangely set blue eyes of hers, and how before long she would
be battered and bruised and ridden with MacDougal's offspring.
He tried to shake off the images, for as sure as God he was
actually beginning to mourn for Helen, and the terrible life she
must have entered into.

Where had John MacDougal taken her to, anyway? Up to
now he had only assumed from Bridie that it had been to
Edinburgh, but did Bridie really know? He doubted it, and
fell to wondering where MacDougal had gone for work. One of
the other soldiers gave him a clue when they were all discussing
the latest fever to hit Scotland, canal fever. Many labourers had
gone to work on the Caledonian Canal, but they were mostly
Scottish, fighting Highlanders at that, and no Irishman would
go looking for trouble there.

'Oh, no,' the soldier told him, 'not the Caledonian Canal. It would be the Forth and Clyde Canal. It's nearly finished as well, now.'

'But what are they digging the canals for?' Billy asked.

'Because of all the new factories. Using the canals is a cheap and easy way to move the goods they make in them about the country. The barges can carry coal as well – and wheat and corn from the farmers. Things that are too bulky for the new railways they're also building. So they tell me, anyway.'

'I see,' Billy said, with a sigh, for none of that information had told him at which end of the Forth and Clyde Canal John MacDougal had found a job, if indeed that was what had happened to him and Helen.

It was a long, long time before he even noticed that Bridie had disappeared from Ballina. He had succeeded in putting the daughter they'd had together to the back of his mind. He would not have been remotely interested to know that her name was now Mary Paterson, and as for begetting another daughter with Bridie, now known as Edina Hamilton, he had never even suspected her existence. But with Helen gone, and it seemed Bridie as well, there was nothing else for it but to go back to his wife. He sent word that he would return that evening, and the message back was that his wife would expect him at eight o'clock.

He went reluctantly, remembering that he didn't like the way her jet-black hair sprang straight up from her low forehead, in the same way as the iron-grey hair of her mother's, nor did he like the long sharp nose she had inherited from her father. In fact she possessed only one redeeming factor, when at certain times the come-hither look in her hard black eyes became extremely suggestive, and to that Billy always succumbed.

But before he even set out from the barracks he felt resentful of the Coleman family. They were all very tall, and that always made him feel inadequate because of his own short stature. His resentment built up with every stride he took towards Michael Coleman's shop, which would be shuttered and darkened now that it was almost supper time. His feet, distinctly less enthusiastic with every step, took him round to the door of the house behind the shop. He knocked and, as

46

he expected, waited. They would make him wait. It was some kind of punishment.

He knocked again and waited for a long time, until his ears picked up the sound of distant footsteps. The Colemans were still up, as he knew fine well they would be. Then there was the deliberately slow pulling back of bolts, the smallest flare of light and at last a human voice. 'Who is it?'

'Billy,' he said as pleasantly as he could. 'Who else would you be expecting at this time of night?'

'Hm,' said his father-in-law, opening the door another grudging inch, 'so it's you, is it? My daughter expected you half an hour ago, but as usual she was disappointed. What's the excuse this time?'

'There was a death. Dr Corcoran wanted me to help him.' Billy pushed in past him.

'Oh, ay? Who was it?'

God, they were a nosy lot, these Colemans! As well as prising all the gossip for miles around from their customers, they also knew every soldier in the Donegals. That was how Margaret had spotted him in the first place, because his face was new.

'Tim Donelly,' Billy said shortly, and sat down.

'Tim Donelly?' Michael Coleman said disbelievingly. 'But he's the biggest, strongest man in the Donegals!'

'He *was*.' Billy sighed. 'Poor bastard, he doesn't look very big or strong now. But he had a wife. She's coming to claim his body.'

Mr and Mrs Coleman pursed their lips at this announcement. Billy Burke had brought with him, as ever, a breath of the real world. Only Margaret looked at him with a different light in her eyes, before she dropped them circumspectly to her sewing.

The long silence went on and on, the women stitching away assiduously and Mr Coleman flapping the newspaper angrily from time to time while the peats died a slow fragrant death in the fire. Utterly bored and frustrated, Billy looked round the room, starting at the wooden floorboards covered by a rug at the fireside, and supposed its existence proved he was now part of the middle class of Ireland. There had never been a rug, let alone floorboards, on the mud floors of the cabins back home.

His eyes roved round the papered walls, their dull sepia merging into the uninspired pictures hanging upon them, to the sideboard which was Mr Coleman's favourite show-piece. Billy often wondered why, and not only that but what tree it had been cut from, for it was a screaming shade of orange, as was the table which was Mrs Coleman's pride and joy. Worst and ugliest of all was the terrible clock on the wall. Taking pride of place above the mantelpiece, it was an ornate cheap timepiece whose only credit was that, by fair means or foul, it really did keep time. It struck nine o'clock now, and as if by a signal Margaret and her mother disappeared into the nether regions of the house.

Fifteen minutes later they reappeared with a tray, with one tattie scone on each of two plates, and two tattie scones on two others. Margaret handed these to her father and Billy, and to complete the meal there was a pot of jet-black tea.

'Make yersel' at home, lad,' said Mr Coleman, suddenly genial; the ladies sighed in relief, and Billy felt completely trapped.

That feeling persisted all the time the Colemans merely tolerated his presence in their house. Margaret made love with him whenever he demanded it, but it was in a perfunctory, soulless way, so that at the end of four long, weary years of it Billy felt no closer to her than he had done when he married her. He had turned to his music for consolation a long time ago. It was the only thing in the world that made him happy now.

Christmas was almost upon them, when in the barracks one day Dr Corcoran received a visitor, and spent a long time laughing and talking to him and slapping him on the back. 'This is a very old friend of mine, Burke,' he introduced him. 'Dr Iain Mitchell from Edinburgh is coming with us on our rounds this morning.'

Billy took to Dr Mitchell right away, mainly because when serving in the officers' mess that evening he heard him reciting a long poem about an old Scottish man of the mountains suddenly confronted by a beautiful young girl. As the story unfolded it became bawdier and bawdier as every part of the old man's anatomy, and the girl's, was brought under the spotlight of the Scottish doctor's wry humour. It caught the attention of every man in the mess, and by the forty-fifth verse they were holding their ribs and howling with laughter.

'He was always good for a laugh,' Dr Corcoran assured Billy when he supported the two drunken doctors to their quarters, 'but remember, he's a damned fine doctor for all that. Anyway, you're to help him now, Burke. I'm off home for a spot of leave.'

At the end of a fortnight Billy would have died for Dr Mitchell. Even the mortuary was an entertaining place when he was in it, and when Dr Corcoran came back he looked at his friend quizzically and asked, 'Well, will he do?'

'He'll do,' Dr Mitchell replied.

'You see, Burke,' Dr Corcoran said, putting an arm around his friend's shoulders, 'this poor bloody fool here has joined up with the Scots Greys. He thinks he's not too old for action yet, and he wants a good dresser with him on the field. Wellington is screaming for help on the continent to stop Boney advancing any further. The Scots Greys are going. Dr Mitchell is going, and he wants to know: will you go, too?'

Billy's heart leapt up and then plummeted again. 'But how can I, sir?' he asked. 'I'm in the Donegals.'

The two doctors smiled at each other.

'There's such a thing as a transfer,' Dr Corcoran said, 'if you would be willing.'

Billy considered, but only for a second. There was very little to keep him in Ballina, to be sure. Margaret had succeeded in becoming pregnant at last, and was now far advanced. As a result, the Colemans had long ago banned him from the house again, and this might be at least a temporary escape from his unhappy life.

'It'll take a month or two to arrange.' Dr Mitchell shook his hand. 'You should hear by February.'

His transfer papers and his orders came through on St Valentine's Day, as the snow fell thick and fast. Margaret's child was due within a week. All day long Billy debated it, but in the end set off unwillingly on the short journey down to the shop to tell the Colemans of his imminent departure.

Outside the barrack gates the short journey suddenly became a long and hazardous nightmare. He floundered on while the wind blew the suffocating flakes horizontally now, and he could scarcely draw his breath. He made out a small yellow light, which seemed to be coming nearer and nearer, and struggled to meet it.

'Oh, my God, lad – is it yersel'?' Michael Coleman gasped, and in the wavering light of the night lantern Billy saw that the snow had frozen to his beard and his moustache, so that the man could hardly speak. 'How can we get a doctor? Margaret's in labour. I was going for the camp doctor.'

'You're unlucky, then,' Billy told him. 'Dr Corcoran had to go out earlier today, and he's not back yet. He's probably stuck somewhere in the snow.'

'Ye're nearly a doctor yersel'! And it's your child Margaret's labouring to bring into the world!' Michael Coleman used his superior height and strength to drag Billy back to the house. Inside, Margaret's screams were shrill, with no pauses in between them. 'For God's sake,' Mr Coleman moaned, 'get upstairs and help her! It's all yer fault!'

When Billy arrived in the bedroom, it was to discover a baby boy already delivered by Margaret's sweating, dishevelled mother. She was in the act of cutting the cord, and the baby lying on the bed was roaring lustily at the top of his voice.

'You must bring down the afterbirth,' said Billy, taking a hesitant step towards his wife.

'Get oot o' my way! I wouldna see ye in it.' Mrs Coleman pushed him aside. 'I ken all about afterbirths,' she added, delivering an almighty punch to Margaret's stomach that did the job with cruel efficiency. '*That*'s the way to deal wi' afterbirths,' she said contemptuously.

Billy retreated downstairs, told his father-in-law of his transfer and departure to Europe, promised to visit upon his return, and left. Battling through the snowstorm seemed very little to endure after what he had endured already that night.

* * *

50

The Scots Greys, and Billy with them, arrived well-fed and fresh in Europe to be taken into the command of the Duke of Wellington, who had the might of the Prussians on his side, too. Whatever Billy had expected active service to be like, it was not the very inactive camping on muddy sites waiting for someone to tell them when the next skirmish was coming.

Nevertheless, there was always the next skirmish, and the next, right through the cold wet spring, but Billy was glad of them because then he could help his beloved Dr Mitchell in the makeshift tent that was his operating theatre.

Soldier after soldier was carried in, some to die and some to be patched up as best as Dr Mitchell and Billy could manage in such primitive conditions. As soon as another batch was stretchered in, Dr Mitchell sorted them out. 'Left,' he would say. 'Left, left, left,' and these were the hopeless cases to be put to the left-hand side of the tent, while they worked on the others they thought they could save before putting them to recover on pallets of straw on top of the bare grass on the right-hand side of the tent.

'This is why it is so important to dissect dead bodies, Burke,' Dr Mitchell told him while he severed the shattered leg of a Scots Grey. 'Doctors have to know where the arteries are so that they can be tied before the poor devils bleed to death. Yes, we have to know about the arteries, besides all the other parts of the body.'

'Yes, sir.' Billy bandaged up the stump and removed the remains of the leg, laying it on a growing pile of severed limbs in one corner. He could see the sense of it all. He enjoyed watching the operations and truly believed that, with a little more training from Dr Mitchell and from Dr Corcoran when he got back to the Donegals, he could be a doctor himself one day.

'Get some of the orderlies to remove that heap.' Dr Mitchell nodded at the limbs. 'It doesn't do the wounded any good to see what may happen to them when they enter this tent.'

For four months the doctors and their dressers followed in the wake of the army until they came to a place called Waterloo, a village south of Brussels in Belgium, and Dr Mitchell told Billy that he thought this was where the last battle would be. So it proved, on the eighteenth day of June, in the pouring rain. The rain mingled with the blood that was shed that day, and the battlefield was a gory place to be.

Dr Mitchell and Billy worked on to the very end of it. The Battle of Waterloo saw the vanquish of Napoleon Bonaparte and the end of the war as well.

'It's not all over for us, though, Burke,' Dr Mitchell told him. 'I need some mementoes – a few arms and legs and anything else you can find left behind on the battlefield. I've a young son coming up, nearly ready to go to Edinburgh's medical schools. He's going to be a doctor, too, you know. So get out there and see what you can find.'

'Yes, sir,' Billy replied with enthusiasm. A hardened young man before, he was now completely callous – about the human body, at least – and he searched for what he knew the doctor would want: unblemished parts, as far as possible. Later he helped the doctor to swathe the discarded limbs in hospital blankets, pack them in a trunk with any large chunks of ice remaining in the dispensary, and they guarded the frozen cargo all the way to Edinburgh, where it started to drip.

'Here we must part.' Dr Mitchell shook his hand. 'You'll be going back to Ballina? Give Dan Corcoran my regards.'

'I suppose so,' Billy said sadly, and a few days later presented himself at the barracks, only to be told that the Donegals were to be disbanded.

'What does that mean?' he asked another soldier.

'The regiment is finished, along with a few others. War, and the threat of war, is over now, and the country can no longer afford to keep us.'

Billy still couldn't believe it when he was issued with a set of ill-fitting clothes and let loose to find some other way in the world. He had thought he would be a musician with the Donegals for ever. Disillusioned already, he went back to the Colemans'.

'Isn't he lovely?' Margaret dandled the child on her knee and then held him up for inspection. 'Look at him! He's the most beautiful boy in all the world!'

Billy couldn't agree with her. The baby was big, and too fat.

His black hair was growing low down on his forehead in the Coleman way, and he grizzled all the time. 'What did you call him?' he asked instead.

'Michael, of course. Michael Coleman. You see, I reverted to my maiden name, too ... *Well*, Billy, how were we to know that you would ever come back from such a dreadful war?'

So he was as good as dead to them, he thought bitterly.

'What will ye do now?' asked the senior Michael Coleman. 'There's no work to be got here.'

'Join you in the shop, perhaps, sir?'

'Oh, no! No, no, no! In these hard times there's scarcely a living for one man in the shop, never mind two. The folk havena the money to buy much now. But,' he looked Billy in the eyes, 'in the hope that things will improve I'm going to have a new sign up above the shop door: "Michael Coleman and Son".'

'Yes,' Margaret slid her hard black eyes round towards him triumphantly while she cuddled her ugly baby, 'that's what it was all about – "Michael Coleman and Son" – that was what we wanted. That was it and that was all. Goodbye, Billy Burke.'

Dazed and bewildered, Billy tried to find work, but the area was as agriculturally barren as ever, with more people to the square mile than the land could possibly support, and every day more and more soldiers were returning, disbanded too, to compete for the few miserably paid back-breaking jobs in casual labour.

Billy found himself desperate, nearly starving and walking for miles every day in the forlorn hope of a few hours' work, and in the evenings joining the other men hanging about miserably outside the Spread Eagle, for certainly none of them had a black penny to go inside.

'John MacDougal had the right idea,' Fingal Gall said, 'when he went to work on the Forth and Clyde Canal.'

Ah, Billy thought, so that *was* where John MacDougal had taken Helen! 'It must be finished now,' he said, with a sigh. 'There's no hope there.' All the other men agreed with him, shuffling their feet and muttering angrily.

'Well, I picked up a bit of a newspaper off the road today,' Fingal told them. 'They're going to build another canal still, to link up with the Forth and Clyde, called the Union Canal. They'll be starting soon. They're going to need labour, so I'm off, as sure as God. We'll all die, if we stay here.'

'I'm coming with you!' more and more voices swelled in agreement.

'So am I,' said Billy, and the next morning was one of the Irishmen migrating to Scotland. In his case, it was to be for ever.

6

DR MITCHELL ARRIVED home from Waterloo to the welcoming cries of his family. 'Are you all right, dear?' his wife asked him anxiously. 'Are you all in one piece?'

'Better than that, Fiona. I've got a few more legs and arms than I left with,' he said, laughing, and swung her round in his arms.

'No, you haven't, Father!' The four younger children scampered around him to make sure. 'You've still only got two arms and two legs.'

'The extra ones are in that trunk, Gavin,' he said, turning to his oldest son. 'Help me to carry it down to the cellar. That should keep them nice and fresh. Tomorrow we'll start dissecting.'

Gavin grinned at his father. In his view he was a good old boy, who up to now had done his best to show him the bones and muscles and tendons of any dead animals that had come their way. Human beings were a different matter, though. It was not so easy to get hold of a body.

In fact it was almost impossible. The surgeons in Edinburgh bemoaned the lack of specimens for dissection needed to train medical students and the latest scandal reported in the newspapers was the inception of mercenary grave-robbers anxious to supply their needs.

Bits and pieces of bodies left lying about on a battlefield were an entirely different and legitimate matter, an opportunity no doctor with any enterprise would miss, in Gavin's admiring opinion. Trust his father not to come back empty-handed from the war!

'The whole family's coming for dinner tonight, Father. They all want to welcome you back.'

'I suppose that includes your Uncle John Stafford?'

'Yes, sir.'

'Oh, well,' his father sighed philosophically, 'we shall just have to make the best of it, I suppose. He hasn't married again in the interval, by any chance?'

'By no chance. Who would have him?'

'Your mother's poor sister did once, my boy.'

'He made short work of *her*.'

'Well, well,' Dr Mitchell laughed and then sighed, 'try and keep a civil tongue in your head tonight, for your mother's sake.'

Later, when all the other guests had left, and the younger members of the family had gone to bed, Dr and Mrs Mitchell and Gavin sat politely in their drawing-room with Reverend John Stafford, wishing he would go. So far, the minister had drained only one glass of brandy and was now gazing fixedly at the decanter on the sideboard.

'You'll have another, John?' Dr Mitchell smiled quietly.

'The work of the Lord is always a lighter burden on my back after a meal like that, Fiona, and a drop or two of your brandy, Iain.' He grasped another full glass and turned his attention to Gavin. 'So you're going up to the university when you're a bit older, laddie?'

'I am, Uncle John.'

'And have you considered what you will study in Edinburgh?'

'Not exactly.' Gavin wriggled uncomfortably on his chair.

'If you take my advice, it will be God's word.'

'You mean, become a minister? Like you?' Gavin veered so near to impertinence that both his parents shot him warning glances.

But Reverend Stafford had not noticed it. He sailed on grandly into his little lecture. 'The landladies always welcome students of divinity. They know they are safe with us. What's more, I have thought of a plan. I can come here every night and give you some tuition – that is, if your father and mother don't mind having to feed me?' He smiled at the ridiculous idea that they could possibly object.

Gavin's father choked a little on his brandy, his mother looked appalled and Gavin himself reflected that he had not yet made up his mind what career to follow. Now, in the sheer horror of contemplating Uncle John in the house every night, he was galvanised into an immediate decision.

'You will not be put to that bother, sir,' he said firmly. 'The only tutor I shall ever require will be my own father. In a doctor's family, at least one child cannot help following in his father's footsteps, and in this case I am that child.'

'May the Lord forgive you, Gavin Mitchell! Oh, dear God, listen to our pleas! Forgive this young man and send him Your guidance, we beg – a *medical student*, indeed! Don't you know that medical students are the most decadent, the most notorious, of them all? The High Street of Edinburgh is thronged with them at the dead of night, carousing and getting into every kind of vice and wickedness!'

So, Gavin thought, it wasn't swotting twenty-four hours a day, after all. It sounded more like fun, instead.

'And how would *you* know about the High Street at the dead of night, John?' Dr Mitchell's eyes danced with laughter. 'You frequent it, perhaps?'

'Certainly not!'

'Well, you're on dangerous ground. I was a medical student once myself, you know.'

'Oh . . . yes. Of course you were. I mean no –"

'It's time for bed.' Mrs Mitchell put away her embroidery and stood up, effectively putting an end to the conversation. 'Up you go, Gavin,' she said, while the doctor ushered out their last visitor for the evening.

'He killed my poor sister, working her hands to the bone for him. Now he would make a slave out of me!' he heard his mother saying indignantly on the way upstairs, and his father's laughing reply, 'Pompous hypocrite!' before their

57

bedroom door shut, and he was left alone with his momentous decision.

So, he was going to be a doctor! He had said himself that it had always been almost inevitable, and for the next few years, after the dominie's school was out, it was taken for granted that he should accompany his father whenever he was called out to visit his patients.

Before he was even secure in his Latin declensions he knew all the instruments – and what they were for – in his father's big bag, had watched him using most of them, and before the dominie ever got round to telling them about the birds and the bees he and the other boys had watched Farmer Brown's huge bull, Jock, with his hooves up on a cow's back.

'What's he doing?' they all asked Jimmy Young, the bad boy of the school, who was only too pleased to tell them, and to translate the bull's activities into human terms.

'Rubbish,' Gavin said. 'My father never did that to my mother!'

'Wait a year or two and you'll be doing it yourself,' Jimmy said, laughing. 'I have.'

'You're a liar!' the boys shouted, and chased him away.

They found out later that he was no liar when they watched the cow delivering her calf, and when it was all over Farmer Brown heaved a sigh of relief. He stood there in his nicky tams, his coat which was really a sack with three holes in it for his head and his arms, and winked at them. 'Ay, he knows his stuff, old Jock,' he said.

Mrs Mitchell's cosy picture of the stork circling their garden in search of a suitable gooseberry bush under which to leave her children was one of Gavin's boyhood illusions shattered in a blinding flash of truth.

When Billy Burke and the other immigrants landed in Glasgow their first task was to find work of any sort to keep body and soul together until such time as they could get to the Union Canal, for the news that met them was that there had been a delay in starting it. If they did manage to find a labouring job they stayed in it as long as they could, and Billy himself worked at road-building for the best part of three years, always managing to get nearer and nearer to Maddiston, where the canal work was due to begin.

When he finally arrived on the outskirts he came to a collection of huts, each one more wretched than the last, made with a few sticks and a lot of rotten straw, a cross between pigsties and beehives. Any smoke that did not escape out of the doors escaped from spaces in the walls, to give them the appearance of haystacks on fire. But the children playing about seemed happy and healthy enough, and their Irish accents told him he had arrived. This was where he would live while he worked on the Canal.

He found shelter in one of the huts with five other of his countrymen, all good-natured, even if they fought and shouted when they were drunk. They had to work hard, digging, blasting, picking, hauling and loading great stones into place for landing-stages and to secure the canal banks, and when the day's work was over they took pleasure in deliberately trampling through the laird's cornfields on their way back to their huts.

'This will be a navigational canal,' one of them told him, 'because people will be able to sail flat-bottomed boats up and down it, and barges will be dragged along it. So they call us the "navigators", navvies for short, and the laird's lady and gentlemen visitors are frightened of us. It amuses them to watch us working – and dying, if a rope frays or a horse slips in the mud and crushes the rider. They think it's funny. Ay, they're very wise to keep their distance from the navvies.'

For Billy the work was hard in the extreme. He was much smaller than the other navvies, but the muscles in his neck, shoulders and hands acquired exceptional strength for the size of him. He found that once their wages began coming in regularly it wasn't all work, work, work. There were compensations, especially on Sundays, when as well as plenty of potatoes to eat there was the poteen to drink.

'Och, ye can always go to Maisie,' the men told him when they saw him becoming restless, especially with a drink inside him. 'We all do.'

'Where is she, then?'

'The last hut.'

'But what about her man? Won't he object?'

The men laughed. 'He's dead. But even when he was living she would have given him a clout over the head if he did. She's a navvy, too.'

So Billy made his way to Maisie's hut one Sunday, and found her lying down, a great rough woman, drinking whisky. 'Get away out!' she shouted in her man's voice to children he assumed were hers. 'Away ye go. Here's a man come to see me.' She turned to Billy. 'And what might you be wanting?'

'What have you got?' he asked, handing her a shilling from the half-crown that was his whole week's wages.

'All right, then.' She grabbed the shilling and lay back again. 'I see ye're new. Next time, bring a drink as well. Then ye can have longer.'

Another four years of his life went past in this fashion, and at the end of it he was nearly thirty years old and getting past the age for navvying. The Union Canal was nearing completion, he was still penniless, but he had survived, although with one bitter regret. In all that time he had seen neither hair nor hide of John MacDougal and Helen.

Now and then he stayed all night long with Maisie. She had become quite fond of the little man who entertained her with his pleasant ways and the tunes he played for her on his home-made pipe. Then, one fine early morning on his way from her hut he stopped short. He stood still, frozen in shock. It was as though his heart was squeezed so hard that it hurt. He could scarcely breathe, for he simply couldn't believe his eyes when, out of one of the other huts, came Helen.

Oh God, oh God, it couldn't be . . . but it was. She was changed, of course, but he still knew her and he still loved her, the one and only passion of his life, with her long narrow face and her blue eyes high above her cheek-bones. She still hadn't seen him when she went to the common pump, put her head under it and allowed the water to run through her hair.

'Oh, *Helen*,' he murmured, as he went up to her.

She pushed her wet, matted hair back from her forehead as

she straightened up, exposing large purple bruises on her cheeks. Billy's heart contracted with anger and pity, and in that moment he knew he wanted only to love and protect her for the rest of his life. 'Oh, Helen,' he said again.

'So it's you, Billy Burke?'

'Are you all right, alanna?'

'No, I'm very wrong, very wrong.' Tears flew from her eyes, to his bitter distress. 'He beats me and torments me, and I hate the two great lumbering sons he ground out o' me. Oh, God,' she sobbed, 'what am I to do?'

'I'll be telling you now what to do, Helen,' he said gently. 'Where is he?'

'Oh, Christ, at this hour? Dead to the world and snoring, as usual.'

'And there's nobody else here but us . . . There's nobody to see us, so walk away, Helen, *now*. Walk away from all this with me. We'll go away together and start a new life.'

By this time Billy's elder daughter, Mary Paterson, was twelve years old and utterly enchanting. 'She's our little princess,' Joe Paterson agreed with his wife, and their four sons – especially Joseph, the oldest – agreed with that.

Nothing was too good for Mary. Molly Paterson sewed her dresses, washed her, attended to her through her 'difficult' times, and over and over again brushed out the startlingly yellow curls that tumbled down her back.

'Oh, don't cut them,' Joe pleaded.

'I never will,' she replied.

All went well for another few months, until one day when Joseph was almost fifteen years old and he and Mary were walking together a little distance away from the cottage. 'Lift up yer skirts,' he panted.

Mary lifted up her skirts without any hesitation. She wanted to please – and besides, she had been brought up to believe she was beautiful from her head to her feet.

'Oh, Jesus,' Joseph said, and plunged into her.

She blinked, a little surprised. But it wasn't sore, and a few months afterwards when Joseph left to take up work on a neighbouring farm and his brother Danny turned to her instead, she had become quite used to it and was completely amazed when Dada Joe came upon them one day and flew into a towering rage.

Danny was quickly despatched and she was left alone and in peace again until, when she was fifteen herself, she met Dada Joe quite by accident in the hayloft. His face flamed dark red and he seemed breathless when he spoke. 'Mary . . .'

'What is it, Dada?' she asked innocently, but she wasn't as innocent as she looked when she went right up to him. She was missing the attentions of the boys, but it was Dada Joe she had always loved best.

Then her whole life became a whirl of secret lovers' meetings, whenever the opportunity arose, and always their favourite rendezvous was up in the hayloft. It was there that Molly's worst and most dreaded suspicions were confirmed when she, the only mother Mary had ever known, crept silently up the ladder until her head and shoulders were in the hayloft, too.

'What's this, Joe Paterson?' Her face was contorted with anger.

'It's only Dada,' Mary told her. 'He isn't doing any harm. He loves me.'

'He's not your father, and I'm not your mother! It was a little viper we found on our doorstep fifteen years ago, after all we've done for you. You corrupted two of my boys. Now it's their father, is it?' Molly screamed. 'Get down this ladder, and out ye go. Get away from here. I never want to see your face again!'

The next Mary knew she was on the road to Edinburgh, thrown out in what she stood up in, and that was all. She would never forget that long walk through the night, when she wondered briefly who her real father had been, and then dismissed him. Her real mother was scarcely more interesting, except that at least she had had some sense. In Mary's opinion she had been quite right to get rid of an unwanted child. It was what she would do herself, if ever she were that unlucky.

But so far, at least, she was not. She reached Edinburgh, and before it was properly light felt herself pulled towards the High

Street, she didn't know how. It didn't take her long to see that she had landed up in the right place. The smells didn't worry her, although they were worse than the little farm had ever produced. She forgot them in the wonder and excitement of the tall, crowded tenements twelve storeys high on both sides of a street which was soon teeming with people – people who shouted, and ran, and pushed past her. She loved this wonderful town. Oh, yes, it was the right place for her!

She pressed her nose up against a bake-shop window. Ah, if only she could eat those delicious smells! She would die soon if she didn't get something to eat, for she had eaten nothing since the three o'clocks the day before. There was an elderly woman presiding over the breads and buns inside. Mary eyed them hungrily while the woman eyed her. Eventually she came out.

'Well, what do *you* want?' she asked. 'Dinna press yer nose against my window unless you want the goods.'

'I do,' Mary said, 'even a crust. But I've no money.'

'Ye could work for a living.' The woman looked her up and down closely.

'I would, and willingly,' Mary said, 'if someone employed me.'

'I'll give you a try. You can sit here in the window. Watch over the bread and put all the money in the till. The prices are on the tickets, and I've got it a' coonted, so ye needn't try to cheat me, my lady.'

The woman went away and didn't come back until six o'clock that night, to count the money and the bread that was still unsold. 'Ye've managed, then,' she sighed, 'and now I suppose I'll have to shut the shop. The woman who usually comes in at six o'clock to do the night shift is ill, and I canna do it mysel' with my man at home ill as well.'

'I'll do it,' Mary offered, 'if you can tell me where I can find lodgings. I've nowhere to go tonight.'

'Well . . . Ye helped me out today, right enough, so ye can sleep on the floor here until the bakers arrive in the early morning, and then let them in. Sweep the shop floor and wash down the shelves, ready for fresh bread. What's yer name, anyway?'

'Mary Paterson.'

'Mine's Mistress Meg Dod. What about tomorrow, Mary? Can you stay on?'

'What about the wages?'

'Oh, I'll see ye all right, lassie, on Saturday. That's when I pay the wages. I might even keep ye on for the day shift, for a while. I'm finding it all too much wi' my man ill as well.'

So Mary, who had been plagued all day by the appetising smells, was left with a two-day-old scone to chew, with the rats for company on the bakehouse floor, and all the following day she sold the bread the bakers brought through until a thin middle-aged woman arrived at six o'clock, and stared at her.

'Where's Meg Dod?' she asked.

'Her man's ill. I've been working here since yesterday morning. She said you usually come in at six o'clock.' Mary took off the large white apron Meg Dod had given her to wear, and the woman put it on, staring at her all the time.

'God, ye're awful like someone I used to know,' she said. 'Her name was Bridie.'

'Never heard of her. My name's Mary Paterson.' Mary smiled. 'You wouldn't happen to know some place I could stay the night, would you?'

'Well, there's no one in my land all night while I'm here working. Ye could stay there, and I'll see about the rent when we get paid on Saturday. I'm Mabel Milligan, and anyone will tell ye where World's End Close is. Number eight. Here's the key.'

Mabel Milligan's eyes followed Mary out, taking in every detail of her face and figure. She might call herself Mary Paterson, but she was Bridie's child, little Mary, and nobody would ever persuade her otherwise. The likeness was striking: the same clear complexion, the same height and outline, the same glorious hair. If anything, she was even prettier than Bridie, for Mary's eyes, the same blue, were bright and sharp. There was nothing simple about Mary Paterson.

God, Mabel Milligan thought, she'd waited a long time for this. Fifteen years. That was why she had offered Mary a home so quickly. She couldn't let slip an opportunity for furthering her future nest in Ireland, for Mary Paterson might know what had happened to her baby sister. Unfortunately it would not be until Sunday when they were both off work that she would have a chance to question the girl in detail.

On the other hand, Mary might not even know, as she did, that her sister was living with a rich family. If not, it was a secret Mabel was not at all willing to share – nor the money she hoped to gain from this knowledge.

'How did ye come to be called Mary Paterson?' Mabel began when they were buttering their breakfast tea-cakes, toasted so that they would not taste so stale.

'That's what I was called by my Ma and Dada – ' Mary laughed ' – Joe and Molly Paterson. I didn't choose it.'

'No, of course ye didn't, dearie. Do ye have any brothers and sisters?'

'Brothers. Four of them, but no sisters.'

'No?'

'No.' Mary suddenly began to feel wary of this long-nosed woman's questions. All right for now, but she was a nosy bitch, and as soon as she could find somewhere else to go she'd be off. But she would give her something to satisfy her in the meantime. 'In fact, that's why I've run away from home,' she said, smiling sweetly. 'I got tired of nothing but boys' company. A girl likes to have other girls for friends.'

'I ken.'

So, Mabel Milligan could get no more out of her and, highly delighted with herself, Mary had found a job and a place to sleep only three days after arriving in Edinburgh. Three months later she realised Meg Dod's profits had multiplied by ten, and that was all because she, Mary, sat in the window attracting the customers in. It was about then that she met Janet Brown, one day when she was out in the High Street on an errand.

'I've seen you in that shop window,' Janet said. 'I look at you every day. You're so pretty.'

Mary was used to gentlemen telling her that, especially the

students from the university, but women usually only looked at her in a nasty way. She decided to make a friend of Janet. It would be fine, as she had told Mabel Milligan, to have another woman to talk things over with.

By this time the first batch of bread and buns and cakes were all disappearing long before six o'clock, and some of the gentlemen customers were making exciting propositions. She could take her pick and charge her own price and she could never get over how easy it was to make all this money; in fact it was so much money – which she kept well hidden from Mabel Milligan – that she decided to look for other lodgings.

She found a large room with a Mrs Lawrie, and asked Janet to go with her. Within a couple of months they both gave up their daytime jobs, Mary hers in the bake-shop, and Janet hers helping out on a fish-stall, and began devoting all their time to their new profession.

Mrs Lawrie didn't approve, and told them so. 'Ye'd better find somewhere else,' she said. 'I canna have ye bringing men in here at all times o' the night. It'll gi'e ma hoose a bad name.'

This time Mary found a room off the High Street all to herself and Janet, not so bold, met another girl to share lodgings with, but they met every day for a drink and a chat.

They were down in the Grassmarket, Mary buying a fur tippet, and Janet trying to decide whether to buy pink or blue garters from the Jew, when Janet suddenly remembered something she had been meaning to tell her. 'There's another girl looks just like you in Edinburgh, ye ken, Mary.'

Mary's face hardened. There couldn't be another girl like her! 'Like me?' she asked sharply. 'Where?'

'Och, they say she lives over in the New Town, far away from us.'

'And you've seen her, this other girl?'

Janet nodded her head, anxious to make amends. 'Ay, I've seen her. But she's not nearly as bonny as you, Mary. Her hair's all twisted up, not like yours.'

'Ay,' Mary smiled and tossed back her yellow ringlets, quite mollified, 'it's queer how many women dinna ken what a man likes.' She strutted along the Grassmarket in her new fur tippet, swaying her hips, Janet trying to copy her as best she could, 'But she'll be one o' those high-ups from the likes o' Charlotte Square?'

'She'll never bother us,' Janet assured her as they climbed up Candlemaker Row and back into the High Street. 'Forget I ever told you.'

But, except for a little something niggling away in the back of her mind, something Mabel Milligan had said, Mary had forgotten already. There was the exciting prospect of the evening's work to think about instead, and how many men she could entice back to her room – or just into one of the closes outside Swanston's tavern if they were in a hurry for her favours, and they usually were.

Nowadays she chose only the better-class men, those who had the sort of money she was now charging. She smiled at the even more exciting prospect of the rest of her life. She was only sixteen now, and she calculated she could carry on for twenty years at least, by which time she would be very rich indeed, and therefore a lady.

Yes, she thought, sticking her delightful little nose in the air, she would be a rich lady, rich enough to buy a house in Charlotte Square herself, if she had a mind to. It was a wonderful life.

'Let's go to Swanston's, Janet,' she said, laughing.

7

WELL INTO HIS seventeenth year, Gavin divided his attention equally between the pretty girls in and around Gilmerton and his expeditions with his father that last summer before going up to the university.

'What is it today, then, Father?' he asked as they buckled their mare to the gig.

'Our dilemma for today is with the Wishart family, or, rather, one of their two little girls. It seems she has fallen into a bramble bush.'

'Will they pay you for this?' Gavin asked.

'I've been going to speak to you about doctors' fees for a while.' Dr Mitchell smiled and sighed at the same time. 'They'll pay if they can, even if it's only sixpence a week. The Wisharts always pay their debts in the end, but there are families here who can never hope to discharge them. Never forget that being a doctor is a vocation, my boy, and although I've always been as poor as a church mouse I've never passed by a human being who needed my help, payment or no payment.'

More doubtful every day now whether he had chosen the right path in life, Gavin followed his father into the Wisharts' house and they examined the child's legs. Every prickle of the bramble bush had found a place to pierce the child's skin, as he could plainly see, for every one had poisoned and was beginning to ulcerate.

'These wounds require tincture of iodine to burn out the poison, Mrs Wishart,' Gavin's father told the distressed mother, and in an aside to his son, 'Of course, it will be very painful, but it must be done. Hold her legs for me.'

He proceeded to flush out the ever-widening wounds with the dark brown fluid, while the child screamed, her mother fainted and her father beat a hasty retreat with his younger daughter. It took two or three more visits and further applications of iodine before Dr Mitchell pronounced himself satisfied that the poisoning had stopped, and the ulcerated areas could now be treated by the village nurse.

'On the outskirts of Edinburgh there's an outbreak of the "Indian fever", as the folk there call it. Cholera, Gavin, and it's deadly,' Dr Mitchell said a few weeks later. 'They need every available doctor who can spare some time. We'll go over there this afternoon.'

Visiting the bleak little houses full of dead and dying bodies was enough to convince Gavin that he certainly was choosing the wrong profession. Even the living were somehow grey and wrinkled surrounded by their own excrement, for there was nobody there to help them and the stench was stifling. His father went amongst them, encouraging them and handing out phials of laudanum.

'What else could anyone do?' he said sadly on the way home. 'There's no hope for them, without nurses and proper care, and the hospitals in Edinburgh are over-stretched already. Laudanum will see some of them, at least, into a less painful grave.'

'What causes it, though, Father?'

'If the authorities know, they are doing nothing about it. Nobody knows for certain, but I believe their water supply should be examined. It is probably contaminated. What is it *now*?' he added when his wife rushed out to meet them.

'It's the younger Wishart girl this time,' she told them. 'Her father's been here in tears. The child has gone blue and can't breathe.'

'Bronchitis,' Dr Mitchell diagnosed when they had hurried there. 'Putrid membrane in the windpipe,' and without more ado, for there was very little time left as Gavin could see, he plunged his instrument directly into the child's throat. There was a minute of agonised waiting before they heard the sheath hissing with regular breathing, and the little girl's face lost some of the blue colour. 'She'll be all right now,' the doctor said, and gave the parents directions for cleansing the tube until he came back the following day.

But there was a third call to the Wisharts' house that same summer. By then both children had had measles, and now the younger one had a recurrence of bronchitis and Dr Mitchell and his son found the elder one with raging double pneumonia.

'We'll have to break the fever first of all,' he said. 'Gavin, find the friars' balsam in my bag. Mother, we need two boiling kettles, one to put the balsam in, so that the steam goes round the room and makes it easier for them to breathe. The other kettle is for you to make up two bread poultices. You have plenty of bread?'

'I'll go and get another loaf,' Mr Wishart said.

It was very late that night and they were still attending to the little girls. The younger was breathing more easily in her sleep, but the other was still fighting for her life, with the bread poultices on her chest for one hour and then on her back for the next hour, until at last Dr Mitchell gestured to his son. 'What do you see on her forehead?' he asked.

'Beads of sweat, sir.'

'Thank God the fever is breaking,' he told the parents. 'Keep up the poulticing, and we will need a basin. Now,' he said, lifting the child up the bed so that her head was almost over the edge, 'listen!'

In a few minutes they could hear the drops of sweat falling down the child's long hair and into the basin, but it was well through the following morning before they dared to leave the Wisharts' house to go home and fall wearily into bed themselves for a few hours. Gavin couldn't fall asleep, even so.

He went over and over all the instruments his father possessed, their purposes, the occasions on which he had seen them used, and after an hour of such deep thought rose up totally refreshed. He went down to the kitchen to find his mother.

71

'Father not up yet?' he asked jauntily, accepting a large plate of bacon and eggs.

'Your father has had years of practice, Gavin. He has the sense to rest when he can. Being the only doctor for miles around isn't easy, you know, and we all get older every day. I've made a fresh pot of tea, and there's more toast coming.'

'Oh, it's not so bad, Mother! I've seen most of it now. There's not much I won't be able to tackle.'

'No? Then you won't be needing to go to the university at all, I suppose? The university of life is good enough for you, I daresay? Don't you ever again let your father – or me, either – hear you bragging like that, laddie!' Mrs Mitchell said indignantly. 'You're not too big to get a good skelping yet, you know.'

On September the nineteenth Gavin was seventeen, and the week after that the day dawned when he would go to the university at last. Having experienced, or so he thought, most of what a doctor might have to face and having had a glimpse into anatomy besides, thanks to his father's supply of extra limbs, he got ready to set off early in the morning to walk to Edinburgh feeling fairly confident.

At the last minute his mother crammed a boiled ham and a plum cake into his bag of clean clothes, weeping all the while. His young brothers and sisters scampered round them laughing and sparring with each other so that they never actually managed to say goodbye, but once they realised he had gone they climbed on the gate and shouted his name and waved until he was out of sight.

'Oh, my God, Iain,' said Mrs Mitchell, dabbing her eyes at the window as they watched their first-born marching jauntily off down the road, 'just look at my wee bit laddie!'

'He's a wee bit laddie now, right enough, but wait and see, my dear! This time next year he'll be a grown man.' Dr Mitchell put a comforting arm round her, and laughed. 'He will that, if I remember rightly, after a year in Edinburgh on his own two feet!'

The corn was ripening a dun yellow in the fields on either

side of the road Gavin tramped along. It was midday when he was walking up the Potterrow within sight of the grim-looking building where he had to matriculate. There he came face to face with an old man in stained white breeches and a coat which had once been black but was now green with age, from which sprouted a cravat closely resembling the cloth with which Mrs Mitchell washed her kitchen floor. Gavin took him for the bursar, since BURSAR was written on the door.

'Umph-hm,' said the bursar, glowering, 'and what can I do for *you*? This is where students enrol for the university, ye ken.'

'Good,' Gavin said. 'I've come to the right place, then! I wish to enrol in the faculty of medicine.'

'Ye'll need to let me see yer papers first,' the bursar said suspiciously, 'and ye canna set yer foot inside any faculty o' this university without yer fees.'

'Here's the fees,' Gavin handed over one packet of the money his father had given him that morning, 'and a letter from the schoolmaster to prove I am fit to matriculate, along with another from Reverend John Stafford in which he states that I have come from a Christian home.'

'Hm! Well, it'll be Professor Monroe ye'll be with, of course, if all this is satisfactory!' It seemed it was, for the bursar took the money and then threw his papers back at him. 'The *annus medicus* begins on October third,' he said. 'It's anatomy to begin with. Ye'll have nowhere to stay, I dinna suppose?'

'I'm going to look for lodgings this afternoon.'

'There's some advertised on the wall behind ye but, as ye'll see, they're mostly spoken for.' The old man smiled unpleasantly. 'Ay, ye'll have a struggle coming up as late as this. Most o' the students have been here for a week already.'

'I'll soon find somewhere,' Gavin said confidently. 'But first, can you direct me to Surgeons' Square?'

Such few glimmers of pleasantness as ever had been on the bursar's face disappeared instantly. 'What dae ye want to go there for?' he snapped.

'To enrol with Dr Knox as well. He's the *real* anatomist, isn't he? We all know that.'

'Get oot o' my sight,' the bursar gasped. 'We dinna speak

73

about the Outside Schools here in these hallowed halls, let alone an upstart like Robert Knox. The minute I clapped eyes on ye I kent ye spelled trouble. Find yer ain way, ye cheeky wee bugger!'

Dr Robert Knox himself answered Gavin's knock on the door of 10, Surgeons' Square. An imposing and unforgettable figure in a lavender suit with snow-white lace at his throat and his cuffs, thinning silver hair on his head and a black patch over one eye, he read Gavin's papers with interest, took his fees and welcomed him to his classes.

'Well, well, Mr Mitchell, you've got the very last place. My classes are full up now. By the way, they begin on October 3rd,' he said.

'But, sir – '

'The same day as Professor Monroe's?' Dr Knox smiled. 'Yes, but I begin at nine o'clock in the morning. He doesn't begin until twelve.'

The afternoon had waned when Gavin knocked at the doors of the first, second, third and fourth addresses he'd been given to try for lodgings, and every one had been slammed in his face. It was the evening now, and the only welcoming place seemed to be an inn with SWANSTON above the door.

Inside, with a jar of beer in his hand and his burning feet propped up on another chair, he noticed that a vision of positive loveliness was eyeing him with interest. His pulses quickened when she came and sat down beside him, her yellow tangled curls bouncing off her wickedly half-exposed breasts, for by this time she had allowed her new fur tippet to fall down round her arms.

'I'm Mary Paterson,' she told him. 'Are you going to buy me a drink and tell me who you are, and why you're looking so glum?'

'Gavin Mitchell, a medical student, and I can't find any lodgings.'

'A medical student, eh?' She laughed as their eyes met. Hers were blue, as blue as the sky, he thought poetically.

She was a good-natured girl, he decided before long, and so very pretty! She was everything he had ever dreamed about.

Within the first five minutes he had fallen madly in love with her.

Of course, he had been in love before, but that was only with wee lassies. This Mary Paterson was a proper woman, as it was very plain to see. He didn't even stop to ask himself how she came to be so practised in the art of introducing herself to strange men, or what his mother might have said about a female person drinking whisky in a tavern. All that was in his mind was, how could he see her again? It proved much easier than he could have dared to hope.

'And you can find no lodgings?' She smiled at him. 'Well, don't worry, Gavin Mitchell. You've found a place now. You can come and stay with me.'

Billy Burke and Helen scarcely paused in their flight until they got to Peebles, exhausted, penniless and homeless. But the most desperate of situations sometimes have their compensations, and Billy was Helen's. During this time she got to know him, and then to love him, for to her he was nothing but gentle and kind.

They were very much in love when he was taken on as a weaver and some money started to come in regularly. Though they had only one room to live in, a straw mattress to sleep on and a very meagre diet, they were happy.

Helen washed her hair oftener. She washed their clothes from time to time, and now and then even borrowed a flat iron to smooth them out. Billy would have felt they were getting somewhere if it hadn't been for the shooting pain in his left testicle. The ache wasn't constant, but when it came every so often he was agonised with worry, very depressed, and the more he brooded about it the more he became gloomily convinced that it had only been there since his intimacy with Maisie when he'd worked at the Union Canal.

Helen didn't understand why, when he was usually so good-natured, he should retreat into these black moods, and when she whined at him his Irish temper got the better of him and he would slap her. But a good booze on a Friday and Saturday night usually cured it all, then he would make love to her again, and call her his 'Nellie', and when he did she knew everything was all right.

This went on for eighteen months, when he was laid off from the weaving. By great good luck he got work as a baker next, before his luck ran out again five months later. He could find no other work in Peebles, and they took to the road once more, this time heading for Edinburgh.

In Leith he thanked God and the Reverend Mr Watt, who had made all the boys at his manse learn the rudiments of various trades, amongst them the patching of shoes, because there he got a job with a cobbler. But this time he and Helen could find nowhere to live.

'Ach, to hell with it,' he told her one perishing cold Friday night. 'I've a brother Constantine living in Edinburgh now. We'll go and see him. He might give us a corner to sleep in, so he might.'

'But where is he?' Helen asked, her face fretful and peevish on the long road up to the town.

'I don't know, but there can't be many men in Edinburgh by the name of Constantine Burke. We'll ask, and in the end we'll find him.'

'Och, what are you staring at *her* for?' Helen clutched his arm jealously when they got to the High Street and saw Mary Paterson swaying towards them. 'She's a slut, that one. Anyone can tell.'

'Well, then, she might know a lot of men in this town. I'll ask her. 'Do you know a man by the name of Constantine Burke, miss?' Billy gazed at the girl. Christ, what a beauty!

'Never heard of him!' Mary laughed and walked on.

'You only asked her so you could get a good look at her,' Helen sniffed, but Billy paid no attention. He was back in Ireland, with his memories. 'She reminded me of Bridie,' Helen added, and got his attention at last.

'Begod, that's clever of you, Helen! I was trying to remember.'

'Trying to remember? When she had your baby? Mary, she called her, and a bonny baby she was when John MacDougal and I last saw the pair o' them on the way to this town. I wonder what ever happened to them?'

'Now, don't let's be speaking of the past, alanna,' Billy said. God, Helen could be an awkward ugly tath at times ... 'We're trying to find a roof over our heads tonight, for God's sake.'

They found Con at last, high up in a tenement in Tanners' Close, at the West Port end of the Grassmarket, dirty and smelly and dark. 'Sure, and it's not exactly how I would like it,' he told them after introducing them to his slatternly woman, 'but at least it's high up away from the pigs. We'll let you stay for the night, but you'll have to sleep on the floor. Have you got work, Billy?'

'I've been working with a cobbler in Leith.'

'In Leith?' Con looked at him in amazement. 'Why in Leith? There are plenty of feet in plenty of shoes up here in the town, man!'

Yes, indeed, and plenty of beautiful women who could be bought, thought Billy, completely unaware that the first child he and Bridie had had together was one of them, and that she was the beautiful woman he'd just spoken to. He made up his mind that Edinburgh was where he would stay.

'Downstairs on the ground floor there's a land called Log's Lodgings,' Con told him, as though he had read his thoughts. 'Tomorrow I'll take you down there. The man who runs it doesn't charge much, so he doesn't. His name is William Hare.'

8

LIZA FRASER SMOOTHED down an already irreproachable white pinafore, settled her cap firmly on her head and entered the dining-room positively rustling with starch. She offered the silver tray to Mr Hamilton first.

'Your letters, sir.'

'Ah, yes, Liza.' Mr Eden Hamilton, Advocate, did not take his nose out of Saturday's *Scotsman*, and Liza laid down the tray beside his plate. As usual, the pile of letters looked formidable and as dry as dust. 'Do you know what the Editor has written for his leading article today?' he asked, without raising his eyes.

'No, dear,' Lady Alison said mildly, taking her letters off the tray and riffling through them idly until she stopped short at one of them with a frown. 'What?'

'Here we are arrived at the first day of October 1825 – 1825, mark you – and he is still bemoaning the lack of bodies for the anatomists, when we all know that nobody is safe lying in his grave! It would fit him better to ask why Edinburgh people, every time there is a death, must keep watch with lanterns over their loved ones laid to rest in the churchyards.'

'None for you today, Miss Edina,' Liza said on the way out.

'Did you hear me, Alison?' Mr Hamilton rustled his newspaper agitatedly and finally lowered it sufficiently to look at his wife over the top of his spectacles. 'There is even a joke going round about it: "The surgeons makes no bones about wanting

79

fresh meat." Christopher North said recently that the students themselves are at it, especially the students of Dr Knox.'

'Did he, dear? I fear I cannot take much interest in what Christopher North said, this morning. There is something here much closer to home, I'm afraid. It is a letter from England, Kendal to be precise.' She paused delicately and then dropped her bombshell. 'From Cornelia.'

She sat back with the air of one who must resign herself to weathering the storm, while Mr Hamilton gazed at her for some minutes in absolute horror. It was a storm that would break at any minute now, with even the *Scotsman* cast aside.

'You cannot mean my most detested cousin, Cornelia Forbes? Mistress Cornelia Sharpe, wife of that scoundrel Cardew Sharpe, who was the only one who would have her after all her scandalous affairs?'

'The same,' Lady Alison said as firmly as her gentle voice allowed.

'But I thought we had got rid of her years ago when they went off to Kendal to hunt with the hounds or whatever they do there?'

'*You* got rid of her, dear. I am the one who has been answering her letters ever since.'

'Do you mean to tell me that you have been in correspondence with her all these years? It is like a ghost come back to haunt us! Why, if you have said nothing about it all along, are you worrying me with it today?' Mr Hamilton betrayed his growing suspicion. 'What can *she* possibly have to say?'

'She says she could not for the life of her spare a minute of the time she must devote to her golf and her husband's horses to come here herself —'

'Thank God Almighty for that,' Mr Hamilton said devoutly, passing his handkerchief over his brow.

'Eden!' Lady Alison frowned before she continued. 'But their oldest son is coming here to go to the university. He wants to be a doctor . . .'

There was a stunned silence in the dining-room while Mr

Hamilton struggled to digest this wholly unexpected and unwelcome information, and Edina seized the opportunity to speak. 'Which one is he, again, Mama?'

'Cardew, dear. The same name as his father.'

'Do you mean to tell me, Alison, that he is actually coming *here*, to this house?' Mr Hamilton spluttered. 'A medical student, and you know what *they're* like, as well as being Cornelia's son?'

'No,' Lady Alison smiled, and her husband subsided a little, 'he is not coming to stay in this house, Eden. It seems he has borrowed a house in Queen Street from a friend who is abroad. But it's funny . . . I always thought young Cardew was an officer in the army. He must be twenty-two now, at least.'

Edina had always known about these distant relations in England, but they were rarely discussed in the house in Charlotte Square, which made them even more interesting now, especially in view of Cornelia's 'scandalous affairs'. There had never been a whisper of them until Papa let it slip just now. Perhaps this son of hers might be a chip off his mother's block, with any luck. He would liven things up.

'He will only come to visit occasionally, my love,' Lady Alison said comfortingly. 'In the meantime Cornelia is asking us to meet him off the stage-coach on October third – dear me, that's on Monday – and trusts that we will make him feel at home in Edinburgh. You will not have to go. Edina will come with me, won't you, dear?'

'Of course, Mama.'

'Cornelia is a lady who has spelled trouble all her life – and she is still doing so, as you can see, to this very day.' Mr Hamilton eyed Edina gloomily. 'Always in debt, always begging money from your mama, always a shady character.'

'But very charming,' Lady Alison murmured.

'I suppose there is no help for it, then?' her husband added with a sigh.

'None, Eden,' Lady Alison said firmly. 'We must do our Christian duty.'

Edina hid a smile. Papa was indisputably head of the house, the one who read the prayers every morning, as befitted the head of a staunch Presbyterian household, but Mama could always get her own way with just one quiet word. 'There is nothing to worry about, dearest Papa,' she said. 'He will probably want to go straight to the house in Queen Street anyway, since he is late for the start of the university term. It starts on the third, doesn't it?'

Mr Hamilton took a square look at his daughter for the first time that morning. For him it was proving a morning of one shock after another. 'Good God, Alison! The child's hair!'

'Now then, Eden, I wish you would not think of her as a child – she will be sixteen next month and of marriageable age. As for her hair . . .' Lady Alison smiled lovingly at Edina, at her heart-shaped face surrounded by a glorious cloud of shining blonde curls cascading almost to her waist, and into her clear blue eyes. 'Her hair has always been so beautiful as to be both a pride and a problem. It is unthinkable to cut it, and it takes a very long time to coil it up in the ladylike way your daughter must be presented to the world. Therefore, from now on I am allowing her to wear it undressed until after breakfast. Kathy can see to it afterwards. She has become quite expert at attending to Edina's toilette.'

'Your "daughter",' Mama had just impressed upon Papa, when Edina had found out one day, years ago, when the family bible was left out carelessly, that she was not their child at all. On the flyleaf she had found the insertion under the date of their marriage. 'Edina Grace Hamilton, found Candlemaker Row, adopted', and further than that she had never wanted to know. If they had been happy to adopt her as their child, Edina was more than happy to adopt them as her parents.

Together, she and Lady Alison beamed at Mr Hamilton with such radiance and undeniable affection that as usual he was forced to retreat in the face of it. They were both as charming as they were beautiful, he had to concede, and if Edina's eyes had not been quite so brilliant, if they had been a shade more grey with the eyebrows a little heavier, like his wife's, he could have been persuaded for ever that she really was their own child, and not the pitiful abandoned baby found in a doorway, now growing up. He had not had such disturbing thoughts for many a long day . . . It was all his cousin Cornelia's fault, of course.

After breakfast Edina wandered off to the kitchen to speak to Kathy, Liza's daughter, who had been brought up below-stairs in the house in Charlotte Square. Kathy was nineteen now, pretty and plump and cheerful, and Edina thought of her as one of her oldest friends as well as her personal maid. She found her looking out dusters. 'What are you going to do?' she asked.

'After I've done your hair, I'm going to clean the windows.'

'Well, then,' Edina sighed, 'we had better go upstairs and get the brushing and the combing and the horrible pins attended to.' Seated at her dressing-table she pursued her theme. 'How happy I should be if only I could wear my hair down like this always, Kathy.'

Kathy smiled patiently and took up the hairbrush. 'No, you wouldn't, Miss Edina. Did I tell you about a terrible girl I saw the other day when I was in the High Street speaking to Janet Brown . . . ?' The brush stopped momentarily while Kathy frowned into space. 'Janet – she's not the girl she used to be, whatever's come over her. Anyway, a girl with long fair hair stopped to say something to Janet, and oh, what a sight it was, just a wild tangle!'

'No, you didn't tell me, Kathy. What about her?'

'Well, you would look just like *her* if I didn't brush your hair with the bay rum and cantharides sprinkled on it. It would never lie in those beautiful waves. On the other hand,' said Kathy, 'she was bonny and just like you, so I dare say the gentlemen excuse her.' All this time Edina's head had been bent while Kathy wielded the brush from the roots of her hair almost to the floor. 'You may sit up now, Miss Edina,' she said, and in the mirror they both surveyed the froth of curls critically. 'Now it is the smoothing down.'

The brushing went on inexorably until the upraised ringlets were tamed. The bay rum filled the room with its aromatic scent, and once again Edina watched the miracle of its smoothing and polishing properties in the mirror. 'That was a strange thing to say, Kathy,' she said. 'What did you mean, "the gentlemen will excuse her"? What was she like, that girl in the High Street?'

'Oh, just some painted taupie. A woman of the streets, by the look of her. And I wouldn't give tuppence for Janet Brown these days, either.'

'Kathy!'

'Pardon me, Miss Edina. It just slipped out.'

'We are not supposed to know about these things, Kathy.'

'No, Miss.'

'But of course, we all do. Who is she anyway, since she looks so like me?' Edina asked, her interest quickening.

'Oh, she is not like you at all!' Kathy said, shocked. 'You are a lady! It was only that her hair reminded me of you. I never found out what her name was. Janet Brown might know, though. Now that's finished,' she said as she slipped in the last pin.

'Isn't it a bit early to be cleaning the windows?' Edina asked on the way back downstairs.

'The better the hour the better the deed.'

'You're up to something, Kathy Fraser. And you're blushing!'

'No, I'm not,' Kathy protested with a giggle, her face scarlet.

'Well, I'm coming with you to clean the windows.'

'I can manage myself. Besides, what would Lady Alison say if she saw you?'

'She would say I was doing something useful,' Edina said as they began to polish the windows, Kathy sitting on the windowsill, one plump elbow with dimples in it bare to the passers-by as she pushed her duster energetically back and fore, Edina rubbing the inside of the glass with another duster. 'Anyway, Kathy, I have something to tell you. Mama and I are going to meet some cousin or other next Monday off the stage. He's coming from England.'

Kathy took her curly brown head back inside the window. 'Ah.'

'You needn't say it like that! He's far too old – twenty-two at least.'

At that point a young man with broad shoulders, a tall frame and a plain face bursting red with anticipation came striding past. His grey surtout could not disguise his true calling in life, as he strode along with a heavy-footed measured tread, and when he saw Kathy he stopped short in feigned surprise.

Edina saw that he had stopped here before to speak to her maid, and that this explained why the windows were being polished at such an early hour. Kathy's head ducked out again. 'So it's you again, is it, Frank Clarke? Do you always come this way on your Saturday mornings off?' She giggled. '*Constable* Frank Clarke, I beg your pardon!'

'And here you are, Kathy Fraser, cleaning the windows again? They must be the cleanest windows in Edinburgh!' The young man strode across the pavement to hold a more intimate conversation.

Edina stepped back from the blue satin damask curtains, dropping her duster as she went. Kathy's attention was entirely devoted to Constable Frank Clarke, off duty, and she didn't even notice her going.

'Oh, Jesus,' Billy said delightedly when Con took them downstairs to meet William Hare and his wife, 'it's you, Maggie Log! I remember you from the Union Canal! Meet Helen. She's a Scottish lady I met first in Ballina. Helen, this is a lady who could wheel a barrow of stones with the best of us.'

It was plain that Maggie took an instant dislike to Helen, her being Scottish and all, and therefore not to be trusted like one of their own. 'Well, I'm after being Maggie Hare now,' she said, her tone surly. 'This was Log's house. It fell to me when he died, and then I married Hare.'

'Ay, Log died suddenly.' William Hare grinned horribly, so horribly that Helen clutched Billy's arm, terrified at the brutality of the man's face.

'Sure, and you can get a room with us,' Maggie Hare said, smiling at Helen in a superior way when she saw she had nothing to fear from her. 'We've got seven to rent. And what are you doing now, Billy?'

'Cobbling. Helen hawks my wares on the streets for me,' he said, throwing down his bag of lasts and hammers and nails on the stone floor with a clang.

'You've landed on your feet here, then,' Hare said, 'with the

85

tannery next door for the leather. I'm a hawker, too, with a donkey in the cellar. You could use the cellar as well for your cobbling, and it would only cost you sixpence a week more.'

'We'll take it,' Billy said.

But once they were in the foul room Maggie Hare showed them to, Helen began to cry. William and Maggie Hare were Irish. Billy was Irish, and she was the only Scot. She felt intimidated, overcome by them all. For the first time she even thought back to John MacDougal and wondered if she had made a terrible mistake.

'Don't cry, Helen.' Billy put his arms around her. 'What's wrong?'

'I don't like them, Billy. They're evil.'

But she changed her mind that night when they were invited with some other neighbours into the Hares' room for a booze. Billy played his pipe while they all danced and laughed, and when Constable Frank Clarke on his midnight rounds heard the noise of the jigging and the reeling and the drunken bawling coming from Tanners' Close, he paused only to think how cold and thirsty he was, and how merry they were in there.

He swung his lantern into the darkness of the next wynd where rats were scampering and mused wistfully on how unexciting had been his career so far. He would never get promotion at this rate, and above all he wanted to be promoted, and quickly, for more money so that he could ask Kathy to marry him. Terrible things went on down here in the Grassmarket and the rotting closes and wynds off it: murder most foul, he wouldn't be surprised. But the trouble was he was never there when it happened. At least, not so far.

Within a week Billy Burke and William Hare were old friends, drinking their morning drams together and trying to clear their heads afterwards.

'It's not easy.' Hare belched and sighed.

'Cheer up,' Billy said in his easy way. 'We should go into partnership. Two heads are always better than one.'

'What could we do?' Hare unconsciously handed over the leadership.

'Carry on as we are, you with your lodgers and me with my cobbling, but we could make more money together.'

'How?'

'I'm after thinking.' Billy swigged down another mouthful of raw whisky. 'That donkey of yours seems to be eating its fill and doing very little. We could be using it.'

'How?'

'Well, with the donkey and cart we could be carriers. We could meet every stage and carry the luggage.'

'Share the last dram with me, Billy. That's clever, so it is.' William Hare poured out the last of the whisky while their two women snored on the straw mat before the dead fire, each one as drab as the other.

Billy's eyes met William Hare's and they each thought the same as they clinked their glasses. A little more money, by fair means or by foul, and they could do a great deal better than *that*.

On Monday morning Kathy helped Edina into her new violet velvet pelisse with its lace ruff, and placed upon her head the bonnet to match, trimmed with white feathers between the double brim. The violet kid boots went on next, and after that the Limerick gloves. Last of all, Kathy handed her the large ermine muff and Edina set off with her mother to meet her English cousin.

'I am so glad you have chosen those quiet colours today,' Lady Alison said, herself attired in restrained dark blues. 'We must remember he is from a remote country place, and hardly likely to be able to keep up with the fashions.'

They were approaching the White Horse inn, the last staging-post for the English coach. They were early, of course. Lady Alison was always well before time. The English coach was well in time, too. They had scarcely descended from the carriage before it roared up the Canongate, slowed down to squeeze inside the courtyard and came to a lathering halt. After a small delay its passengers straggled down the steps and stood about in groups waiting for their boxes and baggage to be unstrapped.

Edina's eyes were drawn to the roof of the stage-coach, to

87

what seemed to her an uncommonly heavy load of luggage. Piece by piece it was handed down until she saw that it had all been stacked round the largest box of all. To her horror, she saw it was a coffin. There could be no doubt about it. Even from here, it obviously measured six feet by two.

'Dear me!' Lady Alison said. 'I never saw such a thing – a coffin on the roof of a stage-coach?' By the time it had been manhandled down, all the other passengers had gone with caddies carrying their luggage. A donkey and cart was at a little distance and four people were left standing by the coach, three men and a girl. 'That tall young man must be Cardew Sharpe,' Lady Alison said. 'Go and see, dear.'

The nearer Edina got to the little group the more clearly she saw that Cardew was not only in the fashion but strikingly in its forefront. He seemed to be giving orders to the two other men. He had his back to her, and this gave her the opportunity to admire the work of his tailor in fitting his pale blue frock-coat so perfectly over his broad shoulders and then bringing it in to a narrow waist before it flared out again over moleskin trousers, which were so tight-fitting that Edina could see no other way he could possibly have got them on unless he had been poured into them.

He turned his head a little, and she considered it was fortunate for him that curly hair such as his should be so fashionable for men, but in the same instant she doubted that it was unruly enough to make him wear his top hat on the back of his head at such a rakish angle. No, there was no doubt about it, Cardew Sharpe was a rake . . . and extremely interesting. But what business could he possibly have with the two terrible men he was speaking to with such authority as she drew near?

'Dr Knox, the Anatomist, prefers his subjects fresh,' he was saying. 'Therefore,' addressing the less sinister of the two, 'I require this to be delivered immediately to 10, Surgeons' Square. Here is a guinea for your services, and you will be paid another when you bring back a card within the hour as my receipt to 57, Queen Street.'

'Indade, your honour, and it's right now this very minute we'll be taking it,' the man said, gesturing to his companion to shoulder the coffin into the donkey-cart. 'Is that not so, William?'

The other man grunted as they heaved the long box on to the cart and turned his face their way. It was the most brutal face Edina had ever seen. The deep, black eyes, set wide apart, did not match. One was higher than the other above cheeks that were sunken and scarred. But it was the black eyebrows and the pointed chin that made him look like the Devil himself. Never in her life had she seen such a face of black evil before.

'Miss Edina Hamilton?' Cardew's voice brought her back to reality. 'You have come to meet me, you and Lady Alison? Let us go across to your carriage.' He swept Edina and the other lady with him. 'Lady Alison?' he flashed a dazzling smile, 'may I introduce my sister to you? Mrs Frances Love, who has come with me to be my housekeeper.'

'How do you do, Cardew?' Lady Alison looked amazed. 'I'm sorry, but I did not recall that you had a sister this age! We are pleased to meet you, Mrs Love.'

'Oh, my mother adopted children as she adopted horses and dogs. Surely you remember? Frances was one of them. Unhappily, she was widowed recently, and Mother thought that coming here to look after me might help her during her bereavement.'

'Yes, indeed,' said Lady Alison, smiling. Edina stole a glance at Mrs Love's ample curves most becomingly clothed in striking black-and-white satin stripes. On her head was poised positively the most interesting bonnet ever seen in Edinburgh, made of white satin, trimmed with long black plumes. The only thing that seemed a little out of place in these widow's weeds were Mrs Love's very ample breasts. Her dress was so low-cut that three-quarters of them were quite uncovered. 'You will come to Charlotte Square with us for some refreshment?'

'Thank you, no,' Cardew said. 'We will go straight to 57, Queen Street. I'm a day late already for the university, and there's a lot to do.'

'Then permit us to drive you there,' Lady Alison said. 'It's too far to walk with all your things.' Cardew handed in Mrs Love, who sat down beside Edina, and then took his seat beside Lady

Alison while the coachman strapped on their luggage. 'Perhaps you will call on us at a later date instead?'

Edina hoped it would be sooner rather than later when she met his laughing eyes looking from her to Mrs Love. He really was a very attractive young man, she thought, and felt her face flushing a little. Turning her head to hide it she met the gaze of an old woman with a long nose, small chilling eyes and an avid expression staring at her fixedly, and standing so close to their carriage that she could have touched her. The flush soon faded from Edina's cheeks. She felt threatened and even frightened for as long as the moment lasted.

Mabel Milligan almost fainted away as the carriage moved off. Oh God, she thought, here it is at last, my lucky day, for if that isn't another Mary Paterson, who else ever could be? I've seen the baby Bridie left in Candlemaker Row, grown up as I always knew she would grow up, a lady.

But you're a fool, Mabel Milligan, just standing there and gaping when your chance came. Somehow you should have followed that coach. As it is, you *still* don't know where she lives. As it is, you don't even know if your chance will ever come again. It's too late now. You should have followed in a sedan chair.

Almost in tears, Mabel Milligan kicked herself all the way back to World's End Close.

'*Is* she his sister, do you think?' Edina asked her mother when they said goodbye to Cardew and Mrs Love at 57, Queen Street.

'Of course, dear. Cornelia was always a little foolish, but she would not permit impropriety of that sort. Oh, dear me, no!' Lady Alison shivered a little and pulled the fur rug up over their knees. 'The time is coming when the carriage must be put away and we must take the coach, Edina. I felt it quite chilly just then. There is a new coach being built for us. Indeed, I hope it is nearly finished. We shall go and visit the coachbuilders before we go home, and see.'

'What colour this time, Mama?' Edina tried to summon up

some interest. Lady Alison's passion was her colour schemes, in her house and in everything connected with it, so that a new coach was almost commonplace.

'Chocolate-brown. But it is the upholstery that I am most worried about. I ordered a soft shade of butter-yellow, and I can almost guarantee the upholsterers will not have supplied us with such a leather.'

But on the contrary they had, Lady Alison pronounced herself satisfied, and at last they could go home.

'Did you meet Cardew Sharpe?' Mr Hamilton asked them when they sat down later to dine.

'We did, Papa,' Edina smiled, '*and* Mrs Love.'

'Who's she?' he asked.

'Cardew's adopted sister, it seems,' Lady Alison frowned, 'although I must say she never spoke of adopting a girl in any of her letters.'

'An adopted sister! A likely story!' Mr Hamilton snorted. 'So we're away the trip again, are we? He's a chip off the old block, is he? Another Cornelia come among us?'

'And you haven't even seen her yet, Papa!' Edina laughed. 'Wait till you do.'

'It wasn't so much Mrs Love, Eden,' Lady Alison laid down her fork and knife, 'as it was the coffin Cardew arrived with.'

'Ah ha! So he arrived with a coffin?'

'Strapped to the roof of the coach, Papa, and he got two horrible Irishmen to deliver it to Surgeons' Square.'

For a minute there was a silence at the table while they all three considered its grisly contents. Lady Alison was the first to speak. 'Eden! You can't mean there was actually a body in it?'

'Why else would he be sending it to Surgeons' Square? He's going to be a medical student, isn't he? He's making sure of his acceptance into the university, believe me.'

'But where would he get a body, Papa?' Edina began to feel quite unwell.

'That is the question. Your mother says he was in a regiment – perhaps not for long, although we won't go into that – and I believe when old soldiers die, and they have no relatives, their bodies are the property of the regimental doctors, to do with as they will. Perhaps he acquired it from one of them.'

'Oh, Papa . . .' Edina's face went white. 'There is another way the students are getting bodies. Christopher North said so in the *Scotsman*. They dig up graves.'

'That is quite enough talk of that sort,' Lady Alison said firmly. 'We are at our meal.'

'If you will excuse me, I don't think I can eat any more anyway,' Edina said. 'I think I'll just go to bed.' She bade her parents good-night and went upstairs to her room, where Kathy joined her.

'You look a bit pale,' her maid told her, 'but cheer up, Miss Edina. I spoke to Janet Brown today and found out the name of that girl in the High Street who looks so very like you. It's Mary Paterson.'

'But that doesn't get us very far forward, does it, Kathy? How could we see her?'

'You never could, Miss, without a veil to hide your face,' Kathy said sternly. 'You never know with women of that sort what might happen. Janet Brown says they drink in Swanston's tavern almost every night.'

'Then we must think of a way to get out to the Royal Mile some evening and go there. Now I'll never rest until I see this Mary Paterson with my own eyes.'

'Your mother – and mine – would kill us!' Kathy was scandalised.

'All I hope is that we don't come across that terrible woman who stared into our carriage, straight at me.' Edina shuddered, and told Kathy the story. 'I wonder why? How could she know me?'

Kathy shook her head.

9

HARE PRODDED THE donkey on with a stick and Billy followed behind, his hands keeping the coffin from sliding off the little cart all the way up the High Street and then, turning left, all the way up the South Bridge until they came to Surgeons' Square. It took some courage, because of all the dirty looks they got, and even more courage to knock on the stout official-looking door set back in huge square stones between Grecian pillars.

'Ach, damn it to hell,' Hare muttered while they waited. 'Everyone knows that even grave-robbers are welcome, so why not us with respectable goods?'

Two men opened the door to them, and at the sight of their white aprons Billy burst into nervous speech. 'Would you be kindly directing us to Dr Knox, sorr? A gentleman off the English coach asked us to deliver this coffin to him.'

'Come away in.' The one with the curly blond whiskers almost embraced him. 'Go and get Dr Knox, Mr Bain.'

Mr Bain went away, and Blond Whiskers continued to smile at them. 'My name is Mr Fergusson,' he said, 'the senior student under Dr Knox. Dr Knox always has to approve the subjects, you understand, but if you ever come on a similar mission again most likely Mr Bain will see to you. He usually receives the specimens.'

Dr Knox was an ugly sort of fellow, Billy thought when

Bain fetched him, with one eye and going bald, and very fancy dressed, not like any doctor *he'd* known. He wore a purple suit, an embroidered vest, white shirt and a high cravat on which a diamond glittered. He stood well back until the two younger men opened the coffin and laid the body on a slab. Then he stepped forward, examined the corpse and muttered for a while to Mr Fergusson, with his back to Billy and William Hare, before he marched out of the room again.

Mr Fergusson wrote out a card and put it in an envelope. 'Do you know Queen Street?' he asked. 'You're to go to Number 57.'

'It's a bloody long way to walk back over to the New Town,' Hare grumbled as they set off. 'We'll be wearing out our boot leather, I'm thinking.'

'You needn't be worrying about your soles with a cobbler in the house now,' Billy laughed, 'and there's another guinea in it when we get there.'

'Ay, to be sure, it's good money! Did you notice there were no questions asked? It makes you wonder what those grave-robbers must be making.' Hare looked at him sideways.

'Not grave-robbing, William.' Billy shivered. 'Dead bodies don't scare me, but the idea of breaking into a grave does, and it after being sanctified.'

'God, you're all to hell with religion, Billy Burke!' William Hare said disgustedly.

Just before nine o'clock on the first day of term, Gavin looked around the sea of young faces in Dr Knox's lecture hall and saw that what he'd been told was true: there was not an empty seat to be had. Except for some uneasy shuffling of feet and the odd cough, there was a nervous silence.

He glanced at the young man beside him, at his head of bushy red hair and his surly expression, but to Gavin's great surprise he held out his hand. 'I'm Joshua McLean,' he whispered, 'commonly known as Josh.'

'Gavin Mitchell.'

'Where are you from?'

'Gilmerton. My father's the doctor there.'

'You're lucky. My father's a minister.' Josh fell into a gloomy silence, and at once Gavin had visions of Uncle John Stafford and the horrors of his Bible class every Sunday at home, where he taught the young of the parish in the bleak Scottish faith to live a life of penance which would save you from damnation on the Day of Judgement, and if the resurrection men did happen to disturb your last sleep at least you would know nothing about it. No wonder Josh didn't sparkle with joy if that had been his background.

At nine o'clock exactly Dr Knox made his entrance. No actor in the land could have made a better one, dressed as he was that day in pure white, which drew everyone's eyes to his black eye-patch, and held them there.

'Gentlemen,' he began with a confident smile, 'let me welcome you to the science of anatomy, of which I am the king. When you have been to Professor Monroe's class later today, you will find *that* is no idle boast. Indeed, you will hasten back tomorrow morning – sharp at nine – with the greatest possible relief.

'Here, you will be provided with subjects for dissection, without which it is impossible to study anatomy at all, although Professor Monroe will attempt to do so. Here, I will demonstrate to you every bone, muscle, nerve and sinew in the human frame so that you will understand their function. Until you do, you cannot hope to treat the sick, which every young man of you present today is dedicated to do.

'*And*, gentlemen, it requires dedication, the closest attention and maximum study before you can hope to take your Hippocratic oath in three years' time.'

His lecture went on for one hour precisely. After that he swept off the platform and signalled the students to follow him on a tour of the mortuary and dissecting rooms, not to mention the rows of jars and bottles in which were pickled bits and pieces of humanity.

'God, I need a drink after all that,' Josh said, leading the way straight to Ross's ale house. 'By the sound of it, this afternoon's going to be even worse.'

'Why are you beginning this course, then?' Gavin asked him as they downed their first chopin of small beer.

'Anything to get out of the manse!' He smiled bitterly. 'This was the first thing I thought of.'

'But what if you hate it? How will you pass?'

'Oh, I'll pass all right. Wait and see.' Josh sighed. 'If I don't get away from the kirk I'll go stark, staring, raving mad.'

The minute they saw Professor Monroe they realised they were in for a ghastly afternoon. Already Dr Knox had told them that Monroe's grandfather, known as Monroe Primus, had been the first professor in 1720. Monroe Secundus had succeeded to the Chair and to his father's lecture notes, and now here was Monroe Tertius about to dish out the same lectures as had his father and grandfather before him.

He dithered and darted about from subject to subject, his main objective being to impress upon them the vileness of the extramural schools and their teachers, Dr Knox in particular.

Dazed, Gavin and Josh escaped at last, both now in the depths of depression.

'Well, it has to be got through.' Josh sighed, squaring his shoulders determinedly.

'I suppose so.' Gavin parted from him and retreated thankfully into the arms of Mary Paterson and a little well-earned light relief, for Mary in his bedazzled eyes was a girl after his own heart.

Her one objective in life was to have a good time, and she always seemed to have the money to pay for it, not only for herself but for him as well. In fact she insisted on it, scorning anything so demanding as cooking at home. She took him to the taverns of the town for every meal, and she had her first little drink with breakfast.

To this he had no objection at all. In fact, the small glass of ale in the morning seemed to clear his head for the rest of the day, and there was no doubt it was needing to be cleared after their carousing of the night before.

Edinburgh had turned out to be a wonderful place, with plenty to eat and plenty to drink and a beautiful woman to go to bed with every night, one whose mission seemed to be to teach him the practicalities of sex, where before he hadn't even dreamed up half of the theory.

Gavin was so besotted it never occurred to him to ask what she was doing when he was at the university, or how she came to be so well-off. She was always there to meet him, always smiling and bright, and all he prayed was that his health and strength could hold up against all this. He was in seventh heaven.

On Tuesday morning he set off eagerly to Dr Knox's, and again every seat was taken. At the last minute another student lounged in, attired in clothes that easily outshone Dr Knox's, and flashed a brilliant smile at Gavin and Josh on the front bench. They eyed the tightest pair of breeches they had ever seen with the utmost suspicion.

'Move up a little, you fellows,' he said airily. While they grudgingly shifted an inch or two, he introduced himself. 'I'm Cardew Sharpe, by the way, soon to make a deep impression upon this university.'

'Oh, yes?' Josh sneered.

'How did *you* get in?' Gavin asked him. 'Dr Knox said he was full up.'

'Ah, yes,' Cardew smiled, 'but then, you see, I knew the password. I brought him a body.' They gazed at him disbelievingly, and at that moment Dr Knox came in so there was no more opportunity to talk until later in the tavern.

'Sit still, chaps,' Cardew smiled at them when they found a table, 'I'll get them in.'

Josh seized the chance to whisper a warning. 'Cardew Sharpe doesn't know me, but I know him. My older brother is the minister in a church in Kendal. That's where this fellow came from originally. How he got himself into the Lancers nobody will ever know. But once in, he wasn't long getting thrown out. Cashiered, over a shady game of cards and some scandal over a woman.'

Cardew delivered the drinks, and Josh went on the offensive right away. 'And how did you manage to get a body? Where did you get it from?'

'Oh,' Cardew waved an indolent hand, 'here and there, you know. Here and there.'

'You can't get a body just here or there,' Josh said. 'Nobody can.'

'Perhaps it was a relative of yours?' Gavin persisted. 'You have taken it over here for burial?'

'There are bound to be questions asked, you know,' Josh warned him. 'Even at Surgeons' Square, if that's where the body has been taken.'

'Right first time, old boy,' Cardew laughed, 'and no, Gavin, it was not a relative. It was an old soldier who happened to die the same day that I left the regiment. The doctor in charge owed me a favour, for an introduction to a certain lady.'

Josh shook his head, drained his glass, got up and left. But Gavin stayed on for another drink with this entertaining – no, outrageous – man. He liked him. He was different from anyone else he had ever met.

Over in Charlotte Square Kathy was talking to Edina. 'So what happened when you met your English cousin, Miss Edina?' she asked. 'What was he like?'

'I don't know if I would quite trust him, Kathy. No, I don't really think I would . . . But oh, he's absolutely gorgeous! Do you think twenty-two is *very* old?'

'Well, I can see he's certainly made a conquest here,' Kathy said soberly.

'I don't know what you mean by that, but you'll see Cardew Sharpe for yourself – soon, I hope. Mama invited him to call. Perhaps he'll bring his sister, Mrs Love, as well.'

'So he has a sister?'

'Widowed, and acting as his housekeeper.'

'Well, well! Pretty, is she?'

'Now then, Kathy! But all the same I know what you're thinking. I even asked Mama if she thought they really were brother and sister. Mrs Love is so very pretty.'

'And what did Lady Alison say?'

'That Cardew's mother would not stand for anything improper.'

'But –'

'I know what you're going to say next. Does Cardew's mother even know they're here together?'

'Well, he sounds very interesting to me, Miss Edina. Do you think I'll get the chance to see him when he comes?'

'I'll make some excuse, don't worry.'

But they had to wait a week before Cardew Sharpe presented his card at 13, Charlotte Square, at four o'clock precisely, when the Hamilton family were just about to have afternoon tea in front of a blazing fire. The silver sparkled in its glow, and Lady Alison was in the act of pouring the milk from the little silver cow-creamer when James knocked at the door and came in with his card.

'Yes, James, who is it?' she asked.

'Some young sprig o' fashion, my lady. I've never seen him before.'

'*Lieutenant* Cardew Sharpe?' she read it out loud. 'Quite young, really, to be a lieutenant. But my memory didn't fail me altogether. He *was* in the army, as I thought. The seventeenth Lancers, it says here. Strange . . . Is he alone, James?'

'He is, my lady.'

'I'll be in the study.' Mr Hamilton reached out for his cup and saucer.'

'Sit still, Eden. I'd like your opinion, dear. Just show him up, James, if you please.'

Edina admired the way their visitor clicked his heels and bowed when he shook Mr Hamilton's hand. In fact, she admired everything about him.

'You have not brought Mrs Love with you today, Cardew?'

'She sends her regrets, Lady Alison. You see,' Cardew smiled round at them all, 'she considers she is still in her period of mourning. Not only that, but as my housekeeper she believes her place is firmly at home. I'm afraid you won't be seeing much of Fanny – oh, excuse me – Frances.'

'Dear me. That's very sad,' Lady Alison was saying, when there was a knock at the door again. This time it was Kathy.

'Will you be needing more hot water, my lady?'

'Yes!' Edina leapt into the breach. 'Bring some more, Kathy. This pot's nearly empty.'

'Very nice, too,' Cardew said, just loud enough for Kathy to hear on her way out, and when he held out his hand for his cup of tea Edina noticed that the cuff of his sleeve was rather frayed.

Perhaps that was what Mama was frowning at.

Helen got a few pennies to herself from Billy's share of the two guineas for delivering the coffin. She went down to the Jew's shop to spend them on a cracked mirror and the remains of a pot of rouge some lady must have grown tired of.

Back again in Tanners' Close she was shocked at her reflection in the glass. God, she'd turned thin, nearly as thin as that scrawny bitch Maggie Hare. Her face was away to nothing, and her hair was clapped to the sides of it, not fluffed out pretty as it used to be when Billy made love to her nearly every night and called her Nellie. If she'd thought of looking for a brush at the Jew's, she could have brushed the lice out of it. Maybe she should even wash it, but she turned faint at the thought of so much trouble.

Freezing cold outside, it was. The water would be like ice and it would take hours to heat. No, she'd wash her hair some other day, but today something would have to be done, whatever it was, for lately Billy hadn't been acting like a husband at all. She put a spot of rouge on her cheeks and rubbed it round and round, surprised at the way it made her blue eyes seem to sparkle again. It was only the other night at another booze she'd caught him squeezing a neighbour woman, and she knew right then she'd lose him if she didn't make the most of herself and hold on somehow.

He was still holding on wonderfully for his thirty-four years, still young-looking with his sandy hair as thick on his head as ever, and attracting the women as he'd always attracted her with his merry eyes and his soft Irish accent. God, he could charm the birds off the trees. Well, maybe tonight . . . If she did herself up a bit . . . If she washed herself . . . it might help. Right enough, the water was as cold as charity, but Helen persisted. Surely the shock of it would scare away all those lines running down her face? They never used to be there.

Afterwards, shuddering because there was nothing in the place to dry herself with properly, she knew she needed a drink to square herself up again before she resorted a second time to the rouge-pot. She found a half-bottle hidden in Billy's pile of broken shoes, tried to dry off on the straw mat in front of the fire, and by the time Billy came home she was glowing and feeling just right. She pulled him down beside her, sure she'd get a response from him when she cuddled up and stroked him.

'Don't be doing that,' he said, moving away.

Helen sat up on one elbow. 'What the hell do you mean?' she said, staring down at him. 'It's been three weeks! More!'

'I just can't. It's not that I don't want you. I love you, Nellie. But it's sore. It hurts.'

'Jesus Christ,' Helen said, and reached for the rest of the half-bottle she'd hidden at the side of the fire. All these good years she'd had with him, now to come to this!

The cold weather was not affecting Gavin in the least. He scarcely noticed it during the days, when, bleary-eyed, he went through the motions of attending classes, and when at last he came awake in the evenings he certainly didn't feel cold in the company of Mary, a sensation in scarlet, while they danced and sang and drank the night away. He seriously believed all his birthdays had come at once, and Farmer Brown's Jock back at Gilmerton must feel the same as he did, one happy bull.

November was drawing to its bitter close when the ugly word 'examination' began to be bandied about daily amongst the students.

'Have you got any books, Josh?' Gavin asked him.

'Books? Of course not. My father gave me only the merest pittance to last me all term.' Josh scowled and shook his shock of red hair, which was longer and therefore bushier than ever.

Well, he hadn't spent a penny at the barber's either, Gavin thought, and he never stayed longer than for one drink at Ross's ale house. How, then, did he spend his miserable pittance? 'So, if you have no books, how do you spend your evenings?' he asked curiously, and to his great amazement Josh's face turned brick-red. 'You can't be studying.'

101

'I am, amongst other things. I study my notes.'

'Notes?'

'I go back to my lodgings every evening and write down what I've learned.'

'God help me,' Gavin said, horrified. 'I haven't written a single thing,' and, quite alarmed now, he pursued the subject with Cardew, even going so far as to accompany him to Queen Street. 'Are *you* ready for these examinations?'

'Not really, old chap. I've done a bit of reading, of course. Why?'

'I haven't bothered to buy any books. I'll never get through,' Gavin said dolefully.

'Well, there's *Lizar's System of Anatomical Plates* in five volumes I found here in the library of this house,' Cardew said when they got to Number 57. 'Hang on, and I'll bring one of them out to you.'

'*Five?* Like this?' Gavin sagged under its weight. 'Oh, God, how am I to get through five of these in time? If I don't pass these examinations my medical career is over before it's begun! Where am I going to get the time?'

Cardew laughed heartlessly. 'You'll have to stay in tonight and every night, old chap, from now on. No more the taverns of the town!'

'It's all very well for you, Cardew. Your sister stays in with you, anyway. But what about Mary? She always wants to go out.'

'Yes . . . It's a pity you didn't have a sister like mine! She's worth her weight in gold, as I keep telling her.' Cardew smiled.

'No!' Mary stamped her foot in the middle of struggling into her red dress. 'Not again tonight! Ye're not sitting with that book again tonight?'

'I've got to. I've wasted the whole term as it is.'

'So that's it, Gavin Mitchell! Ye've been wasting yer time wi' me. Is that what ye're saying?'

'For God's sake, Mary! You know it isn't. I'm supposed to

be a student, but when did you ever see me with a book before this week?'

'And ye expect me to sit at home and never open me mouth for hours on end again? Does this mean ye're not coming to Swanston's with me?'

'I can't. The examinations are tomorrow and now I'm absolutely desperate. If I don't pass I'll be sent down.'

'What does that mean?'

'Sent home in disgrace, and I won't get back.'

'Hm! Ye've only lasted this long because I've been paying for yer food and yer booze! All ye ever gave me was yer company for a few hours at night.'

'Yes. You always seem to have plenty of money, Mary.'

It was definitely the wrong thing to say, Gavin realised as soon as he said it.

'That's because I'm working for it all the time ye're away at yer precious university!' Mary's mouth was stretched to a painted red string across her face, and her nose seemed suddenly very sharp, as sharp as her angry tongue. 'Well then, I'll go out by meself! I'll just carry on working! I might as well.'

The little room they had been living in shook with the force of the door slamming on her way out, and with a groan Gavin read the same page for the fourth time. It was beginning to make sense. Four hours later distant bells were ringing in his head when he vaguely recognised bits of lectures and applied them to all his father had taught him at home.

If only he had been reading all term he wouldn't be in this mess now, he would have been able to contend with tomorrow, he was thinking in a despairing panic, when the door crashed open again and Mary stood swaying on the threshold, held up by a massive sailor.

'Ye'll have to get oot,' she slurred. 'This is ma hoose, and ma bed, and here's someone else to share it all night with me.'

'But it's midnight, Mary!'

'That's your bad luck.' The sailor took a menacing step forward.

'Ay Get yer stuff together and go,' she shouted, and then as an afterthought, 'and take that great bugger o' a book wi' you!' It took very few minutes to gather his things together, and while he was doing it Mary turned maudlin. 'Och, Gavin,' she mumbled, 'it was me or a book . . . Mary Paterson or a bloody book! Christ, what a comedown!' She began to cry.

'Ye're all right, darlin'.' The sailor led her towards the bed as Gavin escaped to trail miserably up the Royal Mile.

Oh, God, what a fool he'd been! All for the sake of a tart! The fresh air hitting his brain, sober for once at midnight, made him see even more clearly that he was now in a desperate, desperate situation, for there was nowhere he could go with his book and his bundle except to the doorway of the university. He would have to huddle down in there and try to get some sleep.

The following day, frozen and hungry, he went through the nightmares of first the written examination and then the practical, vowing all the time that if God would only help him now, this one time, he would never, ever, be so stupid again.

Later, how he had ever passed, even if only by the skin of his teeth, he did not know, but one thing was certain, he could never have managed it without all the help his father had given him before leaving Gilmerton. In a bitter attack of conscience as he trudged back home he recollected his mother's last piece of advice, to put his dirty washing with the Gilmerton carrier at least once a fortnight, and he hadn't even sent a letter home, far less his dirty washing, to warn them of his arrival today.

But all the same, his young brothers and sisters were out playing, waiting to see him coming down the road, and his mother and father were in the window with Uncle John Stafford beside them. They all dashed out to welcome him back.

'Gavin!' his mother shrieked, and turned pale. 'What on earth have you been doing to yourself?'

'Ay, he's a bonny mess, right enough,' John Stafford agreed with the utmost satisfaction. 'Don't say I didn't warn you! God alone knows what he's been up to in that cesspool of iniquity, the medical faculty! Let me tell you, my boy, the good Lord *has* been watching over you – *He* knows – so whatever –'

'Don't talk such rubbish, John.' Dr Mitchell shook Gavin's hand and led him inside. 'Are you hungry, laddie?'

'Famished, Father.'

'Well, he'll have to go hungry for a long time yet,' his mother said, glowering at John Stafford. 'Gavin will be having a bath before he does anything else under this roof.'

'So there's no point in waiting, John,' his father took his cue and the minister firmly by the arm, 'not today. Some other time, perhaps.' He directed the Reverend Stafford to the front door. 'Now then, Gavin,' he added when he had shut it behind him, 'tell us how you got on.'

'I passed,' he said, aware of how nearly he might not have given such an answer, and breaking out in a cold sweat at the very thought of it.

'Ah, yes,' Dr Mitchell said with a smile. 'I kept telling your mother there was never any fear of that.' At that moment there was a scream from the kitchen and Mrs Mitchell came back through with his grubbiest shirt dangling between the tip of one finger and a thumb.

'What do you call this, Gavin Mitchell? How long did you wear this, to disgrace us all?'

'I forgot about the washing, Mother. I just wore everything I had, and when it got dirty the clothes I'd taken off the time before looked a lot cleaner, so I put them back on again.'

'Do you mean to tell me you've worn the same clothes in rotation for three months? What will people think? And look at those sleeves! Your wrists have shot three inches out of them!'

'He's a growing lad, Fiona,' said Dr Mitchell, smiling.

'A growing disgrace, you mean.' She reached for the fine tooth-comb and her eldest. 'You'll come and sit here at my knee, my lad, while I go through your hair, to begin with. I've seen what's in your bundle. God knows what I might find in your hair next! What sort of lodgings were you in, for pity's sake?'

'I was staying with a Mistress Paterson, Mother, but I won't be able to go back there again. She's taken in a sailor instead.'

'Sit still! Well, I'm very relieved to hear it, I'm sure.'

10

WILLIAM HARE SAT on a stool by the peat fire in Log's Lodgings drinking whisky and contemplating the worst problem in his life: money, or, rather, the lack of it.

The past, before he came to Tanners' Close, he kept shadowy. Nobody needed to know that he had been in the secret society of Ribbonmen, a killer hired by the rebel workers against the landlords back home in Ireland, nor a hop-picker in Kent, nor of being at one time in the Armagh Militia, where he had suffered the penalty of cat-o'-nine-tails with several hundred lashes for drunkenness before he deserted.

He kept all that to himself when he disappeared into Scotland, eventually arriving at the tail-end of the construction of the Union Canal, and from there drifted to Edinburgh. Then, quite by chance, he met Maggie Log and her husband one night in a tavern of the town. Log had been a long, skinny drink of water he soon got rid of once he found out the man was a landowner and had this lodging-house, a pigsty and Maggie besides. One vicious punch and Log fell to the ground, cracked his head and died. It had all been quite easy.

Log's Lodgings in Tanners' Close stood between rotting houses down below the Castle, but there was no sense in looking a gift-horse in the mouth. He and Maggie occupied the room at the back facing the pigsty, and it was the swine that were the immediate trouble. They wouldn't fatten for sale until Hogmanay. He needed some further source of income, and his mind kept going back to that coffin he and Burke had delivered to Surgeons' Square.

They had only got two guineas for the carrying of it, but as he'd overheard Dr Knox telling his two students ten guineas was the going rate he paid for bodies, so long as they were fresh. Ten guineas! By Christ, it was a fortune!

A knock on the door roused Maggie, who had been lying drunk on the hearth-straw all through these deliberations of his, and Hare went to answer it. She admired the tall quickness of him, like an animal somehow, and shivered to remember how frightened she had been of him before Log died. He fascinated her like snakes fascinate rabbits, so when he had taken her standing up in the close one night she hadn't asked him for a penny. Then when he wanted to marry her after Log died, she'd said yes. Shortly afterwards she'd had the baby, and a perfect nuisance it was.

Her eyes glanced towards it in its box. Sometimes she wished she could just push the cushion she always kept over the box right over the baby's face, but Hare wouldn't let her.

'It's meself, Billy Burke,' said a voice from the door. 'Helen can't sleep for the noise that old man's making on the other side of the wall. Can I be buying a drink from you to calm her down?'

'Here, take this bottle to Helen and then come back, Billy. We'll have a drink together and a bit of a talk.'

'What are you going to be talking to *him* about?' Maggie asked when he went off. 'He's just another Paddy.'

'He's got a head on his shoulders, that's why.'

Then Billy was back and peering in at the baby's box, cooing and admiring it, when it was a horrible baby she dosed regularly with a drop of laudanum, when she had the money, to keep it quiet. 'What do you call it, the little beauty?' he asked.

Maggie scowled. 'It hasn't got a name,' she said.

Hare brought a stool and filled a glass. 'That's old Donald that's making all the noise,' he said. 'He's been living here for a long time, an old soldier, and paying me with the pension he gets every quarter. He owes me four sovereigns to date.'

'Will he ever see the next quarter?' Billy asked doubtfully. 'It's dying he is.'

'That's what's on me mind,' Hare said. 'He's going to die still owing me four sovercigns. How will I ever get my money?'

The two Irishmen considered the problem while they emptied their glasses, and Hare filled them up again.

'You could sell him,' Billy said, 'to the doctors at the university. They would do anything, pay anything, for a body, as we saw when we took that coffin and no questions asked. It's not like robbing a grave. It's more like calling in a debt.'

'And what about the undertakers?' Maggie Hare asked. 'All the other lodgers will know there's been a death. There will have to be undertakers and a coffin and all, or else there might be trouble with the police. We can't have that.'

'Let me think about it, William,' Billy said. 'I'll think of something.'

'Think fast, then. I'll split the money with you, of course.'

Then Helen appeared at the door clutching a shawl around her night-flannel. 'Billy, Billy, they're all shouting that he's dead! The old man's awful quiet now, and they say he's dead!'

'Come away in, Helen,' Hare said soothingly. 'You've had a bit of a shock. Sit here by Maggie and have a dram, while Billy and I go and see.'

'He's dead, right enough,' Billy said.

'Well?'

'I've thought of a plan, William. Trust me. At dawn you'll go for an undertaker. Paupers get them free. Now, I've been brought up to go to all kinds of churches. I know the Bible inside out, so I do, and I'll hold a wake by the side of the coffin when you come back with it. Then the undertaker will hammer down the lid and go for a helper. We'll open the coffin again, take out and hide the body and replace it with something else.'

'With tanners' bark, from out in the yard. By God, Billy, it's brilliant!'

After dark they walked to Surgeons' Square with the donkey pulling the cart loaded with the body in a sack, and next day ten shillings was hardly anything to pay out of ten guineas for a whole gallon of whisky. They called in the neighbours, and Con and his woman, and paid for a fiddler to give Billy a rest now and then from his pipe. The day after, Billy mended no shoes and Hare hawked no herring, but he did remember to feed the swine on the pratie peelings from the party.

Lady Alison was much too diplomatic to ask her husband's opinion of Cardew Sharpe after his introduction to Charlotte Square. She knew better. If she bided her time his considered opinion would come out anyway, and it did at the dinner table, a few weeks before Christmas.

'Yes,' he said, when Cardew's name came up in the conversation, 'a very merry fellow.'

From that Lady Alison concluded he didn't like him, and Edina pricked up her ears. 'Merry, Eden?'

'A tricky sort, I would say, my dear.'

'*Tricky!* Do you mean a trickster, Eden?'

'He's a very personable young man. Very likeable. Worms his way into your confidence.'

What was Papa saying? Edina wondered. He couldn't mean a confidence trickster, surely? No, not Cardew Sharpe. He was much too handsome.

'Indeed he does worm his way in,' Lady Alison agreed with a sigh, 'but we'll have to invite him and his sister here at some point during the festive season, that is if Mrs Love will accept. Her period of mourning must surely be up by then.'

'Just as you please, my dear.' Mr Hamilton smiled, although Edina considered it was sardonically. 'It is always entertaining, once you have the measure of a man of that sort, to watch him in company.'

'Oh, he is not of *that* sort – not like his father, Eden! He's not like his mother, either.' Lady Alison sighed.

'Much cleverer I would say, Alison, and more charming with it. A dangerous combination. What do you think, Edina? Should we invite him?'

'I do think we should, Papa. Then whether his sister comes or not, we can see if she is a good housekeeper. If she is, he will have a new coat, or new sleeves in the one he wore here, or she will have turned his cuffs, at the very least.'

'Ah, yes . . . indeed, Edina.'

'Sometime, when you can tear yourself away from your studies,' Dr Mitchell smiled at him briefly, 'there is a gentleman I want you to visit, Gavin, at 13, Charlotte Square. Eden Hamilton is a very old friend of mine. He was a law student when I was a medical student, and I often drop in on him when I'm in the town – although I must say, for lack of time, it is usually in his rooms in Parliament Square.'

'Yes, Father. Is there any particular reason?'

'No, no. But it would be only courteous.'

'Well, I'll try, Father, if I have time. But as it is, I'm going to have to go up a day earlier in the New Year, to find other lodgings.'

'Oh, don't put yourself out.' Dr Mitchell laughed out loud. 'It is just that your mother has licked you into shape again over these Christmas holidays, and I would like you to visit Mr Hamilton as long as you are presentable.'

'You needn't worry. Mother says if I don't send home my washing regularly this time she'll come to Dr Knox's in person to find me.'

'She will, too, so learn a lesson. And in future, my boy, drop us a line now and then. We would like to know if our son is still in the land of the living, you know.'

Early in the New Year Gavin set off for Edinburgh again, a sadder and a wiser man, and landed back in the bursar's office.

'It's no' *you* again! What are ye wanting this time?'

'I never did find lodgings in September.'

'What did I tell ye?' the bursar crowed. 'He, he, he! But if you're still in the faculty o' medicine, ye *must* ha'e found somewhere?'

'I did,' Gavin said crisply. 'A hole and corner of sorts. Now I wish to move on to something better. What have you got on your books?'

111

'Nothing. The students, unless they're silly wee buggers like yersel', all stay in the same place for the whole session.'

'So, it's a case of tramping the streets again, is it?'

'Ah, weel, haud on a second,' the bursar seemed to soften. 'I did hear that the third-year student in Miss May's left in a gey hurry. There might be a place for ye there.'

'Oh, thank you. Where will I find her?'

'She has the basement hoose at 177, High Street.' The old man's shoulders heaved, while he looked down at his books and managed to keep his face straight at the same time.

Gavin's suspicions of Miss May continued all the way to her house, but when he went down the steps to her door, and a dainty elderly lady opened it to him, they were instantly allayed. The bursar hadn't been making a fool of him, after all.

'Yes?' She smiled pleasantly, her eyes sparkling behind her spectacles. 'Is it a room ye're needing?'

He nodded. 'Gavin Mitchell, first year medicine.'

'We've never had a medical student before! Follow me,' she said, and just for a second the uneasy thought darted through his head that he might be a very small fly walking into a spider's web, no matter how he towered above her.

Miss May couldn't have stood much more than four and a half feet tall, and he deduced from her severe limp that her right hip was dislocated, probably from birth. However, her smile continued as she showed him to a small, very spartan room with a large key in the inside lock.

'The best view in the house.' She waved her hand at a grimy two-foot-square window. 'It looks out on to the High Street.'

His eyes roved over the narrow iron bed, the washstand which had lost one leg but was propped up with books, and the hooks on the wall for clothes. A rickety table and chair completed the furnishings. But Miss May was right about the window: it *did* give a very good view – of tramping feet, for it was half-below the level of the street. The room was so freezingly cold that he knew it was damp, but perhaps if that window could open to let the air in it might dry up.

'And can it open?' he asked.

She pulled back the snib and the window creaked out an inch

or two on rusty hinges. Gavin judged that some oil would soon cure that, and, what was even better, he could easily climb out and in without Miss May being any the wiser. All he had to do was lock the door from the inside.

'I'll take it,' he said, and at once her smile narrowed.

'Six o'clock on the dot for the evening meal,' she snapped. 'Any later, and ye get nothing. Breakfast at seven o'clock sharp, and the same applies. No drunkenness, no animals, no women. This is a Christian household. Is that understood, Dr Mitchell?'

He smiled, immensely flattered. 'I'm not a doctor yet, Miss May. My name is Gavin.'

'Then the title Dr Gavin will remind ye morning, noon and night what ye're here for, and it'll impress the wee wifies hereaboots that I've got a doctor in the house. The kirk chimes will tell ye when it's six o'clock. Come through then. Just follow yer nose.'

He did follow his nose at six o'clock, hoping that his sense of smell which had never let him down before was betraying him now, for he smelled mutton, his pet aversion. He found himself in Miss May's living-room and there was another lady there, a younger, taller, but otherwise exact replica of his new landlady down to the spectacles on her nose.

'This is my niece, Miss Irene May,' she said. 'Ye're to address her as Miss Irene.'

He bowed politely, but sure enough in the ashet in the centre of the table bits of mutton were floating greasily, crashing into a carrot now and then, the steam from it all almost choking him.

'We love stewed mutton.' Miss May hopped up on to her chair and took up her ladle. 'Isn't that so, Irene?'

Miss Irene smiled at Gavin wanly, managing to convey at the same time the despairing message of a damsel desperately praying to be rescued.

'Cardew!' Gavin almost fell on his friend's neck in sheer relief the following morning. 'How are you?'

'Broke to the wide, old dear,' Cardew answered glumly.

113

'Christmas was expensive enough but Hogmanay, as they call the New Year here, has cleaned me out.'

He fell into a deeper and ever deeper depression as the days rolled on. Dr Knox was now determined upon the practical application of his surgical teaching. His classes were as over-flowing as the ureters pouring from kidneys and down into bladders, and any stones daring to lurk in the bladders themselves were removed at top speed in the operating theatre at Surgeons' Square. 'Watch my hands, gentlemen!' he kept shouting over his shoulder. 'Check your watches! Speed is of the essence!'

Dr Knox, being an Outsider, didn't have any beds in the Royal Infirmary. Instead, a selected band of students were permitted to follow him into patients' homes, amongst them Gavin, Josh and Cardew, since they occupied the front bench under the great man's nose.

'To the Grassmarket!' he commanded one morning. 'A Mr Jock McCullough at Number three, Lady Lawson Street. It's near Tanners' Close.'

'Nobody down here will ever pay him,' said Cardew, demonstrating his preoccupation with his penniless state, while he waved his handkerchief delicately under his nose. As they passed the end of Tanners' Close two men were coming out with a donkey and cart. 'By Jove, those are the fellows who delivered my coffin!'

And a rascally pair they looked, Gavin thought, when they arrived panting at 3, Lady Lawson Street. Dr Knox arrived immediately afterwards in a chaise, along with two huge men with purple noses and another man carrying a bag of instruments.

'That'll be his instrument man, and the two heavyweights his footmen. Their job will be to stop the patient from leaving the table before he's finished,' Josh speculated as the whole procession followed the doctor in through the lobby, a crowd of curious children in their wake.

'Dr Knox! Dr Knox! He'll put ye in a box,' chanted the children, and plump little Mrs McCullough rushed out at them with her sweeping brush. 'Awa' ye go,' she skirled, 'or I'll skelp yer wee bums for ye!'

They all arrived in the kitchen. A shaky table stood in the middle of it, and the patient lay in the box-bed up against the far wall.

'Gentlemen,' Dr Knox addressed his students, 'this is Mr McCullough, a rat-catcher by profession. One of the verminous creatures bit a chunk off his right leg, with the unfortunate consequence that I must cut off the rest of it before he dies of poisoning.' The two large footmen carried Jock McCullough to the table and poured raw whisky down his throat, clearly grudging him every drop. 'Are we ready, Mr McCullough?' Dr Knox handed him a plug to bite on.

'Ay, sir.'

At once the two big beasts fell on poor Jock, one pinning his chest and the other holding down his legs, and at dizzying speed Dr Knox's scalpel was exposing the bone and in a flash had sawed through it.

'Twenty-three seconds.' Cardew snapped his watch shut, while Dr Knox still worked at top speed to wash the stump with rose-water and egg-white, before he sewed the skin flaps over it with silk stitches.

By this time both the McCulloughs had fainted. Dr Knox's two henchmen slapped their wrists while the other man cleaned the instruments in the hot water Mrs McCullough had provided before she keeled over. Dr Knox gathered them together and fitted them back into his bag, and twenty-five minutes after he had entered 3, Lady Lawson Street he was giving his students directions for the venue of his next operation, and getting into his chaise again amid the cheers of the large crowd outside.

In no time at all it was Easter, and Gavin went home again, exhausted but more kindly received by his mother this time.

'The long summer vacation is not far off,' his father reminded him. 'By the way, I've written to Mr Hamilton.'

'Oh! Oh yes, Father ... I must admit I forgot all about him.'

'Well, perhaps you'll have time to go and see him before the summer term is over. Anyway, stick in, Gavin, and the next time we see you that'll be your first year over.'

Back in Edinburgh Cardew, looking fairly cheerful for a change, greeted Gavin with an invitation. 'Come and have supper on Friday night. Two friends of mine have turned up with a new idea. I wish you'd come and see what you think.'

Supper parties were all the rage now, vast affairs of roast pork, wild duck, steak-and-kidney pies and cold collations of poached salmon, boiled ham and salt beef, washed down with a wide variety of suitable wines.

Somehow, when he rang the bell at 57, Queen Street, Gavin didn't think Cardew would be quite up to that mark. His sister, clad in a very low-cut dress made out of some almost transparent black material, opened the door to him and curtsied deeper and longer than was strictly necessary, to give him plenty of time to admire her magnificent breasts.

'Mrs Frances Love,' she murmured out of honeyed lips in an accent he recognised as from the north of England. 'You must be Mr Gavin, sir. Please follow me.'

When she led him to the drawing-room he found Cardew and his two friends already there, goblets in hand, laughing and roaring and slapping their thighs. He could see that it must be a very important occasion for Cardew, attired as he was this evening in an exquisite cravat, chestnut tailcoat, nankeen breeches and long calf boots. Gavin wondered briefly if he had been raiding his absent host's wardrobe, because all year he had worn nothing other than his tight breeches and his pale-blue coat.

Cardew placed his glass on one of the brace of drum tables and rose up with alacrity from one of the light striped armchairs to introduce his two middle-aged friends.

'Two of the Light Dragoons, on leave and far from home,' he said, smiling and pressing a glass into Gavin's hands. 'Captain John Foster and Lieutenant Richard Cunningham.'

John Foster was bleary-eyed already, he saw, and it was plain from Richard Cunningham's hairline, a mere quarter of an inch above his eyebrows, that he had never had much of a brain to begin with to addle with anything. His head was too flat to contain one.

'Now that you're here, old chap, we can go in to supper.' Cardew was clearly anxious to proceed with the business in hand before his friends got too befuddled, and they went through to a dining-room every bit as elegant as the drawing-room.

So, Gavin thought, while he himself had been pigging it in the bowels of the town along with most of the other students, this was how Cardew had been living! In high style, and it must be costing a fortune.

Mrs Love had set silver candlesticks up and down the whole length of the gleaming walnut table, and crystal glittered pink and mauve and green in the light of the candles. She brought in a large ashet of oysters and laid it down in front of Cardew.

'The Muscadet, my dear,' he murmured as he served them. She circled the table pouring out the wine, making the most of the opportunity to bend very low over the gentlemen as she filled their goblets. The temperature at the supper table rose sharply.

'Never knew you had a sister, old bean.' John Foster's eyes goggled out of his florid face when she left the room.

Cardew shot him a warning glance and put his finger to his lips. 'Still in mourning for her husband, poor little creature. That's why she cannot dine in public. We shouldn't upset her.'

Mrs Love came back with a large roast of beef, which she placed on the sideboard to allow it to settle and its aroma to permeate the room. 'For this, a good red wine, gentlemen.' Cardew stood up, lording it at the head of the table when he carved it. 'Perhaps a Chassagne-Montrachet 1817?' Mrs Love glided off to fetch it, returning with a young girl bearing dishes of vegetables, the gravy-boat and golden Yorkshire puddings, while Cardew left his chair to go over to the side-table between the long graceful windows, where warming dishes lay in wait.

'Devilled kidneys here,' he lifted the first cover, 'quail in

117

here,' lifting the second, 'and what's this, Fanny?' he asked, lifting the third.

'Veal.'

'Thank you, my dear. Now, gentlemen, please help yourselves to whatever you fancy. Your very good health!' He raised his glass and drank a mouthful of wine before he sat down.

Yes, Gavin thought, Cardew was definitely out to impress.

It was almost nine o'clock when Mrs Love brought in a frivolous confection of cream decorated with crystallised fruits and flowers, and later, when she had brought the port and sugared almonds, Gavin was staggered at such a display, considering Cardew's moans and groans of poverty ever since he'd known him. He was convinced by now that this supper had only been staged to impress the two Lancers. Cardew was up to something. There was something he wanted very badly from these two men.

'Now then, John and Richard,' he said when they lit their cheroots and Mrs Love and her little maid had cleared the table and retired, 'the time has come to show me.'

'I don't know.' John Foster glanced at Cunningham, who stared pointedly at Gavin.

'Oh, you needn't mind Gavin,' Cardew said impatiently. 'You can tell he's no man of the world. None of the Edinburgh sharps would look at him.'

Feeling rather nettled by this, Gavin struggled to keep his mouth shut and joined them at the card-table. As if by magic and out of nowhere two packs of cards materialised on the table in front of the officers. The two men split the decks, shuffled, riffled, riffled back again and fanned the cards with an expertise that was enough to convince Gavin their brains were all in their fingertips. He was in the presence of masters of whichever game this was.

'Here it is.' Richard Cunningham suddenly turned over all four aces.

'Watch my hands.' John Foster echoed Dr Knox as another four aces arrived on the table from out of thin air.

'Do it again,' Cardew commanded. 'Did you see it, Gavin?'

'No.'

'Well,' Cardew fetched another two packs, one for Gavin and one for himself, 'within the next few hours these two sharps are going to teach us to do the same.'

'They might teach you, Cardew,' Gavin said sometime before midnight, 'but I can make nothing of it. I might as well go home to bed.'

'But what do you think of it, old chap? Do you think we'll do?'

'Do? For what?'

'We're going to the largest card-school in Edinburgh tomorrow. I haven't been exactly idle since I came here, you know, so I can get John and Richard a pass into the club. We should clean up thousands.'

'You do mean thousands of pounds, don't you?'

'I do,' Cardew said confidently.

'And have you thought of what will happen if you're found out? You won't be cleaning up much in prison, except perhaps your cell,' Gavin told him.

All day on Sunday he agonised over his friend, and what might have happened at the card party, now that he understood where Cardew got some of his ready cash from. He had always wondered. But on Sundays Miss May and Miss Irene always served up slices of cold ham with pickled beetroot, which put him in a better frame of mind to go to his narrow bed and sleep.

After the Christmas booze courtesy of old Donald, and the selling of the swine at Hogmanay, the Burkes and Hares were long since resigned again to praties fried in what was left of the ham fat, and if they were lucky the odd rabbit one of them managed to whip undetected off a stall. Hare even sold his donkey and cart. It was understood between the four of them that any money they made was strictly for drink, and by now drink was in very short supply.

'Joseph, the miller, is ill,' Hare informed the rest. 'I've just been to see him.'

'What's wrong with him?' Maggie Hare asked.

'How should I know?'

'I'll go and have a look,' Billy said, and came back to tell them it looked like the beginning of typhoid fever.

'He's not going to get better of that, then,' Maggie said.

'Oh, Billy, I'm frightened of the fever.' Helen started to cry. 'He could give it to all of us!'

'He should be put out of his misery, so he should,' Hare said. 'What's the use of prolonging it for him, and running such a risk ourselves?'

'You mean, the poor man would be better off out of this vale of tears?' Billy looked at him significantly.

'He would.' Hare licked his lips.

'So what are we waiting for?' Billy's testicle was very sore that day. It was making him jumpy, not like himself at all, at all. 'Let's get on with it and buy some grog again, for God's sake!'

'You're sure you know how to do it? We can't have blood splattered around the place.'

'There won't be any blood. My way can't fail.'

'With not a mark on him?'

'Not one.'

They sent Maggie and Helen off with their last remaining shillings to a gin shop, with instructions to get a couple of bottles, to have a drink themselves and spin it out, to give them time.

'That is,' Hare scowled at them ferociously, 'unless you want to stay and watch?' They scuttled off and Hare went to whisper in Joseph's ear that he had some whisky, just a little for medicinal purposes, if he cared to come downstairs for it?

'Oh, God, I'm grateful to you.' Joseph rattled and coughed in his nightshirt, and sank before the fire.

'Take all you want,' Hare said, placing the whisky bottle at his head. Joseph drank it like water.

'Bless you both' were his last words, as he took more whisky and fell to weeping and mumbling to himself before he slumped over on to his back.

Billy nodded to Hare, who fetched the pillow off the bed, pressed it over Joseph's face and sat on it, while Billy found he needed all the great strength he had in his shoulders and his arms to hold down the man's legs, kneeling on the floor to do it. Then the gasping started, and the futile flailing of the arms.

'Christ! His head's twitching something awful,' said Hare, beginning to panic. 'It's all I can do to keep my arse steady.'

'Press harder, then!'

'How long?'

'Ten minutes. Fifteen, to make sure.'

'Will the doctor ask any questions, do you think?'

'Knox? He won't ask any questions, don't worry about it. I was speaking to a student in an inn. He said Knox had four hundred students but he never had enough bodies to teach them with. Subjects, he called them. But if there *is* any trouble we'll say we found Joseph lying dead outside a grog shop. We'll sprinkle him with whisky, as well, before we carry him up,' Billy panted.

'It's too weak I'll be to carry him at all if he doesn't hurry up.' Hare shook the sweat out of his eyes. 'We're going to have a job to disguise it's a body we're carrying, besides. You should have thought of all that.'

'I did. There's an old tea-chest out in the shed. We can pack him in that.'

'His head's stopped moving, Billy, and his arms are slack.'

'There's still a thrill in his legs. Hold on. It won't be long now.'

They fell silent, and listened intently. At last it came, the muffled rattle that told them he was dead.

Hare got up and removed the pillow. Sure enough, there wasn't a mark on Joseph, not the smallest blemish. They crammed him into the tea-chest, and later that night they sold him for ten guineas. It was riches at last.

'Maggie and Helen will have to get a guinea each out of this,' Billy told Hare as they stopped in an alley for a celebratory swig from a new bottle. 'They're in on this. Later on, they might even help us.'

'Later on? So we're in business?'

'Old Donald and Joseph were easy. They were in Log's Lodgings already. Next time it'll be harder. Now, if we want a good time, we'll have to go out and attract the subjects in.'

The subjects, Hare thought. Every fresh one, ten guineas. Christ, did ever a man have such a partner as Billy Burke? Billy was the boyo, the very best.

11

EDINA HAMILTON HAD by no means forgotten Cardew Sharpe, but in the whirl of engagements and parties which her own sixteenth birthday party led to he had become pushed a little to one side. There was another pile of invitations for her with the morning post.

'Let me see them, dear,' Lady Alison said, and together they bent their fair heads while they went through them. 'Goodness me, here's one from Perthshire! I see it's from our old friends the Ellwoods, coming in July to stay at the Crown Hotel in Princes Street, and asking you to meet their daughter Christina there the day they arrive.'

'Oh, Mama, there's a little note inside it from Christina, as well, wondering if I will go back to Almondbank with her when their holiday here is over.'

'Do you want to go?'

'I'd love to go to the country.'

'Then there's no reason why not. Is there, Eden?'

'No, my dear.' Mr Hamilton had been listening with one ear to the conversation. 'I've got a letter here too, from an old friend, Dr Iain Mitchell from Gilmerton. We were students together, long ago. He comes to see me now and then, although not for some time now.'

'Yes, of course, I've heard you speaking about him and his

large happy family before, dear. He practises in Gilmerton, does he not?'

'I suppose I shouldn't be so surprised, when we see Edina here a young lady now, but the passage of time always takes me unawares. Here's Iain's oldest son Gavin, now a young man of almost eighteen and a student in our university.'

'What sort of student, Papa?'

'Medical, and he may come to see us if he has time before the summer vacation.'

'You must write back, Eden, and tell him his son will be most welcome.'

One glance at Cardew's face on Monday morning after the Saturday night card party told Gavin that the very worst had happened.

'They had men posted all round the room watching,' Cardew told him in despair, 'and that idiot Richard Cunningham let a card drop out of his sleeve. The three of us were thrown out, of course, never to be readmitted, but he got an awful pasting into the bargain. The last I saw of him and John Foster, they were heading for the Border double-quick.'

'Three bloody fools!' Gavin was totally unsympathetic. 'You got off lightly.'

'I'm still to the fore,' Cardew agreed gloomily, 'but only just. I've got to lay my hands on some spondulicks shortly, I can tell you.'

'Well, don't look at me. I'm nearly broke, myself. What will you do?'

'Haunt the Musselburgh racecourse by day, and burn the midnight oil trying to think of something else by night. There *is* another little scheme I've been considering,' Cardew admitted. 'You'll be going home, of course?'

'Yes, thank God, away from boiled mutton and the worry of you and your little schemes for a while. However, you'd better tell me before I go what this latest one is likely to be.'

'Well, I've found out from some of the older chaps about all the tourists who come to Edinburgh every year, not knowing where to go or what to look out for. I fancy my chances as a courier, once I've brushed up a little on the local history. What do you think of that for a wheeze?'

'Better than your usual, certainly.' Gavin frowned at his friend, but on the whole he couldn't see that Cardew would get into as much trouble as usual showing visitors around the town.

He felt quite happy as he walked the six miles back to Gilmerton. He'd survived his first year at the university after all, he was thinking, when he arrived back home to find his family in an uproar.

'It's your father,' Mrs Mitchell gasped. 'Oh, what a shock we've all had!'

Within a few minutes he discovered they were tears of joy pouring down his mother's face, for Dr Mitchell had come into a country house and a large sum of money, left to him by an aged aunt. As far back as Gavin could remember, his father had never had a good word to say about his Aunt Gertrude Mitchell. Now, at her death, she was the subject of his highest praise.

'It's a beautiful house in Almondbank,' he told his family. 'As soon as I can arrange for a *locum tenens* to come we'll go for the whole summer. Gertrude was always sensible. Her house, Eastwood, is right on the River Almond. We'll take our rods, Gavin, and the golf clubs. Fiona, you can start packing,' and in the commotion all the other letters were swept away, including Mr Hamilton's invitation.

It took another week before they had arranged it all and the Mitchell family set off for the first real holiday of their lives. Mrs Mitchell spent the first few days wandering about the house, unable to believe that it, and its beautiful old furniture, was theirs now. The younger children had never had water to play in before, either, and it proved to be a huge fascination.

'You're to go nowhere near the big river,' their parents impressed upon them, 'only the little stream at the bottom of the garden.'

'But we want to go fishing as well!'

'You can,' Gavin told them. 'That little stream is part of the big river. It's got fish in it, too. If you promise to stay where Mother can see you, I'll make fishing-rods for all four of you.'

125

So Gavin and his father had peace to golf or to fish the river all day long, and it gave them both a great deal of satisfaction to look up occasionally at their new house. It wasn't the only big house in the trees. There was another, half-hidden by a bend in the river, and out of it early one evening two young ladies walked towards them along the footpath.

Edina had already been staying with the Ellwoods for a few days when the glorious weather tempted the two girls out to walk along the river in the cool of the early evening. Two men were just starting to cast their rods.

'Do you know those men?' Edina asked her friend Christina Ellwood. 'They look like father and son.'

'I've never seen them before. They're fishing the stretch below Eastwood. A Miss Gertrude Mitchell used to live there, but she died recently.'

'Perhaps these people have bought the house?' Edina asked, but her mind was elsewhere, remembering the name Mitchell from something Papa had said. As they drew nearer to the men she looked at the younger one curiously.

'Perhaps,' said Christina with a giggle. 'I hope so. That is quite the most handsome young man I've seen for a long time.'

Gavin looked up and saw the two girls approaching from around the bend. Some part of his anatomy jolted and then sank, for from that distance one of them looked exactly like Mary Paterson. But how could *she* be in Almondbank? He felt the blood draining from his face and his heart.

Then, as they got nearer, he saw to his astonishment that she wasn't Mary Paterson at all. The rod dangled aimlessly from his hand and the line became hopelessly entangled in the weeds at the riverside, but still he continued to stare.

Mary Paterson had never looked like that . . . Her skin had been coarsened with powder and paint, whereas the complexion of this apparition of beauty had the pure bloom of a morning rose. Mary's hair had been wild and, he had to confess, not always very clean, but these blonde tresses hung in a deliberate mass of glorious ringlets tied up with blue ribbons under a frivolous little parasol of the same colour.

Dr Mitchell, having glanced in surprise at his son's neglected

126

rod and line, turned round to see him smitten by Cupid's dart, and rose to the occasion with his usual resourcefulness.

'Good-evening, ladies,' he said, and smiled at the two young ladies. 'It's been a lovely day.'

'Good-evening, sir.' They smiled back.

'Allow me to introduce ourselves, since I believe we are your new neighbours. I am Dr Iain Mitchell, and this is my son Gavin.'

'How do you do?' Gavin took Edina's delicate hand in his, and bowed politely as Christina Ellwood made the introductions. He felt quite breathless. Edina Hamilton. It was a beautiful name. Everything about her was beautiful.

'My mother is going to leave her card, sir, and invite you to our house very soon,' Christina was saying to Dr Mitchell, while recognition dawned in Edina's brilliant blue eyes.

'Dr Iain Mitchell and Gavin?' she said. 'You are a medical student, Gavin? Now I remember Papa saying he had written to you, Dr Mitchell, to invite Gavin to visit us any time in Charlotte Square. My father is Eden Hamilton.'

'It's a small world,' Dr Mitchell said when after a few more minutes of polite conversation they were out of earshot. 'Pretty girls, were they not?'

They were, Gavin thought, especially Edina with the blonde hair, the one who danced when she walked, the one who, he could hardly believe, he had mistaken at first for Mary Paterson. Upon the merest acquaintance, which he intended somehow to rectify, they were as different as chalk from cheese.

'You've met your fate, Edina Hamilton – lucky girl!' Christina Ellwood laughed. 'Gavin Mitchell couldn't keep his eyes off you!'

'And you were right, Christina – he *is* quite the most handsome young man I've seen for a long time. But there is something worrying him very much. I wonder what it is.'

'Everything comes to an end, you know.' Dr Mitchell sighed as the fishing-rods went back into their long canvas sheaths, and what were left of the Grey Duns, the Blue Duns and the

127

Bloody Marys he'd spent so many winter evenings tying were put back into their compartments in the fly boxes.

'Too fast,' Gavin agreed with him.

Mrs Mitchell took a last lingering look around Eastwood before she put the dust covers back on again, and the family journeyed home to Gilmerton; even the children were quiet and pensive.

'Well, life must go on, I suppose.' Dr Mitchell tried to make light of it, but within hours he was called out to visit a sick patient. The days settled down into the old routine, and once more Gavin left for Edinburgh and the start of his second year.

'Ye're back, then,' Miss May observed when he got to 177, High Street, in a mixture of what he diagnosed as surprised relief and disapproval.

'I am,' he agreed, adding in a firmer tone, 'I won't be in for the evening meal. I'm going to visit a friend.'

'Please yersel', I'm sure,' Miss May humped her back towards him, 'but remember, no women, and I lock the door at nine o'clock, as ye ken.'

And you won't get into my room to see if I'm in by nine o'clock, you snippetty little hen, he said to himself and smiled as he walked over to Queen Street fingering the key in his pocket. Little did Miss May know that her two-foot-square window had been his exit and his entrance more often than her front door.

Once again Cardew waved him in and planted a glass in his hand. 'Don't you dare tell me about your holiday,' he said. 'I can see for myself you've grown another foot taller and another foot broader and you're as brown as a berry. Did you visit any interesting watering-holes?'

'Not one. But what about you, Cardew? How did you survive?'

'Barely, and that thanks only to the tourists. In the end I sent an SOS home and they sent me a few shillings as well. But I've got another wheeze. I planned it all when you were away.'

'No,' Gavin groaned.

'Don't worry. We'll get hold of Josh over a tankard of the foaming.'

'Josh? What's Josh got to do with anything?'

'He's got everything to do with this. His father's a minister, isn't he?'

'Further than that Cardew refused to be drawn, no matter how often they recharged their glasses, and it was well after midnight when Gavin weaved his unsteady way back to his lodgings and fell in through the two-foot-square window.

Five minutes later his head was out of it again as he vomited into the High Street. He might have been wiser, he reflected miserably, to have stayed for the stewed mutton after all. It might have lined his stomach. He would have to remember all that, now that he was back at the university.

Constable Frank Clarke paced his midnight rounds swinging his lantern into the darkness of the wynds and closes around the West Port. Here in the Grassmarket the fog hung and swirled between the dim lamps, and he wondered rather wistfully how he could win a rise in position so that he could protect the fine shops and houses of the New Town instead, where Kathy Fraser was living. Would he ever manage to save enough to marry her?

He hated these Old Town slums, rotting and stinking of slops thrown from windows or forestairs, but if promotion ever came his way it would have to be through the hard work he did here, crammed as it was with beggars and drunken folk clogging the closes and the gutters.

They must be having another spree in Tanners' Close. He could hear the noise from where he was standing. How, he asked himself, could people like them afford to buy all that booze? The more he thought about it, the more his interest quickened, and before his late night shift was over he had made up his mind to keep a much closer eye on the folk in Tanners' Close.

'What's that you've got in your basket, then, dearie?' he asked an old beggar woman a few days later in the Grassmarket.

'A few laces for ladies' stays, and some shoelaces. Nothing

129

much or heavy. I've come all the way from Gilmerton, you see.
It's poor pickings there. You have to come to the big city to
earn a crust.'

'Yes. You come every week?'

'I collect my pension every week, and then travel on to
Edinburgh. Abigail Simpson's my name – oh, thank you, sir!'
she said as Frank dropped a coin in her tin.

'Take care of yourself, Abigail. I'll be looking out for you
next Thursday.'

'It's ambitious I am,' Hare told Billy. 'I'm a man in a hurry.
We should try and get a subject a month.'

'Why not? But bringing them in from the street won't
be easy.'

'Maggie and Helen will have to help. We must tell them how
to spot the right subjects.' Hare went to fetch them.

'No young, strong men, even if they *are* drunk,' Burke warned
them. 'Women, yes.'

'Children?' Maggie Hare asked.

'None younger than eleven. They'd bring hardly any money.'

'Give us the patter, then. What do we say?' Maggie asked
Hare.

'Just offer them a place to rest, food, drink – yourself.
Anything to get them back here.'

Helen looked at Billy when Hare said the bit about offering themselves to all and sundry. She didn't like it, but
Billy seemed to be in pain again, and it was better to
cause no fuss. 'We look like beggars ourselves,' she said,
glaring at Hare. 'We'll need some pretty things for a job
like that.'

'Go to the Jew's shop, then,' Hare snarled, and threw down
a guinea between her and Maggie.

Weeks later, after all their fruitless efforts in the streets, fate
provided them with their third victim in a row in their own
house. English, nameless and turning yellower by the minute,
he'd been in one of the beggars' rooms in Log's Lodgings itself
all along.

'Jaundice,' Billy informed them.

'Well, I'm not sitting on that damned slippery pillow again, whatever he's got,' Hare said.

'You take the legs, then. I'll do the rest,' replied Billy, and when they got the man on his back Billy's powerful hands covered his nose and his mouth until the struggling stopped. He felt for a heartbeat. 'He's a goner,' he told Hare, 'and now we've found a new method.'

Dr Corcoran had been right enough, all those years ago. They were rich again, rich enough to buy neat suits for the men and more new bonnets and tippets for the two women. Hare even bought a clock, Helen got her brush at last and a comb that had nearly all its teeth in it, and down at Rhymer's she and Maggie had a lot of fun.

When they went to do their shopping Maggie sailed in first like a duchess, lifting her petticoat from the sawdust on the floor. 'Butter and a pound of the best tea,' she began. 'Then there's tobacco for me husband, and a gallon of whisky.'

David Rhymer eyed her curiously but for the moment said nothing. These two women had been owing him for weeks.

'A shin of beef and some lentils,' Maggie continued, 'and see to it that it's all brought to Log's Lodgings in a tea-chest.'

'I've got some heavy stuff, too,' Helen looked down her nose at him, 'so you'd better make that two tea-chests. Tatties and a bag of coal. And I'll need an oxtail, flour, suet and onions,' she said, opening her tattered purse.

Rhymer saw that it contained more than enough to pay for all this. 'We'll have a little dram in the back first, ladies.' He smiled. 'Och, ye look beautiful this morning in yer frilly bonnets! Ye'll be forgetting all yer old friends soon, and going to do yer shopping in Princes Street.'

'And how would we get there?' Helen asked. 'It's too far away.'

'Two ladies like yerselves wouldn't be out of place in a carriage.'

'It was my husband, William Hare, came into the legacy,' Maggie insisted, beginning to fidget. 'He was never uppity, like that, and he wouldn't allow us to be, either. Now, how much do we owe you?'

When they left the shop Helen asked, 'Why all the hurry? He was good for another drink!'

'Hm! He was asking too many questions in a roundabout way. Besides, I promised Hare we would go looking for subjects.'

They passed Hendersons' stables in the Grassmarket and went on up the West Bow, which was crowded as usual with men selling sheets of songs, and oranges, and hot chestnuts and magical cures. Helen lingered at the potions stall, but Maggie pulled her away. 'We've spent enough already today,' she said. 'Let's leave this crowd and go up to the Lawnmarket and into some of the closes. There's sure to be someone sleeping off drink or sheltering from the wind.'

Up there a crowd was gathered round an organ grinder and his monkey, so they managed to slip into Brodie's Close unnoticed. 'God, look at that! What did I tell you?' Maggie asked Helen triumphantly. 'This must be our lucky day. Let me do the talking.'

'Are you sick, lassie?' she asked the young woman propped up against the wall, an empty gin bottle by her side. 'My God, it's blue with the cold you are! Me sister and me'll warm you at our fire and get some hot food down you. Will you manage to get to your feet?'

'I've no feet to get to. I go about on a wheel-cart,' the woman mumbled, flinging up her skirts so that they saw her stumps. Maggie and Helen fled with the woman screaming after them, 'And some bastard's stolen it!'

Professor Monroe's lectures went from bad to worse as time went on. Where Knox had four hundred students in cramped conditions, Monroe had not two hundred all told. But he was the university lecturer, and his classes Gavin, Cardew and Josh were forced to attend if they wanted a university degree. They tried to liven up Monroe's lectures whenever possible in debates, except that debates with the Professor always deteriorated into the absurd.

Another problem Monroe had, besides not knowing what he was talking about, was a lack of bodies. One reason for that was his unpopularity, and the other his reluctance to part with money.

One deadly dull morning, after he had finished his daily tirade against the Outside classes and Dr Knox, the worst offender of all, he called for his clerk. 'Bring in the subject for today,' he said, and the students sat up. A subject? How could a subject have been delivered to Monroe, instead of to Knox?

In came the clerk carrying a dead dog.

'Sir,' Cardew stood up at once, 'that is not a human being.'

'Indeed? Well, it is of no consequence. The creature has a head, two arms and two legs.'

'I have never seen a dog with two arms, sir,' Cardew persisted.

'Nonsense! In a dog we call them forelegs and not arms as in humans. That is the only difference.'

'I cannot agree that a dog is the same as a man, sir,' Cardew prolonged the fun. 'Besides, we did not come here to study the anatomy of animals.'

'What have I been telling you about Dr Knox? Corpses are not easy to come by – wherever he gets so many from!'

The students all suspected where the bodies came from, although nobody actually said so. It was quite common to see shady characters with sacks on their backs at dusk up at Surgeons' Square. Knox and his rival Liston from another extramural school would both come out to speak to them, and one evening as Gavin and Cardew were passing they overheard Knox's conversation with one of them.

'Five guineas. That's my last offer.'

'Ye're no' getting her for that! I'll try Liston, over the road.'

'Damn your teeth. Six, then.'

Cardew took the greatest interest in the body-snatchers. He always spoke to them, and none of them took exception to him. It made Gavin think again about the body that had been Cardew's admittance card to the university in the first place. Perhaps the body-snatchers recognised him to be a brother of the night.

He was still thinking about it off and on as the year

proceeded, and one night early in November he strolled over to 57, Queen Street at Cardew's invitation to find Josh already installed, his face suffused with brandy, and his inhibitions gone with its fumes. Cardew poured out more brandy and pressed the goblets into his friends' hands, before joining them on the armchairs and resuming the conversation.

'What were you saying about your father's church in Dalkeith, Josh?'

'That it was built in 1802.'

Cardew became impatient. 'No, no, Josh! I'm not really interested in the church itself! It's the graveyard, and any likely burials taking place there in the near future.'

'My God,' Josh seemed to go limp, before he roared with laughter, 'you're going to be a body-snatcher! And in my father's graveyard!'

'You've done it before,' Gavin accused him. 'That was how you managed to bring a body to Edinburgh. It was all a story, that a doctor in the regiment owed you a favour.'

'It was a case of desperation then, and it's a case of desperation now. I've run out of the readies again.'

'Well, I'm game,' Josh said, putting down his goblet and getting to his feet. 'Announcements of deaths are always in the newspapers. Just let me know what your plans are, and I'll take you to the spot.'

'You're in a lather to go,' Cardew said when Mrs Love came to show Josh out with a deep curtsey. At the sight of her ample breasts under his nose Josh turned bright red. 'Ho, ho, ho, you old billy-goat! You're off to see the trading ladies again, aren't you? Don't catch the pox!'

'No, he's not!' Gavin protested when Josh fled.

'Of course he is! That's where all his money goes – didn't you know?'

Edinburgh was a perfect sink of inquity, Gavin thought. Uncle John Stafford had told no lies. And now, half in sympathy with Cardew's penniless state and half out of loyalty to Dr Knox to whom Cardew would sell the body, here he was about to become a Resurrection Man himself.

*   *   *

Miss May and Miss Irene never missed a Sunday at the kirk. They were there most of the day, attending every service. It was an arrangement that suited Gavin perfectly. It gave him time to clear his head after the night before, to get in a little studying, and best of all to enjoy the cold boiled ham and beetroot which was all they had time to prepare for dinner.

And now recently, on Wednesday evenings, Miss Irene had taken to donning a very unbecoming black bonnet and going out.

'The minister is starting a fund for fallen women,' Miss May enlightened him. 'The Society meets in the kirk on Wednesday nights. Miss Irene wouldn't miss a meeting. It's sic a fine minister we ha'e! It's a great pity ye dinna feel ye can join us on Sunday mornings!'

'Pressure of work, Miss May. It takes a great deal of studying to become a doctor, you know.'

'Aye,' she sighed. 'I see by yer locked door every night ye do plenty of it,' and the following evening at the dining table her conversation was all about the whole day she and Miss Irene had been hard at work too, pickling beetroot. 'We do thirty jars a year, Dr Gavin, when the beetroot is at its best and its cheapest.'

'You can count them if you like,' Miss Irene said drearily. 'They're all laid out on the kitchen dresser.'

'I'll take your word for it,' Gavin assured her hastily.

'But perhaps ye'd help her to put them up on the top shelf in the pantry?' Miss May asked.

'Certainly, ladies. When?'

'Now.' Miss Irene pushed back her chair. 'Follow me.'

Before he got the chance Miss Irene had scuttled up the short ladder in the pantry herself, and he found himself handing her up the jars of beetroot. She paused after a few minutes and looked down at him, her eyes sparkling behind her glasses in some sort of excitement. Then the ladder swayed, she fell and Gavin let go his jar of beetroot with a crash in favour of catching her.

'Oh! Oh! Oh! Will ye look at that?' Miss May appeared like greased lightning to clutch the pantry door with one hand, while pressing the other to her bosom. In horror Gavin stood transfixed with Miss Irene still in his arms. 'My God, the wee wifies aroond here were right enough! They aye said this would happen! They aye said not to trust ye, ye were too handsome – and *noo* look at ye! Making my niece a fallen woman hersel'!'

'I assure you, madam, I was not! My intentions were never dishonourable – '

'In that case they were honourable. Irene, go and get the ring. To think o' it! My Irene to wed a doctor!'

A moment later Miss Irene was rushing back to flash a ring with a nasty little blue stone in it under his nose. 'Now we're engaged,' she told him. 'When shall we get married?'

Dazzled by the sheer expertise and the speed of the whole manoeuvre, Gavin could only collect his wits together sufficiently to delay the happy day.

'Not until I'm qualified,' he assured his future bride.

Abigail Simpson collected enough pennies in her tin that Thursday to say to herself 'Bugger the begging' and in the White Hart someone put another sixpence in her tin, so that when at last she staggered out into the Grassmarket late in the afternoon she wasn't seeing very clearly, just enough to make out a tall dark man and a woman.

'Are you all right?' he asked her. 'It's not sick you are? Or hungry?'

'Hungry,' Abigail said.

'Poor soul,' the woman said. 'She reminds me of my mother, so she does. We can't let you go hungry, dearie. Where is it you live?'

'Gilmerton.'

'No, no, you can't go all the way to Gilmerton on an empty stomach. We'll give you something to eat first, and a rest by a warm fire.'

So here she was, with these kind people taking her arms and leading her down some stone steps, through a narrow passage and into a room with stone walls, very like her own in Gilmerton. She felt at home at once, and they gave her a little plate of tattie soup to eat and coaxed her to more whisky. Ah, they were grand people, Mr and Mrs Hare!

After a while another man and his wife came in, a man with sandy hair, and they had more drams while he played some lovely tunes on his pipe. As sure as God they were lulling her to sleep, like lullabies they were.

'Just you stretch out on that mat, dearie,' Mr Hare said. 'Take a nice long rest. Mrs Hare and Mrs Burke are away out for some more whisky.'

Abigail lay down on her back. 'Thank you. I'm that sleep – '

Ten sovereigns Abigail fetched, and the news that Dr Knox approved of the freshness of the bodies they always sold to him spurred on Hare and the Burkes to go out looking for more the very next day, leaving Maggie at home alone with her baby.

Andrew Kay, a chimney-sweep, came down past Tanners' Close, and saw that here were the worst and dirtiest chimneys so far, so he went down a dark, filthy passage and knocked at the door.

A woman with a baby in her arms came out. 'Well?' she said.

'I'll clean yer chimneys,' he said with a cheeky grin.

'Come in,' said Maggie, and led him to a room facing a pigsty and gave him a stool to sit on. She put the baby into a box and brought a bottle. 'What about a drink?' she asked.

'I don't usually. I'm only fourteen,' he said, taking the glass.

'Your mother must be proud of you, doing a man's work.'

'I'm alone in the world,' he told her and took another dram, pleased to be called a man.

'Well, just you wait a while. Me husband'll be back soon. He has the money.' Maggie poured some more whisky into his glass and went to sit opposite him, and before he had time to blink she had lifted her petticoat and was exposing a red garter on her skinny leg. 'You've had a girl before?' she asked.

'No!' He felt his face going red under the soot. The hag must be thirty or forty, by the look of her.

'All boys want it at your age,' she said, coming towards him undoing her bodice, and he got up and ran out so fast that he nearly knocked her over.

'Little bastard!' she yelled after him. 'Too frightened me man would come home and give you a bashing!'

But all the same she didn't dare tell Hare she'd lost them a shot, and she remained puzzled. Why wouldn't any man, fourteen or forty, want her?

Constable Frank Clarke, bent on his own mission, was getting to know the folk on his rounds, and their miserable lives. He went about it gently, genuinely concerned for them, trying to help when he could, and always stopping to have a word with Daft Jamie, everybody's favourite in the Old Town.

He couldn't have done more to further his cause although he didn't know it, for the people of Edinburgh took the simpletons of their town to their hearts and never ill-treated them. James Wilson didn't know he was daft, so he didn't mind his nickname in the least.

'Ay, ay, Jamie,' Frank said when he met him. 'Have you any riddles for me today?'

'I've got a good one for a penny, Constable Clarke.'

'Well, what is it?'

'Och,' Jamie laughed, 'I'm no' daft! Let's see your penny first.' Frank handed him the coin. 'In what month o' the year do the ladies talk least?' Jamie obliged.

'I give up. What month would that be?'

'February, because it's the shortest!'

'I can see you're not daft, Jamie, and you've got a good pair of eyes besides. When did you last see old Abigail Simpson from Gilmerton?'

Jamie screwed up his face in an effort to remember. 'I like Abigail,' he said, at last.

'So do I. But when did you last see her?'

'It's a long time now, Mr Clarke. Weeks and weeks. Three weeks.'

Three was probably as far as Daft Jamie could count, Frank thought. He himself had counted five Thursdays gone past without a sign of her.

12

'JUST THREE DAYS dead, would you believe it?' Cardew laughed,
telling Gavin about his two 'associates', as he called them,
returning from an expedition with a ten-pound-sack for Dr
Knox. To avoid suspicion they had propped up the sack
between them on the seat of their cart, so everyone would
think there were three of them on the driving seat.

For the life of him Gavin couldn't see the sense of that, but
Cardew was determined to persuade him with such tales of
heroic and hilarious caperings.

'They were halfway to Edinburgh in the freezing cold,'
Cardew went on, 'when they came to an inn, so they hid
the sack under canvas in the back of the cart and went in
for a drink. Unbeknown to them, a tramp came along and
lay down under the canvas, too. Ha! Ha! Ha!'

'I've heard this story before,' Gavin said, to no avail. Cardew
was determined to tell all.

'Out came the Resurrection Men, took what they thought was
their corpse and set him up again between them. A mile or two
up the road, their corpse came to life. "Christ," he said, "I'm
cauld enough to die!" Imagine their fright! They left the cart
and didn't stop running till they got to the Cameron Toll!'

'For goodness' sake, Cardew, if you're determined to do it
let's get it over and done with!' Gavin begged him. 'When are
you going?'

141

'Friday night, old man. Josh showed me the newspaper. There are to be no less than three burials all on that same day. It's too good to miss, and there isn't a moment to be lost. I think I've located a horse and cart. Come with me and see what you think.'

'Not much,' Gavin said, inspecting a huge old cart which was falling to pieces and an even older horse who looked at them out of ancient stubborn eyes.

When Friday night came, it came with a welcome mist and Josh with a collection of terrible old clothes. They put them on and half an hour later were rumbling slowly along on their way to Dalkeith, Josh at the reins since he was the only one who knew the way. The further they went the darker it became and more frightening, with only a fitful moon lighting the road from time to time and a rising wind making the trees and bushes wave and sway alongside them like ghostly giants.

It took hours to reach the churchyard and at last Josh threw down the reins in disgust.

'Aren't you going to tether him?' Gavin was already seriously worried about the homeward trip, if there was to be any.

'Tether *him*?' Josh said in a furious whisper, leading them inside the gates, where they could just make out the three freshly dug graves. 'He's not going anywhere, believe me. Where on earth did you dig him up from, Cardew?'

Cardew took two heavy spades, two grappling hooks and three sheets out of the cart. 'Never mind about digging up horses,' he said as grimly as his quivering voice would allow. 'It's three humans we're here for,' and they crept along the wall to the graves, while all the time the church spire glittered in the moon and seemed to watch them.

'Right,' Cardew muttered through chattering teeth, 'lay down the first sheet,' and Gavin spread it out while the other two dug the fresh soil aside furiously. 'The grappling irons,' he muttered next, and between them they heaved out the first coffin, working at top speed to lift the lid and remove the body.

'Lay out the next sheet, and then put that body in the cart,' Cardew instructed Gavin, and in about an hour they had the graves ransacked, all three bodies safely side by

142

side in the back of the cart, and had climbed back up themselves.

'Nothing to it, was there?' Cardew tried to joke.

'Bloody body-snatchers!' roared a voice, and out from the church where they had no doubt been enjoying a quiet drink came three solid men, each carrying a firearm as big as themselves.

'Oh, God, that's my father's voice . . .' Josh relasped into a state of shock.

'Josh!' Gavin dug his speechless, terrified friend in the ribs, 'for Christ's sake, *go*!'

But Josh, when he suddenly came to life, dropped the reins and rolled over to join Cardew and the bodies in the back, out of the line of fire.

'Tell him it's you!' Gavin yelled, taking the reins himself and desperately trying to whip up the horse, bullets whining about his head all the while. Death stared him in the face. 'Tell him to stop!'

'Look at him,' Josh whimpered. 'Just look at the size of him! You can see for yourself that speaking to him is like farting against thunder!'

It was only by sheer luck that the old horse recognised the sound of shooting for himself at last, took to his hoofs and set off at a gallop. Gavin didn't know what to worry about most all the way to Edinburgh – whether the horse would fall down dead of a heart attack due to this unaccustomed activity, or whose beloved mother or son or wife they had stolen and thrown in the back of the cart.

By the time they got to Surgeons' Square and Cardew opened the door with a key he'd 'happened' to borrow, he and Josh had disposed of the shrouds. Stealing a body wasn't a capital offence. Stealing one in a shroud definitely was.

'Off you go!' Cardew waved the other two away. 'I'll stay here all night, and see Dr Knox first thing in the morning.'

'That was the worst night of my life,' Gavin told him next day. 'You can count me out of the Resurrectionists from now on.'

'That's all right, old boy. I got thirty guineas, no questions, and Fanny and I will survive again.'

*　　*　　*

The Registrar of the Edinburgh Royal Infirmary assigned Gavin, Josh and Cardew surgical dressers to Mr Caldwell for the month of December and now, halfway through their training, the real hard work began. They saw cancer, opium, blood, rose-water, stitches. They heard the screams of pain, observed Surgeon Caldwell remaining precise, cool and fast, and developed a surface hardness themselves to conceal their own terror.

It was a relief to set out on their course of midwifery with one of Edinburgh's famous obstetricians, Professor James Hunter. It followed the usual pattern: lectures, demonstrations, visits to lying-in wards and visits to private houses with one of Professor Hunter's midwives.

This interlude spent with mothers, the unmistakable warm sweet smell of birth and the satisfaction they all felt when a child was safely delivered into the world was a happy time for all the students. When something went wrong with the delivery and new, cruel-looking forceps with large blades had to be used, sometimes to bring out the child in pieces, the sadness they felt was beyond belief. None of them could harden themselves to that, except Josh, who was determined to master the forceps, utterly dedicated to saving the lives of both mother and child.

Gavin's favourite midwife was without doubt Effie Justice, a long, skinny woman who had never been seen to smile, and believed that all men were fiends sent straight from Hell with one specific purpose, and that was to rape women, call it nothing less.

'Ach, my poor lassie,' was her usual opening gambit when a woman was in labour. 'Been at it again, has he, the dirty beast! It's well seen none o' *them* ha'e to go through it, or the world would soon come to an end! There'd be no bairns born *then*! Never you mind – '

'Step aside, Effie,' the Professor would say. 'Pay no attention to her, my dear,' to the terrified prospective mother. 'She's only here because she's the best midwife in the town!'

Effie would retreat a foot or two with a sourer look than ever on her face, but when the birth was taking place she proved she was worth her weight in gold.

144

'There ye are, Mistress,' they heard her say one day, as she put a new-born baby into the mother's arms, shaking her head. 'I'm sorry to tell ye, but ye've brought another o' them fiends o' Hell into the world! It's a boy, sent to bother some other poor lassie one day! But now ye ken what caused it ye'll no' be back to see us yersel', will ye? Ye'll keep well clear o' the beast?'

'I don't know,' said the proud mother, her eyes fixed on the door her husband would soon come through.

'And as for you,' Effie went out to fetch the young father, 'for God's sake put one of these on when ye're an animal brute again,' and pressed something like a small deflated balloon into his hand.

'She wouldn't know,' Cardew whispered behind his hand, 'but the damned things keep bursting anyway.'

'Mr McLean,' the Professor addressed Josh, who was for once shaved clean and had had his hair cut, 'follow me. There's something here to interest you.'

'By Jove,' Cardew said, 'Professor Hunter's treating our friend like one of his own. What's the reason for that, I wonder?'

'I can tell ye,' Effie sniffed. 'Mr Josh put himself on call long ago, so that if the Professor wanted a helper through the night he was here. He's one o' the dedicated kind, Mr Josh! Dedicated to these poor lassies and their bairns! He's no' like the rest o' ye.' She marched out contemptuously, adding, 'all *ye* can think about is getting them, dirty wee beasts!'

On the Tuesday, a week before the long summer break began, Gavin cast around wildly for somewhere to go, in an effort to escape his fiancée, Miss Irene. It was useless to say he had to swot, because she knew he had sat his written examinations already, and there was only one practical to go.

He washed in a strong solution of Windsor soap, donned his best clothes, even finding a clean shirt and cravat to put on, and told her and Miss May that he was off to visit friends in Charlotte Square, a statement which impressed them so much that they sat open-mouthed while he made good his escape.

'Who's this, Miss Edina?' Kathy asked, seeing him approach,

and together they watched the young man in a green frock-coat and narrow pantaloons.

'I know who I hope it is.' Edina blushed.

'You mean Mr Cardew, I suppose? Well, I'll go and see.'

But Kathy never came back, and after a while Edina could bear the suspense no longer and went through to the drawing-room. Papa was speaking to the young man in the green frock-coat, and his attitude was quite different from the one he adopted to Cardew, she noticed with a smile.

'Edina, my dear, allow me to introduce the son of one of my oldest friends, Mr Gavin Mitchell, a medical student here.'

'We've met already, Papa, although it was a long time ago, on the banks of the River Almond. You've taken a long time to get here, Gavin.'

'Not from want of will, I assure you, Miss Edina. But this second year has been a very busy one, unfortunately.'

He was holding on to her hand far longer than he should have, and his heart was breaking. He should never have come here to Charlotte Square, to cause himself so much pain, now that he must wed another. He was hopelessly in love with Edina. It was worse than that, he told himself in a daze on the way back home. The fact was he knew he would love her for ever, with all his heart and soul, until the day he died.

'What was the matter with that young man, Edina?' Mr Hamilton asked. 'He became very tongue-tied as soon as he saw you.'

'I think he's in trouble of some sort, and it's not over yet,' she said with a sigh.

Once again the Mitchell family went to Almondbank for the summer. Dr and Mrs Mitchell looked better within a week, the younger Mitchells ran as free as gypsies and only for Gavin was it a cruel travesty of the year before.

No visitors came down from the Ellwoods' house. In fact, from its closed-up appearance, it seemed that no one was home. No amount of fishing calmed his soul, and after a few times round the course with his father he threw down his golf club and swore he'd never play the wretched game again.

'He's got all the classic symptoms,' Dr Mitchell told his wife. 'He's in love, mark my words.'

Instead he went for long solitary walks in the woods behind Ellwood, alternately dreaming of Edina or sitting on the trunk of a tree with his head in his hands in utter despair. He was engaged to be married to a girl he neither knew nor liked, when all he wanted now or ever was to marry Edina Hamilton. He was trapped in a box, with no way out.

Billy Burke and William Hare had been keeping the home fires burning by disposing of Betsy Dawson and Effy Wood, and now the time had come to look for another subject.

Constable Frank Clarke was escorting Fat Jean and her apple barrow safely back to her house as he sometimes did if she was the worse for drink, and this afternoon Fat Jean had got it into her head that he was only doing this because he was in love with her.

'Come in, won't you, and have a drop of gin?' she asked him.

'You know I can't, Jean. I'm on duty.' He shook his head.

'You've made it your duty to follow me, many a time. I know what you want. You want to come in and spend all night with me.' She smiled drunkenly, her fat cheeks creasing alarmingly to join in with the rings of fat on her neck.

Frank felt sorry for her, but he thought it was her own fault she was so fat. She spent every penny she earned on her stomach. He'd seen her himself wolfing down three-cornered puff tarts and cream cakes and treacle pies outside the bake-shop, and the pity of it was she could have been such a pretty woman.

'Don't wait until you're on duty the next time, then,' she said coyly. 'And you should bring flowers. The other men all bring me flowers.'

He remembered the last time she'd bragged to him about an admirer sending her flowers by special delivery. That was in May, shortly after he'd seen her buying daffodils from a cart. But he would never hurt her feelings by telling her that, so he just smiled and left her at her door.

Left to herself Fat Jean drank all the gin and fell asleep

147

dreaming that she was a duchess in a rose-garden. She woke again in the late afternoon, sour-mouthed, sober and as usual dying of hunger. After she'd eaten what was in the house she went down to the cellar and piled more apples on to her barrow. She had very little money left, but at this time of day she often did good business, because she knew the right places to go with her barrow.

This evening she parked it near the Rotunda on the Mound. People liked to eat apples while they enjoyed the panoramas of famous cities and views of battles, but after a while she realised the orange sellers had got there before her, and that was why she was getting no trade.

She trundled on with her barrow, passing a Punch and Judy show, and here a few children did come and buy an apple or two. Then it got too dark for the puppet-show to continue. A man started to pack it up, and Jean took up her barrow again. But her feet were sore, and she was tired when she arrived in the Grassmarket.

Here a few lamps were lit, and the night-life was just beginning. Two painted sluts swayed along in front of her until they disappeared down a close with two men after them. Suddenly Jean felt very lonely. She would never be a duchess, men would never follow her down any close and all she'd made was sixpence and a ha'penny.

Well, she could hide her barrow in a close and cover it with sacks. Then she could go into the White Hart and cheer herself up a bit. Ten minutes later she was waddling up to the long brown bar and shouting, 'Gin and pies,' above the rest of the noise in the tavern, and went to sit at a table in the corner. As soon as her order came she set about the pies first. Next she had a couple of gins, and then she was looking up into eyes that smiled, nice kind eyes.

'May I sit here, miss?' the man said with a touch of an Irish brogue.

'I don't mind if you do.'

'It's Jean, isn't it?'

'How do you know my name, sir?'

'Everybody knows you, with your hair like a flame, and your

skin like a peach. Well, what would you be after drinking, Jean? Gin? Brandy, maybe?'

'A brandy would be very nice, sir. Of course I never drink as a rule, but tonight I felt a twinge in one of my teeth. Brandy would cure it, I'm sure.'

'What a pity if you had to lose a tooth, and you so young and beautiful.'

'Do you really think so?' Fat Jean simpered.

'I really think so, and I also happen to know that champagne is a sure-fire cure for the toothache. Just by chance a friend of mine is having a whole case delivered tonight off a French boat, docked in Leith. We're having a booze. Would you be joining us?'

'Why not?' said Jean. 'But you haven't told me your name yet.'

'William, but everyone calls me Billy. My friend is called William, too. William Hare. It's his house we're away to now, in Tanners' Close.'

'It isn't much of a place, is it?' Billy whispered when they got there. 'I'm moving out soon, meself, and going to Charlotte Square. But wait here, and I'll go and see if me friend's got the wine.'

What a gentleman he was, this Billy! She felt a bit light-headed and wondered if she was needing something to steady her up a bit, like food. Would he give her something to eat? Sausages, maybe?

Within minutes he was back. 'William's just coming,' he said. 'He's been chilling the wine. Ah, William, this is Jean.'

But the nightmare face of William Hare sobered Jean suddenly and completely. Now she knew why she had been brought here. They were going to rape her, her being so beautiful. She got to her feet. 'I'm sorry,' she said. 'I can't wait for the wine. I have to meet someone.'

Hare went to stand between her and the door. 'Och, he wouldn't mind waiting until you had a drop of the bubbly, would he?'

'He *would* mind. He doesn't like to be kept waiting, and if I'm late he'll come looking. He's Constable Frank Clarke.'

In their desperation to be rid of her when they heard that, Hare even unbolted the door for her, and Jean ran wobbling down the filthy passage outside and into the street. She made for a night lantern swinging towards her.

'Frank! Frank Clarke! Two men were trying to rape me!' Her voice quivered, and she quivered, all over.

'Where?'

'In Tanners' Close.'

'Now, Jean, I can see you're upset. And you're drunk again.'

'No, I'm not!'

'I can smell it on you. Come, I'll take you to your door again. You never found out their names?'

'One of them was called Billy, and the other William Hare. See, Frank? I'm not drunk after all, am I?' Fat Jean began to cry.

'You're all right, Jeannie.' Frank left her at her door and walked back down to the Grassmarket.

Was he on to something at last? Fat Jean had been talking about Billy Burke and William Hare, two gentlemen he'd been wondering about a lot lately. All those boozes and parties! And what about the loaded barrows of goods he'd seen their women trundling up from Rhymer's? Where were they getting all the money?

Fat Jean seriously believed they had waylaid her in order to rape her. Could it be that they wanted her body for a different purpose? To sell it, perhaps? Poor Jean was better off left with her illusions, but he would have to watch over her more closely from now on.

Frank steadied himself. Speculation was useless. He must have solid, rock-hard proof. He must get the evidence. He must just keep on waiting and watching patiently, he told himself, groaning, as he turned into Tanners' Close.

Everything was quiet down there. Nothing moved, except the rats and the thin-ribbed cats. When he lifted his eyes he saw the high, far lights of the Castle, and beyond them the tranquil stars.

*   *   *

May Milligan was getting up earlier every day now, when before she had lain back in her bed and taken her rest after the night shift at Meg Dod's bake-shop. This was so that she could prowl up and down the Royal Mile in the hope of seeing Bridie's other daughter again, the one who had been left new-born in Candlemaker Row.

But there was never any luck, and Frank Clarke was the only one observant enough to notice her. That she was looking for something or someone there could be no doubt, as he confided to Kathy. Long ago he had seen the sense of telling her about most of his activities, especially off-duty, in case she got any wrong ideas.

'You're not on duty tomorrow night either, are you?' she asked him one Tuesday evening in September.

'No. But I intend to be in the Royal Mile. I can't afford not to be, with so much going on there, if I am ever to win promotion and marry the bonniest lassie in Edinburgh. Go on, bonnie lassie, give me a kiss!'

'Thank God you'll be there tomorrow night, Frank,' Kathy said after a long, happy pause. 'Miss Edina is determined to be there, too, to see Mary Paterson – she's so curious about their likeness – and of course I'll have to go with her.'

'It's no place for you, or her, at night.'

'Och, where's the danger, when the long arm of the law will be right there behind us?' Kathy laughed. 'She's gone to endless trouble to hatch a plot so that we can get out of the house.'

'What is it?'

Hatching any kind of plot to go out accompanied only by Kathy in the evening had been extremely difficult, that's all Edina knew. She never gave up, trying in the first instance to pick up the gossip of the town in order to find an excuse to get out to the Royal Mile. But that was usually hushed in her presence because no well-bred young lady should know about such sordid goings-on. Now she knew how a dog felt when it smelled a bone, and, frustrated, she dug on, studying every single line of the newspapers delivered to 13, Charlotte Square until at last her tenacity was rewarded. *There* it was, in black and white!

'The Revd John Stafford,' so said the report in the *Scotsman*, 'should be regarded as a pioneer in one aspect of the saving of souls. Conscious of the plight of some unfortunate women of this city, he has founded the Society for the Protection and Rehabilitation of Fallen Women. His meetings are in the Tron Kirk every Wednesday evening at 7.30, to which all interested, and more fortunate, are invited to attend. Revd Stafford hopes by such means some guidance and succour may be afforded these lost souls, with God's will.'

'Pompous man!' Edina muttered to herself, but all the same Revd John Stafford had inspired her brainwave, and carrying the paper in her hand with the article ringed she entered the drawing-room at the four o'clocks. 'I have decided to join in such a worthy cause,' she told her parents, pointing out the place in the newspaper.

'Good God!' Mr Hamilton's delicate Tantallon biscuit, scalloped and lemon-flavoured, shattered on the fireside rug where it fell from his nervous fingers. 'What next?'

To add to his extreme alarm, Lady Alison was having quite a different reaction. 'It sounds good to me,' she said. 'Very commendable, dear, although I wish the meetings could have been in the afternoons. It gets dark so early now.'

Thus encouraged, Edina lost her tenseness and subsided into one of the armchairs. 'I was so sure you would disapprove, Mama.'

'Nonsense, Edina! We are all just weak women! So many times I wonder what might have happened to *me*, if I hadn't had the good fortune to meet your papa.'

Yes, Mama was at work again, twisting her husband round her little finger! Edina smiled when she saw him smile fondly at his wife, and she realised that they were speaking, perhaps, of her own mother and father.

'Alison . . .'

'I adore you, Eden, and I am very blessed,' Lady Alison said crisply. 'Many other women have not had my good fortune, loving very different men, sometimes with tragic results. You and I have seen that in our lifetime.' She looked at him pointedly, as if reminding him.

152

'Indeed, my dear.'

'Besides, now that she has reached this age it is only right that Edina should know and understand some of the seamier side of life.'

'Must she? I have grave doubts about that.'

'Yes, I must,' Edina said, putting her hand on his. 'All my life you have sheltered me, and I adore you, too. I always will, but have you not sheltered me a little too much? Perhaps the time has come to flap my wings. I'm not going to fly away altogether, dearest Papa.'

'Of course not,' her mother agreed. 'It is tomorrow night? But how will you get there? You will take Kathy with you, of course.'

'Of course. If I may have Fergus and the coach, Papa?'

But Mr Hamilton was not altogether convinced. 'Will you be very careful?'

'I promise you, Papa.'

'Very well, then, I'll give Fergus the necessary instructions,' he said sadly.

Early the following evening, on Wednesday, Edina and Kathy left Fergus and the coach at the Tron Kirk while they walked down the High Street as far as Swanston's tavern, and trooped back and fore idly in the shadows opposite.

'Here they come now,' Kathy whispered at last. 'Janet Brown is the one with the hat on. Mary Paterson, need I say, is the one in red.'

Edina's eyes were all for Mary Paterson, and what she saw sent shivers through her. Tousle-haired, Mary swaggered up the High Street, laughing loudly. Then she opened her painted mouth and sang in a raucous soprano. She was still singing when she reached the door of the tavern, and then she flung it open. 'Here's yer Mary, boys!' she yelled to a welcoming roar.

In the darkness and silence afterwards Edina and Kathy clutched each other's hands. 'We'd better go, Miss Edina,' Kathy urged, 'if you really want to attend Revd John Stafford's meeting.'

'Now, more than ever,' Edina replied shakily.

She didn't know what to think. How could anyone, even her dear Kathy, ever imagine she resembled the terrible Mary Paterson? Yet in her heart she knew she did, and a terrible suspicion came to her that she might have sisters, brothers too, even. She choked it all back. There was the travesty of this meeting to be endured next, to account for this stolen evening.

But strangely enough the two girls found themselves enthralled when they got there.

'Would you look at them all, Miss?' Kathy muttered in Edina's ear. 'Of course, they are all women, and every one of them an old biddy, an old hag, a withered old bitch!'

'You shouldn't say so, Kathy, but it's true.' Edina giggled. 'And he's a pompous little ass,' she added after John Stafford's impassioned appeal, and it was Kathy's turn to dissolve into helpless, silent, hiccuping laughter.

'And now, ladies, I invite your views,' he said at the end of his address, and sat down.

Thereafter followed one strident tirade of vituperation after another, as one ancient virgin gave way to the next, utterly revelling in the fornication they had obviously never achieved themselves.

'I can't stand any more of this,' Edina warned Kathy, and stood up herself. 'Sir,' she said loudly, 'what are we listening to? I did not think we were here to condemn these poor unfortunate women. They are in enough trouble as it it. When is there going to be a suggestion as to how to help them instead?'

'Miss Irene May has a suggestion.' The Revd Stafford beamed at a woman, younger but just as vinegary as the rest, and bursting with emotion. Her cheeks were scarlet. In another minute her spectacles were sure to crack right across in the heat of it.

'Ladies – and, of course, dear Revd Stafford – we must tackle the serpent in the Garden of Eden. And where is the Garden of Eden? At Mrs McClarty's whorehouse! We must go there next Wednesday night and every Wednesday night, until we root out all the snakes wriggling their hips in front of men!'

'Ahhhh!' The force of venom, if not at Mrs McClarty's, was certainly in this church hall.

'We must have banners!' Miss Irene May was screeching.

'Let's go,' Edina said.

'But let's come back next week and see the fun,' Kathy begged.

'You needn't worry, Kathy dear. I wouldn't miss it for the world.'

13

WITH HIS HEART in his boots Gavin went back to Miss May's to start his third year at the university.

'There's only a year until our wedding day,' Miss Irene greeted him. 'You should have taken me to be introduced to your parents.'

'As you say, Miss Irene, a whole year. Anything could happen between now and then.' Gavin did his best to believe it. 'There's many a slip between cup and lip, you know.'

If only he could find one!

'Well,' she sulked, 'the whole summer was lost.'

It was lost, all right, he thought gloomily, wondering what Cardew had in store for him next. But to his amazement, when he met up with his friends again Cardew was on top of the world, looking well and decidedly prosperous in a new royal-blue suit bedecked with a gold chain dangling across his chest from pocket to pocket.

'That tourist idea I had last year was an inspiration!' he told Gavin and Josh. 'I remembered it one day when I was about to throw myself penniless from the Castle walls. Just in time to save my life I heard American voices, French voices, German voices – they were all round me. In fact, I wondered if I was in the next world already!'

'But as we see, you're still here,' Josh said drily.

'It turned out some Americans needed a guide to show them

round the town,' Cardew beamed, 'and so did a lady from London, absolutely rotten with the filthy lucre. I've been at it with her all summer. I'm in the money!'

'Oh dear . . . I trust Fanny suspected nothing?' Gavin asked. 'And you with a new suit, as well.'

'Oh, *I* didn't buy this,' said Cardew with a smile, ignoring that sally. 'Nor the gold chain for my watch. That was thanks to my English benefactress, this Miss Daphne Hogg. I ran into her when the foreigners went away.'

'Miss Daphne *Hogg*?' Gavin and Josh stared at him.

'She didn't go back home with the others in her party. You're bound to meet her soon.'

'Why didn't she go back with the others?' Josh asked suspiciously, laying down his tankard and rising to go. 'What's keeping her here?'

'How should I know?' Cardew laughed, but once Josh had gone his face became serious. 'I have a horrible feeling, Gavin, that she's after *me*.'

'I know how you feel, Cardew. In fact, I know better than you do. I got caught,' Gavin confided glumly, and then went on to tell his friend the story of the beetroot jar, and that he was now engaged to be married to a lady dedicated to helping fallen women.

'My God . . . You're in a fix, then!'

'I am, and if there's a way to get out of it, I can't find it. I've just spent the most miserable summer of my life trying,' Gavin assured him, without telling him the most pressing reason of all to get out of it. The subject of Miss Edina Hamilton, the love of his life, he believed he should keep to himself.

Cardew patted him on the back. 'Leave it to me, old fruit. But we should bring Josh into this as well. Three heads are better than two in a case of this kind.'

A few days later, when the three of them were in Swanston's, Cardew announced to Gavin: 'Josh and I have thought up a plan. It's foolproof.'

'I've known plans of yours before, Cardew.'

'This time I made up most of it,' Josh said, 'so it's bound to be better. We've decided, Gavin, that you must visit a brothel

. . . Cardew, what the hell's the matter with him? Help me to pick him up off the floor, for God's sake, before people take notice!'

'It's all right, Gavin,' said Cardew, dusting the sawdust off him. 'We're perfectly serious. There's one brothel in the town that Josh is particularly acquainted with. He'll go with you.'

'I *was* particularly acquainted with it some time ago,' Josh admitted without so much as a blush. 'Not so much now, but I'm still well known there. We could go next Wednesday night.'

'What's so special about Wednesday night?'

'Well, it so happened I was there last Wednesday night, and the Wednesday night before that. There was a great disturbance outside the place. Women caterwauling, singing hymns and waving placards. The Society for the Rescue of Fallen Women, I believe they call themselves. Something like that.'

'My God!' Gavin was horrified.

'Now, isn't it a splendid plan?' Cardew laughed uproariously. 'Your betrothed will be singing hymns outside when she sees you coming out of the den of iniquity! She won't want to marry you after that!'

'I'll have to think about it,' Gavin said, but already he knew he was desperate enough to try anything.

'Come to supper on Wednesday night before you go, then, both of you. I've got an excellent brandy to fortify you, thanks to Miss Daphne Hogg.'

Gavin was much too miserable to remember very much of the days between, or of Wednesday itself, before Josh dragged him off to Cardew's at 57, Queen Street for supper. It was as if he had suddenly come awake still in the middle of some terrible nightmare.

To begin with, Cardew simply couldn't keep his hands off his housekeeper. He was giving her some instruction about the roast chicken when Gavin distinctly saw his hand caressing Mrs Fanny's silken buttocks. Surely a man didn't behave like that towards his housekeeper, and certainly not if she was his sister besides?

159

It was then that Gavin really looked at Mrs Fanny for the first time, with a deadly suspicion that she was not and never had been Cardew's sister. The dirty dog! All this time he had been living in luxury and contriving to keep a mistress, besides! He tried to cool his resentment. After all, he might be only imagining it, in this atmosphere which was undoubtedly highly sexually charged.

She, in turn, kept stroking her belly, and gazing back at him with her large soft eyes swimming with tears. There was something in the air at Number 57 which Gavin couldn't place or understand, when Mrs Fanny suddenly caught her breath and ran sobbing out of the room.

'Pay no attention to Fanny.' Cardew dismissed her lightly. 'She's upset today. Now here's the famous brandy before you set off.'

They tossed off the brandy fast, and Josh pulled some strange furry objects out of his pockets. He shook out one of them as Cardew refilled their glasses. It was a violent shade of orange. 'This one's your wig, Gavin,' he said. 'Put it on, and here are your face whiskers to match.' He handed him such an obvious imitation of a moustache and beard that it wouldn't have deceived a child. 'Put your hat on as well and pull down the brim,' he said, and did the same with a set of jet-black disguises for himself.

'Haw, haw, haw, your own mothers wouldn't recognise you,' Cardew brayed.

Gavin and Josh shot him venomous looks from under their false shaggy eyebrows and departed. 'It's down here,' said Josh, leading him into a dark little wynd off the High Street. 'Number 6, the infamous Mrs McClarty's.'

'Oh, God,' Gavin moaned when Josh knocked at the door, sensing in a blinding flash that now he had descended to the lowest depths of degradation that Edinburgh could possibly offer.

Just as he was trying to banish all thoughts of Edina and his parents, the door was flung open. Tobacco smoke and music and bright lights billowed out for a second before a large stout woman draped about with pale pink satin shot out an arm

160

like a prize-fighter's, hauled them in and slammed the door shut again.

'Professor Monroe!' she greeted Josh, with a glittering porcelain smile.

'This is Dr Knox, Mrs McClarty,' said Josh, introducing Gavin.

'And ye're both here in the right place for a good time!' she boomed above the music, barring their way into Paradise with her hand held out.

'We'll go upstairs.' Josh paid her and pushed Gavin up a few steps to a sort of elevated balcony. It seemed to run right round a large room, and curtains hung at intervals on its walls. 'Sit here.' Josh pushed him into a gilded chair upholstered in grubby pink velvet in front of a small table bedecked with a pink cloth. 'Look around you,' he hissed.

There was an excellent view of the front door from up here. Within half an hour they saw entering the real Dr Knox himself – who could do nothing to hide his black eye-patch – members of the very town council itself and half the dignitaries of Edinburgh, all of whose disguises were so clumsy that they only drew attention to who they really were.

When Gavin looked behind him he saw that the curtains scarcely veiled small cubicles, and to judge from the sounds coming out of them that was where the business of this establishment was being done.

The flash of a red dress drew his eye to one of Mrs McClarty's girls. It was Mary Paterson leading a man into one of the cubicles, but a very different Mary from the one he used to know. She looked stringy and tawdry and ten years older than when he'd last seen her. In a few minutes she was back out again, buttoning up her bodice.

'Professor Monroe,' Mrs McClarty shouted. 'That's Mary ready for ye now!'

Without a word or a backward glance Josh strode off towards her and Gavin was left alone. Oh God, he thought, it would be his turn next . . . How could he get out of this awful place? His panic increased when a terrible uproar sounded at the front door. Women's voices were upraised and police whistles were shrilling. It must be a raid! Reporters would be at the scene. Oh, the disgrace when they got to know of this in Charlotte Square! Edina seemed to recede further and further from him . . . And how would he ever face his mother again when the first thing she would read in the *Scotsman* was that her son was arrested in a brothel?

He leapt to his feet and ran, desperate to escape, but suddenly his heart stopped beating. Now he knew exactly how a heart attack felt. He couldn't move. To speak would have been impossible. He was frozen into a perfect statue face to face with his uncle John Stafford, newly emerged from one of the cubicles, pulling up his breeches and trying to fasten them without much success, since in the same desperation as Gavin's he had put both feet in the same leg.

If he saw his nephew he gave no sign as he scurried and flurried out and into his breeches again, his shirt-tail hanging out, his round collar all askew. He raced down to the door. Suddenly in full charge of all his faculties again, Gavin arrived on the front doorstep a few paces behind him.

'Oh no, ye don't!' Frank Clarke stopped the minister, while another policeman was valiantly trying to prevent a collection of vinegary, screaming ladies brandishing placards from entering.

Gavin saw at a glance that the most vigorous of them all, the one struggling the hardest and screeching the loudest, was none other than his betrothed. 'I tell you, I'm here to start a benevolent fund for your fallen women,' shrieked Miss Irene.

'That slut,' declared Mrs McClarty, 'is ruining my good name. It's the Liberton Wynd lock-up for her.'

'Don't you understand?' Miss Irene shrieked again. 'I want to save your whores.'

'What good would that do?' Mrs McClarty appealed to the policemen and the growing crowd. 'Where would we all be then? My ladies would be out of work, and half the gentlemen in the town – '

To everyone's amazement Revd John Stafford, still trying to adjust his dog collar but with his spectacles back firmly on his nose, cut her off in mid-flow. He burst from Constable Clarke's arms and rushed towards Miss Irene.

'Unhand that lady at once, sir!' he thundered at the other policeman. 'She is a mission lady from my own kirk!'

'We don't care if she'd dropped down from Heaven itself,' Frank took it upon himself to speak for the Edinburgh constabulary, 'she making too much noise! She'll be waking all the decent folk in their beds.'

'Decent folk?' John Stafford appeared to choke. 'What decent folk? I have been into this Godless fleshpot myself, trying to save the poor fallen women and their customers at the same time! We are all trying to save their souls from damnation!'

He ranted on in his best pulpit fashion for some time, and Josh, presumably finished with Mary Paterson, came to join Gavin with some of Mrs McClarty's other customers. Gavin's eyes, as were everyone else's who were in the front rows witnessing this scene, were mesmerised by the spectacle of John Stafford's passionate championship of Miss Irene. She looked up at him adoringly, drinking in every deceitful word he uttered, flashing triumphant glances at the crowd whenever he drew breath.

It was then that her eyes fell on her prospective husband coming out of the whorehouse. Screaming, and flinging herself about in a truly dramatic fashion, she promptly and carefully fainted straight into John Stafford's arms.

'Hysteria, probably of some sexual disorder,' Josh muttered in Gavin's ear, who scarcely heard him. He had just caught a glimpse of the very last person he ever wished to see – Christopher North of *The Scotsman*, and he was taking notes.

Half an hour earlier, when the commotion in and around Horse Wynd was at its height, Mabel Milligan deduced that since it was a Wednesday evening it would be coming from the brothel at Number 6, and those mission women would be at it again, screaming and shouting.

For once in nearly twenty years of hard work and scrimping and saving for her Irish Eldorado, she deserted her post. There were no customers anyway, there hadn't been for hours, and with all this going on nobody would be thinking of buying a half-loaf. Besides, there was little enough excitement in her life. So she locked the door and ran out to join the crowd.

'It's them missionaries,' the woman next to her explained, 'trying to get a' the men oot o' McClarty's, to shame them. If they get the whores oot as well, they'll tear them limb from limb! Will ye listen to that, noo!'

It was like the screaming of banshees, right enough, but all Mabel could see was Constable Frank Clarke herding out the notables of the town into the milling mob. Then she got a perch up on the steps of the building opposite, and from there she had a bird's-eye view of what was happening.

The men didn't interest her. Suddenly all the whores in various states of undress were being pushed out into the street, Mary Paterson in her red dress conspicuous among them. At the sight of her the crowd hissed, the Society women surged forward in a frenzy, and it was only Frank Clarke keeping them back that allowed her to escape. She scuttled across the road and into the labyrinths around the Grassmarket.

But not all the Society women were taking part in the uproar. Two stood apart. One of them was a beauty, too well-dressed to be here at all, and the other must be her maid. Mabel Milligan jumped down from her perch into the midst of the sweating, screaming women and grasped one of them by her arm. 'Who's that?' she demanded urgently. 'Who's that blonde lady behind us?'

'Oh, *her*!' The Society woman turned her head for a second to see. 'That's Miss Edina Hamilton, a do-gooder. What does *she* ken aboot it? She's only come oot o' her fine hoose in Charlotte Square to see how the rest o' us live. Oh, God, there's Mary Paterson coming now!'

Mabel Milligan went back to Meg Dod's deserted bake-shop. She felt sick with excitement, but it was an excitement of a very different kind from the Society Women's. Miss Edina Hamilton . . . Charlotte Square . . . Christ, she had found her, on this lucky, lucky day.

Then, after all the noise had died away, the dispersing crowd flooded into Meg Dod's brightly lit establishment. By the time Mabel's stint was over there wasn't a fresh pie, a misshaped bread roll, nor even a second-day scone, left in the place. She had sold out.

'You had a lucky escape from that one,' said Josh, gazing disapprovingly at the prostrate Miss Irene. 'Come on, let's get out of here!'

But before Josh smartly and with great presence of mind dragged his friend away to melt inconspicuously into the crowd, Gavin caught sight of Edina and her maid being whisked away in the Hamilton coach. Jesus . . . How much had she seen? Had Christopher North got his name? After two and a half years of what he couldn't deny was riotous living, unless he was forced to study, Gavin knew that now he had hit the very bottom of the barrel of disgrace.

All was undone, thanks to Josh and Cardew – his so-called friends – while he himself was almost the innocent party. He climbed into the two-foot-square window, and out of it the next morning, so managing to postpone the inevitable confrontation with Miss May and Miss Irene for the best part of twenty-four hours.

During the day he collected copies of all Edinburgh's newspapers and read about the incident of the night before, but the names of any men involved were not mentioned. Oh, the relief of it! Now the worst thing he had to worry about was whether or not Edina had caught sight of him at Mrs McClarty's, and he would know the answer to that as soon as he saw her next.

It was six o'clock the following evening before he went back to his lodgings to face the music. He found Miss May at one side of the table, Miss Irene at the other side and his uncle, Revd John Stafford, in between them, each sitting ramrod-stiff on the straight-backed chairs. When he entered the room all three faces turned to him accusingly, all thin, all bespectacled and all utterly contemptuous.

'Your engagement to my niece is off,' Miss May announced icily, and his heart leapt up in pure joy.

Good old Cardew! Good old Josh! He would be indebted to them for ever and ever. It was all he could do to keep the grin off his face, until he saw the horrible blue ring was still on Miss Irene's finger.

'Miss Irene has done me the honour of accepting my proposal of marriage,' John Stafford said. 'The wedding will take place as soon as it can be arranged.'

So she was getting a husband at last! Gavin didn't believe it mattered much to her who he was, as long as she got one. And as for his uncle, quite clearly after the exhibition of last night he was in need of a woman, and it wouldn't matter much to him either who she was, since he was already consorting with whores.

'I shall be requiring the room you occupy just now,' Miss May went on haughtily. 'I will retire. These two can have the rest of the house. It would have been my niece's when I died, anyway, but we won't wait for that. It will be my wedding present to the happy couple now.'

'And she doesn't mean only this house, but the rest of the tenement as well.' Miss Irene spoke her first words with tremendous triumph. 'I shall be a rich woman, as well as a minister's wife.'

'Even if she had been wrapped up in gold paper, allow me to be the first to congratulate you, Uncle John.'

After a short silence during which they seemed to be digesting this revelation, the smiles faded from their faces. 'You'd better pack up and go tomorrow,' Miss May, the first to recover, gasped.

'Better still,' Gavin could no longer help laughing, 'I'll go tonight.'

Nowadays Billy refused to try and sleep without a candle burning constantly by his bed, because if it was totally dark huge worms began to writhe and wriggle on the ceiling above him. Some night one of them would drop on him, he was sure of it, and then he would die or go mad. Then there were the red monster spiders crawling down the walls towards him, changing as they got nearer and nearer to the hideously grinning faces of his victims coming to get their revenge.

He awoke out of a troubled sleep to the smell of a low-burning candle. It reminded him of altar candles, incense, the Mass, the women shawled in black, and the click of beads. He should go to Confession.

It was not the only thing he should do. He should try and please Helen – and soon – if he was to keep her. Last night she had tried to have contact with him again and shouted at him about her 'marital rights'.

'I have needs, too, you know,' she had sobbed.

Oh, God, what if she took up with another man for her body's needs? She might even inform on him out of spite, not knowing that his right testicle was almost eaten away now. The pain, when it came, was excruciating; he could not have survived if it was like that all the time. The strange thing was that it didn't prevent him wanting a woman, but the last time he'd had Helen it was hell on earth.

There was no pain just now, though, and to make sure that it stayed away he drank some raw whisky. It helped. It chased away the dark thoughts. He drank some more, and then he woke Helen.

The scorch of the pain made him scream. Helen thought he was screaming in passion, and didn't take long, as if she had been starving. Afterwards he had another drink, made her light another candle from the bundle at the side of the bed, and gradually the pain eased and he fell asleep. In the morning, standing at the side of the bed, she woke him up.

'I'm covered with blood,' she shivered, 'and it's not my time. Where has it come from?' Helen was pulling down the blankets and looking at the rags on the straw. 'Jesus Christ, Billy? What's this? There's more blood, and black stuff! Has it come out of you?'

'You know about my sore. Maybe it burst last night.'

'You'll have to see one of the doctors.'

'So I will, the next time we're up at Surgeons' Square, honest to God I will, Helen.'

'No. Go today.'

Later that day he lied to her that he'd been. 'It's just a long rest it needs. He gave me some ointment. Sure, and it feels better already.'

'What did he say it was? Is it catching?'

'No, but it'll take a few months.'

'I don't care, Billy, so long as you're all right.'

That night he lay awake and stared up at the silver mesh of cobwebs on the ceiling, thinking about it. All along he had been convinced it was the French disease, caught from Maisie at the Canal. Now he remembered something Dr Corcoran had told him: that leprosy ate you away. But it couldn't be that, or else it would have attacked other parts of him. All the same he was worried sick, and one day when he got the chance he *would* ask a doctor.

Next morning dawned bright and clear, the pain had disappeared altogether and after a few morning drams with Hare, Billy felt on top of the world as he walked up the High Street on the look-out for the next subject.

You couldn't be wanting better ones, he told himself, when he saw coming towards him a plump old woman with the florid face of a drinker leading a young boy by the hand. He didn't even have to give her the patter. The woman stopped and spoke to him of her own accord.

'Would you be after excusing me, sir, but I'm a stranger here and it's all muddled I am.'

'Irish!' Billy said joyfully. 'So am I. How can I help you?'

'It's all the way from Glasgow we've been walking to join me friends, but now I can't find them.'

'Come along home with me and have a rest and a dram. I'll try and find them for you. Bring the boy – your grandson?'

'And deaf and dumb.'

Billy gave the old woman a dram and the boy an apple in Tanners' Close. 'O'Hara, that's the name of your friends? Oh well, that's easy, then. My landlord knows all the Irish in Edinburgh. I'll just go and have a word with him.'

In the stables he found Hare and told him his plan. 'We'll do in the woman first. I'll get Helen to feed the boy in our room while we're doing it. Then we'll attend to him later.'

Before long the old woman was very drunk. They boy

watched while Hare and Billy laid her gently on the bed, and Helen took him by the hand and pulled him gently off his stool.

'Oh, look at his eyes!' she said. 'Such beautiful huge green eyes!' Then she turned to the boy and spoke to him as if he could really hear. 'Your granny's asleep, dearie. She's tired. Come with me and we'll have some nice fish and tatties.'

The boy smiled back at her, and when they were gone Hare bolted the door.

Helen chattered away to the boy and played with him until she judged the time had come to take him back downstairs, but all the while his beautiful eyes had touched her heart.

'We'll need a herring barrel for both of them,' Billy told her. 'Hare's away for one now.'

'Och, Billy . . .' Helen hesitated.

Billy took the boy on his knees and bounced him gently. 'Ride a cock-horse to Banbury Cross,' he sang to him, as slowly his arms met around the boy's back. 'Ride a cock-horse – ' There was a sharp crack and the child's back broke.

The contents of the herring barrel brought sixteen guineas from Dr Knox, but neither food nor drink could console Helen. She cried in their room for hours on end, face down on the bed.

'It was his eyes,' she kept telling Billy.

But Billy thought differently. The murder of the boy had been the first one she'd witnessed, and that was why she was so bitterly upset.

'I've had enough,' Helen sobbed. 'I don't want to be living here.'

'Ach, it's only a holiday you're needing,' Billy soothed her, and her sobs subsided a little. 'Only I don't know where we could be going. What's more, I don't like leaving the business to Hare, but it's anything for my darling Nellie!'

Helen thought of Ann MacDougal, a cousin of her estranged husband's who lived near Falkirk. Ann had been the only person to understand why she'd eloped with Billy Burke, so long ago. 'Could we not go to visit Ann? Oh, please let's go! The Hares will think all the more of us when we come back. They can't do the business without you, Billy. You're the man.'

'What did I tell you?' Cardew crowed when Gavin turned up on his doorstep.

'It certainly worked. I can never thank you enough, nor Josh either. But now I need to ask one last favour, Cardew. Can you put me up for the night? Tomorrow I'll find new lodgings.'

'Of course I can, old bean. Hold on while I get Fanny to make a bed ready.' He was away rather a long time, but he came back smiling. 'It's all right. I gave her a hand to make it up.'

A few minutes later Fanny Love came in with a silver tray piled with sandwiches, and gave Gavin a watery smile. 'I'm going to bed,' she told Cardew.

'Is she all right?' Gavin asked anxiously.

Cardew dropped his veneer of sophistication suddenly. 'No, she is not,' he said, passing a worried hand over his brow. 'She's with child.'

'Good God! What do you mean? How can she be?'

'It's very easy,' Cardew said with a bitter smile.

'But . . . But . . .' Gavin stuttered, for what he was suspecting was too awful to be put into words.

'She's not my sister,' said Cardew, putting him out of his agony. 'We eloped from Kendal.'

'Then why haven't you married her?'

'For a very good reason. She's married already, and no doubt Harry Love will find us one day. Then I have no doubt whatever that he'll kill me,' Cardew told him in despair.

'Don't worry about what may never happen,' Gavin said briskly. 'First things first. What about the baby?'

'Yes, what about it, Gavin? Believe me, this has been the most trying time of my life. Of course, Fanny wants the baby. Of course, so do I, but where is the money to come from at this stage of my career? We both agree it's out of the question to allow it to be born, yet neither of us can take a step to have it aborted.'

'How far is she gone?'

'Seven or eight weeks.'

'Well, you know what Professor Hunter told us. If it must be done, the sooner the better.'

To Gavin's dismay Cardew burst into tears. 'I know,' he sobbed, 'but I could never bring myself to try it, not with my little Fanny.'

He dried his tears eventually and looked up into Gavin's face.

'Josh,' they both said together.

Next day Gavin skipped classes so that he could find new lodgings, but it was like looking for a needle in a haystack, for not only was it the middle of the academic year and rooms were scarce, but he had also become a lot more choosy. There was nothing available in the Royal Mile. Wild horses would not have dragged him down to the Grassmarket, and in the end he found himself walking past Surgeons' Square and further up the South Bridge.

He came to a square of houses set back with a garden in front of them. ST PATRICK'S SQUARE he read on the street notice, and it looked very quiet as he walked along the pavement. There was one with a little notice propped up inside the window, and when he went up to it he read VACANCY.

By now he knew better than to judge anyone by appearance, but he had to admit that the lady who answered the door looked very daunting. She was long and lean, with grey hair, and her face was long and lean as well, with an expression that reminded him of a very sad dog's.

'You're looking for a room?' she asked with a smile, and her face came to life.

'Yes, Mrs . . .'

'Miss. Miss Phyllis Plenderleith. Well, come away in and see the room. It was my youngest brother's until he graduated. Now I cannot get used to the house without some young life in it,' she told him as they walked down the long passage. She opened a door at the bottom. 'This is it.'

'It's very comfortable, Miss Plenderleith,' Gavin said. He was quite unprepared to be shown a room that might have been back in his own home in Gilmerton, civilised, with pictures and ornaments and a carpet on the floor. 'When can you take me? Before you answer that, I should warn you that I'm a third-year medical student, and my name is Gavin Mitchell.'

'From today?' She seemed very amused, and Gavin liked her more than ever. She had kind grey eyes. 'My brother was a medical student, before he became a doctor. Medical students are not *all* bad.'

'I'll go back to my classes and see you this evening,' he promised. 'About six?'

'That's when David used to come home. Don't worry, laddie. I'll look after you.'

A few days later he came out of the Royal Infirmary with Josh, who was carrying a bag. 'It's this afternoon,' Josh told him. 'We're going to 57, Queen Street. I've taken some instruments in this bag, and Cardew's waiting. Not that he'll be any use, of course, for this job. You'll have to be my helper, Gavin.'

'Yes, and that makes me an accessory at the same time, if anything goes wrong.'

'Nothing is going to go wrong,' Josh said with quiet confidence.

Cardew met them at the door, looking sick and pale. 'She's in here,' he said, leading them into a large bedroom off the hall.

Fanny Love lay back in the bed in a white shift while Josh examined her and asked her a few questions. 'Is this your first child, Mrs Fanny?'

'Yes,' she said and started to cry. Cardew left the room.

'Everything will be all right in a wee while,' Josh reassured her calmly. 'You've got plenty of time to have more babies, a lovely young lady like you, don't worry.' He turned aside to Gavin. 'Dilatation and curettage. You know the procedure as well as I do.'

It was three o'clock when he set to work, and the deft, confident way he set about it inspired Gavin to play his part to help him. They were almost finished at half past three when they heard someone at the front door, and Cardew's voice when he opened it.

'My God, Josh,' Gavin muttered, the sweat of guilt and terror breaking out of him, 'if I didn't know better I would say that was Professor Hunter I hear out there speaking to Cardew. *Christ*, what a fright I got.'

The door opened and a white-faced Cardew ushered in the Professor. Josh remained quite unperturbed. 'Everything all right?' the great man asked him.

'Ready for you to examine, sir,' said Josh.

'Good! Good! Yes,' the Professor was clearly delighted with their work, 'we'll make a fine accoucheur out of you yet, Mr McLean, in a hospital already famed for its accoucheurs. But your friends seem to be in shock. Anything wrong, Mr Mitchell?'

'No, sir.'

'You, Mr Sharpe?'

'No, sir.' Cardew was near to tears, torn between patting Fanny's hand and shaking the Professor's. 'It's the opposite from wrong, just to see you here. I must thank you, from the bottom of my heart.'

'Well, well, laddie – you didn't think I would give just anyone permission to take my instruments for an operation like this, did you? Mr McLean pleaded your case very eloquently; I wanted to see how he performed all alone; so he got my permission, provided it was under my overall supervision. It would have been quite illegal, otherwise. Your lady is well, and quite comfortable now.'

'Thank you, sir.' Cardew was all at sea. For the first time he had no idea what to do or say next, so he said what was for him second nature. 'May I offer you a small brandy?'

'You may offer me a large brandy,' the Professor said as they moved across the hall to the drawing-room, 'and tomorrow I shall expect to see the three of you in my rooms, when I will go over all the methods of contraception with you. It looks as though you need it. At the same time you may collect some rubbers.'

'The rubbers were the culprits, sir,' Cardew complained.

'Yes, there's plenty of work to be done in that area,' the Professor agreed. 'So concentrate on your chemistry this year, and see if you can do something about it with your fresh young brains. And now, gentlemen, I must leave you. Mr McLean is coming with me. My wife has taken quite a fancy to him, and she insists he must come to supper.'

14

'I'T'S A GRAND holiday you're after giving us, Ann,' Billy said in his soft, sincere Irish voice, pouring her out some whisky first thing in the morning.

It was funny, but a fortnight ago she wouldn't have dreamed of drinking whisky at all, except at a booze, and all her life it was with a good strong cup of tea she had started her days. But whisky certainly gave a lift to things, and it made Billy and Helen laugh when afterwards she mistook the salt for the sugar and poured it in her tea.

'Och,' Ann said, noticing that nowadays Billy had deep lines round his mouth and dark circles under his eyes, 'it's been a grand laugh having you! I haven't had so many people in this house, or so many boozes, ever. But tell me again about the theatres and the coffee-houses of Edinburgh before you go back – and the *King*! Do you ever see him when he's in the town?'

'Oh no.' Helen took another dram. 'We live quietly, Ann, in a friend's house. He takes in lodgers.'

Ann thought when Helen said it she looked sad again. My, what a change in the lassie! Only thirty-three, but she looked so much older, with her bonny blue eyes all sunk in and a sick pallor to her withered cheeks. She would never have recognised her for the girl who used to drive men wild – her husband's cousin John MacDougal, in particular.

She hadn't thought about Andrew MacDougal, her dead

husband, for years. Life had been steady with him, but never any fun, not like it must have been for Helen with Billy. What a spark he was! Wherever he went there was music.

He didn't dance so much now as he used to do, though. He was always having to sit down with this stitch in his side Helen had told her about. Ah, well, Ann concluded with a sigh, when they went back to Edinburgh later that day, it was back to the hens and the fruit bushes for her. The raspberries and the gooseberries would rot soon if she didn't get them made into jam.

The Burkes arrived back in Tanners' Close to find a strange woman going about the place, up and down the stairs a lot to the Brogans.

'Her name's Mrs Hostler,' Hare told them. 'John Brogan's engaged her for a few weeks until his wife has her baby. She's a widow.' His eyes met Billy's significantly.

Mrs Hostler was very glad of the job, and when she found out that Mrs Brogan liked a wee dram and a chat she was happier still. It gave her a fine rest between washing the clothes and scrubbing the stone floors, and when she found out that Mrs Brogan was scared of the birth she really came into her own. She herself had buried five little Hostlers long ago.

'My hips are too small,' Mrs Brogan said, 'and three times I've had the same dream. If the child is ever born it'll be born deformed.'

'Na, na,' Mrs Hostler reassured her. 'Anyway, I'll hold yer hand when the midwife comes.'

'What was your husband like?' Mrs Brogan asked.

'Och, a wee squinty man he was! But he took me off the streets.'

'Oh?' Mrs Brogan chuckled, leaning back on her pillows. 'Tell me about it.'

When it was time to go, Mrs Hostler was a bit unsteady on her feet, and the streets were running with rain. She took shelter in the passage, pulling her ragged shawl over her head, and a few minutes later a voice spoke behind her.

'Are you waiting for someone, alanna?'

'No, just waiting for the rain to go off.'

'It's not going to go off. You'll get your death standing there in the chill. Me wife'll give you a dram and a warm at the fire until it lets up.'

'Well . . .'

'Come away, dearie. This is our anniversary today. We're having a booze later on, and you'd be very welcome to stay. The more the merrier!'

The man with sandy hair smiled at her, and Mrs Hostler couldn't help smiling back, although she wondered why he was being so kind. She was old and fat now. He couldn't be wanting her for her body. In fact, she had nothing of value except the ninepence ha'penny Mrs Brogan had given her. It was still in her hand.

'We're having blood puddings,' the man told her, leading her back up the passage again and down some more steps into the pitch-black. Then they were in firelight, and a woman turned round with a pan in her hand. 'Helen,' he said, 'here's our first guest.'

Gavin had been in his new lodgings for a fortnight when Miss Plenderleith met him at the front door. 'Where are you going with that bundle, Mr Gavin? It looks to me like your washing.'

'It is, Miss Phyllis. I'm rushing to get it away with the Gilmerton carrier.'

'You'll do nothing of the sort! I never heard the like! I've been waiting for you to give me your dirty washing all this time.'

'I couldn't put you to that much bother, Miss Phyllis. Besides, my mother will create havoc if my bundle doesn't arrive home.'

'Bother? What bother? I washed all my brother's clothes. Washing for you won't be any different, and as for your mother I daresay she would rather have a letter from you than your dirty washing every fortnight. Have you written to her yet this term?'

'Well – '

'I thought not. Scribble a note now, and *then* rush to the Gilmerton carrier, laddie.'

177

Miss Plenderleith was the best landlady in the town, once you got used to her whistling the psalms under her breath all the time she wasn't talking. After only two weeks Gavin believed he would even miss the psalms now, and he would certainly miss Miss Phyllis when he left.

They had long chats together, during one of which she told him that she did all her housework in the mornings and in the afternoons went out to play cards with her friends. 'For money, of course,' she laughed, 'otherwise there would be no point in it. And I cheat, otherwise there would be no fun in it.'

'Rubbish! You wouldn't cheat anybody, Miss Phyllis.'

'Do you want to bet? Would you like a game now?'

He laughed. 'No,' he said as he went out the door. He was still smiling when he crossed the High Street to the North Bridge, and a voice hailed him. 'You look very happy today, Gavin!'

At first he didn't recognise the tall distinguished gentleman speaking to him. Then he realised that was because his eyes had been utterly dazzled the last time he'd been in Charlotte Square. But Edina's father was looking at him quite kindly, he saw to his relief. So perhaps she had never seen him at Mrs McClarty's after all. He began to hope. 'Mr Hamilton sir! I didn't notice you there.'

'Where are you off to? Classes?'

'Not today. I was just going for a walk. Then I thought I'd visit some of my friends.'

'That's good. You can walk home with me, then, and visit some of your new friends. Edina was just speaking about you the other day.'

Edina was speaking about him the other day! Gavin thought his heart would burst with happiness.

'So was my wife,' continued Mr Hamilton, taking the edge off it slightly. 'They've already started discussing the Christmas Ball in the Assembly Rooms, and making up a guest list. They were wondering if you would like to go, and of course Mr Cardew Sharpe.'

Walking along Princes Street now, Gavin couldn't make up his mind whether to feel deflated altogether, or merely jealous, but there was something about the way Mr Hamilton said

178

Cardew's name that left room for a little more hope. 'Are you busy yourself, sir?'

'Well,' he smiled, 'it is a well-known saying that men cannot live *without* women and find it almost impossible to live *with* them! I am surrounded by them. There is my wife and Edina, both of whom can twist me round their little fingers. However, it is Kathy, one of our maids, who is troubling me most just now. You see, she is engaged to be married to Constable Frank Clarke.'

'I see, sir.'

'Of course you don't,' Mr Hamilton sighed as they got to George Street, 'but I'll try to explain. You see, Frank Clarke has confided in me that people have been mysteriously disappearing from the Old Town, and he's convinced that they are being murdered. He doesn't want any of the ladies to be alarmed, but Kathy knows there's something he's not telling her, and she's weepy and sulking because she thinks it's another woman. I told you, it's not easy, living in a household of women!'

'Not under those circumstances, indeed. But I didn't know that people were disappearing from the Old Town.'

'Frank says five have – from his beat round the Grassmarket – three men and two women. The three men were lodging in a house in Tanners' Close, and the two unfortunate women were last seen up at that end of the Grassmarket, too. My great interest in it is the remarkable increase in the number of bodies currently being supplied to Dr Knox. They seem roughly equivalent to the disappearances.'

'Oh,' Gavin said, with a terrible prick of his conscience. 'Your interest, you were saying, sir?'

'If plenty of bodies became legally available to the anatomists, there would no longer be this trade in the Edinburgh underworld. Dr Knox does not seem to care where they come from!' Mr Hamilton paused for breath as they approached Charlotte Square and gave the absent Dr Knox an indignant glare. 'It is unclaimed bodies that should be allowed for anatomical dissection, or those gifted to medicine, as Mr Cardew Sharpe's old soldier gifted his.'

'Is that what Cardew told you? Oh, I beg your pardon, sir!'

'No need to beg my pardon, my boy. I have always been suspicious of what *that* young man said. I know his mother, you see,' he added darkly.

Cardew had never spoken much about his parents, it was true. Now that he came to think about it, Gavin realised he knew very little about his friend. 'His mother, sir?'

'Mistress Cornelia Sharpe. I cannot speak about that woman without spitting! Long ago she wheedled a small fortune out of Lady Alison. Then she made herself a scandal in Edinburgh, applying to every eligible bachelor in the town – every one who had money, of course,' Mr Hamilton added with scorn. 'She even applied to me! She almost came between me and the woman I loved, and still do. Then, fortunately for us all, she mistook the size of Sharpe's pockets, married him and went away to leave us in peace.'

'She thought Mr Sharpe had money?' Gavin hazarded.

'He could have had, but he is as extravagant as she is, drinking like a fish and living like a lord, no doubt on his wits – if not worse! I confess, my boy, I find it hard to trust their son, likeable though he is.'

'But anyway,' Gavin tried to lead him away from the unhappy subject, 'you think there should be a law about the bodies?'

'Along with other lawyers, Scottish and English, I am engaged in drafting the necessary legislation now for what we hope will be the Anatomy Bill.'

'That should stop the body-snatchers.'

'At least the people are being allowed to die naturally before the body-snatchers dig them up, Gavin. No, this is worse even than that. Constable Clarke is hot on the trail of these murderers, and a dangerous job it is. Goodness knows how many they may have killed by this time. It is bad enough not to be safe in the grave. Now it seems we are not safe in the streets either.'

Gavin followed Mr Hamilton into the drawing-room of Number 13 to join Lady Alison and Edina, prettier than ever today in high-waisted pale-green sarsenet. After tea by the fire she went across to the Broadwood to sing 'Caller Herring' in her high sweet voice.

'Come back soon again, my boy,' Mr Hamilton said when Gavin was leaving. 'We had such an interesting talk. Come into my study next time, and we can continue it.'

A few days later Gavin wondered if he might manage to speak to Edina alone, but considered it was too soon to visit Charlotte Square again. Instead he wandered up and down the pavement outside it. At least he was near where she lived.

'Look at him, Miss Edina!' said Kathy, peeping out of the window. 'Oh, it's a shame! He doesn't dare to ring the bell, and him such a beautiful young man!'

'He *is* nice, isn't he, Kathy?'

'A lot nicer than that Mr Cardew, I can tell you. Why don't we go out for a little walk? Then we could bump into him.'

'You're a proper schemer, Kathy Fraser. It was how you met in with Frank Clarke, as I recall. All right, we'll go and get our coats.'

'Miss Edina!' Gavin was saying a few minutes later. 'I didn't expect to see you.'

'Of course not. That was why you were pacing up and down outside the house.'

When he stole a look at her he saw that she was teasing him, and smiling at him enough to steal his heart away altogether.

Gavin laughed. 'All right!' he said. 'Yes, I was hoping to see you, but I didn't think I would be so lucky.'

'Well, Kathy and I are going for a walk to the gardens in Queen Street. Would you like to accompany us?'

As they walked along Kathy fell behind a few steps, far enough to be out of earshot, and Gavin smiled. 'Is she well trained or just naturally diplomatic, your Kathy?'

'Sympathetic. She knows what it's like to be in love, you see,' Edina replied, teasing him again, and he saw that he could say anything he liked to her, after all.

'Your father was speaking about her future husband the other day.'

'Frank Clarke. What else was he talking about? Not the Resurrectionists again?'

'I like your father, Miss Edina, and I agree with everything

181

he says. I just hope he doesn't find out that many of the medical students have been body-snatchers themselves in their day.'

'Ah!' Edina's eyes sparkled with mischief. 'Who did you go with? Tell me all about it!' she said, and at the end of the story she wiped the tears of laughter out of her glorious blue eyes. 'How like Cardew! He's a card, just like his name – and *so* good-looking, isn't he?'

'Very good-looking,' Gavin managed to grind out between his teeth, wondering all the while if she was noticing that he was turning green.

'But at the end of the day I'm lucky to be speaking to you at all. You might have been killed yourself.'

'All I know is that I'm lucky to be speaking to you, Miss Edina.'

'Then we're both lucky. So from now on you can call me Edina when we're alone, and I'll call you Gavin.'

He went back home to Miss Plenderleith's, warning himself not to take too much comfort from the hints she had dropped – 'when we're alone' – and wondering wistfully if that happy occasion would ever come again.

Whilst striding along the main thoroughfares of Surgery and Medicine, Gavin and his two friends now had to explore other avenues – Chemistry, for instance, where new elements such as oil of vitriol were being discovered every day, often in clouds of black smoke, in the laboratories, and they were introduced to a new instrument devised by James Currie to measure if a patient was too hot.

Then there was Botany and the Materia Medica which translated the elements and herbs into healing balms. They were required to roll pills, crush drugs with mortar and pestle, dispense ointments in oyster shells and write out prescriptions in Latin.

By the time the three of them struggled into Swanston's every day they were worn out, but, hard-pressed or not, Cardew was managing to look more and more resplendent as the days rolled on.

'That's *another* new suit!' Josh accused him.

'I know,' Cardew agreed wanly. 'She forces them on me. Miss Daphne Hogg wants to heap it all on me, anything money can buy.'

'She's not still here?' Gavin cried in horror.

'She is. At some point every day I have to take her on a sightseeing tour, and every day she pays me more and more to do it. How can I refuse?' He looked at them like some pathetic cornered animal.

'Say no.' Josh drained his glass and departed briskly as usual.

'She won't take no for an answer, Gavin,' Cardew continued despairingly, 'and now she's trying to find out where I live. Can you see Fanny's face if she arrived at Queen Street?'

'What are you going to do, then?'

'Perhaps if someone else took an interest in her?'

'Not me,' Gavin assured him firmly, 'so don't ask.'

'I meant . . . some other young lady, such as Edina Hamilton, perhaps? The fact is, Gavin, I intend to introduce Miss Hogg to the Hamiltons on Saturday afternoon. I'm absolutely desperate to get her off my back, somehow. I wish you'd come with me,' he added pathetically.

It was a cruel request, all things considered, Gavin thought, a cruel trick of fate, but any path that led to Edina was good enough for him. 'What time and where?' he asked.

'Four o'clock, in Charlotte Square.'

Cardew knew what he was about. Four o'clock, just as it was getting dark, and just in time for tea, Gavin brooded. There ten minutes early he watched the Leerie going around the Square with his torch, setting up his short ladder at the lamp-posts and lighting all the lamps, before extinguishing the torch in the link horn at the bottom of the last lamp-post.

Then Cardew approached, on his arm a grotesque little lady shaped like a pear waddling along beside him. On her head she was wearing what appeared to be Admiral Nelson's hat. It must be the London fashion, Gavin thought as he was being introduced, and they all three went up the steps to the front door and Cardew rang the bell.

'You cannot imagine how excited I am!' Miss Hogg squealed

183

loudly. 'Oh my! A *real* butler!' she exclaimed, tearing off her voluminous plaid cloak and the admiral's hat and throwing them at James to reveal diamonds glittering on every part of her anatomy – in a tiara which the high hat had covered, in an ostentatious necklace, in earrings, in bracelets and in rings on her podgy little fingers.

James, black affronted, showed them into the drawing-room and announced them in a voice of doom.

'Dearest Cardew has told me all about you,' gushed Miss Hogg as she burst upon the Hamilton family and rolled up to them where they sat at the fireside. 'Isn't he just a darling?'

Lady Alison took charge of the situation immediately. 'My dear Miss Hogg,' she said with an element of steel in her gentle voice, 'do come and sit down.'

'Daphne,' Miss Hogg trilled playfully.

'A very pretty name, I'm sure, Miss Daphne,' Lady Alison became almost heavy-handed, 'but in Edinburgh society we do not become too familiar on first acquaintance. You must excuse us if we seem a little old-fashioned compared with those in London. The pace is a little slower here, I understand. Now, may I introduce you to my husband, Mr Eden Hamilton . . . and to our daughter, Miss Edina Hamilton . . . ? Edina, dear, please ring for tea.'

It was superbly carried out, while Edina smiled obediently, Mr Hamilton squinted at the diamonds, Cardew coughed uncomfortably, Gavin grinned his approval at Lady Alison and a mystified expression settled on Miss Hogg's white pasty face.

'I hope you are enjoying your stay in Edinburgh, Miss Daphne?' Edina asked kindly, thereby unwittingly opening a floodgate.

'If only I could stay longer! So many places to see, and dearest Cardew,' she touched his arm possessively, 'has been showing me them all! Where should I have been without him? Oh, it was just so lucky I ever met him!' Her round little eyes became positively fervent.

'Yes, Cardew has told us that he met you when you were a tourist in Edinburgh last summer. You must really like our city, to have stayed so long. But you must leave us now?' Lady Alison tried to stop the flow.

'Oh, I've got to get back in the New Year, your ladyship. Is that how to address royalty in Scotland, Cardew? You forgot to tell me, you naughty boy!' Miss Hogg waggled a roguish fat finger and the diamonds flashed fire. Without waiting for an answer she carried on in her strident voice. 'I've got to get back to the business. I inherited it when my father died. Building houses. I'm worth millions,' she boasted, stuffing a dainty egg-and-cress sandwich into her mouth all at one go.

Mr Hamilton was looking increasingly depressed, and his wife was trying hard not to appear outraged, when Edina stepped into the breach once again. 'But you are short of friends, perhaps?' she said sympathetically, and Miss Hogg's round little eyes became suddenly watery. In a minute the tears had spilled over.

'You must allow us to rectify that for the remainder of your Scottish trip.' Lady Alison leaned forward and patted Miss Hogg's satin lap kindly.

'May I offer you a small glass of brandy?' Mr Hamilton asked anxiously.

'Certainly not, sir. Definitely not. I never drink. I do not approve of it in any shape or form!'

'No, she doesn't,' Cardew agreed with a sigh.

Lady Alison changed the subject abruptly. 'We are engaged in making up our list of guests to take with us to the Christmas Ball, Miss Daphne. It is always a grand affair, held in the Assembly Rooms. We haven't sent out our formal invitations yet, but we do hope that Cardew and Gavin will accept. Perhaps you might care to come, too?'

'Oooh,' Miss Hogg shrieked, quite restored. 'With Cardew? Oh, yes, *please!*'

On the night of the ball the Hamiltons' guests foregathered in the large hall of 13, Charlotte Square. The fire burned cheerfully, its flickerings reflected on the gleaming mosaic of the tiles under their feet, James, Liza and Kathy scurried about seeing to it that no glass remained empty for long, and excited anticipation grew by the minute.

The Hamiltons mingled with their guests, smiling and chatting. Lady Alison was wearing a grey-blue gown which exactly matched her eyes, and a small golden necklace of sapphires. Edina looked like a newly opened rose in pink, with ribbons in her hair. Miss Hogg, the first to arrive, wore diamonds, and Mr Hamilton looked every inch the distinguished lawyer he was in a black suit, his only sign of levity a white lace cravat fastened with a gold and sapphire pin.

Gavin, feeling happy in his new grey coat with striped pantaloons and a white ruffled shirt, wondered how Cardew, the last to arrive, would present himself.

He didn't have long to wait. When James ushered in a glorious figure attired in the scarlet and gold and ermine dress-uniform of a lieutenant of the Hussars, it caused a minor sensation. The ladies fluttered around him, the men looked daggers at him, and Gavin came to the conclusion that Cardew had been raiding his absent friend's wardrobe again.

'You've come alone?' he managed to mutter to him behind his hand.

'Had to, old chap. Couldn't let the two ladies in my life meet, now could I?'

Then there was the flurry of getting everyone into the string of coaches James had lined up in Charlotte Square, the jolting across to the Assembly Rooms in the Old Town's George Square in the rain and the wind, the depositing of cloaks and galoshes in the entrance hall and at last the arrival in the ballroom itself.

'Hm,' Mr Hamilton said. 'Every lord, lady, chieftain and laird in Scotland is here tonight.'

Certainly no tartan had been left out. Gentlemen who should have known better exposed their short fat, or thin and hairy, or bandy, legs under the colourful pleats, taking great pleasure every time they turned to speak to someone to twirl round, so causing a flutter among the ladies.

'Tell me, Gavin,' Edina whispered in his ear, 'do they really wear nothing under their kilts?'

He grinned at her. 'They're not supposed to, you wicked

186

woman,' he said as a terrible grinding noise began on the stage, a hideous skirling sound, a screaming, and the bagpipes were ready to play.

'Gentlemen,' the Master of Ceremonies begged, 'please take your partners for the eightsome reel.'

'May I have the pleasure, Edina?' Gavin asked.

'It will be all mine, sir,' she replied with a smile, and then they were making up the eights, bowing to each other in the rings and the dance began, fast and furious.

The eightsome they were in was composed of young men and women, all fit, and all out for fun. One by one the other rings disbanded and left them to the floor. Gavin let out a wild whoop. The other three men joined in as they whirled their ladies round and round, while everyone standing or sitting round clapped in time to the pipes. At last the piper ran out of breath himself, and the dance came to an end.

'Gavin,' Edina fanned her face on the way to their chairs, 'I found out something.'

'And I have a nasty feeling you're going to tell me.'

'Neither John nor James Finlayson are wearing anything under their kilts,' she reported, giggling.

'I don't know if I should continue to associate with such a perceptive young lady.'

'Don't,' Edina sat down breathlessly beside her mother, 'for at least five minutes.'

'Can I fetch you ladies something to drink in the meantime?'

'No, thank you, dear,' Lady Alison said.

'Some lemonade would be just the thing,' said Edina, smiling up at him, and Gavin's heart lurched as he went to find some. He felt ten feet tall.

The night wore on with dance after dance, then supper in the Supper room, and more dances as the gentlemen strove to do their duty. Gavin danced with Lady Alison, then invited Miss Hogg to take the floor with him and was pleasantly surprised to find that she bobbed about on her little feet as light as a feather. 'I haven't seen Cardew for at least ten minutes,' she said when the dance ended. 'Can you find him for me?'

Cursing under his breath Gavin went to look. He wasn't in the card-room. The same old men who had started the evening there had no intention of giving up their seats. He wasn't in the Supper room, nor even lurking in the Gentlemen's room. Eventually he tracked him down in a dark corridor.

'What's the idea, Cardew, for Christ's sake? Miss Hogg is looking for you.'

'Oh,' Cardew clutched his arm fearfully, 'that bloody woman's been chasing me all night! I daren't tell you what's happened now! I daren't come out of hiding.'

Gavin sighed. 'Let's hear it,' he said patiently.

'She wants to marry me! She's gone on and on and on about it! What do you say to a totally unsuitable woman who asks you to marry her? Oh, God, what am I to do now? Look! She's given me all this money!' Cardew held out his hand with – Gavin did a rapid calculation – at least five hundred pounds in it.

'Aren't you ashamed of yourself? You should never have taken all that money from her, tonight or any other night,' Gavin said severely. 'But you did, so what else was she to think? You've got yourself into a fine pickle this time, bloody fool that you are!'

'But what am I to do?' Cardew panted desperately.

'There's only one thing to do. She hates and abominates drink. You've got to get yourself drunk, my friend, and I don't mean just glowing, I mean filthy drunk. Wait here and I'll fetch you something.'

'Make it champagne, then.' Cardew held out some money. 'Nothing gets me drunker quicker than champagne.'

'Any particular year?' Gavin asked sarcastically.

'Just go . . . Please, old dear.'

It was true. Cardew became drunk alarmingly quickly, while Gavin watched over him. 'You're drunk enough now,' he said, watching this sad deterioration stage by stage. 'See if you can stand up.'

Cardew tried without success. Better still, he had started to sing in a jumbled mumble, with an odd shout now and then. To increase the effect, Gavin undid his jacket and pulled out his shirt. Then he dragged him back into the ballroom.

'Oh, my God!' Miss Hogg cried. 'What's the matter with him? Cardew, my love, speak to me!'

'I'm afraid he can't, Miss Daphne,' Gavin said sadly, as he allowed Cardew to slide to the floor, where he lay on his back smiling foolishly. 'He can't even stand up.'

'He's drunk!' Miss Hogg squealed when Cardew suddenly rolled over and emptied the contents of his stomach on the ballroom floor. 'He said he never drank.'

'Oh, dear! He told you that? No, Miss Daphne, I'm afraid he has the reputation of being the most drunken student in the whole of the medical faculty. He won't be able to see you for a couple of days, I shouldn't think. He won't be able to see anyone. In fact, he won't even be able to see. He's on one of his benders again.'

Miss Hogg's face became very serious, and looking at her thinning fair hair and the lines running down from her nose to her mouth, Gavin realised for the first time that she was much older than he had thought. 'I shall make arrangements tomorrow to go back to London. I think I've had a lucky escape,' she said, wobbling away.

Lady Alison shook her head at the sight of Cardew. Mr Hamilton arranged everything. 'He's one of our guests, Alison. We can't let him go home to his sister in that state. He'll have to come home with us.'

Back in Charlotte Square Gavin dumped his friend unceremoniously on the tiles in the hall. Somehow, between them, he and James managed to get him upstairs, where they stripped off his clothes and left him to it.

'Don't worry,' Edina said, her eyes shining, 'I'll look after him from now on. It'll be an adventure.'

On the way home to Miss Plenderleith's in the pouring rain Gavin couldn't help feeling a little bitter. There was Cardew turning up trumps again, comfortably installed in 13, Charlotte Square, with Edina, the most beautiful nurse in the world, to look after him. There was something wrong somewhere.

15

ANOTHER DRINK PUT Billy in mind of Dr Knox. 'How many have we done in now, counting this Mrs Hostler?'

'It might be eleven,' Hare said. 'I've lost count over the last two years.'

'What I can't understand is why that famous brain hasn't twigged yet that we're uncanny lucky at finding dead folk in the streets.'

'He's twigged, all right, but what he's likely told Mr Fergusson and Bain is, "I want fresh subjects. Ask no questions." He's not interested in us, only in what we bring him.'

'He's got no morals, then, our Dr Knox,' Billy said.

'What do you mean, morals? Let's get the tea-chest.'

It was as easy as ever. Two hours later Mrs Hostler fetched eight guineas, and when that ran out a few weeks later they became much more daring by inviting Mary Haldane and her daughter Peggy, ladies of the night, for a booze.

'Come on ahead.' Burke ushered them into the party and filled them full of drink, so full that they both fell down in front of the fire and never got up again.

But somehow the more money they made the faster it kept trickling through their fingers, and it wasn't long before Mr Rhymer was sending messages to Tanners' Close. 'I would like to see Mr Burke and Mr Hare at their convenience.'

'Can we still charge gin?' Helen asked. 'We have to have it. Look, I've got the shakes.'

'He might stand for another gallon, but that's all.'

'Oh God, Billy, you've got to think of something.'

'I have. I'm going to write a letter.'

'Who to?'

'Ann MacDougal.'

'You can't. She's my cousin.'

'Exactly. So she'll come, and gladly, for a bit of a holiday.'

'I'll have nothing to do with it, Billy. She's my own relative.'

'When did I ever ask you for help, darlin' Nellie? Here, have another gin. It's the only way out, believe me.'

Billy wrote his letter and Ann MacDougal replied. There wasn't much doing on the farm at this time of year, so she would come on the coach next Thursday, the one that got in before dark.

Ann didn't think much of the first part of her journey to the Big Town. They bowled along through farmlands very like her own, but the two other women on the coach were very friendly to make up for it. When the coach halted at the inn stop they shared a lunch of bread and cheese and a penny jug of ale with her. It was almost dusk before they caught a glimpse of tall houses and church spires, and Ann was thrilled to think that tomorrow she would see the Castle, where the King sometimes came for his Christmas holidays, so the Burkes had promised her.

Billy Burke met the coach and carried her basket because it was so heavy and the roads were icy. She'd packed it with tatties, fresh-churned butter, new eggs, fruit jellies and sausages as gifts, and as they walked Billy pointed out the sights on the way to Tanners' Close. Rounding the corner of the Grassmarket, Ann was struck by the heart-stopping sight of the Castle, sparkling with frost in the torchlight, hanging above them on its rock like a painting on a wall.

'Oh my,' Ann breathed. 'Is His Majesty inside?'

'Well, if he isn't tonight, he will be tomorrow. I'll take you up there to see him reviewing the troops, alanna, and the bands will be playing – oh, Ann, until you hear a pipe band you haven't lived!'

'I'll never sleep tonight.'

'Sure, you will, after a fine supper of rizzered haddocks and a few jars. A lot of people are coming in tonight to see you. We'll have another booze.'

So she did sleep, to her great surprise, and when Helen wakened her in the morning with a mug of tea she felt well, very happy and excited. Only she was a little worried that Helen didn't seem to be feeling the same. Her first words proved it.

'It's not a good morning, Ann. We've kept the shutters closed – it's so depressing looking out at the miserable weather.'

The shutters weren't really shutters. They were just boards propped up against the one window in the room, but they certainly kept the room dark, Ann thought, as well as trapping the stale smells of last night's drink and pipe smoke. 'Where's Billy, then?' she asked.

'Och, he's away finding out when the King's arriving. Just you lie still, Ann, and take a rest.' Helen fetched her a bannock spread thick with her own butter. 'There's plenty of time.'

'I'm too excited to lie in my bed for long. I should be getting up and putting on my new pink dress for the King.'

'Och, no, it'll just get crushed. Wait till the weather clears. I'll fetch you a dram.'

Ann was sure she was seeing a chink of sunlight through the shutters, but the dram made her forget it. After another dram she felt wonderful, just lying there and watching Nellie washing last night's glasses. Then, there was another ray. It glinted on a little cracked mirror hanging on the wall.

'I think the sun's coming out now, Helen.'

'No, no, it's only someone burning rubbish.'

They had another little drink, and then Billy came in. He took a big gulp out of the bottle and told them what he'd found out. 'The King's not coming until this evening,' he said, 'so we've plenty of time.'

Mr Hare came in next, and they all had another drink. Ann's head began to spin and she slid down in the bed, only just aware that Helen was leaving the room to go for provisions, she said. Ann thought she heard the door being bolted behind her.

Then a big heavy cat pounced on her, and she couldn't breathe any more.

Charlotte Square began to ice up that Saturday, and James poured brown salt on the steps at intervals all through the day.

'It will be dark early, Edina,' her mother said. 'In fact, it looks like snow, and if it lies we'll never have the new curtains ready for your bedroom by spring. I think we should go this afternoon and choose the material.' They came out upon the top step of Number 13 and the sky was more ominous than ever. 'We shall have to walk to the shop, dear,' Lady Alison said. 'It's much too dangerous for the horses, sliding and skidding along Princes Street, and now here comes the first flake of snow! Let's hurry. We must try to get back before four o'clock. Gavin Mitchell said he would come for tea.'

With that, she put out one foot to descend and, the next minute, a horrified Edina saw her mother hitting the pavement below, landing in a crumpled heap with a sickening thud, and great fat snowflakes began heaping up on top of her. She opened the door again and screamed for James, and somehow they carried Lady Alison inside and up to her bedroom. She left Liza and Kathy undressing her and cleaning the wound as best they could and hurried downstairs again.

'What are we to do, James?' Edina wept. 'Papa will be at his chambers. We could never reach him, and I'm sure she's broken her leg.'

'It's the doctor we're needing here.' James shrugged himself into his overcoat. 'Now just you go and sit with your mama, Miss Edina, and I'll be off to fetch him.'

She felt far from happy to see his slight figure clinging to the railings as he went down the steps before he disappeared into the swirling snow. James was getting old now, she worried. Then she took it in turns with Kathy to watch at the window for him coming back with the doctor. They waited for what seemed an eternity before Kathy shouted to come and look at three figures battling along the pavement.

'Frank Clarke is one of them,' she said, 'and I'm sure Mr Gavin is the other holding up poor old James between them.'

'I didn't get very far,' James gasped. 'Mr Gavin found me in George Street on his way here, and very fortunately for me Constable Clarke was returning home after seeing Kathy here, and turned about. I never got to the doctor's.'

'You'd be very lucky to get a doctor to come out in this, anyway,' Gavin said. 'Help him to bed, Frank. He's chilled and exhausted. Ask Kathy to fetch him a hot brick and a hot drink, and I'll look at him later. Now, Miss Edina, where is your mother?'

Weeping, Edina showed him upstairs, more upset than ever. Her dearest Mama with a broken leg, Papa miles away in the Old Town and now here was a totally different Gavin from the one she was used to, brisk and matter-of-fact and apparently quite unemotional. With a great effort she wiped away her tears before she opened the door and they went inside Lady Alison's bedroom.

As soon as he saw her Gavin became very depressed although he didn't show it. He had seen too many cases with similar injuries find their way into the hospital mortuary to expect anything but the worst. 'Is there a medicine chest in the house?' he asked.

'Over here.' Edina pointed to a handsome piece of mahogany, a small cupboard sitting on top of a side-table, and when Gavin opened it he found inside rows of little bottles, one of them labelled *Laudanum*. He took a large measure from it and smiled at Lady Alison, whose face was crinkled with pain. 'My father's favourite remedy,' he told her, and watched over her until she fell asleep. 'Now, Edina, I must speak to Frank Clarke, if he's still in the house.'

'Yes. Go. I'll watch her.'

'Where's the nearest potter's mill, Frank?' he asked him.

'Burnett's Mill.'

'Could you get there?'

'I'll do my best, sir.'

195

'I need clay, about a bucketful, and fast.'

Fast Frank Clarke certainly was. He disappeared out of the door into the snowstorm immediately and returned in less than an hour with the clay. In the meantime, Gavin gently cleaned Lady Alison's wound, realigned her bones while she was still in a haze of opium, and then sent Kathy to find a board on which to mix the clay while Edina watched in horror.

'Thank God! That's Papa's voice I hear downstairs!' She sprang up and went to meet him.

Gavin carried on with his preparations, hearing the stamping off of snow on the tiles in the hall, a short alarmed conversation with Edina and Kathy, who was removing galoshes and sodden overcoats, and then Mr Hamilton was in the bedroom, with another man behind him, and Frank Clarke.

Never in his life was Gavin so relieved to see his father as at that moment. Greetings and explanations died on their lips when Mr Hamilton took one look at his wife's face and another at the clay at Gavin's feet.

'What's that?' he barked, pointing to it.

'I am going to encase and splint her fracture in this, sir,' Gavin told him. 'It will help the bone to heal in place.'

'You will not touch my wife's leg with that dirt,' Mr Hamilton said, almost weeping.

'Now, then, Eden,' Dr Mitchell explained soothingly, 'it is a technique I learned at Waterloo for broken legs, and taught to Gavin. I treated many such wounds on the battle-field.'

'She is not a soldier, Iain!'

'Of course she is not. But I am a doctor, and my son will qualify in a few months. For certain, no other medical man will get here tonight. Now, what are you going to do? There is no time to waste.'

Mr Hamilton took another agonised look at his wife's face and Edina rushed to his side. 'We must trust them, Papa,' she said gently. 'We have no choice.'

Mr Hamilton gave in. 'Do what you must,' he said, staggering a little as he walked across the room.

'Go and keep an eye on him, Frank,' Gavin said.

'Now, at last, to work.' Dr Mitchell sighed. 'I'll mix that clay with water.'

'I'll fetch the water.' Edina fled.

Between them Gavin and his father moulded the clay around Lady Alison's leg from her toes to her knee while Edina watched. 'What will become of her?' she asked when they were finished.

'We can't promise, my dear,' Dr Mitchell said, 'but if anything will save her, this will. Now we'll leave her to sleep. Your father has arranged for me to stay the night here, for it is out of the question to get back to Gilmerton. I was with him in his chambers when the storm laid on. Miss Edina, you must go to bed.'

'I'll do nothing of the sort,' she replied with spirit. 'I'll take it in turns with Liza here to sit with her all night.'

'Well, well,' Dr Mitchell said mildly, 'but it's going to be a long forty-eight hours, you know, before we can tell which way it's going. Come and help me find my room, Gavin.'

'The green room, third on your left, sir,' Liza said.

'Where are you sleeping?' Dr Mitchell looked at Gavin's white face.

'Nowhere. How could I sleep?'

'You know better than that, son. Go and bed down some-where. Take a glass of whisky and then take two more. You *must* sleep tonight. You know as well as I do there might be a crisis tomorrow.'

The next day the sun streaming through the windows made the snow outside look almost blue, so Gavin knew the frost was holding it. He splashed himself in an ornate basin and rushed to Lady Alison's room, to find his father already in attendance.

'All's well,' he said. 'Her pulse is regular and unhurried and her forehead is cool. A little fresh air in here would do no harm.'

Mr Hamilton came in fearfully, surprised at the general atmosphere of cheerfulness that the two doctors were radiating, and only raised his eyebrows a little at the open curtains and the open windows. 'Come and have some breakfast,' he invited

197

everybody, and afterwards Edina dragged Gavin out for her favourite walk.

'Is it always to Queen Street Gardens, Edina?' he asked jealously.

'It's the nearest thing to the country round here, and that is all I long for, to be in the country for ever! I had such a happy time in Almondbank where I first saw you, but neither Mama nor Papa can understand how much I long to leave the hustle and bustle of the town.'

'I can understand it.' He put his arm round her and gave her a hug, and the hug turned into their first kiss. He felt dizzy with happiness.

'You're a great comfort,' she said, and smiled up at him. He didn't believe her when he saw her eyes straying to Number 57. The green monster took over again. 'Oh Gavin,' she sighed, her eyes still on Cardew's residence, 'do you think she'll be all right?'

'Of course she will,' he reassured her on the way back, and that evening Lady Alison continued so well and the snow was disappearing so rapidly in the sudden thaw that Dr Mitchell was making his arrangements to go home the following morning.

But the next morning it was a different story. Lady Alison's pulse was racing, she was flushed, and she didn't want to talk to anyone.

'She's fevered,' Mr Hamilton moaned. 'She must be bled.'

'With respect, sir, hasn't she lost enough?' Gavin asked.

'I certainly wouldn't recommend it,' his father agreed.

'She must be cooled down with cold compresses,' Gavin insisted.

'You are ignoring the cause of her fever, my boy,' cried Mr Hamilton, distraught. 'Her leg.'

'That may have been the original cause, certainly, but not now. The skin above the clay is neither swollen nor angry.'

'Maybe so, maybe so.' Mr Hamilton stumbled out of the room, unable to bear any more of his wife's ramblings.

'Oh God, Father!' Gavin sank his head in his hands.

'You must be strong, son. You know if that leg swells, she is lost. But you can only treat the symptoms as you find them.'

198

'I know that, too,' Gavin said numbly.

'Well, I have enough confidence in you to leave you with it. Your mother will be out of her mind with worry by this time, and my patients cannot be left any longer.'

The next twenty-four hours passed in a black pall for Gavin, alone and in charge of it all, before Lady Alison's fever broke, her leg didn't swell, and her ravings ceased.

'Oh, Gavin!' Edina wept on his shoulder, while her father could hardly contain himself. 'How can I ever repay you, my boy?' he asked.

'Allow Edina to come to Gilmerton for a few days at Easter, sir. My mother would love to have her as our guest.'

'Of course,' Mr Hamilton agreed at once. 'You have our blessing, for I'm sure I am speaking for my wife as well.'

The midwife was there, and his wife was in labour when Brogan came downstairs to sit with Burke and Hare. 'What happened to Ann MacDougal?' he asked, his pale eyes fixed on them, staring, unflickering.

'She wanted to go home the next day,' Billy invented swiftly. 'She didn't like it here.'

'Sometimes I see the two of you carrying a heavy tea-chest after dark,' Brogan went on. 'Another thing, Mrs Hostler never came back to help my wife. She just disappeared too, like Ann MacDougal.'

'Well, you know what these old women are. She's lying drunk somewhere, more than likely.' Jesus God. What was the matter with the man, and him just sitting there, staring at them? Billy was rattled, and desperate for a drink.

'Your wife'll be grand in an hour or two,' Hare said calmly, 'and when she's up and about again we'll have a fine booze for your wee son.'

'Yes, it's certain to be a boy,' Billy agreed, buttering him up.

'I've been thinking,' Brogan said, 'that when she's up, we'll be moving.'

'Moving?' Hare looked stunned. 'Out of this house?'

There was only a nod from Brogan, and neither Billy nor

199

Hare dared to ask why. When he left, Billy gulped down neat gin. 'God,' he said, 'that Brogan has an awful way of saying nothing and thinking deep. He put the fear of death into me, just staring and staring like that!'

'Och, the frights are on you, so they are. Drink up, man.'

'But it's strange he's moving, with no good reason. Is he suspicious? He wanted to know about Ann MacDougal, but he couldn't have known about Mrs Hostler. Yet he seemed suspicious about her, too.'

'Let the bugger move, him and that lush of a wife of his, and now a screaming brat.'

'So long as he doesn't wag his tongue to someone like this Constable Clarke, forever poking around here,' Billy said, his face gaunt with pain.

Christ! It was sore, today . . .

But the Brogans were still there for the booze to wet their baby's head, and Mrs Brogan was back to her usual self, greedy for whisky and food, as well as boasting about her new son, and Billy, not daring to dance for the threat of pain in his ball, sat down beside her. 'What's wrong with John Brogan that he's so quiet lately?' he asked her.

'I don't know, but he keeps waking up in the middle of the night at the drop of a hat or the squeal of a cat. Now he's saying we've got to move – and me just up out of my child-bed.'

It was for fear of the police, Billy was sure of it. 'Where to?' he asked.

'He's found a place at – ' she paused. 'Och, I forget.'

Brogan must have warned her well not to tell anyone where they were going. Billy's worst fears were confirmed. He got up and moved about to try and ease the pain, drinking as he went to achieve oblivion. In the end he almost achieved it, falling down into a corner. He wakened at dawn to see a litter of empty bottles, spilled food and vomit on the straw before the dead fire.

Oh, God! He needed air! Shivering, he went out to the entrance of Tanners' Close.

'A good morning to you,' said a cheery voice.

Jesus Christ! *The policeman*! 'And the top of the morning to you, sorr.'

200

'Got a bad head this morning, have you?'

'Ay.'

'You're lucky – I've not had an ale since the day before yesterday,' said Constable Frank Clarke and passed on his way.

The day had started dark, under the shadow of the Law as you might say, Billy thought. It continued under a sky like granite, and he and Hare were on the prowl for subjects when they stopped outside Meg Dod's bake-shop, drawn by the smell of her penny pies.

'It's a new idea I've got,' Billy said. 'With a poke of those pies in our hands, and us offering one, a subject would trust us straight off.'

'I always said you were clever, and if we don't find a subject we can eat them ourselves,' Hare said when he came out with the paper bag of pies, the grease marking it already. But the smell was glorious, and they began the long wearisome task of searching the wynds and closes off the Royal Mile for drunken or starving people. 'Sure, there must have been a clean sweep to the Watch House or the Lock-up House last night,' he remarked an hour later, when all they could find was a dead cat in White Horse Close.

'Who's that woman serving in May Dod's?' Hare asked.

'Mabel Milligan they call her.'

'Would you be knowing anything about her, Billy?'

'Not much. Helen says she's a skinflint. She lives alone.'

'Hm,' Hare said thoughtfully. 'Well, if she's a skinflint she must have money. It stands to reason.'

Billy said nothing. Hare was in a murdering mood today, all right. They wandered about for another hour before they decided to go into Rhymer's and stand at his back counter for a jar.

'Maybe someone likely will come in,' Billy said as they ploughed through the sawdust on the floor, smelling the coffee beans and the wheels of cheeses as they passed through the grocery part on into the bar.

Four men stood drinking there under the smoking lamps – the organ-grinder, a street singer, a butcher still in his bloody

201

apron and Daft Jamie – all young and strong and healthy. None of them were any use, thought Billy, sighing.

They went and sat down at one of the tables, and the familiar murderous look came over Hare's face as he stared at Daft Jamie. 'He might be a likely one,' he said.

'You're off your head. For one thing he's far too strong. Look at him, for Christ's sake! Shoulders on him like an ox, and him only eighteen or so, in the prime of his life!'

'He's daft, and he's drinking.'

'It must be the first drink ever to pass his lips, then. Jamie doesn't drink, as anyone in the town will tell you. They all know him, even the rich, and they all love him. If *he* went missing they would raise the same hue and cry they'd raise to find the King.'

'Hm,' said Hare, still staring at Jamie.

'The medical students know him as well, and even Knox himself. They'd offer rewards for his murderer in every newspaper. Going up to Surgeons' Square with Daft Jamie's body would be as good as signing your own death warrant. No, no!' Billy said indignantly, 'you can count me out of that one.'

'Oh, fuck it,' Hare said. 'Forget it. It was only a thought.'

'Stop thinking then.'

'These pies, Billy – shall we be getting a wee tea-chest for them now? This poke's falling to bits.'

Billy choked over his whisky, laughing. 'Ach, you're as daft as a brush, so you are!'

Arm in arm, chuckling and singing, they wended their way home to Tanners' Close, and it wasn't until the following morning that Hare spoke his mind to his wife Maggie. 'It's Daft Jamie I have in mind.'

'Are you daft yourself?' She shot up in the bed.

'You could help me. A lovely woman like you could lead a lad like Jamie here like a lamb to the slaughter.'

'What does Billy say?'

'I'm away to see,' he said, taking a fresh bottle of whisky with him. 'You were too far gone last night to listen to the plan,' he whispered to him as they sat on the straw mat in front of the Burkes' fire. Helen was still asleep in the bed.

'You never heard the bit about the laudanum. Between that and whisky, we'd soon overcome him.'

'I'm still worried about the medical students, and Knox.'

'Knox isn't caring about justice, as you very well know. All he cares about is fresh subjects. When were we ever asked one single question?'

'I'll be thinking.'

'You've only got until tomorrow to think. That's when we'll do it. This is our last bottle of whisky.'

Billy shuddered. 'All right, then.'

Daft Jamie still didn't know why his mother had thrashed him with his father's big leather belt when he was only twelve. He'd only been out playing with the other boys, he hadn't run away because his father had just died, when she went out with a search party to look for him.

When he got home and found the door locked he broke it down, he was so hungry. Somehow the cupboard with all the plates in it, and the oats and the butter and tatties, just came tumbling down in his desperation for food. So when his mother got back at last and found him sitting in amongst the smashed teapot and bits of bacon, she'd belted him until he'd screamed. He didn't mind about the pain, but his mother didn't love him any more. It broke his heart, and made him run away, after all.

Although he had a club foot he hated wearing shoes. He ran messages or did odd jobs barefoot. A lot of people seemed to be sorry for him, and one day when he had earned a few shillings he went down to the Jew's shop and bought a brass snuff-box and a spoon. He wouldn't lend them even to his best friend, Bobby Awl, who some said was as daft as himself. Jamie earned the snuff for his box by telling riddles in the taverns, but he never drank the whisky or the ale. It made him feel too dizzy.

This morning he made his way down to the Grassmarket because he was hungry again, and the customers in Rhymer's often bought him a pie in return for his riddles. He had just reached the shop when a woman came up to him and smiled.

'Why, it's Jamie!' she said. 'Don't you remember me?'

'Ay,' he said, for he had seen her often. Perhaps it was his mother, but he was doubtful, because this woman was smiling. 'Are you my mother?'

'No, laddie. But your mother's in my house in Tanners' Close, waiting to see you, and she's got drams to celebrate seeing you again, and plenty of snuff.'

Later, it was the laudanum in Jamie's dram that did it.

'He's asleep,' Hare whispered, and gripped Jamie's nose and mouth, but the boy was awake in a flash, threw Hare to the floor and shot out a great fist. Hare ducked, Billy kicked Jamie where it hurt the most and so they got the better of him.

While Hare was gripping the nose and mouth again, Jamie bit his hands until the blood ran down his wrists, but still Hare held on although he was screaming like a woman. Billy pressed down on the boy with all his might, but even after he was dead the body still moved.

'Jesus,' Billy panted. 'Jesus Christ . . . That was the worst one yet.'

Hare couldn't speak. He just held up his bloody hands, and it was late that night before they got up enough strength to carry Jamie in the tea-chest to Surgeons' Square. Mr Fergusson gave them ten guineas without even opening the chest.

'What did I tell you?' Hare asked.

Next morning, with the help of Bain, his assistant, Fergusson unpacked the body and the medical students gathered round. 'It's Daft Jamie, sir,' he said as Dr Knox joined them.

'He must have met with an accident,' one of the students said. 'He was as healthy as a horse two days ago in the Grassmarket. I saw him. He asked me a riddle.'

'Rubbish,' Dr Knox said. 'That's not Daft Jamie! Mr Bain, help Mr Fergusson to take him into my private dissecting room.'

'Yes, sir.'

'Now, both of you are sworn to secrecy here,' Dr Knox reminded them, 'and, of course, this *is* the corpse of Daft Jamie. I don't know how he landed here. I don't want to know. But everyone will recognise his face, and everyone has seen his club foot. Therefore, gentlemen, I would be obliged if you would remove the head and the feet before presenting the subject to the students for dissection.'

'Yes, sir.'

'And make sure you dispose of them properly.'

'Yes, sir.'

16

WHEN THE TIME was up, Gavin went to remove the clay from Lady Alison's leg.

'Oh, thank goodness, Gavin,' she said. 'It's been so itchy.'

'Have you had any pain any time your toes touched the ground?'

'No, dear. I'm sure it is better now.'

'Well, then, would you like to see your leg again?' Gavin smiled, but his stomach was churning for fear his handiwork had not been a success, and he could see that Mr Hamilton and Edina were holding their breath, too.

'Oh,' Lady Alison exclaimed as she lifted it up, after he had gently removed the clay, and compared it with the other. 'Look! It's perfect, and the wound has healed!'

'Yes,' Gavin said. 'Now, the next thing is not to put all your weight on it for a while yet. Let's make sure the bone is knitted together properly, first. You must walk with a stick to help you for a week or two.'

'I'll do anything you ask, Gavin.'

'Would you even allow me to take Edina home with me to Gilmerton?'

'I'd trust you with anything now. Even my daughter.'

'And so would I, my boy,' Mr Hamilton agreed.

'Then can you be ready to go on Saturday, Edina?'

'I'll do anything you ask,' she echoed her mother with a smile, and Gavin thought, If only she meant it . . .

The daffodils were nodding their heads and the woodlands of Gilmerton were carpeted with primroses when Gavin and Edina went walking in the real countryside.

'This is what I meant, Gavin. I love it here. I wish I could live here all the time,' Edina said, and then seemed to change tack. 'I suppose after you qualify, you'll go on to specialise in something? Which branch of medicine are you most interested in?'

'You mean, do I want to become someone like Dr Knox or the professors? I can't think of anything I'd hate more than that, Edina.'

'Oh . . . I thought you would like to stay in Edinburgh. I thought you liked it there.'

'I'm happy enough in the lodgings I have now, yes. My landlady is another mother to me.' He went on to tell her stories about Miss Plenderleith until they reached the little humped-back bridge. She was laughing at something he'd told her, and looking up into his face. 'It could be slippery here with all this moss, Edina. Give me your hand.'

Neither of them quite knew how it happened, but next she was in his arms and he kissed her tenderly, and once over the bridge and all the way home he kissed her again at intervals of about three minutes.

'I love you,' he told her. 'I have from the very first moment I saw you, and *that* was here in the country. There's something about it, isn't there? And if you were trying to fish out the answer – will I go on, or will I take a practice – that depends.'

'On what?'

'On whether you play your cards right, Edina Hamilton.'

They were both radiant when they got back to Dr Mitchell's house, and Mrs Mitchell did her best to keep the younger children from bothering them.

'No, leave them,' Edina said with a laugh. 'They can teach me some of their games. I never had any sisters or brothers of my own, you know.'

One evening Gavin was sitting beside his mother and Edina was entertaining the Mitchell family playing the piano and singing.

'Oh, Gavin, look at her! Listen to her!' Mrs Mitchell exclaimed.

'I am.'

'Such a lovely girl. I've been over her, metaphorically speaking, with a fine tooth-comb – '

'I'm sure you have, Mother,' he said wryly.

' – and I can assure you there isn't one unpleasant bone in her body. She was made out of music.'

He felt struck to the heart by her words. There had always been a special bond between them, and he had always believed it was because he was her firstborn. Now that bond pulled tighter than ever before, for she had put into a few words everything he'd tried to express to himself about Edina. 'Made out of music, Mother? Yes, that's it, exactly.'

'So . . . ? Gavin . . . ?'

'I am not at that stage yet, Mother. I love her with all my heart, but what can I offer her? I have to face the finals first.'

'I don't think I would wait so long, if I were you.' His mother patted his hand. 'I can tell by the way she looks at you. Opportunity knocks but once, so don't lose her, son, or you'll lose the light of your life.'

The very morning they were due to go back to Edinburgh the postman came with an invitation for the Mitchell family.

'What do you think?' Mrs Mitchell asked them. 'It's to the marriage of Revd John Stafford and someone called Miss Irene May, in Edinburgh. Do you know her, Gavin?'

'I've seen her,' he admitted, 'and with Uncle John, too. I believe they met through the Society for Fallen Women.'

'Oh, dear,' Mrs Mitchell said. 'I suppose we'll have to go, Iain?'

'Is there no way to get out of it?'

'Not that I can see.'

'Well, you and Father can go, and my brothers and sisters,' Gavin said. 'Give them my regrets, but I'm going back to the last stage of it all now, and the finals in June.'

'And you'll be studying every minute, I suppose?' His father winked at Edina.

'It's no joke. If I don't get through, I can't get a practice, and if I don't have a practice, I can't have a wife.'

'Ah . . .' said the Mitchells, and Edina blushed becomingly right down to her toes.

Now that they were senior medical students, they had plunged into studies of Mental Disease, Diatetics, Medical Jurisprudence and everything else a student should know before daring to face the finals. New students asked their advice about where the best taverns in the town were to be found, about the professors and did they know anyone with second-hand books?

Cardew was the only one of them still frequenting the anatomy rooms by the back door with his contributions from the graveyards, for which he received the usual ten guineas to keep him and Fanny in the lifestyle to which they had become accustomed, but his real talent was for being caught, and this was where the big scandal started.

Gavin had just been to a lecture in diatetics, at which Dr Archie Green had told the class all he knew about the art of planning a diet. In his own case it was all home-grown and manured by his horses, due to his deep distrust of modern farming practices, in a cycle of absolute purity. The horses manured the ground, half of what it produced went back into the horses, and so round and round it went.

He always took a suitcase with him when invited to friends' houses for a meal, sat on the doorstep with his own supper laid out in the lid, and told anyone who happened to be passing that the only things missing, which he intended to add to all this, were eggs. He would get hens next, and, providing they scratched around the barley grown in pure dung, that would be following the Lord's command when he told the people of Israel to go forth and enter a land flowing with milk and honey.

Gavin found the air in Brown's Square positively perfumed after all that, and was just breathing in great gulps of it when he spied his friend on the other side of the road, his hair blowing wild and his eyes rolling in his head like those of a terrified horse. He galloped across the road and grasped Gavin by the arm.

'My God,' he said, 'come with me and get a brandy in the nearest hostelry! I cannot go another step. All I want to do is get drunk. I'm in the worst hole of my life.'

'What's happened to you, Cardew?'

'Come here and I'll tell you,' he said, dragging Gavin into a filthy tavern.

'Not here, surely!'

'Yes! Yes! In here, old boy!'

His story unfolded between large mouthfuls of brandy interspersed with gulps of brown ale, and it concerned Mrs Fanny. Gavin and Josh had known for months that only one of the four bedrooms in Cardew's ménage was in use. They also knew how Cardew financed the house in Queen Street. Nevertheless the next bit of information that he delivered now to Gavin came as a bolt from the blue.

'Imagine my horror when a wolf came to the door last night, old thing!'

'A wolf?'

'In sheep's clothing. Rags and tatters. But a wolf, none the less. I'm talking about Fanny's husband, Harry Love. He's found us after all this time. And you'll never guess how.'

'Go on, then – how?'

'Only last week, in a drinking-hole in Carlisle of all places, he overheard a conversation. You'll never guess who between,' Cardew groaned.

'Who?'

'The two card sharps who came here, Jack Foster and Richard Cunningham. They spoke about Fanny, and they mentioned my name.'

'But not your address, surely?'

'No?' Cardew's smile was ghastly. 'Do you want to bet? He had a gun, you see.'

On the third of May Mr Hamilton took up the *Scotsman* with an exclamation of dismay. That was not unusual, but his expression of horror as he read the front page was enough to alert his wife.

'What is it, Eden?'

'How long is it since we had the vaccination?'

'It must be twenty years,' she said, after consideration. 'Why?'

'There has been a case of smallpox found in Edinburgh. Everyone who has not had the vaccination within the last five years must go to the Vaccine Institute, where it will be done free of charge. It is compulsory.'

'Oh dear,' said Lady Alison, 'you have never had it done at all, Edina. You will certainly have to go. Do you understand about vaccination?'

'Cowpox is introduced into people, isn't it, for immunity? I know that Jenner discovered it.'

'Another Englishman who got his Scottish medical degree by post!' Mr Hamilton snorted, snapping back the newspaper. 'However, there is not the time to discuss that, and no time to be lost. This entire household will go to the Institute either today or tomorrow. Make the arrangements, Alison, my dear.'

In the afternoon Liza, Kathy and the rest of the staff were bundled off to the Institute willy-nilly.

'The rest of us will go tomorrow morning,' Lady Alison said. 'I know your father when he is in this determined mood. It is easier to give in gracefully. So let us hope that the weather is better than this tomorrow. It is so cold, what with the haar from the sea lying over Edinburgh all week.'

'It's very chilly, for May,' Edina agreed with her, looking out over the town. 'But not too chilly for Gavin, it seems. Here he comes across the square.'

'Have you been to the Institute?' Lady Alison asked when he came in.

'All the final-year students have been roped in to help the doctors give the vaccinations. There's a rota. I had it done myself when I was there earlier today.'

'Well, it's our turn tomorrow,' Lady Alison told him.

'I'm very glad to hear it.'

'Aren't you supposed to be studying every minute of the day?' Edina asked.

'The day's been broken anyway, with this smallpox scare. So I've come to take you out while it's still daylight. Cardew asked me – no, *begged* me – to call when I had a spare minute, so I thought we'd kill two birds with one stone.'

They set off on their usual walk, and had scarcely got to Queen Street when they noticed a strange man opening the door of Number 57 and going in.

'Who's he?' Edina asked. 'I wonder if Cardew's in? I didn't like the look of that man at all. What if Mrs Fanny's in alone?'

Janet Brown watched her friend Mary Paterson getting up out of the ramshackle bed and going over to peer in the brown-spotted mirror, humming as she always did as soon as her eyes were open. Music just seemed to flow out of her, and as if she didn't attract enough attention as it was in the taverns she would think nothing of standing up on a table and giving everyone a song.

'God, what a bloody sight!' Mary said when she saw herself.

'It's the rouge,' Janet said. 'It's all run. We'd better heat some water and wash our faces with the Windsor soap. Then we can put on some fresh paint.'

'I've half a mind not to,' Mary said half an hour later, surveying her reflection again. Now that it was clean her skin was still clear and pure with only her natural colour glowing on her cheeks and lips. But there were dark patches under her eyes, and sags here and bags there, and funny lines between her nose and her mouth which were never there even a few months ago. God, it didn't take long to lose your looks in this game! 'Oh, to hell with it!' she said impatiently. 'Pass me the paint-pots, Janet. I'm so thirsty, and not for water, either.'

'But nothing's open yet. Where could we go?'

'Mrs Lawrie will be up. She was good to us when we stayed with her. She'll give us something, surely to God.'

But Mrs Lawrie had nothing stronger to offer than tea, oatcakes, and a lot of advice. 'You shouldn't be walking alone in the Royal Mile every night, not after the news about Daft Jamie disappearing. It's more than rumours, now. Everybody's speaking about it, and saying he was murdered.'

'Och, away!' Mary scoffed. 'Who would want to harm Daft Jamie? No, no, he'll just be hiding up somewhere with that Bobby Awl.'

'You're wrong, Mary. When Bobby Awl was interviewed for the newspapers he said he didn't know where his friend was. There's a warning out to be careful. You shouldn't be going with just any men, like the pair of you do, not knowing half the time who they are. They could be murderers.'

'Well, I'm getting out of it,' Janet told her. 'I'm getting married to David Rowan in November.'

'And I'm going to her wedding.' Mary tried to smile, but her teacup was rattling about in its saucer something wicked.

'Yes,' Janet said. 'She's promised not to utter one curse, as well. Haven't you, Mary?'

'Not a bloody one.'

'Och, *Mary!*' Mrs Lawrie clucked her tongue. 'Look at you! You've got the shakes. I wish you'd give up the life you're leading. Stop drinking, and get married like Janet's doing. With your looks you could marry an earl and live in style with plenty of money!'

'An earl hasn't asked me lately!' Mary laughed as they rose to go, and when she came to think about it, walking up the road with Janet, where, too, was all that fortune she had been going to make? What with buying clothes and booze, it all seemed to disappear like snow off a dike.

When they got to Swanston's it was crowded with students, blaring with noise and thick with the fumes of tobacco and spirits. It was all the breath of life to Mary, and her own spirits rose accordingly as she led the way to a little table in the middle of the bar-room.

Janet bought the first drinks. If all went well as usual, she would not have to buy any more. Sure enough, when she got back to the table with the glasses Mary was chatting and laughing with a crowd of students already, and she tossed off her gin as if she were parched.

'Can I buy you another?' one of the students asked. He was tall and well dressed with blond whiskers and spoke the New Town way. Scottish all right, but posh. 'My name's William Fergusson, by the way.'

'Is it now?' Mary smiled, and sent out her signals. She ran her tongue over the red of her mouth so that the paint gleamed invitingly, and dropped her tippet from her shoulders to reveal plump young breasts scantily covered by the bodice of her red dress. William Fergusson flushed and grinned; the other students sniggered and dug each other in the ribs. 'Well, what about me calling you Billy, for short? Yes, I'll have a drink with you, Billy, and anything else you fancy, long or short.'

Her meaning could hardly have been clearer, and all the students whistled and laughed. From a table tucked in the corner two men watched the whole performance, one sandy-haired and the other, bigger and darker, looking like the Devil incarnate, even more so now that he had grown a small black pointed beard.

'I'd like to get my hands on that one,' he said, staring at Mary.

'And how could we be doing that?'

'Easy! You can see for yourself. Fill her full of drink, and then . . . We could have some fun with her first, before we put her in a box,' he added with a fiendish smile.

Billy compared her with the two drabs back home in Tanners' Close. Oh, for just one night with a woman like Mary Paterson, and he seriously believed he might be cured. 'Helen and Maggie would go mad,' he said despairingly. 'Of course,' he brightened a little, 'we could always send them out with plenty of money to the White Hart.'

'She's leaving, anyway,' Hare growled, as Mary stood up, put on her tippet slowly and ostentatiously so that her next clients had every opportunity to admire her, and swaggered out with William Fergusson.

'That's him who takes our subjects and pays us the money in Surgeons' Square. He's away up a close with her.'

'Sure, and he's the lucky one!' Hare said longingly, and then his eye fell on Janet. 'We might get her friend along with her as well. She doesn't look that bad, either. But it won't be easy. How can we arrange it?'

Suddenly Billy got a terrible bad feeling, more like a superstition. He didn't want to arrange it, and he didn't know why. He only knew that this was the first time the hairs were standing up on the back of his neck at the very thought of it. But he couldn't tell Hare that. He would think he was going soft all of a sudden.

'You're right,' he said. 'Mary Paterson would be the worst one of all to pull in Edinburgh. She's too well known all around the town.'

'A ten days' wonder, that's all it would be. Could we ever manage it?'

'I'm after thinking,' Billy said.

Harry Love was fairly sober when he entered the house in Queen Street. That was because he had hidden and waited a long time for Cardew Sharpe after having the front door slammed in his face last night. He'd been watching the house most of the day. He'd seen Sharpe sneaking out earlier. He knew Fanny would be alone in the house, but that was no use. He wanted to confront them together and then blow their brains out.

His patience was rewarded when Sharpe came back furtively, glancing frequently over his shoulder. Harry Love crept up cautiously to the front door and looked up and down the street. Nobody was coming except a young couple in the distance. He pushed the door experimentally, and could hardly believe his luck. Sharpe had forgotten to shut it properly. In the excitement that gripped Love when he tiptoed into Number 57, he forgot to shut it, too.

First he deposited behind the front door the heavy object he had been carrying about with him, and then he stood still

216

in the hall listening for a minute or two until his ears told him where the noise was coming from. He began to creep up towards it.

'I'm sure that was Harry Love,' Gavin whispered to Edina when they in turn reached the open front door.

'Who's Harry Love?' Edina whispered back.

'Mrs Fanny's husband.'

'I never heard of anything so scandalous and exciting!' Edina smothered a giggle when they peered inside. 'Look, he's nearly got to the top of the stairs.'

'You wait here, Edina.'

'Not on your life,' she muttered, following Gavin following Mr Love.

Mr Love tiptoed to the bedroom door and flung it open. Gavin and Edina were behind him as he stood swaying there for a while, unable to believe what he was seeing.

It was too late by that time for Gavin to prevent Edina from seeing it, either, when Mrs Fanny stared, speechless, at her husband around Cardew, who had taken off more than his breeches.

'Oh! Oh! It's himself!' she screeched at last.

'So this is it!' roared Mr Love, stumbling back out of the bedroom, so incensed that he didn't even notice anyone else was there. He blundered past Gavin and Edina.

'He's away for his gun!' Mrs Fanny clutched at her breast and then snatched at her clothes, with total disregard for poor Cardew hopping about with one leg back in his breeches.

'Help me on on with these damned breeches,' he commanded Gavin.

But Gavin had no intention of entering into any such struggle when he saw the narrow pantaloons. Besides, with his back to Edina he was doing his best to press her up against the wall, so as to obstruct her view.

Mrs Fanny was busy smoothing the ruffled sheets, obviously hoping that such small facts as Cardew in her bedroom and her own nakedness might just escape her husband's notice. Far from putting any of her clothes back on, she went next to the dressing-table and began brushing her hair in a demented

217

fashion, and Gavin felt Edina's whole body shaking behind him in the force of her mirth.

Then in burst Mr Love again, this time with a huge blunderbuss.

'Cardew! Cardew! He's going to kill us,' Mrs Fanny screamed.

'Put away that damned firearm, Love!' Cardew bellowed in his best officer-of-the-army style.

'After me trusting you, you dirty whore!' Mr Love was beside himself, so beside himself that he pointed the gun holding it by the trigger. It went off in a monstrous report, raking the bed, the dressing-table mirror and finally his own foot. He fell down on the floor and lay still.

'Harry! Harry! Are you dead?' Mrs Fanny flung herself on top of her husband. 'Oh, my God, he's dead! Look what you've done to my husband!' she accused Cardew. 'You've killed him!'

'Me? Did I kill him, Gavin?' he appealed to his friend, who by this time had shut Edina out of the room and was down on his knees examining Mr Love. 'The silly bugger shot himself, and then died of shock. Besides, it's the best thing that could have happened. We're rid of him, for good.'

'Well . . .' Mrs Fanny wavered.

'He's certainly dead,' Gavin confirmed. 'Edina and I were witnesses. You can't get away with this, you know, Cardew. Not this time. You'll have to report it.'

'The students are back after Easter. There may be some I haven't even seen yet. I might land one of them,' Mary Paterson said as she and Janet Brown went into Swanston's.

Janet doubted it, but she went up to the bar and ordered two gins. Out of the corner of her eye she saw Mary introducing herself, accepting a drink and knocking it back, before the students left in a body. 'They're away to a lecture,' she told Janet, and was just about to order a third gin when a man came over and said, 'Ladies, please allow me.'

He wasn't young; thirty-five or so, stockily built, with a thin mouth and sandy hair, and he was wearing a nice dark frock-coat and a white cravat. Perhaps he was a clerk with a free morning. In any case, he was good for one dram at least.

'Thank you,' Mary said. 'Won't you sit down?'

They found out from the music in his voice that he was Irish, and he liked to laugh and joke. 'Are you alone in the world?' he asked them after a while.

'I'm not,' Janet said. 'I'm getting married.'

'I'm still looking,' said Mary.

'I'm single myself,' he told them, 'but I've got a good pension, and staying with friends just now until I buy a house of my own. I've been looking in Charlotte Square.'

'Charlotte Square!' Mary said. 'God, you must be rich!'

'Rich enough to be keeping one of you.' He smiled, looking at Janet.

That surprised her. In fact everything he was saying surprised her, because clients didn't usually volunteer any information about themselves. After another gin he invited them to his lodgings for breakfast. Breakfast? Was that what he called it, Janet asked herself, and started to refuse.

'Och, I'm that hungry I'd love some breakfast,' Mary said. 'The bigger the better.'

Well, Janet thought, perhaps this Mr Burke was the man Mary had been looking for, to keep her for the rest of her life, especially when he presented them both with a bottle of gin. She'd better go along, she supposed, and when she saw the terrible room in which he was lodging she wasn't surprised that he wanted to move.

But the fire was bright, there were finnan haddies on the pan, an egg poaching on top of each one, and with bread and tea they had a splendid breakfast. Then Mr Burke got out a whisky bottle and poured them a drink, and shortly afterwards Mary fell asleep with her head on the table.

'She'd be better lying down,' Mr Burke said, and lifted her on to a bed. Then he poured out another dram, and Janet was beginning to feel a bit drowsy herself when the door opened suddenly and a mean, drab woman came in.

219

'Helen!' said Mr Burke, and the way he said it made Janet realise that here was Mrs Burke.

'What the fuck's going on here?' she shouted. 'Little wonder you have no time for your own wife nowadays when you go with the tarts of the town! You're a runking faithless pig, Billy Burke!'

She ranted and shrieked and cursed and then stood over Mary with her hands upraised, as if she was about to claw the skin off her.

'Please, ma'am, my friend's done no harm,' Janet sobbed. 'She just got fou, that's all.'

Helen gave her a look that scared her stiff, and then whirled round to hit and scratch her husband instead, until he lost his temper and threw a glass at her. The last Janet saw before she escaped and ran for her life was Helen Burke with the blood streaming down her face.

But what about Mary? She couldn't just leave her there in that hell-hole, and she was too scared to go back and try to rouse her. She thought of Mrs Lawrie, who was so wise and motherly. She'd know what to do.

'Annie,' Mrs Lawrie ordered her big husky maid, 'go with Janet immediately and bring Mary back here.'

Once out on the road again, Janet couldn't quite remember how to get to Tanners' Close. She thought of Mr Swanston, who would know all his customers, and she and Annie went in to ask him about the sandy-haired man who'd taken them away earlier. But Mr Swanston was busy. They had to wait and wait, and to pass the time they had a little drink. Janet's head was swimming again when at last Mr Swanston gave them directions.

That terrible Helen was still there with a blood-encrusted wound on her temple, and another even uglier woman and a tall, dark, hideous-looking man. The sight of him sobered Janet quickly and completely.

'Where's Mary?' she asked, with Annie close behind her.

The man seemed to be sizing up the situation. Or perhaps he was sizing her up. Or perhaps she and Annie, together.

'Out with Mr Burke,' he said, 'getting sobered up.'

The two women sniggered, and Janet sensed the evil in the room. So did Annie. 'Come away, Miss Janet,' she said. 'Mary Paterson can find her own way home.'

17

THE HUE AND CRY about Daft Jamie died down, but a lot of Edinburgh people could not forget it, Mr Eden Hamilton least of all. 'James Wilson was a strong, healthy young man,' he told Gavin in his study. 'I try not to discuss the details of such things before the ladies, but there is no doubt in my mind that he was abducted and murdered.'

One of Mr Hamilton's ladies was more worldly-wise than he realised, Gavin thought. For a girl brought up in such polite, genteel society Edina had little to learn. 'It seems so, sir,' he said aloud, wondering how he could steer the conversation round to the land of the living, and to his own immediate concern in it ... with her.

'Frank Clarke never saw anything of the Daft Jamie affair,' Mr Hamilton continued, 'in spite of extra vigilance. He cannot be everywhere at once, of course, and yet his instincts keep leading him back to the West Port and the mean streets and closes in that area, Tanners' Close and Irish people who live there in particular.'

'I understand your concern, sir, and that you are really asking me if I have recognised any of the cadavers in the dissection rooms. I can assure you, I have not.'

'That was two years ago, long before this recent explosion. You may recognise some of them now.'

223

'Do you want me to keep an eye on the specimens that come in, sir?'

'You see, Gavin, the medical profession is a thing set apart from the rest of us. As a senior student you have the authority, where we have not.'

'The authority, yes. And in my case, the incentive. I would do anything for Edina and her parents,' Gavin got it in at last.

'My dear boy, you needn't remind me of what you did for my poor wife when she broke her leg! Just tell me the bargain. Well do I remember your father at your age. It was a case of favours done. You scratch my back, and I'll scratch yours.'

'The very great favour, sir, is in asking you if I may court your daughter. I love her with all my heart, and hope to be able to support her very soon now. But I'm afraid she may have someone else in mind.'

'Someone else? What nonsense! Young men and young ladies come and go in this house, of course. My wife and daughter entertain endlessly. But there is no one else in the marriage stakes, or else I would have been told,' Mr Hamilton protested.

Then he hesitated, a strange, sad expression on his face, and seemed about to say something else. It worried Gavin more than words could say, for Cardew was probably their most frequent visitor, always alone, and probably cadging money from Lady Alison, who seemed to forgive him anything.

'Of course you have our permission, Gavin,' Mr Hamilton said at last. 'I wish you the best of luck.'

'I'll need it all,' he said, visualising Cardew's naked legs like a pair of tree trunks and the considerable equipment in between, the sight of which had entertained Edina so much.

'To go back to it,' Mr Hamilton said as they emerged from the study and crossed the hall, 'you'll have a look out from now on?'

'I will, sir.'

'We are sitting on the edge of a volcano,' Mr Hamilton declared, opening the drawing-room door. 'Did you hear that, Alison? Mark my words, soon it will erupt.'

'We have a more immediate eruption upstairs,' Lady Alison

said. 'An eruption of smallpox. Edina's vaccination has gone wrong.'

'Great God!' Her father clutched Gavin's arm.

'You cannot go into her room,' Gavin said on the way upstairs. 'Neither can anyone else until I have examined her.' He went inside and shut the door. From the foot of the bed he looked at her flushed face, and then went round the side of the bed and lifted her hand. 'You have a sore throat?' he asked, feeling her pulse.

'What a great fuss they are making! Yes, my throat is sore; so is my head, and so are all my bones. It feels like a very bad cold.'

'Yes,' he said, and his eyes were soft and gentle, 'the vaccination has taken, there's no doubt about it. If you had not had it, and really caught smallpox, you would have taken it very badly. These are only a few mild symptoms of what it might have been like.'

'Then I do not have the smallpox?'

'No, but at the same time you may be starting a nasty cold, so you will stay in your bed until further notice and your own doctor sees you.' He pulled the bedclothes up round her and tucked them in.

'I'd rather have you, Gavin. I trust you.'

'I would be no use to you, Edina. I could not be impersonal enough, if at any time something really did go wrong. A doctor does not treat his nearest and dearest.'

'Bend down, and tell me that again. Am I really your nearest and dearest?'

'You know you are.' He kissed her, and she wound her arms round his neck. 'Some day I wish you could be even closer than that.'

'Then ask me now. I'll say yes, and yes, and yes, and yes,' she said, and confirmed it with kisses.

'You'll marry me?'

'Oh yes, please, darling Gavin!'

After some time he went over and opened the door. 'It's all right,' he told her anxious parents. 'Come in. She hasn't got smallpox.'

225

'I haven't got smallpox,' Edina said with shining yes, 'but I've got a fiancé. We're going to be married, Gavin and I. Look at me! Don't I look better already?'

William Hare pushed Helen and Maggie through the door with a fine fat purse to go to Swanston's. 'It's a kind of peace-offering,' he said, 'after all that fighting over Mary Paterson. Away you go and enjoy yourselves. You deserve it – especially you, Helen, with a black eye coming up. Billy and I will be out when you come back, delivering the body.'

The women decked themselves up in their tawdry finery, and went off arm in arm. At the door Maggie shouted back. 'You're not feared, then, in case we get a click?' The men heard the sound of their giggles as they went down the passage.

'Where have you put her?' Billy asked.

'Under the bed.' Hare dragged the body out, still fully clothed, and they sat and gazed at her for a long time, drinking steadily.

'God, she's beautiful,' Billy said, an icy shudder going through him.

Hare sat down beside her on the mat, lifted her skirt and pulled down her shift. They marvelled at her full breasts and her tiny waist. Already she was stiffening with her legs apart. With a muttered curse, Hare had her then and there, on the hearthstraw.

'Now it's your turn,' he told Billy, fastening his breeches afterwards.

But there was no answer, and when he looked up Billy Burke was crying. 'I can't,' he said.

'Why not? What's wrong with you? It was kind of exciting.'

There was a terrible feeling inside Billy. It had nothing to do with his testicle. The pain was in his heart, as minute by minute he watched Mary Paterson's face changing in death, and from out of the past came the memory of Bridie's face, young and sweet and smiling . . . But not with blood trickling out of the corner of her mouth like this.

'What in the name of God have you done to her?' he asked

Hare in terror. 'Look at her mouth! There's blood coming out of it.'

'Ach, to hell with it,' Hare said, in a thoroughly bad mood now, 'we're not getting rid of this one, yet. We'll hide her in the coal-cellar for a day or two. We got some money for the Docherty woman last night, enough to keep us going in the meantime.'

'And how are you going to explain Mary Paterson in the coal-cellar to the women?' Billy asked.

'They won't go in, not when I tell them I found rats in there.'

When they came back, Helen and Maggie were standing in the middle of the room. 'Oh, yes,' Helen said, suspicious again, 'what's been going on in here, then, when you thought we were safely out of the way?'

'What the hell does it look like?' Hare looked up from wiping coal dust off his hands, with an expression so vicious that she shrank back. 'We've found rats in the coal-cellar. They're savage. You'd better not go in there. Where's the drink? You did fetch back drink?'

'No, we didn't. What about the tart?' Maggie asked.

'Packed, and ready to go.'

Oh, God, Billy thought. If it hadn't been for the queer feeling he'd had at the time, he might have been on top of Mary Paterson now, this very minute. Then Helen would have taken a knife to him, there was no doubt of that. But with the constant agony in his ball, every day now, he wondered seriously if he would care anyway. He sent Helen out for some more whisky with his share of the Docherty money, and when she came back she silently put a drink in his hand every time his glass was empty.

While he waited he tried to ease his body on the bed, but it kept on twitching. The sweat poured from his forehead and the palms of his hands, and as he stared up at the cracked ceiling there was a humming in his head. The humming that heralded the worst nightmare any man could have, and he screamed and screamed and pressed back on the stone wall behind the bed, trying to stop it coming.

Helen heard him when she came in. So did Hare. They met together by the bed. 'I'll stop his noise,' Hare said, with a hard punch of his fist that knocked Billy out of the bed and woke him up.

'You bastard!' Billy opened his eyes and gave Hare a look of pure hatred. It was enough to remind William Hare that Billy Burke was the mastermind here. 'That's the finish of the tart, and it's the finish of her stay under this roof. We'll deliver her today. I don't care if it's in the broad daylight.'

'Och,' Hare tried to lighten Billy's mood, 'give him some whisky, Helen. It was only a nightmare. He'll be all right.'

Left alone with her man, Helen was worried. Billy was in a queer old mood today. She wondered what had happened to cause it. But it was better not to chatter when he was in a state like this.

'Helen,' he said after a long time, 'do you ever pray?'

'I used to.' She used to pray that he would be a proper husband to her again. 'But it never worked. They say praying is like knocking on His door. He never heard me.'

'Nor me, but then I'm not a good Catholic now, never going to mass or to confess. How could I confess, anyway? How could I trust a priest with my secrets?' he groaned. Helen poured another drink when the Hares came in. 'Never again must we be without drink in the house,' Billy told them all.

'Then we're agreed,' Hare said. 'The grog's more important than bread or anything else. If we became careless, just because we haven't had a drink to stir the brain, it could be the end of us.'

But Billy still hadn't forgiven him. 'Anyone finding a body here could be the end of us, you mean.' He glared at him. 'One more drink for us, and a good sprinkling over the body in the box to pretend she was drunk enough to die, and we're off to Surgeons' Square.'

William Fergusson stood chatting to Gavin while Mr Bain took delivery of this latest tea-chest from Burke and Hare. 'Wait there,' he told the two Irishmen, 'until we get the body ready for Dr Knox to see.'

A few minutes later Bain came rushing back. 'You'd better come and have a look at this,' he muttered with his back to Burke and Hare so that they couldn't hear what he was saying to the two senior students.

'What is it?' Fergusson asked.

'There's something wrong, isn't there?' Gavin sensed it.

'Far wrong,' Bain said. 'The body's still warm. And look at her!'

William Fergusson looked stunned. 'That's Mary Paterson,' he said when the body of the naked young woman was laid out on the slab. 'Good God! I met her in Swanston's not long ago.'

Mary Paterson! Gavin gazed down at her and tried to steady himself in the worst shock of his life so far. Uneasy feelings of shame and grief overwhelmed him, followed by a horrified realisation of her likeness to Edina. Too shocked to answer William Fergusson, Gavin followed him to the back door to hear him question the two carriers. 'Where did you get the body?'

'In a close off the Canongate. At first we thought she was drunk,' Hare said. 'You can smell it on her.'

'Ay,' Billy said, thanking God that they had always had the wit to sprinkle their victims with whisky, 'the poor taupies die of drink.'

'A very handsome body,' Dr Knox pronounced when they fetched him, handing over ten guineas and dismissing the two men. He came back to take a closer look, not the only man there to think with pity that the red dress had never done justice to the planes and curves of her magnificent body. Her head lay on a block and her streaming gold hair hung down almost to the floor.

'No,' he spoke again. 'This one is not for dissection, gentlemen, not at the moment anyway. Such perfection should be captured first by our art students, for they will never have a model like this again. Then I shall put an intimation in the *Courant* for the public viewing, under my jurisdiction of course. I want her put into spirits immediately, and preserved.'

'When will you do it?' Gavin asked Fergusson when the great man marched off.

'You heard him, the sooner the better. Now, tonight.'

'Would you allow me to bring a gentleman here tomorrow morning to see her? He is Mr Hamilton, a friend of mine.'

'Of course, soon all Edinburgh will come to see her anyway,' Fergusson sighed, and went to work.

'The body I'm taking you to see was still warm when we first saw it,' Gavin told Mr Hamilton the next day. 'But that is not the most surprising thing. She was another well-known figure in Edinburgh, probably the most notorious prostitute of the Royal Mile, Mary Paterson.'

'Indeed. Whoever is doing it must be getting desperate now. First Daft Jamie, and now Mary Paterson. Who delivered her, still warm?'

'The usual carriers, sir. Here she is.' Gavin pulled aside the curtain hanging round Mary in the empty room.

'*Oh, my God . . . Oh, my God . . .*'

Cleansed of all the paint, and wiped clean by death of all its tell-tale lines, the dead woman's face was that of a young and lovely girl. The sharpened angularities had been filled in again, the delicate features restored to girlhood and the ashen lips were curved in an innocent smile.

Gavin was as stricken as Mr Hamilton. They were standing there in silence looking at Mary Paterson, but they were seeing Edina. Neither of them could take it in, and the silence went on and on until Mr Hamilton broke it.

'I tried to tell you once, Gavin,' Mr Hamilton's face was almost as ashen as Mary's, 'but I couldn't. You see, Edina is not our own child. My wife found her, a baby, abandoned in Candlemaker Row. But perhaps there was not just one child abandoned by the mother. It looks as though there could have been two.'

Gavin sat him down in a chair and made him sit with his head between his knees for a while. Then he went to find Fergusson. 'Mr Hamilton doesn't feel well,' he told him. 'I've got him sitting down for a few minutes. Have you a spot of brandy?'

'Drink this, sir,' Gavin said when he went back with it, 'and don't worry. Edina is Edina. It doesn't make any difference.'

'We have never told her,' Mr Hamilton said, his colour beginning to return. 'What was the use? She would only fret about her real mother, and her real mother left her to die. In fact, the first time I saw Edina I didn't think she could survive. We thought that to tell her would be too cruel. I still do.'

'I agree with you. She will never know it from me.'

'Gavin, all I can tell you is that whoever her parents were, and for that matter wherever Mary Paterson came from, no child ever brought more joy into a home than Edina . . . always singing . . . always happy. She's given us nothing but love and happiness.'

'Gavin smiled. 'I'm a lucky man,' he said when they stood up, with one last look at Mary Paterson. 'She's given me that already.'

The next time Gavin saw Cardew he could detect no change of expression on his friend's face when he repeated his question. 'Cardew, you did report the accidental death of Mr Love, didn't you? Didn't you?'

'No, damn me!' he burst out, 'I didn't. I couldn't afford to, for one thing. I sold him to Professor Monroe. He only gave me eight guineas for him, too! He said the feet were twisted and one-eyed specimens were not in the greatest demand.'

'How could you be so stupid? The neighbours are bound to have seen and heard the noise. They'll talk.'

'That's just the problem.' Cardew seemed ready to weep. 'They did.'

'What?' Gavin said, aghast.

'I was just pocketing the eight guineas when two policemen arrived and backed us into Monroe's dissecting room. He told them a direct lie when he said that there hadn't been a hanging in the town for three weeks, and the cadaver of that went to Dr Knox. My God! When Harry Love was in behind the curtain not two feet away!'

'I don't know how you manage it.' Gavin shook his head. 'You have a perfect talent for trouble.'

231

'The policemen said they were just warning him to be on the look-out for anyone offering him a body with one eye missing and feet full of lead balls. When they left, Monroe asked me what I had to say for myself. But,' he added mournfully, 'it was a waste of breath. Baying at the moon. Or as Josh would say, farting against thunder. He listened to none of my stories.'

'Who would?' Gavin snorted. 'Not even Professor Monroe!'

'He said young gentlemen should not sell bodies to our noble institution. They should donate them to further the cause of humanity instead. Then he had the audacity to make me give him back his eight guineas.'

'Well, you got off lightly.'

'Got off lightly! Got off lightly?' Cardew howled. 'You haven't heard the half of it! He's blackmailing me next! In return for his silence I have to give all his lectures for him, *from now to the end of the year*!'

'What about the finals?'

'What indeed? And just when I'd met such a fascinating chap! He's a chemist. Been experimenting with the old rubbers, you know. It's a line I'm very interested in. He and I agreed there's a fortune in rubbers. All we needed to do was find out how to make them so that they stay on – in the height of passion, old boy – and never burst. Now I won't be able to help him with his experiments. He'll go and patent the damned things on his own.'

'You've lost another fortune, then, Cardew,' Gavin said drily.

'Yes. And Fanny's pregnant again. I feel like topping myself, old fruit,' Cardew said tragically.

'I've got visitors,' Helen told Maggie Hare. 'James Little and his wife and bairn. She's a daughter of that MacDougal man I was married to before I met Billy.'

'What about MacDougal? Where is he?'

'Dead.'

'And your two bairns?'

'I forgot to ask. Anyway, the Littles want to stay.'

'They could have the Brogans' room, then. Can they pay?'

'It doesn't look like it. He's a lot older than she is, an old soldier and out of work. But we'll pay for them as long as they're here.'

'As long as they *last* here, you mean?' Maggie sniggered. 'Good for shots, in the end?'

Helen laughed with her, to keep her sweet, but in her heart she felt sorry for the Littles, poor and homeless and somehow innocent, just sitting side by side on the bed in their slit of a room, staring hopelessly into space.

She went out to the end of the close to cheer herself up watching the world go by, and there coming down the street was that nosy Constable Clarke with a tiny old woman. What could he be wanting with the likes of *her*?'

Frank Clarke had taken a shine to the birdlike creature as soon as he saw her coming down the West Port on her spindly legs. She reminded him of his mother, God rest her soul. 'Are you looking for somewhere, Mother?' he asked her.

'I was looking for me son, Michael Docherty,' she said in a soft Irish voice. 'Someone said that he might be down here in the Grassmarket, and that he sometimes goes to a place called Rhymer's. Could you direct me to it, sir?'

'I'll take you to it, dearie,' Frank said slowly. Michael Docherty . . . Where had he heard that name before? Wasn't he one of the men who had disappeared about a year ago? 'Have you anywhere to stay if you don't find Michael?' he asked.

The poor old lady was too tired to tell her the truth just yet. 'No, sir. But don't you be worrying about me. I've come all the way from Glasgow and I'm still here to tell the tale. I'll be all right in Edinburgh, too. I'm used to looking out for meself.'

Frank looked down at her. She was as thin and as frail as a matchstick and her wispy hair was grey, although she could only have been about fifty, he thought, and in that moment he made up his mind he wouldn't let her far out of his sight. 'Well, here's David Rhymer's,' he said. 'Now behave yourself, Mrs Docherty. Be a good girl!'

'I'll try.' She smiled, as chirpy as a bird.

It was the strongest temptation of his life to follow her in, but somehow he resisted it, loitering up and down the Grassmarket

233

for a good half an hour. Then he saw her coming out again, in the company of those two Irish fellows, Burke and Hare.

They had their arms linked in hers. They were almost carrying her between them, and she was skirling and laughing all the way up the road from Rhymer's. Frank supposed they had given her a few drinks. She was fairly enjoying herself, anyway – but all the same he shadowed them to the end of the passage in Tanners' Close, frowning. It was not the first time he'd marked that house.

For the public viewing of Mary Paterson's remains, Dr Knox covered her body with a white sheet, exposing only her face and her long golden curls trailing almost to the floor. She lay on a marble slab in a small, bare room, and outside the door he posted Mr Bain and another student as guardians.

'Let in no more than two at a time,' he ordered, 'and, Mr Fergusson, you will be present beside the body at all times.'

'Yes, sir.' William Fergusson sighed and resigned himself to a long, boring day when half the people of the town would file past Mary, having read Dr Knox's intimation in the *Courant*.

He believed that Dr Knox should never have made this generous offer to the townsfolk, to come and see her. But he had, and advertised it in the newspapers besides, so that all other activities in the Surgeons' Hall were halted for the day.

Dr Knox, having issued his invitation to Edinburgh, and now his instructions to his faithful students, marched down the pillared hall past the long queue which, he discovered, was already spilling outside and continuing up the South Bridge as far as Rankeillor Street, and went home.

Mabel Milligan was fifth in the queue. She simply could not believe what the newspapers said. She had to come and see for herself if it was really Mary Paterson or not. If it was, then why had she died? Or had she been killed? And if she *had* been killed, was there a possible threat to Bridie's other child . . . *before she had time to act*?

She lifted her brooding eyes to glance round at the queue of people behind her, and her gaze came to rest on Miss Edina Hamilton herself, and her maid with her. In that moment Mabel

Milligan knew that her lucky day had come at long last. Today was the day to act.

Edina and Kathy had come early for this public viewing. It was the talk of the town, but, thinking that her parents wouldn't approve, Edina hadn't told them where she was going. She felt guilty enough about that, and worse every minute, the more jittery Kathy was becoming.

'Well, you were the one who said Mary Paterson was very like me, Kathy, so naturally I want to see her close up,' Edina whispered.

'I don't think this is a very good idea,' Kathy kept arguing, her voice trembling. 'I've never seen a dead person before.'

'Is that all that's worrying you? Well, you won't have to see one now,' Edina whispered back. 'When we get to the door, just wait for me outside.'

The gloomy, eerie silence continued in the hall, as the people shuffled forward slowly. Edina was not afraid of the dead, nor death itself, after long debates with herself on the subject over the years, but standing there in Surgeons' Hall she was suddenly aware of something a great deal worse, of evil somehow, and danger. She looked round at the sea of faces, but there was nothing amiss there. Then a woman walked out of the small sanctuary alone, her eyes met Edina's and in a flash she knew that this was where the evil was coming from. But the woman hurried by to the outside door without stopping.

The incident had been unnerving, and, still upset, Edina went in alone to view the body. There was utter silence in the presence of death. Even the young man sitting in a chair in the corner didn't lift his eyes when she entered the room. She went up to the body and looked down at Mary Paterson.

William Fergusson never knew that Edina stood still for such a long time because she simply couldn't get her legs to move. He stared straight ahead with his arms folded, completely disinterested, while she endured long moments of shock when she almost thought she must be looking in some grim mirror, before she somehow managed to steady herself.

How, she never knew afterwards. She was looking at Mary

Paterson, but she was seeing herself, Edina Hamilton, dead. Then in an instant Edina tumbled to the truth: Mary Paterson could be her own sister. Mary Paterson probably was her own sister – and to such an end, but for the grace of God, she might have gone herself.

Outside, Mabel Milligan picked out the most handsome coach waiting there, chocolate-brown with gilt on its doors. 'Whose coach is that?' she asked a chair man she knew.

'The Hamiltons', 13, Charlotte Square.'

'What a coincidence! That's where I'm going at four o'clock this afternoon.'

'Yes?' The chair man pricked up his ears. 'And you want me to take you? I'll come for you at a quarter to.'

When they got home, Edina dismissed Kathy and lay down on her bed to think. No two girls could look so much alike as she and Mary Paterson unless they were closely related. In fact, they had to be sisters, with the same mother and father. With that realisation, the awful feeling of danger and doom returned.

Why had Mary died? Why had she finished up at Surgeons' Hall, where all the candidates for dissection finished up? The answer was plain. *She had been murdered.* No girl as healthy as Mary the last time she saw her was going to die any other way, and in spite of herself Edina began to cry. She cried and cried until she cried herself to sleep, and when she woke up it was to hear the wheels of their coach stopping outside, and Mama's voice as she came in.

The little clock on her bedroom mantelpiece tinkled out the time. Half past three. Nearly time for the four o'clocks, and long past time to confront her parents.

Gavin woke up that morning at Miss Plenderleith's to realise that the finals were now looming terrifyingly large on the horizon. He gazed glumly at his landlady over their porridge. 'After nearly three years, I know absolutely nothing about Medicine, Miss Phyllis.'

'My brother discovered the same,' she said, unmoved, 'and just at exactly the same stage, too.'

236

'What am I to do?' he asked despairingly.

'The same as he did. Get a grinder. Mr MacIvor, four flights up in Advocates' Close.' She removed the plates whistling 'The Lord's my Shepherd' under her breath, and disappeared into the kitchen.

Gavin went to Mr MacIvor five nights a week from then on, unable to believe all the things he had forgotten already when Mr MacIvor reminded him of the intricacies of the human body. He took him up the arm and down the trunk and then up and down the leg. He revised the brain, bladder stones, jaundice, angina, consumption and smallpox.

From there they moved on to surgery. Mr MacIvor made sure Gavin was able to recognise at a glance what instruments – forceps, knives, trusses and saws – for which operation, and brushed up the writing out of prescriptions in Latin, long since lapsed, until the night before the terrible day in June arrived. Gavin said goodbye to his tutor and in an effort to quell his nerves and drown his sorrows he went out to the White Hart with Cardew, who had bounced up again after his most recent tragedy.

'Too late to worry now, old thing,' Cardew assured him, fetching more drinks and a plate of chicken legs with crusty bread. 'Eat, drink and be merry, even if tomorrow we die. That old buzzard Monroe is allowing me to sit the finals, after all. Of course I haven't a hope in hell of passing.'

Next morning, with a headache that defied medicine, Gavin set off to the university on foot to try and clear it. What happened next was all a blur as he hazarded a guess at the diagnosis and treatment of a case drawn up by one of the six professors, who were ranged up in front of the students, clearly enjoying themselves. He answered their oral questions as best he could and finally wrote in his best handwriting his chosen thesis on how the weather affects the body, if not the brain.

It seemed to him to be a fairly innocuous subject to choose, yet one of worldwide interest. Towards the end of it, before the last bell rang to down pens and close papers, he even waxed lyrical about everyone's response to the sun. A man's whole working day, he argued, could be affected by the weather. On grey days he might have little inspiration, let alone energy, to give a good day's work. But sunshine relieved the body, made the tissues moist, relaxed the bowels and produced such a state of well-being that a man gave of his best.

'How did you get on?' he asked Cardew afterwards.

'Naturally, I chose contraception for my thesis, and went as far back as BC and the use of animals' intestines, don't you know. All in all quite a brilliant study, though I say it myself, of a subject close to every man's heart, not to mention his penis.'

'I don't know why I associate with you, Cardew.' Gavin laughed. 'I'll be damned if I do! You're an out-and-out disgrace!'

18

'WHERE HAVE MAMA and Papa been?' Edina asked Liza, who was still in the hall brushing the rain off their coats before she hung them up.

'To see Mary Paterson, I'm sorry to say,' sniffed Liza. 'Lady Alison is very upset.'

Edina soon saw for herself that Liza was telling the truth. She found her father quiet and pale and her mother dabbing her eyes with her handkerchief. She would have to take the bull by the horns. 'I went to see Mary Paterson today,' she told them.

Mr Hamilton froze in his chair. Lady Hamilton tried without success to pull herself together. 'Oh, *Edina* . . . Why?'

'Because everyone said I resembled her so much. Because I wanted to see her close up for myself. Because I have sometimes wondered, dearest Mama and Papa, who I really am.'

It was a thunderbolt, she knew that. But it had to be said, and now the effects of it upon them must be stopped as soon as possible.

'You see,' she hurried on, 'I've known since I was about ten years old that I was not your natural-born daughter. Papa, it was naughty of me to go into your study where for once you had left the family Bible out. I read the flyleaf, and discovered that you had found me in Candlemaker Row.'

'But why did you wait so long to tell us?' Lady Alison asked.

'I never would have at all, if you had not been so upset today.'

'Your real mother, Edina, and your father – '

'Hush, Papa.' She took their hands. '*You* are my real father, and you are my real mother, Mama, that's all I need to know. I suppose from your sad faces that you have also seen Mary Paterson?'

'Yes,' Lady Alison said with a sob.

'Then you both know that there must have been two abandoned children, not just one? Poor Mary Paterson was not so lucky as I.'

Mr Hamilton blew his nose loudly. 'That is just what is alarming us, my dear. I suspect that Mary Paterson was murdered. Whoever it was could have done it just to sell her body, that seems the most likely reason. But was there another reason, something in your early background, perhaps?'

'Oh, we have put in a terrible afternoon of worry,' Lady Alison exclaimed as there was a knock at the door and Liza came in with the tea-kettle and some hot water.

'Kathy's coming with the tray,' she announced. 'She went to answer the door.'

Five minutes later Kathy came in. 'It's someone for you, Miss Edina. A woman, and she says she's from the Society for Fallen Women. I've put her into the back sitting-room.'

'Did she give her name?' Lady Alison asked sharply.

'No, my lady. I didn't bother to ask. It's Mabel Milligan, who works in Meg Dod's bake-shop, and *she* was never at the meetings for the Fallen Women, was she, Miss Edina?'

'Ah.' Mr Hamilton stood up. 'Women can be dangerous, as well as men. I shall come with you.'

'Oh, Papa! Sit down and drink your tea! Kathy will come with me. We'll soon deal with her.'

'I'll give you ten minutes, no longer, to deal with her.' Mr Hamilton frowned.

They opened the door of the back sitting-room and Edina went in and round behind the table, while Kathy took up her position on a chair beside the door, and their visitor remained seated with a scowl on her face.

240

'Miss Milligan?' Edina asked.

'It is,' the woman said, clamping her mouth shut like a mousetrap, and giving Edina such a look of venom that she recognised her as the woman who had been in Surgeons' Hall that morning, and her fear returned.

'You wish to speak to me, Miss Milligan?'

'Alone.' The woman jerked her head in Kathy's direction.

There was some pent-up excitement in Mabel Milligan. Edina dreaded it and at the same time she knew she must find it out. Whatever the woman wished to say, it was urgent. She could tell by the way her face was twitching. She made up her mind. 'You may leave us, Kathy.'

'But, Miss Edina!'

'Leave us, Kathy,' she repeated determinedly, 'and wait in the hall.' As soon as the door closed she spoke again. 'I understand you have come on behalf of the Fallen Women of this city?'

'Ay, ye could put it that way, I daresay,' the woman sneered. She was becoming more sinister by the minute. 'It's about one Fallen Woman I've known in me time, if no' two.'

'I'm afraid I don't understand you, Miss Milligan,' Edina said coldly. 'What exactly are you saying?'

'Ye saw for yersel' today, did ye no'? Ye're only the sister o' a tart. Mary Paterson was a whore, and that makes ye no lady, so dinna try yer airs and graces on wi' me. I knew yer mother as well. Bridie, she was, from Ireland. She ran away with an Englishman and dropped both her babies on the way. If it hadn't been for that bairn finding ye, I would have been yer Ma today. I would have kept ye.'

'What bairn?' Edina asked with a shudder.

'Oh, never mind her! I'm going away back to Ireland mesel', to buy a farm. I'm just a hundred short o' two thousand. Let me have it, and I'll keep my mouth shut.'

'You want me to give you a hundred pounds to pay for your silence?'

'Ay. I'll take it today. I'll wait.'

'Indeed you will.' Mr Hamilton came out of the withdrawing-room behind the back sitting-room followed by Lady Alison, who went and sat down beside Edina and put her arms round

241

her. 'You will wait until I send for the police. That's slander and, worse than that, blackmail. My wife and I were both witnesses. Do you know who I am?'

'Yes, sir, Mr Hamilton sir . . .' Mabel Milligan tried to glib it out and brazen it out at the same time. 'Ye're a lawyer. Knowledge o' this in the town wouldn't do *you* any good, either.'

'The only person it could harm is my daughter herself, and she already knows that we adopted her. You haven't a shred of proof where from, or from whom. You will never go to Ireland. You will go to prison instead.'

'Rich folk like you could easy spare a hundred.'

Mr Hamilton pulled the cord at the side of the fire. 'James,' he said when their man appeared, 'I'm afraid we're going to have to call the police.'

'Very good, sir.' James whisked out of the room and Kathy burst in, all agog.

'No, no!' Mabel Milligan saw that Mr Hamilton meant what he said. 'All right, I'll go! But I'll get my own back for this, see if I don't!'

'Show this woman out, Kathy,' Edina said and swept past their visitor. 'She will not be back.'

Mabel Milligan made as if to turn on her, but Kathy grasped her from behind and forcibly ejected her. 'Out ye go,' she said with great satisfaction, and slammed the door.

'I hope it was all worthwhile,' one of the chair men said with his eyebrows raised when she landed on the pavement, perhaps more suddenly than she had anticipated.

'Oh, I've got the money to go back to the High Street, if that's what ye mean,' she snapped, and got in the sedan and drew the little curtains to shut out the world.

Still thoroughly agitated, disappointed and on the verge of tears when she got to the High Street, Mabel Milligan got out of the sedan and did something even more unusual. She went into Swanston's tavern. Never one to drink, she thought she needed something drastic now to pull herself together before it was six o'clock and time to go to the bake-shop.

She ordered a small brandy, and the price the man behind the bar demanded for it was shocking, just shocking.

'That's Mabel Milligan, out o' Meg Dod's bake-shop,' said Hare, recognising her long thin figure. 'All alone in the world she is, and loaded.'

'Terrible it is, the price of drink.' A man materialised beside Mabel. 'Let me buy it for you.'

'Why should ye?' she said rudely. 'I dinna need yer money.'

'Well then, let's just say it's in memory of a bag of penny pies you once sold us. Jasus, I can taste them yet, so I can! But come over and join us, won't you? We can't let a lady stand when we have a spare seat at our table.'

An hour and four brandies later Mabel had forgotten every care and woe she had in the world. She had also forgotten the bake-shop as Burke and Hare helped her down to Tanners' Close, on the way to a party there.

Och, this was the life! This was really living! It *was* her lucky day, after all.

Burke and Hare laughed to each other behind her back. She was easy meat.

A week after the final examinations the medical students converged at the notice-board shortly before nine o'clock in the morning, in a silence best described as very highly charged. Some shuffled their feet and looked ready to cry, others looked upwards, clearly at prayer, and one actually vomited.

'God help me,' Josh said with quiet desperation, his face so pale that it appeared luminously green in contrast with his carroty hair.

Gavin looked round for Cardew, but he was nowhere to be seen, and just then the dark green door marked PROCTOR was flung open. Well, he thought, when it remained open and nothing else happened for at least five minutes, it's a start, I suppose.

Then the proctor appeared in the doorway with a large sheet of paper in his hands and there was a hiss from the crowd, for a nasty, officious little man he was too, with his strange round peaked cap on his head and under it a total lack of humour;

243

and he might just as well have cut short his theatricals, however immensely important this moment was for him, since every eye was fixed on the paper.

But no, he had to stalk over to the notice-board, and with maddening slowness pin it up deliberately and precisely by its four corners, one, bang – in went the pin – two, bang, three, bang – and at long last, four. After that he was swamped, drowned in the tide of students surging forward, and shouts of triumph or groans of despair filled the air.

Gavin was in the last wave, and found himself trying to read the results with eyes which simply would not focus for a few nervous seconds. Then he saw that they were divided into three categories; distinctions at the top, passes in the middle and failures at the bottom.

Joshua McLean and William Fergusson had both obtained a distinction. He found his own name, simply unable to believe 'Gavin Mitchell' fairly high up on the list of passes, and just as he was marvelling at the goodness of God up galloped Cardew, nerveless as usual, and able to pick out his own name at ten paces.

'What did I tell you, dear soul?' He stabbed a finger at it, last on the pass list. 'Now we're all doctors. We're MDs!'

'Not until we pay the bursar ten pounds,' Gavin reminded him. 'You can't be capped or get the scroll otherwise.'

'I say, if you're going that way, do you think you could pay my fee along with yours, one of you chaps? I'm a bit short of the readies this morning.'

'Not a chance,' Gavin assured him.

'Don't even ask,' Josh echoed.

The ceremony in the large College hall was quite a family occasion. Josh introduced them to his father, Reverend McLean, who was instantly recognisable as one of the three bullies with guns who had done their best to kill them at the Dalkeith kirkyard, but his plump little mother seemed pleasant, if tried.

Across the hall Gavin saw an older, faded version of Cardew

with a large purple nose escorting a lady who looked imperious, to say the least, in the Hamiltons' party. It was easy to trace both blood lines in their son.

'My father, Major Sharpe,' Cardew introduced them, 'and my mother, Mrs Cornelia Sharpe.'

'So you're Gavin,' Mrs Cornelia said with a tinkling, condescending laugh. 'Some doctor's son, I believe?'

'Yes,' said Dr Mitchell, joining them at that psychological moment, 'and I'm *some* doctor, believe me.'

'Really, Cornelia!' Lady Alison led her back to her seat.

'Darling,' Edina giggled as Gavin escorted her back to hers, 'she's a scream! Cardew's just like her!'

Dr and Mrs Mitchell with Miss Phyllis Plenderleith and the rest of their brood took their seats at the back of the hall, and after more milling about for a minute or two the audience finally settled.

Suddenly there was a knock, and in came the procession of university and town dignitaries preceded by the University Mace. There was a prayer first, for all young doctors and their patients, and then the Dean explained what would happen next, a clerk read out the names of all those successful who had paid their ten pounds, and one by one they all filed up on to the stage to collect their diplomas. Suddenly, it was all over.

Josh melted away and was next seen in the company of Professor Hunter, his wife and a very pretty dark young lady. Dr Mitchell addressed the rest of his family, the Hamiltons and the Sharpes. 'Now! Off to the Crown Hotel,' he said, 'for the celebration lunch.'

'No, you don't,' Mrs Mitchell grasped Miss Phyllis's arm when she retreated, 'you're coming with us, after all you've done for our boy.'

The party sat round a large oval table. The only one missing was Mrs Fanny, and Gavin was on tenterhooks in case Lady Alison asked her so-called mother, Mrs Cornelia, why she was absent. Happily, she never did, and the gathering was a great success, improving bottle by bottle as Dr Mitchell kept the champagne coming. Mr Hamilton made a speech on behalf of himself and his wife informing everyone that their beloved daughter Edina Grace was now formally betrothed to Gavin, with their blessing.

The two mothers dabbed at their eyes, Gavin and Edina smiled at each other, the Mitchell children giggled and Major Sharpe was by now incapable of saying anything except 'By Jove, don't you know' every now and then.

'I'll have to get him into a bed.' Mrs Cornelia prepared to depart.

'Such a pity.' Lady Alison smiled serenely, and over at another table Josh and the dark young girl exchanged hot, amorous glances.

'But before we all go,' Dr Mitchell stood up, 'I have an announcement to make. I have decided to retire, now that there is another Dr Mitchell in the family. The rest of us can hardly wait to go and live in Almondbank, so if Gavin will accept it the Gilmerton practice is now his.'

'If I will accept it, Father!' said his overjoyed son.

'And the house.' Mrs Mitchell smiled at Edina, who got up and kissed everyone, including Cardew.

'A carriage has arrived for you, Dr Sharpe,' she heard a waiter murmuring in his other ear.

'Yes,' Cardew said, 'I must go,' and they all went out with him on to Princes Street to wave goodbye.

At the same time Professor Hunter and his party with Josh arrived on the pavement beside them.

'What are you going to do now, Josh?' Gavin asked him.

'I'm going on, to specialise in obstetrics.'

'Under me,' said the Professor, who had overheard them, 'and he's coming to live with us while he's at it. Of course, to make things legal, he and our dear daughter Belinda will first be married.'

'Congratulations, Josh,' Gavin had time to say as Cardew leapt up into the carriage. Inside sat Mrs Fanny, more beautiful and more voluptuous than ever, now that she was at least six months pregnant, by Gavin's calculations, and still by some miracle undetected by the older Sharpes.

'Well, we're off, dear boy.' Cardew smiled down at him.

'Cardew! You won't – you won't –' Gavin gazed at Fanny's bump.

'Of course not. We can marry now! We're going to have dozens of little sprogs, simply dozens!'

'But . . .' Gavin lowered his voice. 'Your ventures into rubber?'

'No, no! I've gone the other way! It was a question of giving up gracefully in the end. If you can't beat it, join it! Let it all keep happening, the more the merrier,' said Cardew, guffawing. 'Just think of all those dear ladies in London who'll want their little embarrassments removed! There's an absolute fortune in it, old boy.'

'You're going to London?'

'All the way to Harley Street!' Cardew promised as the carriage moved forward. 'Well, a few streets removed, to begin with. I'll put up my brass plate. DR CARDEW SHARPE,' he yelled out of the window, 'and under it, *WOMAN CARE*. Clever, isn't it?'

'The Lord works in mysterious ways,' Miss Phyllis remarked as Gavin escorted her home. 'How did that young man manage to get through?'

'In his own way he's quite brilliant, Miss Phyllis, with a sheer genius for turning disaster into victory. He survived the three years entirely on his wits, with scarcely a penny from his parents.'

'Quite a character?'

'I shall not look on his like again.'

'There's always one in every year, Gavin.' Miss Phyllis went on to tell him about the escapades of one of her brother's friends. 'They usually settle down, in time,' she added.

'You do know that I would never have got through without you?' Gavin assured her when they got back to her house and he gathered together his things.

'Ye'll aye come back and see me, dearie?' Miss Plenderleith's long lugubrious face lit up in a smile.

'Always.' He bent and kissed her; then, taking up his bundle, he headed back to Charlotte Square and to a new life, now that

he had become a Doctor of Medicine of the great University of
Edinburgh.

That summer, after all the students had gone away and the
hordes of visitors arrived to see Auld Reekie, Billy Burke
and William Hare did quite well. Together they portered, and
separately Hare sold as many herring as he could carry, while
Billy mended shoes. They hadn't turned their hands to anything
more serious for quite some time, not since Mabel Milligan, and
Hare was getting restless now that the dark nights of October
had come again.

Ann Little, Helen's friend, had been down to the Burkes' one
morning, and came back to her husband angry. 'Helen's getting
one of the pigs ready to roast, and that old woman Docherty
they picked up months ago is hollowing out a turnip for a
lantern, making the teeth grin. You would think she was one
of Helen's family, and not me.'

'It's Friday, the thirty-first of October, Ann – Hallowe'en –
and old Mrs Docherty's a fine old soul. She does all the work
when Helen's out hawking shoes.'

'Well, they're going to have a booze, a big one, by all
appearances. So why haven't they asked us?'

'They've been good enough to take us in and pay for us.
Beggars can't be choosers,' said James Little, shrugging, as a
knock came to their door.

'We've still got our guest downstairs.' Billy smiled at them.
'You know she's Irish, so in her honour we're inviting a lot
of Irish friends round to see her. It's going to be noisy for
you and the wee one, so Mr Hare has kindly invited you to
stay in his room overnight. You'll come to a booze with us
tomorrow? There'll be plenty of ham left over.'

'That's kind of you, Mr Burke,' James Little said. 'We
wouldn't like to be in the way,' he added as Ann got the
baby ready and wrapped him in a shawl.

'You?' Billy laughed. 'In the way? Follow me now, because
it's dark, so it is.'

'It *is* dark out here,' Ann said as they crossed over to Hare's
house. 'When I was a bairn I used to be so frightened on

Hallowe'en night, with the ghosts coming out and the witches . . . Do you believe the dead return this night?'

'No!' Billy almost shouted, and stopped with his hand on his heart.

'That's only talk for bairns, Ann,' James Little said, but he looked at Billy curiously.

The wind had risen to a gale. The moan of it was like banshees wailing up the close and along the passage.

'It's in here,' said Billy, showing them in. 'Mr and Mrs Hare won't be needing their bed tonight, so you can have it. We'll see you in the morning, then?'

'Goodnight, Mr Burke,' they said as the door closed. Ann put the baby to bed and she and James sat on the edge of it. 'There's no more to be said, then, is there?' Ann sighed. 'And no more to be done except wait for tomorrow and hope that Helen and Burke don't forget us, and save us a bit of that pig.'

'The smell of it's going clean round my heart,' James agreed, 'and now that's them started the jigging. I can hear the music. The whisky will be flowing like water, too, down there. I could do with a drink, right now.'

'Well, we daren't complain, James . . . It's a roof over our heads, and it *was* thoughtful of them to see that our sleep wasn't disturbed.'

'Yes,' James said, 'if that was the real reason why they moved us.'

'What other reason could there be?'

Michael Docherty, her son, had died of the drink, so Mr Burke and Mr Hare had told her, but now that she had got over it Mrs Docherty was having the time of her life. Neighbours were arriving, people called Law and Connaway and a young lad, Murphy. Mr Burke was playing his pipe and all the folk were dancing, and when he wasn't playing he was singing the old Irish songs so that she could join in.

Then they began to tell stories, some of them enough to scare the hair off your head, and it being Hallowe'en and all, and some of them so funny, she thought she'd die laughing. Once when she was dancing with Mr Hare she stubbed her toe, but she didn't even feel it with so much drink in her, and Mrs Burke kept filling her up with more. Ach, sure, and she'd sober up as soon as she got some of that pig inside her!

How the fight started she didn't quite know, but soon Mr Burke and Mr Hare were going at it hammer and tongs, so that all the other guests were frightened and just melted away. There was just this awful shouting and scuffling and panting, and Mr Hare was winning, when she really liked Mr Burke better.

Mrs Docherty left her stool by the fire and tottered up to them. She caught a punch from Mr Hare for her pains, fell to the floor and was unable to get up. But she could still yell.

'Get the police,' she shouted at the top of her voice when she saw Mrs Burke and Mrs Hare leaving, although how that Mrs Burke could leave her poor husband when Hare was going to kill him for sure, she didn't know. '*Murder*!' she screamed, and kept on screaming. '*Murder*!'

Then she was grasped savagely by the throat.

19

'By GOD, THAT was the best one yet,' Billy said, 'and it's not even midnight.'

'Practice makes perfect,' Hare agreed. 'How many's that we've done in now? Fifteen, sixteen?'

'More like twenty, and that's not counting the ones you and Maggie have done on your own behind my back,' Billy's tongue lashed out suddenly.

'Well, that's a bad mark on her throat, so it is,' said Hare, trying to change the subject. 'Could we just say it was from stuffing her in a box?'

'They'll never ask, anyway,' Billy said, undressing the old woman. He doubled her up so that she stiffened in the position; then he pushed her under a pile of straw near the bed before he went to unlock the door for Helen and Maggie.

'What a racket!' Maggie said. 'They must have heard "Murder!" for miles around.'

'I'm going to get Bain here, to show him what we've just "found" in a wynd,' Billy said.

'No, that isn't safe,' Helen said. 'Deliver to him tomorrow instead.'

'It's a feeling I have,' Billy argued. 'We've got to get rid of her.'

'Forget it,' Hare urged him. 'We've no more tea-chests anyway,

251

and besides, here's Murphy again. That lad's becoming a perfect nuisance. What about *him*, Billy?'

'Not tonight, but I'm after thinking.'

They had more drams, until young Murphy grew sleepy and curled up by the fire, but by that time the Burkes and Hares had climbed into the bed together and fallen asleep.

Hugh Alston, a few doors away, slept no more that night. Some hours before, when he'd heard that cry of 'Murder!' he'd got up to look for a policeman, but none was to be seen. Perhaps it had only been a drunken brawl, and God knew there plenty of them at the West Port, but all the same he was still awake at daybreak.

At nine o'clock in the morning the Burkes and Hares got up, and Billy went to ask the Littles to come for their breakfast: cold roast ham and hot bread and porridge – and maybe a wee dram?

'Och, that's right good of you,' James Little smiled, all his black thoughts of last night melted away. Ann dressed the baby hurriedly and downstairs they went behind Billy. 'I've lost a wee stocking belonging to the bairn,' she said. 'Maybe I left it at your house, sometime?'

'We'll soon look for the stocking, don't you be worrying,' he said.

Hare was pouring whisky when they arrived. 'What happened to the little old lady?' Ann asked.

'Madge Docherty? Some lady!' Helen sneered. 'I had to kick her out. She was getting too free with Billy.'

'At her age?' Ann looked hungrily at the cold ham and the hot porridge. Burke and Hare and their women never seemed to go short.

For their part Burke and Hare glowered at her, and filled her full of food and drink, her and that long drink of water she called her husband. They sent silent signals to Maggie and Helen, who both got the same idea at the same time about needing to run for some more bread and a few sausages.

Ann stuffed her face for a while with cold ham, and then sat back. 'That was lovely, Mr Burke. I couldn't eat another thing.'

'A pipe of tobacco, then?' he offered.

Ann sat puffing it for a minute or two and then handed it over to her husband before she pulled her child on to her lap. 'Look!' she said. 'One of his little feet is blue with the cold without his stocking.'

'Warm him up at the fire, then,' Hare snarled. 'We'll look round in a minute.'

James Little took the pipe out of his mouth and handed it back to his wife. 'It's funny,' he said. 'Daft Jamie never smoked. He only took snuff. Yet they said he was reeking of drink and his feet had been cut off.'

There was a strange cold silence in the filthy room. Billy was the first to recover. 'His feet cut off?' he asked incredulously. 'How do you know that, Mr Little?'

'I heard the students talking in Swanston's. Whoever killed him cut off his feet and his head, but still they knew him right away, and the smell of snuff besides confirmed it.'

'We never – ' Hare began indignantly, and then changed direction. 'Och, they're all drunks, these poors that get murdered! That's how they're so easy caught,' he said, getting up with a full bottle of whisky and sprinkling it over the heap of straw on one of the beds.

That was when nameless suspicions first entered Ann Little's mind. No sensible man emptied bottles of whisky over the floor, over the furniture, and especially over a heap of straw.

'Are you mad?' James Little asked him, shocked.

'Och. I'm just emptying the bottle so that we can get another, isn't that right, Billy?' Hare's smile was a stretch of the lips over wolf's teeth, and Ann, with a queer feeling on her that they should find the stocking and go quickly, got up and began to search under the bed.

'Jesus Christ, you'll be setting the house on fire, and you with a lit pipe in your mouth,' Billy yelled.

'It's gone out,' she said, and now she knew for certain that there was something very far wrong. Billy flung out saying he was going for more whisky.

'You'll excuse us for a minute,' Hare said. 'I'll go and see if the women remembered to fetch tea-chests for Mr Burke's shoes.'

253

'They've got eyes like hawks, those two,' he panted, running after Billy. 'We'll have to do them both in now, this minute.'

'Yes, they've got eyes like hawks,' Billy said savagely, 'and you're the one who's left them alone with Madge Docherty's body. Get back and stop them searching, for Christ's sake!'

Left alone with the child and James half asleep on his stool at the fireside, Ann got up and raked desperately at the foot of the bed for the little stocking. Then she lifted the straw. 'James! James! Wake up!' she screamed. 'Look!'

'It's Mrs Docherty!'

'With blood on her face and her throat!'

'Let's get out of here! Quick!' her husband said urgently.

Horrified, James Little with his wife and baby fled out into the passage and bumped into Helen coming back in carrying a tea-chest. 'Do you know there's been a murder done?' he asked.

'Don't inform, if you have any mercy in your hearts,' Helen begged.

'But what happened to that old woman?'

'Her heart gave out, with all that drinking and jigging. Billy's away out now, looking for her son Michael, so that she can get a proper burial.'

'I don't believe you,' James Little said, 'not with all that blood on her, and stripped naked like that and hidden. That's only a story about Michael Docherty as well. We all know he's been dead for months – but how did he die? – that's what we would like to know.'

'Ann, you're like one of my own,' Helen sobbed. 'Say nothing and it's ten pounds I'll give you every week.'

'Blood money?' Ann said.

'So you sell them,' James Little said. 'Come, Ann. We've heard enough.' He dragged her out into the close, with Helen trying to stop them, sobbing and pleading.

'What's all this, then?' Maggie Hare came into Tanners' Close from the Grassmarket, carrying another empty tea-chest.

'They found the old woman,' Helen sobbed.

'Ay, it was a terrible thing to happen, and at a booze, too. She died of consumption,' Maggie told them.

'It was her heart as well,' said Helen quickly, with a glare at Maggie.

'If you were going to make up a story, you should have had the sense to make up the same one,' James Little said. 'Come on, Ann. We're leaving, and we won't be coming back.'

Maggie put down the tea-chest and barred their way. 'You're a right bitch, Ann Little. I should never have taken you in, you and that old wreck of a husband of yours! Christ! I'll smash your faces in, so I will!'

'And after Billy and me *paying* for you, even,' Helen screamed at them, keeping Maggie at bay.

'Run!' James Little grabbed his wife's arm and they scuttled away, leaving the two women fighting each other. Their mutual bitter hatred came out at last, and they clawed each other's faces, kicking and spitting, until Helen fell to the ground clutching a handful of Maggie's hair, her face a mass of blood.

'You Irish sow!' she yelled. 'I never trusted you! If it hadn't been for Billy, you would have killed me, too!'

Maggie reeled back with two blackening eyes and the look of the devil on her face. 'You're right there, by God!' she shouted. 'I hate you, you skinny Scottish whore!'

'We've got to find some place to go, James,' said Ann as she wept the following afternoon. 'I'm tired of trailing about begging and homeless with wee Jamie in my arms. I couldn't go through another night like last night, sleeping in the street. Oh God, I'm tired out . . . Would we not be better to go back to Log's Lodgings?'

'Never. That's an evil house if ever there was one. We were lucky to get out with our lives. We'll find somewhere.' James Little spoke the hopeless words as hopefully as he could. 'We're bound to. The biggest mistake we ever made was to go to Tanners' Close in the first place.'

Frank Clarke overheard them from the next close. By now he was desperate, so desperate that any word about Tanners' Close he was going to investigate. He came out on to the Grassmarket behind them. 'Are you in trouble?' he asked in a sympathetic voice.

At the sight of the uniform Ann immediately shrank away. James stood to attention. 'No, sir.'

'Well, I am,' Frank told them. 'I'm in trouble. I've lost a little old Irish lady, Mrs Docherty by name. I saw her going into Tanners' Close weeks ago, and I haven't seen her coming out. I'm worried about her.'

'As well you might be,' James Little said, and started to talk.

Frank couldn't believe it. Before him stood a man and a woman who looked like beggars. For a minute he just stared at them, these two who had just given him the lucky break of a lifetime. Now he would get his promotion, and then he could marry Kathy. He could have kissed them. As it was, he put his arms round them both.

'Say no more here,' he said. 'Save it for the police office. I'll take you there and you'll get a nice cup of tea.'

He got them to Riddle's Court and into the office where a woman took charge of the baby and fed him, Mr and Mrs Little got their cup of tea and a rest, while he outlined their story to Sergeant-Major Fisher. It was half past three in the afternoon.

'You're off duty now, Clarke?'

'Yes, sir. Back on again at eight tonight, and the same tomorrow.'

'We'll have to let this family sleep here tonight, I suppose. They could be called as witnesses, if all this comes to something, so we can't let them just go off. God knows where they might wander to.'

'No, sir.'

'Do you know of an empty land we could put them into tomorrow?'

'Well, there's Mabel Milligan's. She disappeared all of a sudden, although everyone knew she was talking of going to Ireland to buy a farm. She didn't even bother to warn Meg Dod, though.'

'*Didn't* she, by God?' Sergeant-Major Fisher opened his eyes very wide. 'I wonder, did she ever get there, after all?'

* * *

Gavin, married now on a golden September day to Edina, had been practising medicine for about six weeks when he spoke to his wife at the breakfast table that same Thursday morning. 'David Chisholm and I have come to an arrangement. At this rate neither of us is ever getting a break, so we have agreed that if I keep an eye on his practice one weekend a month he'll do the same for me.'

'Thank goodness! I'm sure Edith Chisholm will be as relieved as I am to hear such common sense! When does this arrangement start?'

'Tomorrow, sweetheart. Just in time for Hallowe'en. Now, I wonder, *where* shall we go for the weekend? Charlotte Square, perhaps?'

'Stop teasing, Gavin Mitchell! I'll go and get our bags packed.'

'I'll stop teasing when you stop looking so pretty at eight o'clock in the morning.'

'Happy, you mean. I love you, Gavin.'

'And I love you.'

It had been a long, wonderful honeymoon, but Edina came right down to earth again with a bang as soon as she saw Kathy's distraught face the following morning at 13, Charlotte Square. 'Whatever is the matter?' she asked her as they were going upstairs to unpack in Edina's old room. 'Tell me at once! Is it Frank?'

At the mention of Constable Frank Clarke's name, Kathy broke down altogether. 'Is it Frank?' she echoed bitterly. 'When do I ever see him nowadays? He spends all his time on the murder cases.'

'Calm down, dear,' said Edina, rubbing Kathy's heaving shoulders. 'Try and explain.'

'He knows who's doing them. Two Irishmen called Burke and Hare.'

'*Those* two? They're the ones who took Cardew's coffin to Dr Knox!'

'But he can never prove anything, and he's far more interested in all that than ever he is in me.'

'That's rubbish, Kathy, and you know it! He's determined,

257

just so that he can get promoted, just so that he can get enough money to marry you! You *are* a goose!'

Kathy smiled a watery smile. 'You don't know how much I've missed you,' she said sadly.

'Well, now I'm here. But not for long.'

'How long can you stay?'

'Just till Sunday. Let's see . . . This is Friday, so if we can arrange everything today, we can put my plan into action tomorrow night.'

'But what about your mama and papa – *and* Mr Gavin?'

'We'll think of something. In the meantime Frank needs help, and we're the very two to give it him. Listen to this . . .'

On Friday morning Constable Frank Clarke escorted James and Ann Little and their baby down to World's End Close and opened up Mabel Milligan's old land for them. 'There's been a fall of soot,' he said. 'The place is in a mess.'

'Don't worry about that,' said Ann Little with a smile as she looked round the little room. 'It's a home, at last.'

'I'm sure to see the chimney-sweep some time this morning. I'll tell him to come at once. His name is Donald Affleck.' With their thanks ringing in his ears Frank left them to their new life.

'We can do nothing until the sweep comes,' Ann said. 'We can't light a fire, even if we had sticks and coal. I can't heat up water to wash this place, even if we had some water. We can't even have a cup of tea, and we've no tea, either.'

'Cheer up, Ann,' James Little smiled. 'We left Log's Lodgings in such a hurry that we didn't pay them out of my pension. We've just got enough for water, a bag of coal, some tea and milk for our Jamie. We might even get some penny pies, if there's anything left over once I pay the sweep.'

'Constable Clarke didn't waste any time,' Ann said when there was a knock at the door and a voice shouted, 'Sweep!'

'The lum must have been full, judging by all that lot,' Donald Affleck told them. Then he had a look up the chimney. 'But there's still something sticking there, so I'll sweep it again. You stay in here and give me a shout out of the window when you hear my brush in your lum so I'll know I'm in the right one. It's hard to tell in these old tenements.'

About ten minutes later they heard the scratches of his brush up the chimney. 'Right!' James Little shouted up. 'Go ahead!'

'Oh, my God!' Ann screamed when something hard came down in a cloud of soot. 'What's that? Is it a bird?'

'It's a box,' her husband told her, and quickly wrapped it up in a sack just before Donald Affleck tramped back into the room to inspect the chimney again.

'That's better,' he said. 'I can see the sky now. Was there a stone or something stuck up there? I felt something hard coming away.'

'You're right.' James Little nodded. 'It was a stone. I threw it away.'

'Well, you can start cleaning up now,' said Donald Affleck as he mentally counted the coins James put into his black palm, 'and I'll be going.'

They listened to the tramp of his boots dying away and then James took the box out of the sack. 'People don't put tin boxes up the lum unless they're hiding something,' he told his wife.

'So what is it, then?' And when he finally prised open the lid, she cried, 'Oh, my God, James! It's money! It's a fortune!' Tears sprang from Ann's eyes.

'It *is* a fortune,' he said seriously, when he counted it. 'It's a hundred pounds short of two thousand. It must have belonged to Mabel Milligan. That means she never went to Ireland, after all.'

'Poor soul! We can guess what happened to her, James . . . But what are we going to do with her money?'

'Well, we're not going to draw attention to ourselves by spending it, that's absolutely certain. Give me time to think about it. Then I'll probably invest the bulk of it in a bank for Jamie's future.'

'And for the future of all our other children. Oh, James, I knew I wasn't wrong to marry you!'

*   *   *

259

On Friday afternoon, Frank went to Charlotte Square to see Kathy. 'And about time, too,' she said. 'If you hadn't come here this afternoon I was going to come looking for *you*, Frank Clarke.'

'Yes, Frank,' Edina said. 'We've got a proposition for you.'

'And you'll never get a better offer,' Kathy told him.

They spent the next hour talking about it before Edina left them to go out with Gavin, and at eight o'clock that night when Frank went back on duty he spoke so convincingly to Sergeant-Major Fisher that Edina's plot was accepted and extended.

'And these two young ladies are willing to act as decoys tomorrow night, Clarke? Well . . .' he considered, 'it's a very long shot, but something must be done before the Edinburgh police lose credibility altogether, with Christopher North speculating in the newspapers every day.'

'Yes, sir. But our decoys will need protection, or else it cannot be contemplated. One of the young ladies is my future wife.'

'Leave it with me,' Sergeant-Major Fisher said.

Frank, sweating with excitement, came out of the police office to start out on his beat just in time to see Mr Hamilton and Gavin parting company. 'Dr Gavin, sir,' he said, touching him on the arm.

'A gentle approach, Frank,' Gavin joked. 'Not the touch on the collar?' Then his smile faded when he looked into the policeman's face. 'What is it, man?' he asked. 'What is it?'

'You are not to do it, Edina. It's far too dangerous.'

'It probably won't work anyway. Desperate last resorts seldom do. But *please* don't stop us now when it's all arranged! Kathy and I will be surrounded by policemen, six deep.'

'Very well. But you're not going out on such a hare-brained exploit without me,' he said sternly. 'Did you really think I wouldn't find out about it, Edina?'

'I didn't stop to think, that's true.' She smiled at him so ruefully and lovingly that all he could do was groan and smile back when she added, 'And it's in such a good cause, isn't it, dearest Gavin?'

'Kathy and I are going out guising tonight, Mama,' Edina told her mother. 'It'll be just like the old days. But don't worry. Gavin and Frank are coming, too.'

'It's so cold, dear. Wrap up well, then. We will be here to welcome the children as usual, won't we, Eden?'

'Yes, my dear,' Mr Hamilton agreed, looking at their daughter in such a way that she knew he had been told all about tonight's plan. 'Just be very careful, Edina.'

'Do you think there are plenty of apples to give them when they sing us their little songs?' Lady Alison asked anxiously.

'Plenty, my dear,' Mr Hamilton replied, looking at the laden bowl.

In the showy but tatty red dress Edina swayed down the High Street far more convincingly than Mary Paterson had ever done. Kathy walked beside her, looking remarkably like Janet Brown, who had left Edinburgh to get married some time ago.

'I always loved dressing up. How do I look?' Edina asked, thoroughly enjoying herself.

'Just like a taupie. More like Mary Paterson than Mary Paterson herself. It's that red dress I got at the Jew's, and this one's not much better.' Kathy looked down at her own dress, a screaming shade of blue.

'Well, where is it?'

'Here. This is it. Swanston's.' Kathy shivered, for it was from Swanston's that Mary Paterson had gone out and was never seen again. She looked round for their protectors. Thank God Frank was there, up the street a bit, and she jerked her head to show him that they were going in.

There had never been a sudden hush in Swanston's, not even for Mary, not in all these years, not while the drink was flowing fast. But there was now, as Edina parted the crowd of men like a scythe cutting through grass and sat down in the middle of the bar-room at the same little table as Mary used to. It was as if she knew it by instinct.

'*Jasus God*,' Billy swore, and choked. Then he crossed himself, with all the colour drained out of his normally ruddy face. 'It's a ghost, so it is! It's her, come back to haunt us!' He

261

waited in horror for the blood to stream down her nose and ooze out from the corner of her painted smiling mouth, as it had done the last time he had seen her.

'For Christ's sake, get a grip!' Underneath the table in the corner Hare was kicking him viciously and repeatedly on the shins. 'Do you want to give the game away altogether? Everyone can hear you.' But still Billy sat, terrified. 'Mary Paterson is dead,' Hare hissed. 'We sold her long ago. That's not Mary Paterson, just a bloody good imitation of her. Jesus, it is! But that's Janet Brown that's with her, all right.'

Billy shuddered so violently that he could hardly raise his glass to his lips to down the raw whisky in an effort to cure his shakes in one gulp, but even after that he remained cold sober and speechless. There had been too many nightmares, fifteen or sixteen at least before he lost count, and now here was one spilling over into real life. He was going mad. He always knew he would, before it was all over.

'Get up and get going!' Hare kicked him harder than ever. 'That's twenty guineas sitting over there staring us in the face! I would go myself, but for some reason folk are feared o' me.'

Another whisky brought Billy almost out of the jaws of hell, far enough to find himself in the most flaming temper of his life. He tossed off another one, thinking furiously about this tart here who had the effrontery to imitate Mary Paterson and nearly scare him to death. *He would have her*, he vowed, a veil of red in front of his eyes and murder in his heart.

Wound up now almost into a state of trance, he passed by the table in the middle, noted the drinks on it, ordered another round and sat down beside the two drabs. 'Have a drink on me,' he begged in his soft Irish accent while he smiled into Edina's eyes – and oh God, it was easy, after all. She smiled back and winked. She actually winked. 'There's a Hallowe'en booze goin' on at my house later,' he said, 'and a bit of a dance, so there is.'

'A dance!' Edina giggled. 'Lead the way!'

She smiled boldly and wriggled her bare shoulders back into her fur tippet as if to the manner born, and with a very subdued

Kathy beside her swaggered out behind Burke who was joined by Hare.

Yes, she thought. These were certainly the two awful men she'd seen carrying Cardew's coffin. They must have sunk to much lower depths since then, and for the first time that evening she had a few misgivings. But she pushed them away.

It was a strange procession down into the Grassmarket minutes later. Edina and Kathy linked arms hilariously with Burke and Hare. A little distance behind, Frank and two other policemen shadowed them from doorway to doorway, and behind them more policemen closed ranks.

While they were in Swanston's Gavin went on down to the West Port of the Grassmarket, according to plan. He was well acquainted with that part of seedy old Edinburgh, he thought with severe pangs of conscience, for it was here that he had once shared a room with Mary Paterson . . . However, all that was safely buried in the past, thank God.

He came to Lady Lawson Street, and the past came back to hit him between the eyes again when he remembered Dr Knox cutting off poor old Jock McCullough's leg in Number 3. There were policemen all along this narrow venomous street, he saw thankfully, and Tanners' Close was the next street along.

'We've got Log's Lodging surrounded, Dr Mitchell,' one of the young officers whispered. 'Sergeant-Major Fisher is in Tanners' Close itself with six men and the police surgeon, Dr Black.'

'Well, I've got to be in there as well,' Gavin whispered back. 'My wife is one of the decoys, God help us all.'

'Yes. A very brave lady, sir.'

'Is there any way I could watch her? Is there a window in that terrible house?'

'Only one, but it looks out on to a pigsty. Follow me. There are no pigs in it, fortunately. But it still stinks,' he added.

'Jesus Christ, it stinks, all right!'

'Flatten yourself against the wall, sir. If you look inside you'll see their women. Drinking, of course.'

Any nervous hilarity Gavin was feeling at floundering round in the muck of the pigsty deserted him as soon as he got a

263

glimpse of the filthy fireside straw with the two hags stretched across it, a bottle between them, and the unspeakable room beyond. His Edina couldn't possibly be entering a hovel like this.

But entering it she was, as he saw to his horror.

20

W HEN THEY LEFT the comparative safety of Swanston's with Burke and Hare, Edina's courage almost deserted her. It wasn't so bad while they were going down the High Street where there were other people walking along, all dressed up, but down in the Grassmarket, away from all the noise of the guisers and the merriment of the Royal Mile, there was an eerie silence. Here there were no guisers. There was no money down here for any such frivolity, and the darkness felt cold and hostile.

Burke especially tried to keep their spirits up, chirping away like a sparrow, but Edina's pricked ears caught beyond his chatter the wail of some child behind a tatter-curtained window, the scrape of a fiddle somewhere else, and the little grating sound a swinging sign made in the wind outside a darkened tavern called the White Hart.

She managed to make out the sign and to peer at the name 'Crooked Lane' before Burke and Hare rushed them past it and took them into Tanners' Close. They gave her no time to contemplate the dark void they were stepping into before they were walking along a passage rank with filth – and, she knew, lined with silent unseen policemen.

They stopped at a door and Hare knocked on it three times. There were scufflings inside, and then a woman opened it.

'Me wife, Helen,' Burke said by way of introduction, and

put an arm round her to steady her. 'Where have all the others gone, Nellie darlin'?'

'Maggie's just gone out with Ned Murphy for some whisky, and left me to peel the onions and the praties.'

'That's it – ham and onions and praties. Nothing like it.' Burke rubbed his hands in anticipation and Hare rushed about, stirring up the fire and drawing ragged curtains round beds heaped up with straw that was none too clean.

Scattered about the floor was more straw, mixed with a litter of tea-leaves, rinds of bacon and potato peelings. There were dirty, battered cooking pots on the hearth, and another tattered curtain drooped at the side of a grimy window. Edina judged from the all-pervading stench that they must be next door to a pigsty. She was glad when Helen began drunkenly to peel the onions.

'Sit down, sit down!' Burke set two stools for her and Kathy beside the fire, and Edina tried her best not to look too much round the room, and not to wonder if it was in here that Mary Paterson had met her death.

Then in came Ned Murphy, a cheerful lad of about sixteen or seventeen, with the whisky and his fiddle. The ham began to spit in the frying pan beside the onions and Ned Murphy had played only a tune or two before the first knock was heard at the door.

Hare's face darkened even further when he opened it. A couple stood outside. 'Is it a booze ye're having?' asked the man.

'Come in,' Burke said, shouldering Hare aside. 'It's only a bit of a jig.' Then, with her ears tuned in to their voices and nothing else, Edina heard him muttering fiercely in an aside to Hare. 'You bloody fool! *What did I tell you? We should have got rid of the old woman!*'

There were more knocks at the door and more people – the Laws and the Connaways – came in, and the dancing began. Within half an hour the party was in full swing. Ned Murphy and Burke sang old Irish songs and the lively neighbours joined in. Every time Hare filled up Edina's glass or Kathy's they emptied them gradually and surreptitiously into the fireside straw.

Hare grabbed Edina, wanting her to dance with him, when the door burst open and a terrible drab mean-faced woman stood glaring at the scene inside. Her eyes fixed on Edina in a way that scared her utterly, this time to her very soul.

'Maggie!' Hare said.

'An' what's going on here, as soon as I turn my back? Who's this?' Maggie poked Edina viciously and then began to shriek and curse and spit at her like a demon. 'Do you know he's my husband? The faithless pig!'

'Stop it, Maggie,' Hare said. 'Can you not see what we're doing? Why did you have to come back?'

Then Maggie really rounded on him. 'Some husband you are, William Hare! Always after taupies! Canna keep yer dirty hands off them!' she screeched, and began to kick and punch him and claw at his face with her hands.

It had been a booze and a jig one minute; now it was a drunken brawl. Everyone joined in, and at the height of it Edina saw Kathy being pulled out of the room in a flash by somebody. Billy saw that too, and it was then that he lost patience.

They had inveigled these two subjects here, and now one of them had got away. He had never wanted this booze in the first place, with all the money it cost to feed their faces and pour the drink down their necks like water. It was the day after Hallowe'en anyway, and bloody stupid with a body in this very room, but would Hare give him a hand to take it away? No.

It was all Hare's fault. Everything was going wrong. But better one subject than none at all, now that all the visitors had cleared out.

He came at Edina like a maddened bull and knocked her to the floor. His hands closed round her neck. 'Fetch me a pillow, Nellie, for God's sake,' he panted, and the next Edina knew one of the filthy bed-pillows was over her face, shutting out the air, smothering . . . suffocating her . . . A red mist floated in front of her eyes.

Then the grimy window smashed in, glass flying everywhere, and a man's fist, covered in blood, crashed into Billy's face, and crashed again. There was the sickening sound of Billy's head hitting the stone floor. Then there was air in her lungs again. She gasped and coughed, the red mist moved away, and Gavin gathered her into his arms.

'Are you hurt, Edina?'

'Only bruised,' she began to cry, 'and it was all no use, anyway, was it? They can't be accused of murder without a body.'

'Thank God it wasn't your body,' he said grimly as the room filled up with policemen.

'Body? Body?' Hare glared at them. 'There's no body here.'

'We'll take a look round, anyway,' Sergeant-Major Fisher said, making no remark when he found blood stains and a woman's clothes half-hidden. Frank was poking about in the straw. 'There's blood here, Sergeant-Major.'

'It's my time on me,' Helen said swiftly. 'I moved on to the straw when it came on me in the middle of the night, it not being modest to sleep with my husband at a time like this.'

Then James Little was standing there, tall and erect like the soldier he once was, with Captain Stewart of the Edinburgh Constabulary behind him. 'Look there,' he pointed, 'under that pile of straw,' and when he saw the woman's clothing that Sergeant-Major Fisher was examining he said firmly, 'Mrs Docherty was wearing that dress. I'll swear to it.'

'You're under arrest on the suspicion of murder, all four of you,' Captain Stewart said, 'and you'll come along with us immediately.'

'Not me,' Maggie Hare said. 'I've got a baby to look after.'

'The baby's under arrest, too, then.'

'I swear to God I know nothing about that body under the straw,' Hare shouted.

'You know as much as I do,' Billy said, while Helen's cries rose to a scream.

'Save it, the lot of you. You'll all get plenty of time to say what you have to say where you're going.'

Captain Stewart put the Hares into separate cells, and later in the day they were taken into a room with the Burkes and shown the body of Mrs Docherty under a sheet.

Billy crossed himself. 'God take pity on that poor soul,' he said piously. 'Poor little woman.'

'Who can she be?' Hare asked, and got no answer.

Instead Billy, feeling half-dead without his morning dram, and in great pain, was taken to another room to be questioned. Oh God, he thought, with just one lush I could convince them in only a few words, for I was always the boy to tell a good story.

As it was, he had to tell them the best story he could dead sober, making it up as he went along.

'It was this man all muffled up came to me with a tea-chest asking me to mend his shoes. While I was doing it, he put down the chest near me bed of straw, and when I finished the job he gave me a sixpence and took the chest away. I never noticed until later that he'd left a corpse under the straw. It was a terrible thing to find, by God, in a man's own house.'

'So you never saw the man's face?'

'I swear to God. It's like a nightmare. I can't get it out of my head. I'm that upset, so I am.'

'So you should be,' said Captain Stewart. 'I never heard such a load of rubbish in my life. It's a great pity, for your sake, that the four of you didn't get together beforehand and make up a better story. The same story, even. As it is, I've listened to four different ones already today, so let's see what you tell the Sheriff next, shall we?'

The *Edinburgh Evening Courant* was first with the story, with EXTRAORDINARY OCCURRENCE for its headline. The people of the town stopped in the street to read about a doctor, so far not named, a vigilant policeman, also unnamed, the body of an old woman, and two men called Burke and Hare now held in custody. The article rambled on, reminding the readers of the rumours about strange disappearances recently, especially those of Daft Jamie and Mary Paterson.

The questions in the Tolbooth went on and on. Billy's pain

got worse and worse without whisky to deaden it, until in the end he was so tired and ill he could hardly stand, but still he persisted in trying to save them all.

'None of us should be held here,' he told the examiner. 'And as for young Murphy, he had nothing to do with it. Nobody had anything to do with it when the Docherty woman got so drunk that she lay down in the straw and suffocated herself. We had just decided to take her body to the surgeon, and in lifting her up those marks got on her neck.'

'So you've changed your tune? There never was a man who left the body with you?'

'No, sir.'

'Give him a cup of tea,' the examiner instructed the policeman who was present, 'and I'll go and listen to the next story,' and just for a fleeting, wistful moment Billy wondered if he should ask to see the police surgeon about the pain in his ball.

But the moment passed. The torment was excruciating, but he didn't ask, after all. In his heart he didn't believe his worldly ills would be with him much longer anyway.

In a separate cell Helen told her story. 'An old nuisance she was, that Docherty woman, always calling for tea, and interfering with my cooking. Then, at the party, she was so drunk it was disgusting – handling my man, wanting him to go outside with her . . . I wanted no more of that, and threw her out of the house.'

In another cell, Maggie Hare cradled her baby, a thing she had never done before. The examiner saw a woman every bit as hard as a man, and a child dirty and pallid and certainly undernourished held up before its mother like a shield. 'What can you tell me about the body of Mrs Docherty?' he asked.

Maggie threw him a look of pure venom, and appealed to the policeman standing to attention at the door. 'Will you be listening to that one, now?' she asked. 'And me a weak woman with a wee bairn to look after! When are you coming with milk for me child, before it dies in me arms?'

'It would be better for you if you answered my questions,' the examiner said. 'Again, what can you tell me about the body of Mrs Docherty?'

'I've told you! I'm a weak woman doing a woman's work. I look after me husband and the bairn. I wash the clothes and I cook the food. What would I know of a body? I have nothing to say,' and with that Maggie shut her mouth like a clamp.

The Littles told how Helen had tried to bribe them. James Little repeated that he had recognised Mrs Docherty's clothes. Ann Little described the body she saw under the straw.

The police widened their enquiries. They questioned the neighbours, and Hugh Alston told them about the night – that same night – that he had heard the cries of 'Murder!' and had got up out of his bed to look for a policeman.

Dr Black, the police surgeon, stated that he believed Mrs Docherty had died violently, although it was true that death from suffocation could be caused by alcohol.

At the end of it all Sir William Rae, Lord Advocate, Counsel for the Crown, sighed and shook his head. 'It is not enough.'

'It is not, sir,' Captain Stewart agreed with him. 'There is no proof that Mrs Docherty was murdered by either Burke or Hare.'

'We need prove only one murder to convict them, so we will concentrate on Mrs Docherty. Four different stories from a house divided . . .' Sir William smiled. 'It will soon fall, when I suggest to Hare that he should turn King's evidence. We don't want to lose the whole gang, do we?'

He went to visit Hare in Calton Jail, and explained it to him. 'But you must tell the truth, the whole truth and nothing but the truth. Then you will go free.'

'If I did that I would incriminate myself.'

'No. You would be closely advised which questions not to answer.'

'What about me wife?'

'A wife cannot give evidence against her husband.'

'So only Billy and Helen will be tried?' Hare laughed. 'God, that's a wonderful way of doing things! Turning King's evidence, eh?'

'Christmas week is not the easiest time in the year to get locums,' Gavin sent a message to his parents-in-law, 'so Edina and I must be content to spend the week before that with you, returning to Gilmerton on Christmas Day.'

'Well, you have arrived to see the capital at its most crowded,' Mr Hamilton informed them over breakfast on the first day of their holiday, 'and getting worse every day now as the trial of William Burke and Helen MacDougal approaches. It is set for the morning of the twenty-fourth.'

'A ridiculous day to have a trial,' Lady Alison said. 'Christmas Eve?'

Mr Hamilton rustled over the next page of the *Courant* and imparted the next piece of information. 'Sir William Rae, Lord Advocate, Counsel for the Crown, will be far outclassed by James Moncrieff, Francis Jeffrey and Henry Cockburn for the Defence, of course, and he knows it. So what tricks will he try next, I wonder.'

'What do you mean?' asked Edina.

'Oh, it is all here in the *Courant* today. Hare has confessed. Sir William Rae has promised immunity in exchange. He has got Hare to turn King's evidence to put all the blame on Burke. Hare will go free, and Burke will hang. It is all a foregone conclusion.'

'From what I have read about the case, both men were deep in it together and the women, as accessories, just as guilty,' Gavin said. 'They should all stand trial.'

'It is a scandal, and they have not even mentioned Dr Knox, who is in my opinion the blackest villain of all.' Mr Hamilton flapped over another page in his agitation, and Gavin and Edina exchanged glances which spoke louder than words.

They knew that Dr Knox's students, worshipping as ever, escorted him to and from his lectures every day to guard him from the hostile Edinburgh mob. If it were not for his brilliant teaching, they certainly would not qualify under Professor Monroe. The fault did not lie with Knox for accepting the bodies; the fault lay in the ridiculous lengths to which mercenary people had gone to keep him supplied; the fault lay in the system.

'Fine well did he know that the bodies he was receiving were suspect,' Mr Hamilton went on, 'yet he took Daft

Jamie's and Mary Paterson's, the most blatant of all, without a quibble.'

'Do not excite yourself, Eden,' Lady Alison protested as Liza came in with the morning rolls, crisp under a white cloth.

'I am not in the least excited, my dear! I am only very angry.' He slapped on butter which immediately melted, mostly from his own heat.'I will have the marmalade, Edina, if you please.'

'You will not read the latest news of all in that paper, sir,' Liza announced. 'We heard it from the baker when he came to the back door with the rolls. Early this morning there was a riot. A mob on Calton Hill made an effigy of Dr Knox, marched it up the South Bridge and took it to his home in Newington Place. Then it was hanged by the neck from a bough of one of his trees and set on fire. Dr Knox escaped by his back door. Nobody knows where he is hiding.'

'Justice,' Mr Hamilton said, calm again. 'It was in the hope of seeing justice done that I ever took up Law in the first place. You can always trust the man in the street to see the rights and wrongs of any situation.'

With peace and pleasure thus restored at 13, Charlotte Square, Mr Hamilton left for his chambers, Gavin went up to the Royal Infirmary to see some of his old friends, Josh in particular, and Lady Alison and Edina got ready for a shopping expedition.

'Oh, Miss Edina,' Kathy flung her arms round her neck, 'Mistress Edina, I mean — what do you think! Frank has got his promotion! We are to be married in June!'

'I wouldn't miss it for the world, Kathy.'

That Christmas Eve in Edinburgh was like no other, before or since. The people should have been at home getting ready their houses, their festive fare, and their celebrations of the birth of Jesus. At the very least, they should have been intending to go to the kirk for the watch-night service.

Instead of that, the crowd in the Lawnmarket was enormous, and every human being who could be packed into it was in the courtroom, while hundreds stood outside waiting for the slightest titbit, in spite of the bitter wind blowing from the north-east, straight from Siberia.

They shuddered with every gust, but still they stood, huddled together, and it was somewhere in that crowd that a new song was born. Burke, Hare and Knox were judged and condemned before the trial was half over.

> 'Up the close and down the stair,
> But and ben wi' Burke and Hare,
> Burke's the butcher, Hare's the thief,
> Knox the boy that buys the beef.'

Inside the courtroom it was anything but cold, and many of the ladies present were waving their fans. It was not only the press of people that raised the temperature, and not even the one crime for which Burke and his wife were being tried. It was the indignation and the outrage at so many others who had played a part.

How many? God only knew, they told each other with a mixture of awe, loathing and, although none would have admitted it, salacious curiosity.

Mr Hamilton came home at eight o'clock in the middle of a party Lady Alison was holding for the young folk. He told his family that Lord Henry Cockburn had been on his feet most of the day defending Helen Burke, or MacDougal, as she was known throughout, and making a splendid job of it. But Maggie Hare, vicious as she was, looked like going free along with her husband.

Billy lay on the bed in his cell, waiting while the jury retired, and tried to ease his body, but it kept on twitching. The sweat poured from his forehead and the palms of his hands, and as he stared up at the ceiling there was a humming in his head.

It started far off and came nearer and nearer until he could identify it as the voice of a child. In a pure clear voice she was singing a song of the most shameless indecency he had ever heard. It was grotesque. It made him sweat again, and feel ashamed. Why didn't her mother stop her?

Then there was a rustling, but not the sound of rats. It was more like the rustlings of a woman's skirts. 'Helen!' He started up. 'Helen! Is that you? Where are you?'

Gradually he saw a young girl, but not all at once. First the blonde head with the glorious mop of ringlets, then the blue eyes and the pale oval of her face, and a red, red mouth like a crushed strawberry, running juice.

'No!' he screamed. 'No!'

Then her shoulders appeared, her full breasts, her little waist and her scarlet skirt spread out.

'Go away!' he moaned.

But Mary Paterson didn't go away. She sat down on a stool and lifted her skirt, exposing her long white stockings and her purple garters before she took them off, smiling at him all the time. 'Dada,' she murmured in the child's voice from the red ooze of her lips. 'Dada.'

He had never known terror like this before, gruesome and filthy and coming at him, crawling like slime towards him.

'In Thy holy goodness,' he closed his eyes and prayed, 'help me now. Oh, God, in Thy mercy, help me.'

He opened his eyes and she was still coming towards him, offering herself, smiling with her bloody torn lips, and he screamed and screamed and pressed back on the stone wall behind the bed, trying to escape from his recurring nightmare.

His guards heard him, and came in with a bottle of wine they had smuggled in for him. They had become sorry for the little man who sang for them and told them stories when he was well enough, and like everyone else they believed he shouldn't be the only man there today waiting to be condemned to death. 'Here, Billy, take a swig,' one of them said. 'The jury's back. It's time to go.'

At twenty minutes past nine the Justice Clerk, Lord Boyle, placed a black cap on his wig and in a hushed courtroom delivered the jury's verdict. Burke was first on the list. He was to be detained in the Tolbooth until the twenty-eighth of January 1829, when he would be hanged on the gibbet and afterwards his body should be given to Professor Monroe for dissection.

Then he turned to Helen, and told her that the libel against

275

her was not proven. She was in tears when she looked up at Billy from under her dishevelled bonnet, and those in the court were so still and silent that her sobs could be heard right to the back.

In Scottish law, Billy Burke was not allowed to say one word in a statement. He was pale but composed as the guards led him away, past where Helen was sitting, and whether such a right was granted or not, he took it.

It was probably better than a hundred declarations he could have made from the dock when he stopped beside her and flung his arms round her neck. 'I love you, Nellie darlin',' he said. 'Thank God you are out of this scrape.'

They were the finest words she had ever heard him speak.

A few weeks later Gavin ran a professional if adoring eye over his young wife, happy and glowing at the breakfast table. 'It has worried me, Edina – all that happened in Tanners' Close, and then the trauma of the trial – to think you could never forget it.'

'Who could forget it? But I have put it behind me and, as you see, after four months of marriage I am perfectly healthy and perfectly normal.'

'Yes, thank God! What you have experienced doesn't seem to have affected you at all.'

'Oh, *some* experiences have.' She smiled. 'While you have been snoring away, some experiences have been making me sick in the early mornings.'

'What?'

'Yes, Dr Mitchell. Do you think I might be just a wee bit pregnant?' she laughingly asked, unconsciously using the same words that Bridie her mother had used before her. 'So you needn't have worried, you see. We've got happier things to think about now than murders and trials and places like Tanners' Close.'

HISTORICAL NOTE

I F YOU VISIT the Chamber of Horrors in the Wax Museum in Edinburgh's Royal Mile, you will see the effigies of Burke and Hare and the beautiful Mary Paterson. Although Tanners' Close was demolished in 1902, you can still walk down Candlemaker Row and still visit the Grassmarket, haunted by all three. Burke's skeleton remains on view in Edinburgh's Anatomical Museum at the University.

Helen MacDougal (Nellie) was given police protection out of Edinburgh as far as the boundary of Northumberland and Durham. It is believed she died in Australia in 1868. Margaret Hare (Maggie) escaped with her life to Belfast. In 1850 she was employed as a nurse in Paris. William Hare tried to hide in numerous places throughout the country. He was seen even in Shetland, but it was in London that he died more than forty years later, a blind beggar. He had been recognised and thrown into a lime-pit as soon as he arrived, and his eyes were burned out. Dr Knox was forced to leave Edinburgh, a broken man. He died in London, aged seventy-one, in virtual oblivion. His assistant William Fergusson fared better: he became Sir William Fergusson, Sergeant-Surgeon to Queen Victoria.

Mary Paterson's sister Edina is fictitious, as are Gavin and the other medical students and their families, but all the great figures of Scottish history mentioned here live on into eternity, among them Sir William Rae, Lord Henry Cockburn and not forgetting Meg Dod, whose famous recipes are referred to so often by F. Marion McNeill in her wonderful book, *The Scots Kitchen*.